THE
GOLDSMITH
AND THE
MASTER
THIEF

TONKE DRAGT writes and illustrates books of adventure, fantasy and fairy tales. She was born in 1930 in Jakarta. When she was twelve, during the Second World War, she was imprisoned in a Japanese camp, where she wrote her very first book, using begged and borrowed paper. After the war, she moved to the Netherlands with her family, and eventually became an art teacher. She published *The Goldsmith and the Master Thief* in 1961, and a year later this was followed by her most famous story, *The Letter for the King*, which won the Children's Book of the Year Award and has been translated into sixteen languages. She was awarded the State Prize for Youth Literature in 1976 and was knighted in 2001. *The Letter for the King*, *The Secrets of the Wild Wood* and *The Song of Seven* are also published by Pushkin Children's Books.

LAURA WATKINSON studied medieval and modern languages at Oxford, and taught English around the world before returning to the UK to take a Masters in English and Applied Linguistics and a postgraduate certificate in literary translation. She is now a full-time translator from Dutch, Italian and German, and has also translated Dragt's *The Letter for the King*, *The Secrets of the Wild Wood* and *The Song of Seven* for Pushkin Children's Books. She lives in Amsterdam.

THE GOLDSMITH AND THE MASTER THIEF

TONKE DRAGT

Translated by Laura Watkinson

PUSHKIN CHILDREN'S BOOKS

Pushkin Children's Books
71–75 Shelton Street, London WC2H 9JQ

The Goldsmith and the Master Thief first published in Dutch as *De Goudsmid en de meesterdief*
© 1961, *De goudsmid en de meesterdief* by Tonke Dragt, Uitgeverij Leopold, Amsterdam

© Illustrations Tonke Dragt

English language translation © 2019 Laura Watkinson
First published by Pushkin Children's Books in 2019
This paperback edition first published in 2020

N **ederlands**
letterenfonds
dutch foundation
for literature

The publisher gratefully acknowledges the support of the Dutch Foundation for Literature.

9 8 7 6 5 4 3 2 1

ISBN 978 1 78269 248 5

Text designed and typeset by Tetragon, London
Printed and bound by CPI Group (UK) Ltd, Croydon, CRO 4YY

www.pushkinpress.com

CONTENTS

The Birth of the Twins

*Right, now we shall begin. When we reach the end
of our story, we shall know more than we know now.*

ANDERSEN: 'The Snow Queen'

In Bainu, the beautiful capital city of Babina, there once lived a poor cobbler and his wife.

One morning, two puppies came running into the cobbler's workshop. They greeted him, barking and wagging their tails, and started playing with the shoes that he was mending.

"What's all this?" the cobbler shouted. "Away with you!" And he chased them outside.

The next morning, however, the dogs came back, barking and wagging their tails as before, and once again he chased them out of his workshop. But when he joined his wife in the kitchen at lunchtime, the dogs were under the table, eating together from the same plate.

"What are you doing?" he said to his wife. "Are you feeding those animals? They've already been into the workshop bothering me twice. Get rid of them!"

"Oh," said his wife, "but they're such friendly little things! And have you seen how thin they are? Let them stay. They clearly trust us to look after them."

"Absolutely not," said the cobbler. "We're poor and we have a child on the way. There is no way we can have two dogs."

"But we always have a few leftover scraps that they could eat," his wife replied. "And they can guard our house. Please, let them stay."

"As if we have anything that needs guarding!" said the cobbler, but his wife kept on pleading, so he gave in, because he was in fact just as kind-hearted as she was.

So then they had two dogs, which brought them a lot of problems, but also a lot of pleasure.

A week later, the cobbler found a basket outside his door. There were two kittens inside, meowing sadly.

"We have no use for these little beasts," he said to his wife. "I'm going to get rid of them."

"No, you can't do that!" said his wife. "They're so sweet. Look, they've only just opened their eyes. Let's keep them."

"Absolutely not!" cried the cobbler. "We're poor and we're about to have a child. Besides, we already have two dogs."

"Cats hardly eat anything though," said his wife. "And they catch mice."

Once again, the cobbler gave in, and so they had two dogs and two cats, which gave them a lot of trouble, but also a great deal of pleasure.

Some time after that, the cobbler was hammering away in his workshop when two pigeons came flying in through the open windows and sat on his shoulders, one on each.

"What do you want from me?" he asked. "I already have two dogs and two cats. And in a few days I'll have a child too. Away with you! Scram!"

But the pigeons stayed where they were.

Fine then, thought the cobbler. *I wonder what pigeon legs taste like.*

No sooner had he thought that than the pigeons flew up and away. The cobbler ran outside after them, trying to catch them, but they fluttered up onto the roof of his house.

"Right, then you can just stay up there," said the cobbler, and he headed back inside and told his wife that there were two pigeons on the roof.

"You mustn't eat them," his wife replied. "They came to you of their own free will – and that's good luck."

"Two dogs, two cats and two pigeons," muttered the cobbler. "I wonder what other good luck is in store for us?"

The next night, he received the answer to his question, when his wife gave birth to twins, two big and healthy baby boys.

"Well, well," said the cobbler the next morning, as he stood beside the bed where his wife lay, tired and happy, with a child in each arm. "Twins! And their birth was foretold by extraordinary events. So our sons are sure to become extraordinary children."

The boys were christened and given the names Laurenzo and Jiacomo.

"We don't have any money for christening gifts," said their parents, "but we'll still give them something. They shall each have a puppy, a kitten and a pigeon. Don't we make a lovely family?"

Laurenzo and Jiacomo grew up in good health, and they were as alike as two drops of water or two grains of sand. When they walked together through the streets of Bainu, with their dogs at their heels, their pigeons on their shoulders, and their cats in their arms, no one knew which was one and which was the other. Only their parents could tell them apart – not because of the way they looked, but because of how they behaved.

The brothers were inseparable, and they enjoyed their time together. They were poor, but how many boys are there who have not only a dog, a cat and a pigeon, but also a twin brother to play with? And what better places to play than in the narrow, winding streets and alleys of Bainu, or on the big square in front of the royal palace or in the rolling fields outside the city walls?

The twin brothers had lots and lots of interesting experiences when they were still little boys, and I shall tell you a story from that time.

THE SECOND TALE

To School

*"You look exactly the same as me, as you wear the
same clothes, and the same animals follow the two
of us, both you and me."*

GRIMM: 'The Two Brothers'

The twin brothers led a free and happy life until one day
their father called them to him and said: "Boys, you're nearly
seven years old now, and it's time for you to learn something. I
cannot give you wealth, but I can make sure that you learn to
read, write and do sums. That is a wealth that you will never
waste or lose. So tomorrow the two of you are starting school
at the Brown Monastery."

Laurenzo and Jiacomo stared at him. School? Did that
mean they would no longer be free to wander the streets and
play all day long? Some of their friends had recently started
school. They spent all day inside, sitting on hard wooden
benches, locked up like birds in a cage.

"Oh, Father, please don't send us there!" they both cried.

The cobbler looked at his sons seriously. "You're big boys
now," he said, "big enough to understand that school is good
for you. When you grow up, you'll be happy to have learnt
something – and to know more than I know myself."

"We're going to be cobblers, like you," said Laurenzo. "So
we don't need to go to school."

"But maybe later you'll want to be something different from your father," replied the cobbler. "And just think how nice it will be when you can read letters from people and write letters back to them too."

"And our pigeons can deliver them for us," said Jiacomo.

"Exactly. Do your best, and you'll soon be clever boys who will make me and your mother proud."

The boys did not reply. They really did want to please their parents, but...

"And you'll have Sundays off," said their father, as if he had guessed what they were thinking. "But anyway I'm sure you'll enjoy school."

So it was settled. But that night, in bed, the brothers lay awake for a long time, talking. They both agreed that school sounded like a very bad thing indeed.

"And it's every day too!" said Laurenzo with a sigh.

"If it was just the morning, or just the afternoon!" said Jiacomo.

"I've heard that the teacher sometimes makes you write the same word out a hundred times," said Laurenzo. "What's the point of that?"

"I have an idea!" cried Jiacomo suddenly.

"Sssh!" whispered Laurenzo. "You'll wake Mother and Father."

"We won't go to school every day," Jiacomo whispered back. "We'll go one day and not the next – that'll be enough."

"But we can't do that," said Laurenzo. "You get punished if you miss a day."

"Ah, but we can do it completely differently," said Jiacomo and he began to whisper his plan.

"Will it work?" wondered Laurenzo.

"Of course it will!"

Then they heard their mother's voice. "Boys, are you still awake?"

Then there was silence.

The next morning, their mother took a long look at the two of them. "Good. You both look nice and neat," she said. She gave them each a bag of sandwiches. "That's for lunchtime," she said. "And here's an apple for each of you."

Their father patted them both on the shoulders before heading to his workshop. "Do your best – and work hard," he said.

Then their mother got ready to take them to school.

"Oh no, there's no need to come with us, thanks," said Laurenzo. "We already know the way."

"Just this first time," their mother said.

"All of the other boys walk to school by themselves," said Jiacomo. "We can go with Antonio from the tavern. He's been at school for a while now."

Their mother smiled. "Oh, the two of you are getting so big," she said, a little sadly. "Fine then, if you'd rather go on your own. No, Jiacomo, the animals have to stay at home."

"You mean the dogs can't come with us?" asked Laurenzo.

"No," their mother said firmly. "Dogs don't belong in a classroom."

And so the two boys went on their way. Their mother stood in the doorway and waved them off. At the end of the street, Antonio joined them. And as they reached the next street, their dogs came running after them. They had slipped out when the boys' mother was not watching. The twins told them to go back home, but the animals did not listen.

"They'll just have to come with us," said Laurenzo. "Do you think that's allowed?" he asked Antonio.

Antonio looked doubtful. "The monks might not mind one dog," he said, "but I think two might be a problem."

"But only one of the dogs is going to school," said Jiacomo.

"Why? Are you sending your dog home?" asked Antonio.

"No," said Jiacomo and he started to tell Antonio his plan. "You have to help us," he said, as he finished. "And you mustn't tell anybody about it. Not a soul."

Antonio gazed at the brothers in awe. "I wish I had a twin brother too," he said with a sigh.

A quarter of an hour later, school began. The teacher of the younger pupils, a big monk in a brown habit, stood at the door, smiling and welcoming all the children.

"Aha," he said, "I see we have a new student." Leaning over to a young boy with a dog, he asked, "What's your name, lad?"

"I... I'm Lau... Laucomo. Laucomo, the son of Ferdinand, the cobbler."

"Welcome, Laucomo," said the monk cheerfully. "Are you a friend of Antonio's?"

"Yes, sir."

"Can he bring his dog, Brother Thomas?" asked Antonio.

"His dog? Well, I suppose so, if it's well behaved. But, Laucomo, I thought you were coming with your brother. Ferdinand mentioned two sons."

"I... I don't have a brother," said Laucomo, his face turning red.

"Oh," said Brother Thomas, scratching his head, "then I must be mistaken."

"Yes, sir," said Laucomo.

"That's right, Brother Thomas," said Antonio. "He doesn't have any brothers."

"Go on inside," said the monk. "You can sit next to Antonio, Laucomo."

When the boys were in their seats, Antonio whispered to his neighbour: "It worked!"

Laurenzo, because that, of course, is who it was, did not reply. He felt a little uneasy. He was missing his brother too. Antonio was nice enough, but it should have been Jiacomo sitting beside him.

Meanwhile, Jiacomo was walking across the market square with his dog, singing a happy song. He was very pleased with his plan. He and Laurenzo were going to take it in turns to go to school. That way they would learn just enough and they could have plenty of time to play outside too. At school, everyone would think there was just one boy, Laucomo. Yes, he certainly had come up with an excellent plan! He thought about what he was going to do today. He could play anywhere, as long as it was not too close to home or to school. But how was Laurenzo doing? Jiacomo missed him – until today the two brothers had always played together.

A week later, Brother Thomas said to Brother Augustine, who taught the older students: "That Laucomo is a nice boy, but I don't know quite what to make of him. One day he behaves completely differently from the next. And he can be so forgetful! Sometimes he can't even remember what I told him just the day before."

Which goes to show that the big monk was an observant man.

So far everything had gone as planned. The only problem was that the twin brothers often spent a long time talking in bed at night, and so their father sometimes became angry with them. But how else were they supposed to tell each other what they had been up to all day?

"We learnt a song today," said Jiacomo one night, "about riding on a horse." He sang it quietly to his brother. "And we did the letter T. It's really easy. Do you remember it?"

"Yes," said Laurenzo. Jiacomo had already taught him the letter T on the way home.

"What did you do today?" asked Jiacomo.

"I went to the market with Piedro. And then we played by the river. But it was boring. Piedro's such a baby. He's only just five."

"School's boring too," said Jiacomo with a sigh. "And I had an argument with Antonio. He's so stupid. I'm sure he's going to give us away."

"The letter T," said Laurenzo, "T... T... Two... Twins, that begins with a T too. Two twins. Do you like it? Being on your own?"

"No," said Jiacomo. "Not at school."

"And outside school?"

Jiacomo did not answer for a while. Then he said, "Well, sometimes it's fun at school. But having to go there every day? No, I don't like that at all."

"But being on your own every day is no fun either."

"We have lots to tell each other though."

Then they heard their father's voice: "If you two don't settle down, I'll give you both a whack on the behind!"

The boys were silent. For a while. Then Jiacomo whispered: "You're right. I don't like it, not one bit."

A week after that, Brother Thomas said to himself: "That Laucomo! Why does he write neatly one day and then make a mess the next day? Why does he know his times tables one day and forget them the next? Sometimes he does one thing well, and then he does another thing excellently, but there's never a week goes by when he does consistently well at the same things."

He looked at Laucomo. The boy was sitting next to Antonio in the front row, and his dog was lying under the desk. Brother Thomas could see that Antonio was whispering something to him. Laucomo did not answer. So Antonio nudged him and repeated his question.

"Hey," he whispered, loudly enough to be heard, "are you Laurenzo or Jiacomo?"

Brother Thomas raised his eyebrows. "Are you talking, Antonio?" he said. "Be quiet and get on with your work." But he wondered what Antonio could have meant.

However, he was even more surprised when he spoke to Brother Augustine after school, who had taken his classes out for a walk that afternoon.

"You need to keep an eye on that Laucomo," said Brother Augustine. "I saw him on the street this afternoon, during school hours!"

"You must be mistaken," said Brother Thomas. "He's been sitting in the front row all day."

"I'm sure I saw him," Brother Augustine insisted. "The boy with the dog."

Brother Thomas scratched his head. Something was beginning to dawn on him. "But that's absurd," he muttered. "Hmm, I shall have to keep a very close eye on that lad."

Meanwhile the twins were sitting on the step outside their house, with their pigeons on their shoulders, their cats on their laps and their dogs at their feet, happy to be together again.

"How was it today?" asked Jiacomo.

"You didn't miss much," said Laurenzo. "We didn't do anything new. Oh yes, don't tell Antonio which one of us you are. He can't keep track of it, the dope!"

"Boys! Dinnertime!" called their mother.

"How was school today, Jiacomo?" she asked, when they were sitting at the table. "You haven't said anything about it yet."

"But Laurenzo already told you everything," said Jiacomo. Which was completely true.

Laucomo, thought Brother Thomas, as he stood, large and imposing, at the front of the classroom. *Laurenzo or Jiacomo. Most amusing.* Then he raised his voice. "Laurenzo!" he called.

The boy on the left in the front row looked up. It was Jiacomo, but each of the twins also answered to the other's name.

The monk came and stood beside him. Jiacomo leant further over his slate. He felt rather uncomfortable. If only he and his brother had never started all this!

"Tell me, boy," said the monk. "Yes, now do tell me, what is your name? Are you Laurenzo? Or are you... Jiacomo?"

Jiacomo dropped his pencil. With a red face, he looked up.

"I..." he began hesitantly. Then quickly he said: "Both. I'm both. My full name is Laurenzo Jiacomo."

"Hmm," replied Brother Thomas, narrowing his eyes. "That's quite a mouthful, eh?" He turned around and began walking along the rows of desks.

Jiacomo picked up his pencil, but he could not keep his mind on his work. What had he gone and done now? He had lied to Brother Thomas! But he had of course been lying all along, ever since his first day at school.

Antonio nudged him. "Good one!" he whispered. "But which one are you? Laurenzo or Jiacomo?"

"You should know," Jiacomo whispered back. "I'm not telling you."

"Bah, you're being just like... just like your brother yesterday. Watch it, or I'll say it out loud! Which one are you?"

"Sssh!" whispered Jiacomo.

"Quiet, boys!" barked Brother Thomas.

Startled, the boys pretended to go on working.

A little later, the monk had the slates collected. Then he went and stood at his lectern and said: "It's another ten minutes until you can go home. Now listen carefully, and I'll tell you a story. It's an old, old story, from the days when people still believed in all kinds of different gods.

"In Greece, there once lived two brothers. Castor and Pollux were their names. They were born on the same day, and so they were twins. Their father was Zeus, the ruler of the Greek gods, and their mother was an ordinary woman. The two brothers were so alike that no one could tell which was one and which was the other, and yet there was a difference between them. Pollux was immortal, just like his father, who was a god – so he would live for ever and ever and never die. But Castor was mortal, just like his mother and every other human in the world.

"The two brothers were inseparable and they performed many brave deeds together.

"But alas, a war began, and Castor was struck by a spear and he died in battle. When Pollux saw him lying there dead, he was heartbroken, and he cried: 'What do I care about living for ever if my brother is not with me?'

"Now the ancient Greeks believed that the dead went to a land that was under the earth – a cold and dark land, the Underworld. So that was where Castor went, and Pollux remained behind, all alone.

"But Pollux did not want to be alone, and so he went to his father, Zeus, who was sitting on his throne of clouds.

"'Oh, Mighty Father,' he said, 'why did Castor have to go to the Underworld when I do not? Can't you bring him back to life and return him to me?'

"'That is impossible,' said Zeus. 'Those who have descended into the Underworld must remain there. You are immortal and so, if you wish, you may live with the gods in Heaven and be happy for evermore.'

"'But I can't be happy if Castor is not with me!' Pollux wailed.

"'Fine,' said Zeus, 'then you may choose. Do you want to live for ever with me and the other gods, or do you want to be with your brother in the dark land under the earth?'

"'I would rather be with Castor in the Underworld than alone in Heaven, no matter how beautiful it might be,' replied Pollux.

"'You are a loyal brother,' said Zeus. 'And so this is what we will agree: you may spend one day with Castor in the Underworld and the next day you can both be with me in Heaven.'

"And that is what happened. From then on, the twin brothers spent one day in the Underworld and the next day in Heaven, but they were always together and so they were happy."

Brother Thomas looked around the class as he finished his story: "You might think this is an odd tale. But there is something very fine about it – and that is the loyalty between the two brothers, who were prepared to share with each other even those things that were not pleasant or enjoyable." His gaze rested for a moment on "Laucomo". Then he said: "That's it for today, boys and girls. You can go home now."

Later, Laurenzo and Jiacomo were sitting on the step outside their house again, and Jiacomo was telling his brother about Brother Thomas's story.

When he had finished, they both sat in silence. After a while, Jiacomo said: "Shall we stop it now?"

"Yes," replied Laurenzo. Then all was silent again.

Until they both spoke at the same moment. "What do you think Brother Thomas is going to say?"

"You'll be punished," said Jiacomo.

"So will you," said Laurenzo. "We both played truant."

"Maybe he already knows," pondered Jiacomo.

"The punishment won't be so bad if we're together," said Laurenzo.

"It still won't be much fun though," said Jiacomo.

"No," agreed Laurenzo.

"But then we'll be able to have such a good time together!"

When Brother Thomas came into the classroom the next morning, he froze. He had been expecting it, but still, for a moment, he was stunned. The children were all giggling. Antonio was the only one who looked a bit glum, because he was no longer sitting next to his friend "Laucomo".

"What's all this?" the teacher cried in a loud voice. "Is there something wrong with my eyes? Am I seeing double? Or has Laucomo really split in two?" And he added: "And he even has two dogs!"

The twins, sitting in the front row, looked at him with a mixture of amusement and fear.

"I see," said the monk. "So you've been sharing the work, have you? Then tell me why you've decided to come together today."

"It's more fun when there are two of you," said the brothers.

"Hmm," said Brother Thomas. "You naughty little truants! But the two of you belong together, eh? You've realized that now. And school's not really that bad, is it?"

The boys shyly shook their heads.

Brother Thomas burst out laughing, his belly shaking, and the whole class laughed along with him. "But tell me," he asked, "which one of you is Laurenzo and which is Jiacomo? Or do I have to guess?"

"Yes, guess!" the class cried.

"Let me see," the monk said to the twins. "Who can tell me the story I told yesterday?"

"Me! Me!" cried both Laurenzo and Jiacomo.

Brother Thomas sighed. "How will I ever know who is one brother and who is the other?" he wailed, putting on a sad face.

"Jiacomo told me the story," said Laurenzo.

"Excellent! Now I know who's who. And by the end of the week, I won't make any more mistakes."

But no matter how clever Brother Thomas was, he still got it wrong, many, many more times!

The twin brothers Laurenzo and Jiacomo had a happy and carefree childhood. But when they were fifteen years old and had just become apprentices to their father, a contagious disease broke out in Bainu, and both of their parents died, one after the other. They did not even have time to grieve properly, as their parents' illness had cost the family so much money that they had to sell the cobbler's shop. And when they had done that, they were penniless.

"Luckily we still have each other," they said. "We must look for a job so that we can earn our living."

However, that turned out to be more difficult than they had thought. There were plenty of people who wanted a servant. But no one needed two.

"There are no jobs here in Bainu for the two of us together," Laurenzo said to Jiacomo. "What shall we do?"

"We belong together and we shall stay together," replied Jiacomo. "Let's leave Bainu and go out into the world. We're sure to find work somewhere."

"You're right," said Laurenzo. "Why should we stay here?"

So the brothers packed up their few belongings. They found homes for their cats and pigeons with some kind neighbours. Only the dogs were allowed to go with them. Then they said farewell to their friends and, with heavy hearts, left the city that was so dear to them.

THE THIRD TALE

Out into the World

We are brothers, as you can see.
But when shall I see him – and he see me?

A Dutch folksong

So the twin brothers headed out into the world. And once they were outside the city walls, their sadness began to give way to a feeling of anticipation. Every twist in the road might lead them to a surprise, and behind every hill a beautiful view might be hidden.

They travelled through Babina, along the banks of the River Grior, imagining that they might encounter adventure at any moment. Their dogs trotted along beside them, and back and forth, wagging their tails and covering twice the distance that their masters travelled.

At first the brothers enjoyed their freedom so much that they did not even think about looking for work. There was always something for them to eat and they could easily sleep out in the open, as it was summer. But when autumn came, and it grew colder, they both agreed that they should find a job.

But alas, they had no more luck finding a job together than they had in Bainu!

One day, they came to a place where the road split in two. There was a shabby little hut nearby, and they were tired, so they decided to knock on the door and ask for hospitality. They found an old pedlar living there, who welcomed them warmly and invited them to share his meagre meal. Before long, the brothers were telling him all about themselves and complaining that they had been unable to find a job that would allow them to stay together.

"There's only one option," said the pedlar. "You're going to have to split up."

"But that's exactly what we don't want to do," said Jiacomo.

"We've always been together," said Laurenzo.

"That was fine when you were children," said the pedlar. "But now that you're almost adults and there's no other way, you will each have to choose your own path." He looked at Laurenzo and asked: "What would you like to do? What kind of work appeals to you most?"

Laurenzo thought about it. "I believe that I would like to make something," he said then. "Not shoes, like our father, but objects made of silver and gold. Vases and bowls and beautiful jewellery."

"And what about you?" the pedlar asked Jiacomo. "Do you share your brother's wish?"

"No," said Jiacomo after a pause. "I love beautiful things too, but I don't think I could make them, not like Laurenzo. I don't really know exactly what I'd like to do. I would just like to travel the world, and go on long journeys, and to spend some time here and some time there. And to discover new things, and to meet all kinds of people and to have adventures – that all sounds very fine to me."

"You see?" said the pedlar, looking at one brother and then the other. "You see that you're not the same, even though you're brothers and as alike as two drops of water? So each of you needs to choose his own path."

He saw the worried looks on their faces and smiled at them kindly. "Never mind," he said. "This is not goodbye for ever! There's a fork in the road nearby. Each of you should go his own way and agree to meet here again in a year's time."

The brothers looked at each other as they considered his words.

"Take my advice," said the pedlar. "Look, I have a knife here. I'll drop it and whoever the tip is pointing at should take the left path. Whoever is facing the handle should take the right. But you must both make sure to return here in a year's time. And what you do after that – well, we'll cross that bridge later. So what do you think of that idea?"

"We'll take your advice," said the twins. "If there is no other way, then we shall part company."

The pedlar dropped the knife on the ground, and it landed so that Laurenzo should take the right-hand path and Jiacomo the left.

The next morning, the two brothers said goodbye to their host. They said a very fond farewell to each other and promised once again to meet at the same place in a year's time. Then each of the brothers went his own way, Laurenzo to the right and Jiacomo to the left.

Laurenzo's path took him through a beautiful hilly landscape. For the first two days, he met no one, but on the third day he caught up with an old man, who was struggling to lug a big sack. Laurenzo asked him if he could carry the sack for a while, and his offer was gratefully accepted.

"Thanks. I'm not getting any younger," said the man, "and it was starting to become a little too heavy for me. My horse stumbled yesterday and broke its leg, so I had to continue on foot. Where are you heading?"

"Wherever the road takes me," replied Laurenzo.

"Then you will end up in Sfaza," said the man. "What are you going to do there?"

"Look for a job," replied Laurenzo.

"What kind of job?"

"I don't know yet. Maybe working with a goldsmith."

"A goldsmith? Why?"

"Because that is the trade that appeals to me most," said Laurenzo.

"But why do you need to go to Sfaza for that?"

"Oh, that's purely by chance," replied Laurenzo. "Fate showed me this road. I hope I will find my fortune there."

"Then let us travel together," said the old man. "I love company. Or is your dog enough company for you?"

"I'd be happy to be your travelling companion," said Laurenzo, who had been feeling rather lonely since saying goodbye to his brother.

So the two of them travelled onwards, with Laurenzo carrying the sack.

When evening fell, they came to an inn, and the old man said: "You are my guest, and I shall treat you well, as you carried my sack. And then you may have something from the sack as payment for your help."

Laurenzo assured him that he did not expect a reward, but the old man said: "I know that! But I would like to give you something."

When they had eaten dinner and were sitting in the room that the old man had rented for the two of them, he opened up the sack and, to Laurenzo's surprise, took out the most valuable of objects – silver necklaces, cups and bowls of beaten gold, elegantly decorated rings and brooches, set with precious stones. "I'm going to sell them in Sfaza," said the old man. "But first you may choose something for yourself. Do you like them?"

"They're beautiful," said Laurenzo. "Far too beautiful for me." And he wondered how his travelling companion, who did not look at all wealthy, had come by these costly objects.

"I made them all myself," said the old man, as if he had read his mind. "I am, in fact, a goldsmith by trade."

"A goldsmith!" said Laurenzo. "And is that a difficult trade?"

"Only as difficult as any other job," said the man. "If you have a talent for it, that is."

"There are lots of goldsmiths in Bainu too," said Laurenzo. "One of them is very famous. His name is Master Philippo and he has even worked for the king."

"Do you know this Master Philippo?" asked the old man.

"No," replied Laurenzo. "Although I have heard a lot about him. I have only seen his shop from outside."

"Well, then now you *do* know him," said the old man. "I am Philippo the goldsmith, and I come from Bainu. So tell me which of these things you think is most beautiful."

"This one," said Laurenzo, pointing at a small bowl. "But I couldn't possibly accept it. It's far too beautiful and precious for me."

"Listen to me," said Master Philippo. "I know you a little now, and you seem like a good lad. And you also have a good eye, as that bowl is indeed the finest of all the objects in my sack. So if you don't wish to accept anything from me, then I have another proposal for you. Become my apprentice. If you have a talent for the job, then an excellent future awaits you. What do you say?"

"Oh, Master Philippo!" cried Laurenzo. "There is nothing I would rather do! I truly believe I found good fortune on my path today."

"Excellent," said the goldsmith. "I have to go to Sfaza first to sell these things, and then we'll travel back to Bainu, where I work and live. Is that what you would like to do?"

"Of course," said Laurenzo. "Bainu is the most beautiful city in the world."

"You're right," replied Master Philippo, "although you can't actually know that for sure, as you've seen hardly anything of the world. And now it's time to sleep, as I'd like to make an early start tomorrow. I'll be a good master, but you'll need to work hard."

"I'm not scared of hard work," said Laurenzo. He could not get to sleep at first, as he was so excited about the future that awaited him. The only shadow over his happiness was that Jiacomo could not be with him. *But*, he consoled himself, *we'll see each other again in a year's time.*

Jiacomo had taken the left-hand path. Although he was sad about saying goodbye to his brother, he was still singing. It was a song he had made up himself:

> *"Oh, when will we two see each other again?*
> *When will we meet once more?*
> *When will we see each other again?*
> *And will there be sun?*
> *Or will there be rain?"*

The first two days, like his brother, he met no one. On the third day though, he came to a sheep pen. He asked the shepherd if he needed any help.

"Bah!" said the shepherd, scornfully spitting on the ground. "A boy like you soon tires of looking after sheep and then he runs away and abandons the poor creatures. Go on! Clear off!"

As Jiacomo walked on, he thought to himself: *I hope everyone around here isn't that unfriendly. I've been walking for three days now and I still haven't found a job. Maybe I should just go back to Bainu.* Then he stopped.

No, he thought. *I'll follow this path to the end. I already know what lies behind me. What lies ahead is a surprise.*

So he walked on, followed by his faithful dog. And he came to a vast plain covered with yellowish grass, where rocks lay scattered around, as if thrown by giants. This was the Plain of Babina, where there was dense fog for half the year, and a stormy wind blew for the rest of the time – a hostile, mysterious region, where few people lived. Travellers who had to cross it did so as quickly as possible, afraid of fog and storms, of robbers and will-o'-the-wisps.

Jiacomo headed across that desolate plain. First there was a storm, then mist and finally he got lost. He wandered around for three days, with no idea where he was going, and he thought to himself: *I was longing to travel and to see the world, but that's no good if you never meet anyone to talk to.*

Three days later, the fog lifted, and he saw a man walking ahead of him in the distance. He stepped up his pace and soon caught up with him. He was a big, dark man, and he was struggling to carry a large sack. Jiacomo greeted him and said: "Would you like me to carry your sack for a while?"

"Yes, please," said the man, "I've already walked a long way. My horse broke its leg so I had to put it out of its misery. Where are you going?"

"Wherever the road takes me," replied Jiacomo. "But right now it doesn't seem to be taking me anywhere."

"If you tell me where you want to go, I'll point you in the right direction," said the man. "You can go to Bainu, Forpa or to Talamura, whichever you prefer."

"Bainu – that's where I came from," said Jiacomo. "Which is better, Forpa or Talamura?"

"I can't tell you that," said the man. "I don't know what you want to do."

"Look for a job," said Jiacomo.

"What kind of job?" asked the man.

"I don't know yet," replied Jiacomo.

"What would you prefer," asked the man, "an ordinary, dull job, or one that's full of adventure?"

"Adventure, of course," said Jiacomo.

"You can go to Forpa or to some other place," said the man, "but if you like adventure, I'd say you're best off coming with me. I've only just met you, but you seem like a bright lad. Come and work with me, and I'll teach you my trade. If you have a talent for it, you won't regret it."

"So what is your trade?" asked Jiacomo.

"Hmm," said the man. "You could say that I'm a hunter. I hunt valuable game. My trade is one for skilful, intelligent and resourceful people. I'll explain it to you in more detail later. Come with me. You'll have a good life with me."

Jiacomo looked at him and decided that he seemed trustworthy. "Fine," he said. "I'll come with you."

And so he went with the man, who turned out to be called Jannos, and they took it in turns to carry the sack.

After a while, Jannos and Jiacomo came to some big rocks.

"Here's my house," said Jannos.

Jiacomo looked surprised, as he couldn't see anything resembling a house. But his companion gently pushed one of the rocks. It rolled aside and, after passing through a gap, they came to a small grassy area that was surrounded by more rocks. In the middle of the grass, there was a house made of stone, with two horses grazing beside it.

"Come inside," said Jannos, "and make yourself at home. Now you're my apprentice and your first duty is to tell no one where we live."

As soon as they were inside, he opened the sack and tipped its contents onto the floor. Jiacomo was astonished to see the valuable objects that came tumbling out: cups and bowls of beaten gold, silver coins, elegantly decorated daggers and glittering jewels. He wondered how Jannos, who did not look at all wealthy, had come by these precious items.

"Now I'm your apprentice," he said. "But I still don't know what I can learn from you."

"You'll find out soon enough," replied Jannos. "Your lessons begin tomorrow."

Then he put all of the objects into a large chest, which he carefully locked, and said: "We won't talk about business now though. Go and sit at the table, and I'll prepare a nice meal."

Jiacomo was starving. So he did not ask any more questions, but tucked into the meal that Jannos had made.

That night in bed, he lay awake for a long time. He wondered what trade Jannos was going to teach him, as the man still refused to tell him anything. And he also thought about his brother. How was Laurenzo faring?

Laurenzo was back in Bainu, where Master Philippo was teaching him to be a goldsmith. He learnt how to forge and cast and beat metals, and he learnt how to tell the difference between different kinds of precious stones. He enjoyed his work, even though it would be some time before he could make beautiful objects, as Master Philippo could.

"How long will it take me to finish learning?" he once asked.

"You never finish learning," replied the old goldsmith, "but in about three years or so you'll be able to make some nice pieces. You have a talent for this work."

"But I can't stay that long," said Laurenzo. "I'm supposed to meet up with my brother after a year."

"Then you can return to me after you've met up with him," said the goldsmith. "No one can learn a trade in just a year."

So Laurenzo sat in the workshop every day, surrounded by his animals. In addition to his dog, he now also had the two cats and two pigeons, which he had fetched from his old neighbours, with his master's permission. One cat and one pigeon were for Jiacomo, when he came back to Bainu. Because Laurenzo was sure that would happen one day.

Meanwhile, Jiacomo had also begun his lessons. On the first day, Jannos gave him a bow and arrows and taught him how to shoot. He made a target close to his house, and Jiacomo practised for many hours. A week later, Jannos told him to get onto one of the horses and when the boy could ride, he took him out onto the plain and showed him every path, every rock and every hiding place.

So, when Jiacomo could both shoot and ride, and he knew his way around the area too, he asked his master when he would be able to go hunting.

"You don't know enough yet," said Jannos. "These were just the lessons to prepare you, which have little to do with the job itself, although they can come in handy. Now we're really going to get started. Dexterity, that's something you'll need to develop. Remember, too, that the only reason you have weapons is so that you don't have to use them – unless you're really in trouble."

Jiacomo did not understand what he meant, and he told him so.

"Wait and see," said Jannos and he gave him a small box. "Open it," he commanded.

"There's no key," said Jiacomo.

"That's the point," said his master. "Open this box without using a key."

Jiacomo took a hammer, a pair of pliers and a nail, and he managed to force the lid.

"Not too bad for a first attempt," said Jannos. "Now I'll show you how to do it better – quickly and without making a sound."

Within a few days, Jiacomo was opening all kinds of boxes and chests and doors, without using keys and without making any noise.

"Now for the next lesson," said Jannos, when they were having dinner one night. "I want you to take the salt cellar from the table, without me seeing, and to drink my cup dry, without me noticing. You'll need to be quick and skilful, and you'll also have to spin a nice, entertaining yarn to distract me. No, if you reach out your hand like that, I'll spot it straightaway."

Jiacomo put down his spoon and said: "Tell me now what your trade is!"

"Can't you guess?" asked Jannos.

"I believe I can," replied Jiacomo. "But if it's true, then I can't stay on as your apprentice."

"Why not? It's a fine job trade, with few true masters. Hey, where's the salt cellar?"

"Here, in my hand," said Jiacomo.

"Good work! You have talent," said Jannos. "You know, you could become a decent robber and an excellent thief!"

A thief! That's not an honest job, thought Jiacomo, and he said: "I'm sorry, master, but I don't want to be a thief."

"Don't be so foolish," said Jannos. "You've been training for a while now, and it would be a shame if you didn't finish your studies. Stay at least until you have completed your final test. Then you'll be fully skilled and qualified, so you'll be able to make a living."

Jiacomo had to admit that there was a lot of truth in his master's words. Even if he never practised his trade, it might still prove useful. So he said: "Fine, I'll stay," and he picked up Jannos's cup and downed his drink without him noticing.

"Laurenzo," said Master Philippo to his apprentice, "I have to go to Forpa with two silver necklaces and a golden bowl that the duke has ordered from me. It's springtime now and good weather for travelling, and I can go with an easy mind, as I know you and your dog will look after my house. Keep on working hard, even though I'm away."

He said farewell to his apprentice, climbed onto his horse and went on his way, with the precious objects packed up carefully inside his saddlebag. In addition, he had armed himself with a dagger and a big stick, as he had to cross the Plain of Babina, where robbers sometimes roamed.

"Jiacomo," said Jannos, the thief, to his apprentice, "now it is time for you to make practical use of your knowledge. We'll start with something simple. It's spring and travellers are using the road again. Your task today is to stop a man and rob him of his belongings. Make sure you come home with something good."

Jiacomo hesitantly said that he was not too keen on the idea, but Jannos became angry and yelled: "Don't be so foolish! What good is knowledge that you don't use? You have to show that you've learnt my lessons well and prove that you can indeed carry out the trade of thievery. You're not afraid, are you?"

Jiacomo was not afraid and besides he thought Jannos was right – well, looking at it from Jannos's point of view anyway. Of course Jiacomo had to prove that he could rob and steal, even if his conscience was not entirely easy. So he armed himself, wrapped a piece of cloth around his face, so that only his eyes could be seen, climbed onto his horse and rode to the big road that went from Bainu to Forpa. When he got there, he hid behind a rocky outcrop and waited. His dog had followed him and jumped around him, barking. That would be sure to give him away, so he spoke sternly to the animal and told it to go home. It was not easy to make the dog obey, but finally it went and Jiacomo was alone.

He waited for a long time, but saw no living creatures except for the butterflies on the flowers and the lizards in the grass. Just as he was beginning to wonder if anyone would ever come, he heard the sound of hoofs. A little later, he saw a horse approaching, carrying an old man whose saddlebag looked nice and full. It was Master Philippo, but Jiacomo had no way of knowing that, of course. The young man waited until the traveller was close to him and then he stepped out from his hiding place. He drew his bow, nocked an arrow and shouted: "Your money or your life!"

Master Philippo urged on his horse and was about to flee, but Jiacomo blocked his path and repeated: "Your money or your life!"

The goldsmith raised his stick, but Jiacomo, much younger and stronger than him, pulled it from his hand and said: "Give me what you have and I won't harm you."

"You won't harm me?" said the goldsmith, panting. "Robbing me? Is that what you call doing no harm? You can have what I am carrying, because you are stronger than me. But don't pretend you're doing me a favour by not killing me."

Jiacomo did not reply, but started searching through his victim's bag. He found the necklaces and the golden bowl – a valuable haul!

"So you have what you were looking for," said the goldsmith. "Now clear off, you coward!"

"I'm no coward!" cried Jiacomo indignantly. "My job is a job like any other."

"Then why are you hiding your face, as if you are ashamed? An honest man always dares to show who and what he is."

Jiacomo was indeed ashamed. "Fine. You can see my face!" he cried. "Here you go!" And he pulled away the cloth.

When the goldsmith saw his face, he almost fell off his horse. He stared incredulously at the young man. "Y-you!" he stammered.

Jiacomo, who had been about to ride off with his haul, stopped, surprised by the look on his victim's face.

"You..." repeated the goldsmith. His surprise gave way to fury and disappointment. "You are robbing me!" he said. "Robbing me, when I have taught you and given you shelter, without ever asking for anything in return."

"I don't understand," said Jiacomo.

"You two-faced liar!" cried the goldsmith. "I trusted you, Laurenzo, as I would have trusted my own son. I would never have believed you could behave like this!" Now Jiacomo understood.

"Laurenzo!" he cried. "You are mistaken. I am not Laurenzo."

"Silence!" said the goldsmith. "Just go! I never want to see you again."

The old man was about to ride off, but Jiacomo stopped him.

"I'm truly not Laurenzo," he said. "I'm Jiacomo, his twin brother."

Master Philippo looked at him. Was this boy really not his apprentice? He remembered that Laurenzo had often spoken about his twin brother.

"Honestly," Jiacomo persisted, "I'm not Laurenzo. Is he a friend of yours? Then please don't think badly of him. Be angry with Jiacomo, not with his brother."

The goldsmith believed him. "I'm glad you're not Laurenzo," he said. "Maybe I shouldn't have suspected him, but how could I have known that he and his brother looked so alike?" He looked seriously at Jiacomo and added: "And I had no idea that Laurenzo's brother was a robber!"

Jiacomo stared down at his feet. "Neither does Laurenzo," he said. Then he looked back at the goldsmith and asked: "How is he?"

"Fine," replied Master Philippo. "Better than you, or so it seems. He is my apprentice and he is learning to make the things you steal."

Jiacomo blushed. Then he took out the silver necklaces and the golden bowl and put them in Master Philippo's hands. "Here is your property," he said. "I don't want to rob a friend of Laurenzo's. Give him my best wishes and tell him I'm longing for the moment when we will see each other again. And please also tell him that this is the first and last time I've ever stolen anything."

He turned his horse and galloped away, as quickly as he could. The goldsmith stared after him until he had disappeared from sight.

The twin brothers Laurenzo and Jiacomo lived far from each other and the work they did was very different. Laurenzo was an apprentice to Master Philippo, the goldsmith. He was going to become a goldsmith himself – and that was exactly what he wanted to do. Jiacomo had learnt how to rob and steal, but he no longer wished to become a thief. So he decided to leave his master, Jannos, and to learn an honest trade instead.

The Silver Cups of Talamura

"I want to put you to the test and see what you can do."

GRIMM: 'The Four Skilful Brothers'

1 THE ADVENTURES OF JIACOMO

"So did you get something good?" Jannos the thief asked his apprentice, Jiacomo, upon his return from his first raid.

"Yes," replied Jiacomo. "I stole two silver necklaces and a golden bowl."

"Excellent," said Jannos. "Let me see."

"I can't," said Jiacomo. "I gave them back."

"What did you say?" exclaimed Jannos.

"I gave them back," repeated Jiacomo. "The man I robbed turned out to be a friend of my brother's. He has taught him and given him a roof over his head. I can't take something from a friend of my brother's, can I?"

"You must be insane!" yelled Jannos. "You're a terrible thief – that's what you are!"

"I've proved that I can steal," said Jiacomo, "and that was the point, wasn't it? But I'm not going to steal any longer. I'm leaving."

"What? You're leaving?" cried Jannos.

"Yes, I am," replied Jiacomo. "I don't want to be a thief."

Jannos was furious, but neither cursing nor cajoling could sway Jiacomo from his decision.

"Now listen," the thief said finally. "I've taught you and given you a roof over your head, without ever asking for anything in return. It would be most ungrateful if you left me just like that."

These words got through to Jiacomo and, spotting this weakness, the clever Jannos continued: "So let's come to an agreement. You will carry out a job for me. When you have done that, your debt to me will be paid and you will also have proved your mastery."

Jiacomo really did not want to steal again, but he could not help asking: "So what's this job?"

"In the west, among the rocks and the pine forests that border the plain, lies the Castle of Talamura. A rich and powerful man lives there, who owns many treasures. Among those treasures are thirteen silver cups, beautiful and precious, decorated with magnificent engravings. I have always planned to steal those cups, although the Lord of Talamura knows me and has sworn that he will hang me. This is my task for you: bring me one of those cups. It only needs to be one. If you succeed, your debt to me is paid, and you can call yourself my equal, a master thief."

Jiacomo thought about it. The job was tempting, but he had made up his mind never to steal again.

"Oh dear," said Jannos, shaking his head. "I can already see it on your face. You won't do it. The task's too difficult. You're too scared to accept my challenge."

"Of course I'm not!" cried Jiacomo. "It's just that I don't want to be a thief."

"Well, maybe you're not scared," said Jannos, "but you're simply not up to it. Only a master thief could steal one of the silver cups of Talamura."

"Didn't you train me well enough?" asked Jiacomo.

"I certainly did," said Jannos, "but this is all down to you and to your own ingenuity, and I can't give you that, not in a thousand lessons."

"Tell me more about these cups," said Jiacomo.

"I've already told you they're made of silver," replied Jannos, "decorated with beautiful engravings and with the arms of Talamura on them: an eagle and a squirrel on either side of a pine tree. The Lord of Talamura is very fond of them and keeps them closely guarded against thieves. They are said to stand next to each other on a shelf inside a large cabinet, but there are of course many cupboards in the castle, so I cannot tell you exactly where they are kept."

"What's the castle like?"

"Strong and impregnable. It's up on top of a rock. Day and night, there are guards at the gate, and no stranger is admitted."

"Are there any secret doors? Or hidden passageways? Or weak spots in the walls?"

"The walls are many feet thick, and there are no secret passages."

"So how am I ever supposed to get inside?" asked Jiacomo. "How am I going to steal one of the cups?"

"I don't care," replied Jannos. "I asked you for a cup, and I'm not interested in how you get it. But let's not talk about this any longer. You don't want to steal anyway, and I can see that this task is too difficult for you."

"It is hard, I will admit that," said Jiacomo. "But not so hard that I won't give it a try."

"I'll just come up with another task for you," said Jannos.

"No," said Jiacomo, "this one suits me fine."

"So you'll do it?" asked Jannos.

"Yes," replied Jiacomo. He might not have wanted to steal any longer, but the lure of the adventure and the challenge was too strong for him. If the Lord of Talamura owned thirteen cups, then surely he could do without one of them. Besides, Jiacomo thought he should do something for Jannos, who had done so much for him, without ever asking for payment.

The thief smiled at him. "You are a boy after my own heart," he said. "And I wish you good luck. This is a true test of mastery, which is first and foremost about cleverness. Go and have a look inside my chests – you'll find everything you need, from false beards to crowbars."

Jiacomo picked out everything that he wanted to take and the next morning he dressed himself in the finest clothes he could find. He buckled a sword around his waist and on his feet he wore leather boots with silver spurs.

When Jannos saw him all dressed up, his eyes opened wide. "What do we have here?" he said. "You look just like a nobleman!"

"That's the best way to go visiting a nobleman," replied Jiacomo. He gave his master a graceful bow and then said: "There's an old lute in one of your chests. Can I take that too?"

"You can keep it," said Jannos. "I stole it once, because I was in the mood for a little music. But I've never been any good at playing it."

Jiacomo thanked him. He picked up the lute and strummed a few chords.

"You're really good," said Jannos.

"I've played the lute before," said Jiacomo. "A friend of mine in Bainu had one."

"Well, I hope you can steal as well as you can strum," said Jannos. "And now we must say farewell. When will you return?"

"I don't know yet," said Jiacomo. "As you've told me, haste is rarely wise."

"If you find yourself in danger, then send your dog to me," said Jannos. "And I'll come to help you."

Jiacomo promised to do so. Then he said goodbye to his master, whistled for his dog and jumped onto the horse that Jannos had said he could borrow. And he rode away, towards adventure, playing his lute and dressed like a nobleman, although he was also equipped with certain items that a nobleman does not usually possess.

The plain was beautiful: spring flowers blossomed on the ground, which was usually so bleak, butterflies danced in the air, and the sun shone. Jiacomo sang one song after another as his dog skipped around him, wagging his tail. Later in the day it became misty, but the young man knew his way on the plain so well that he rode on without hesitation. When night fell, he found a place to sleep in an empty sheep pen, and early the next morning he set off once more. Cheerfully, he rode onwards, along one little path after another, and he thought he should be able to reach Talamura before the evening. The only problem was that he still had no idea how he would get inside that impregnable castle.

That afternoon, when he was sitting on the ground beside his horse and having a bite to eat, three rather gloomy-looking men came riding along. One of them, a finely attired young man, not much older than Jiacomo himself, reined in his horse and said: "I say, do you know the way to Talamura by any chance?"

"I do," said Jiacomo, getting to his feet. "Why don't you ride along with me?"

"We're completely lost," said the young man. "These stupid servants of mine wanted to take a shortcut but instead they've had me wandering around for hours."

"It's an easy place to get lost," said Jiacomo. "But I'll put you back on the right path."

The four of them rode on, Jiacomo and the young man leading the way, and the two servants following behind.

"Are you going to Talamura as well?" the young man asked.

"I'm not sure yet," Jiacomo replied casually. "I'll choose whichever way looks best." Good thieves do not reveal too much about themselves. "Are you going to the castle?" he asked his companion.

"Yes," the young man replied. "I'm going to visit my uncle."

When Jiacomo heard that, he thought it might be a good idea to become better acquainted with this fellow. But he was clever enough not to be too hasty. "Now that we are travelling together for a way," he said, "I shall tell you who I am. My name is Jia, Lord of Como."

"Nice to meet you," said the other man. "I am Ricardo, a nobleman of Pava."

"Of Pava? Are you by any chance related to Zebedee of Pava?"

"No," said the young man, "I don't believe we're acquainted."

Which made sense, as Jiacomo had just made the name up.

"Oh," said Jiacomo, "I thought you might have known him. You have the same name, after all."

"My father is Nicolaas of Pava and I have an uncle called Michael," said Ricardo.

"But the Lord of Talamura is also an uncle of yours, is he not?" asked Jiacomo.

"Yes," replied Ricardo, "he's my mother's brother. Do you know him?"

"No," said Jiacomo. "But I have heard talk of him."

"I don't know him either. My parents were at odds with him for some time. But they recently reconciled and now I'm visiting him to strengthen the peace between us."

Aha, thought Jiacomo, *I can feel a plan beginning to form.* He talked on, cheerfully entertaining his travelling companion – and cunningly teasing information out of him.

When they came to a fork in the road, Jiacomo stopped his horse. "Now we must part ways," he said. "I'm riding on to Forpa and you need to turn right to Talamura." And he pointed at the road to Forpa.

Ricardo thanked him and unsuspectingly set off along the road to Forpa with his two servants. But Jiacomo rode straight on, whistling a happy tune.

Ha! he thought to himself. *Ricardo won't find out for quite a while that he's going the wrong way, because you hardly meet anyone on the road to Forpa. So I'll be in Talamura long before him!*

Soon Jiacomo had left the plain and was riding along a rising road, which meandered between hills and through

pine forests. Before the sun went down, he saw the castle before him, steep and stately, on top of a high rock. A village huddled against the cliff face below, with lots of little houses with pointed roofs. As Jiacomo headed along the path that led to the castle, he heard the sound of horns above.

"Listen," he said to his dog. "They're announcing our visit."

Not long after that, he banged the heavy knocker on the castle gate.

Two guards peered out through a slit in the wall.

"Good evening," said Jiacomo. "May I come in?"

"Good evening," replied one of the guards. "No, you may not come in. You must find hospitality down in the village, as no strangers are admitted to the castle."

"But I am not a stranger," said Jiacomo. "I am Ricardo of Pava, your master's nephew."

"Oh!" exclaimed the guard. "You should have said so at once! Come on in. Are you alone?"

"I have my dog with me," replied Jiacomo. "My men will be coming along soon. I rode ahead, as I was keen to meet my uncle."

"Our lord and his lady are expecting you," said the second guard. With much bowing and scraping, they allowed the presumed Ricardo to enter. One of them took his horse by the reins to lead it to the stables, while the other took Jiacomo across the courtyard to a second gate. Then another guard appeared, who opened the gate and entrusted "Ricardo" to a solemn servant. This man led him through a large hall, up a flight of stairs, through another large hall, up another flight of stairs, through a multitude of rooms, up another flight of stairs – and finally knocked on a door.

My goodness me, thought Jiacomo, *if I hadn't met Ricardo of Pava, getting inside this castle would certainly not have been an easy task.*

The door swung open and a large man with dark, greying hair appeared before him and asked: "So you're my nephew Ricardo, are you?"

Jiacomo gave him a deep bow and replied: "My greetings, noble uncle. And I also bring you greetings from everyone in Pava, from my father, my mother and my sister."

"Welcome!" cried the Lord of Talamura. "Is there no one else with you?"

"Just my dog for now," said Jiacomo. "My men will follow soon. I rode ahead."

"Ah, the haste of youth!" said the Lord of Talamura, laying his hand on Jiacomo's shoulder and leading him into the room. "And this, Ricardo," he continued, "is my wife, your aunt."

A finely dressed woman with a kind but somewhat sad face came towards him. Jiacomo started to bow again, but she took his hands and kissed him on both cheeks. "Welcome," she said. "I'm so pleased to see you!"

Jiacomo smiled a bit sheepishly.

"You're just in time for dinner," said the lord of the castle. "Are you hungry? We've planned a feast for today."

"In your honour," said the lady. "But first I shall take you to your room. I'm sure you'll want to freshen up after your long journey."

A little later, Jiacomo was sitting with the lord, his wife and the other residents of the castle at the large table in the beautiful great hall, enjoying the excellent meal and answering his so-called aunt and uncle's questions as well as he could – which, with some help from his imagination, was not going badly. Luckily, the lord was quite a talkative man, so Jiacomo did not need to say too much.

"Tomorrow I'll show you around," said the Lord of Talamura. "We'll go hunting in the mountains and forests."

"Yes," said Jiacomo, "that would be nice – at least if you're happy for me to stay a little longer."

"Well, that was what we agreed, wasn't it?" said the lord, and his wife added: "Yes, I think it would be marvellous if you stayed for a long time. Then I can imagine that I have a son here again."

"Is your son away somewhere?" asked Jiacomo.

"Our son... died when he was a little boy," said the lady.

"I... I'm sorry..." stammered Jiacomo. Why had Ricardo not mentioned that?

There was a brief silence. Then the lady put another large piece of chicken on Jiacomo's plate. "Here, have some more," she said with a smile.

Jiacomo thanked her and began to eat, even though he had completely lost his appetite. He felt like a complete fraud – which, of course, he was.

When the meal was over and the lord had said a prayer of thanks, they all went and sat together in the castle's great hall: Jiacomo, the lord and his wife, and the other residents of the castle.

"Tonight we shall stay up a little later than usual," said the Lord of Talamura.

"But not *too* late," said his wife. "Ricardo must be tired after his journey."

"Oh no, not at all," said Jiacomo quickly. He remembered that he would soon have to put his plan into action. He had to get away from the castle before the real Ricardo arrived in Talamura. He looked around the room. It was beautifully decorated, with heavy carved furniture, sheepskins on the floor and embroidered tapestries on the walls. There were a number of cabinets, but which one contained the silver cups? Or could they be in another room?

Jiacomo expressed his admiration for Talamura and for the room they were in. Then he brought up the subject that had been on his mind all night. "I have heard, my uncle," he said, "that you are the owner of some beautiful cups. Magnificent silver cups. Is that true?"

"Yes," replied the Lord of Talamura, "those cups are my pride and joy. Maybe not the most precious of my possessions, but certainly the most beautiful."

"I would so love to see them," said Jiacomo.

"And one day you shall – but not now. Another time."

"And no one knows where you keep these cups," Jiacomo persisted. "At least that's what I've heard."

"That's true indeed. Hardly anyone knows," said the lord, "except for a few trusted servants – and my wife, of course."

"They are in this room, are they not?" said Jiacomo.

The Lord of Talamura did not reply, and Jiacomo did not dare to ask any more questions, but he followed the lady's gaze and drew his own conclusions. Then he turned the conversation to other subjects and did not mention the cups again.

They spent a pleasant evening together. The Lord of Talamura talked about the journeys he had made in the past, and Jiacomo played a few tunes on his lute. But the more time passed, the more uneasy he felt. He had made a plan, but still he hesitated to carry it out. What would these kind people say when they realized he was a thief? What would the lady of the castle think of him after he had made off with one of the silver cups?

Oh well, he thought. *I have to do it. This is my test. I need to prove that I am a master thief.*

He stood up, walked over to one of the tables and picked up a jug, which was full of wine. And as he did so, very quickly, without anyone noticing, he dropped something into the jug. "Let me fill everyone's cups one more time," he said. "I wish to drink to your health." He went around the room, filling cups, and as he did so he heard Jannos's voice inside his head, saying: "I asked you for a cup, and I'm not interested in how you get it."

"Well, Ricardo?" said the Lord of Talamura. "Are you going to give us a speech?"

"Yes!" cried everyone. "A speech! A speech!"

Jiacomo looked around, his cup in his hand. His cheeks were flushed, and his eyes were sparkling. "I want to drink to your health, my lady," he began, "and to yours, my lord! And to your kindness and to..." He fell silent.

"Thank you!" said the Lord of Talamura, and he raised his cup and was about to put it to his lips.

"Stop!" cried Jiacomo. "Wait a moment, I haven't finished yet! I also want to drink to Ricardo of Pava, to whom I owe my presence here. Poor Ricardo, who may well still be trying to find the way to Talamura!"

Everyone stared at him in surprise.

"However, you had better not drink this wine," Jiacomo continued. "Unless you have had enough of this evening and would rather go to sleep. If you drink, you are drinking to my good fortune alone, as I am planning to stay wide awake and—"

"What nonsense is this?" cried the lord of the castle, slamming down his cup.

Jiacomo took a deep breath. "Don't you understand?" he said. "I'm not who you think I am. I am not your nephew, Ricardo of Pava."

"You're not Ricardo?"

"No, my lord."

"So who are you then? And where's Ricardo?"

"Ricardo is most probably wandering around somewhere on the plain, at least if he has not yet realized his mistake. He might turn up tonight and, if not, he'll certainly be here tomorrow morning."

The lord of the castle did not know whether to be angry or not. "Who are you?" he shouted. "And why are you saying such strange things?"

"I have some even stranger things to say," said Jiacomo. "I pretended to be your nephew because I was eager to get inside the castle."

"And why exactly did you want to enter my castle?"

"Because I wanted to steal one of your silver cups."

No one knew how to respond to that answer.

"I see..." said the lord of the castle finally. "Well, I'm glad that at least you've warned us in advance."

"Oh, but I don't believe he's a thief!" cried his wife.

"I'm not," said Jiacomo seriously. "Stealing one of the silver cups was a test to prove my mastery. I'll only be able to call myself a thief if I pass that test."

"Well, I really don't know what to make of you," said the

lord of the castle. "Have you finished your speech now? Or is there anything else you'd like to tell us?"

"I put a sleeping potion in the wine," said Jiacomo. "In the wine I just poured for all of you."

"I see," said the lord of the castle. "And why did you do that?"

"If you had drunk the wine, you would all have fallen asleep."

"Indeed?" said the lord of the castle. "And then?"

"Then I could have stolen one of your cups at my leisure."

"Oh really?" said the lord of the castle. "So you know where they are, do you?"

"In that small dark cabinet, over there in the corner," replied Jiacomo without hesitation.

"And how do you know that?"

"It was a guess, but a good one. Earlier this evening, when I mentioned the cups, I saw your wife look over that way. And she was looking at the most unattractive and insignificant cabinet in the room, at a cupboard that would not be the first place a thief would search for a good haul."

"You're a clever one," said the lord. "But even if we had all fallen asleep and even if you did know where the cups were, how did you intend to open that cabinet?"

"It wouldn't have been difficult. The key is obviously on the ring that you carry on your belt. Besides, I have a tool that can open any lock."

"I see," said the Lord of Talamura. "So you would have stolen my cups. And then?"

"I would have stolen only one cup. Then I would have gone to the gate and told the guards that I wanted to go out and see if my servants were here yet. And then I would have ridden off with the cup."

"But why are you telling us all of this? Now you can't do it. Is this a joke?"

"No, my lord, I am completely serious," said Jiacomo. "Tell me honestly, if I had not said anything, would I have succeeded in stealing one of your cups?"

"I think so, yes," said the lord of the castle. "But now you must finally tell me who you are and what you want."

"I am happy to tell you my name. It is Jiacomo. And I have already told you why I have come here: to steal one of your cups. However, you have welcomed me so kindly that I would rather not do it. I don't actually want to be a thief, you see, but I would have liked to show my master what I can do. He told me to bring him one of the cups, and he didn't care how I got it. When I found myself sitting here with you and having such a pleasant time, I realized that I didn't want to deceive you. I thought it would be better to tell you the whole story honestly and to ask for the cup. You have thirteen of them, so I'm sure you can spare one. In fact, it would be good if you had one fewer, as thirteen is an unlucky number."

The Lord of Talamura looked at Jiacomo in astonishment. "Well, by all the wild boars in the world!" he cried. "You are a bold one!"

His wife leant over and whispered something in his ear.

"They do say that fortune favours the bold," said the lord of the castle. "In any case, you have certainly won over my wife. I believe she would actually like to give you a cup."

"Really? That's so terribly kind of you," said Jiacomo. "I know I don't deserve it, but my master says that hardly anyone gets what they deserve."

"I think I know who your master is," said the Lord of Talamura. "And if he got what he deserved, it would be the gallows." He stood up and walked over to the small dark cabinet. "I'm not planning to give you anything," he continued, "other than the beating you deserve. But I would like to know if you've been idly boasting. Show me that you can really get this cupboard open. And I'm not going to hand over my key!"

Jiacomo took out his special thieves' tool, and everyone in the room stood up and gathered around to see how he would manage it. The young man set to work and, within a minute, he had opened the door. "There you go," he said, stepping back.

The cups were lined up on the top shelf, gleaming away. They were all the same shape, but each was slightly smaller than the previous one. Everyone in the room cried out in admiration, many of them craning their necks for a better view, as most had never been permitted to set eyes on the cups before. Jiacomo spoke their thoughts aloud when he said: "What a shame that those beautiful silver cups are always kept in the darkness under lock and key, where no one can ever see them." He turned to the lord of the castle and asked: "Might I just take them off the shelf for a moment to look at them? Then at least I will not have come here for nothing."

"You have my permission," said the Lord of Talamura. "As long as you are careful."

Jiacomo took the cups out of the cabinet, placed them on a table and looked closely at them, while everyone, not least of all their owner, kept a very close eye on him.

"It's sad that I can no longer steal them," said Jiacomo. "I almost regret telling you the truth."

"I'd like to give you a chance," said the Lord of Talamura. "If you succeed in stealing one of the cups before we go to bed, you may keep it."

"Challenge accepted, my lord!" said Jiacomo with a smile. "Can we leave the cabinet open?"

"Fine," said the lord of the castle. "It shall not be locked. But put the cups back inside."

"One moment, my lord," said Jiacomo. "Let me just look to see which cup I shall take." He turned the smallest one upside down and placed it on his palm. "It's so funny how they fit together," he continued, as he placed the next cup over it. "Which one shall I take? The smallest, the largest, or one of the ones in between?" He placed the third cup over the two in his hand, and then the fourth, and went on stacking them until they were all on top of one another, with the largest cup covering the other twelve. "I'll take that one," he decided. "The largest of all. And now I shall place all thirteen of them back neatly in the cabinet."

Carrying the tower of cups, he walked to the cabinet and quickly placed them back on the shelf, one by one. As he did so, he counted: "One, two, three..." all the way up to thirteen. Then he closed the door and asked his host: "How much time do I have before you go to bed?"

"Not long," the lord replied. "It's already late." He ordered one of his servants to pour the cups of wine that Jiacomo had served back into the jug and to throw it all away. "We don't want to fall asleep before we're in bed," he said. "Sit down, Jiacomo, and tell me what you've done with my nephew. I hope nothing bad has happened to him, because otherwise I really will have to give you a beating."

Jiacomo sat down and told him how he had met Ricardo.

"A fine kettle of fish," growled the Lord of Talamura. "In any case, you will have to stay here until he arrives. Then he can give you the beating. You're a bright lad and you could achieve something in this world if you were not a thief. Because no matter how clever you are, a thief always ends up on the gallows."

"Oh, don't say that!" cried the lady of the castle. "You won't steal again, will you, Jiacomo?"

"Just the cup," replied the young man.

"And you won't succeed anyway," said the lord of the castle. "We're all keeping a close eye on the cabinet, and besides we're about to go to bed."

"My noble lord," began Jiacomo, almost apologetically, "as far as I'm concerned, you can all go to bed right now. You see... I already have a cup!"

"That's impossible!" cried the Lord of Talamura. "I've been watching the cabinet all this time and you didn't even get up off your chair!"

Jiacomo reached his hand into his jerkin and pulled out a gleaming object. "Here it is," he said. "The smallest of the cups. It was the easiest one to take."

"However did you manage that?" exclaimed the lord.

"When I put the cups back on the shelf, I counted to thirteen, but I only put twelve down. I slipped the last one into my jerkin, and then I closed the door before you had a chance to notice that they weren't all there."

"Well," said the Lord of Talamura, "you did it very skilfully, and so the cup now belongs to you." He sighed and added: "Perhaps you are too skilful – I fear that nothing is safe from you."

"Oh, but I'm not going to be a thief," said Jiacomo. "It's a fun job, but it's not honest."

"I'm glad to hear it," said the lady of the castle. "You're welcome to take the cup, but I wouldn't like to think of you as a thief."

Jiacomo looked at the lord and his wife with a serious expression on his face. "I thank you both," he said. "You've been so kind to me. If there's anything I can do for you, you only have to ask."

"Thank you," replied the Lord of Talamura. "Now let's all go to bed. I suspect my nephew Ricardo will not be here before tomorrow morning, not if he rode all the way to Forpa at least.

So there's no point staying up any longer. Sleep well, Jiacomo – if your conscience is clear," he added with a mocking smile.

So everyone said good night and Jiacomo was taken to the room that was actually intended for Ricardo.

He was sitting on the edge of the bed, taking another look at the cup, when a servant came in with a cup of wine.

"Here you are, sir," said the servant. "My lady would like you to drink this cup to her health."

"Thank you," said Jiacomo. He put the silver cup in his bag and accepted the wine. Although he had already had a few that evening, he did not wish to be impolite to his hostess and so he downed the wine. If only he had not done so...

When the Lord of Talamura awoke the next morning, he felt quite glum.

"Whatever got into me yesterday?" he said to his wife. "Now I've gone and given away one of my precious cups to a complete stranger."

"You don't regret it, do you?" asked his wife.

"Hmm, I wouldn't exactly call it regret," he replied irritably. "I just think I've been a fool. If someone had told me a week ago that I'd give away one of my silver cups, then I'd have laughed at them. But don't worry that I'll ask him to return it. An honest man does not give with one hand and take with the other."

Jiacomo was sleeping so soundly that morning that the servant who came to wake him had to give him a good shake. When he went for breakfast in the great hall, he found not only the lord and lady of the castle there, but also their nephew, Ricardo of Pava. He had arrived early that morning and he was not in a good mood.

71

"There is the impostor!" he cried when he saw Jiacomo. "Hey, if you want to steal, that's your business, but don't send me wandering off down the wrong road!"

"My apologies," said Jiacomo.

"What good are apologies to me?" spat Ricardo. You've slept in a comfortable bed all night, while I was wandering around on the plain. And if I hadn't met a shepherd who pointed me in the right direction, I still wouldn't be here now!"

"You're right," said Jiacomo. "Apologies are no good to you. Would you like to give me a beating? That's what your uncle suggested."

"Yes, mock me, why don't you?" cried Ricardo. "What if you hit me back? Besides, I'm far too tired and hungry to give you a beating."

"Come on," said the lady of the castle. "Don't argue! Why don't you try to make friends? Ricardo, sit down and have something to eat. Then you'll feel better – and be in a friendlier mood."

The breakfast was a rather miserable affair. The Lord of Talamura and Ricardo were not very talkative, and Ricardo kept glaring at Jiacomo. Only the lady of the castle talked pleasantly to everyone. After breakfast, Jiacomo stood up and said that he would like to take his leave.

"Stay another day," said the lady. "It's nice for Ricardo to have a guest of his own age here."

Jiacomo looked first at the lord and then at Ricardo, who pulled a sour face. Then he shook his head. "I'd better go," he said. "I have to take the cup to my master and then, when autumn comes, I'm going to meet my brother at a fork in the road. Let me thank you once again for your magnificent gift."

"Nonsense," said the Lord of Talamura, a little abruptly. "You earned it yourself with your skill. And I would rather give away one cup than have them all stolen. Farewell, Jiacomo, I wish you all the best."

"Farewell," said his wife. "Come and visit us again." Jiacomo promised that he would do so.

"Come and visit me in Pava too," said Ricardo. "And give me a chance to make a fool out of you."

Jiacomo also promised to do that. Then he said goodbye, kissed the lady's hand, fetched his bag, whistled for his dog, and a servant led him to the gate. Soon he was riding away, back to the plain, with the cup in his possession. His mission had been successful!

But in the Castle of Talamura, Ricardo said to his uncle: "I don't understand you! He told you himself that he is a thief and an impostor, but you still gave him what he wanted."

"Silence!" barked the lord of the castle. "He won the cup honestly. The matter is closed." He walked over to the small dark cabinet and put the key in the lock. "I still have twelve left," he muttered. "Let me see if the cupboard looks bare."

It did indeed look very bare, as when he opened the door, he saw that not one single cup was left. The cabinet was empty!

The Lord of Talamura was stunned for a moment, but then he flew into a rage and screamed for his entire household to come at once.

"I have been robbed!" he cried. "A curse on the thief!"

Everyone stood pale and fearful while he uttered the most severe threats. But when he finally paused for breath, Ricardo of Pava said: "Who could have done this but Jiacomo?"

"No!" cried the lady. "I don't believe it!"

But then a servant stepped forward. "My lord," he said, "as I led the young man to the gate some minutes ago, I heard a jangling noise coming from the bag he was carrying. I don't wish to accuse him, but he certainly could be the thief."

"Go after him," the lord ordered. "Go after him, Josefus, and bring him here! And no one may enter or leave the castle until it has been thoroughly searched."

The servant quickly followed the orders, but the lady of the castle scolded her husband. "How could you suspect Jiacomo of such a thing?"

"His behaviour last night might have been a trick," replied the lord. "Someone must have done it: either him or someone who lives in the castle. I have to investigate. If he is innocent, no harm will come to him."

Jiacomo was still not far away, and so it was not long before the servant returned with him.

"Here am I, my lord," said the young man. "How might I serve you?"

The Lord of Talamura looked into his bright eyes and paused before answering. "Do you not know?" he asked gruffly.

"I haven't told him anything, my lord," said Josefus, the servant.

"I have been robbed," said the Lord of Talamura. "All of my silver cups are gone. And not only that – the money and the twelve golden spoons I kept in my cabinet have disappeared too."

Jiacomo gasped. "That's terrible," he said. He felt a little guilty, as he realized that he might have given the thief the idea.

"Either the stolen objects are still inside the castle," said the Lord of Talamura, "or they are outside. If they are outside, then only you could have taken them there."

Jiacomo blushed. "Do you suspect me?" he asked.

"No, of course not!" cried the Lady of Talamura.

"Oh, I understand," said Jiacomo. "After all, I'm good at stealing! But I didn't do it. Here, take a look inside my bag."

The Lord of Talamura began to believe in his innocence. But he wanted to be absolutely certain. "Open that bag," he ordered.

Jiacomo waited a moment before obeying. He was angry because the lord looked so suspicious. Then he emptied out his bag, but not before carefully removing the little cup. His clothes came out, followed by some food, his thieves' tools and, finally, a number of objects that clattered onto the floor. Jiacomo stared at them in surprise. It was three gold coins and a large spoon, also made of gold.

"The coins from my cabinet," said the lord. "And one of my golden spoons."

"How did they get into my bag?" cried Jiacomo.

The Lord of Talamura interrupted him with a cry of "Thief!" He continued: "You lying, deceitful thief! How dare you betray my trust? Thief! What have you done with the rest of your loot?" The lady began to cry.

"But I'm innocent!" shouted Jiacomo.

"Seize him!" roared the Lord of Talamura. "Throw him into the deepest dungeon! I have no desire to look at his face any longer!"

Servants roughly grabbed hold of the young man, but his dog growled and came to his assistance.

"Seize that dog and the boy!" cried the Lord of Talamura. "And lock them up together. I shall take further measures later."

"I'm innocent!" shouted Jiacomo again, but they dragged him away, along corridors and down many, many stairs, and finally left him all alone in a damp, dark dungeon, with no one to comfort him except for his dog, who licked his hands in sympathy.

"Oh," he sighed. "If only I'd never started all this! Now they think I'm a thief, just because I'm good at stealing. When they release me, I want nothing more to do with thieves ever again." But no one came to release him.

The Lord of Talamura came down to the dungeon to ask him where he had hidden the stolen treasure. He refused to believe Jiacomo when he swore that he was innocent. The stolen objects in his bag clearly proved he was the thief, didn't they?

When the young man continued to insist that he knew nothing about it, the Lord of Talamura became furious, and he would certainly have hanged Jiacomo if his wife had not begged him not to. Then he condemned Jiacomo to solitary confinement in the deepest dungeon, with nothing but water and bread, until he revealed where he had hidden the rest of his loot.

"Not that I will release you then," he told him. "You must be punished. But if you remain silent, you will never, ever see the light of day again!"

And so Jiacomo languished in one of the dungeons of Talamura, while the days passed and became weeks, and the weeks passed and became months, and the spring passed and then the summer too.

2 THE ADVENTURES OF LAURENZO

Filled with alarm, he thought, My brother must have suffered some terrible misfortune.

GRIMM: 'The Two Brothers'

Far away, in Bainu, Jiacomo's twin brother, Laurenzo, was working for Philippo, the goldsmith. And the day came when he said to his master: "I must set off for the fork in the road now, to meet my brother."

"Don't leave," said his master. "You have talent and could become a skilled goldsmith. Wait until you are qualified."

"I have to leave – and I want to," replied Laurenzo. "My brother and I agreed to meet after a year. We belong together and I'm sure he's longing to see me just as much as I'm longing to see him."

"Then I shall not stop you," said Master Philippo. "But come back to me. I am old and I have no children, and I enjoy having you around. If your brother is no longer a robber, then you must bring him back to Bainu. He can always find a job around here."

"He told you he wouldn't steal anymore, didn't he?" said Laurenzo. "I'm so keen to find out how he's doing now. Sometimes I think we should never have gone our separate ways. I shall certainly bring him here – at least if he wants to come."

He said farewell to his master and went on his way, taking his dog with him.

Exactly a year after he had seen his brother for the last time, Laurenzo came to the fork in the road. When he saw no sign of Jiacomo, he knocked on the old pedlar's door, as he had before. The pedlar welcomed him warmly.

"Good morning!" he cried. "You're one of the brothers who came here last year and who each went his own way. But I can't tell which one of the two you are."

Laurenzo told him which brother he was and gave him an account of his fortunes over the past year. The pedlar invited him to be his guest until Jiacomo showed up.

The day went by, but Jiacomo did not come and, when night fell, Laurenzo said: "I'm worried. I'm afraid that something has happened to Jiacomo."

"Stay calm," replied the pedlar. "Your brother is just delayed. I'm sure he'll be here tomorrow. Now go to bed and don't worry."

But Laurenzo could not get to sleep that night. It was not until morning that he finally fell into a fitful slumber, and he dreamt that he saw his brother in a dark cellar. When he got up, he said to the pedlar: "I'm certain that Jiacomo has suffered a misfortune. I'm going to look for him."

"Don't worry," said the pedlar. "Just wait a little longer. I'm sure he'll come wandering along soon, and in perfectly good health."

"No," said Laurenzo. "I had a dream. I can feel that he is in trouble. So I don't want to wait. I need to go and help him as quickly as I can."

"Then go," said the pedlar. "God bless you and may you find him soon!"

Laurenzo said farewell, whistled for his dog and headed down the path that Jiacomo had taken a year before.

After a while, he came to the bleak and desolate Plain of Babina, where Master Philippo had met his brother a few months before. But then the fog descended, and he was soon lost.

He wandered around for many hours, losing all sense of direction. Finally, when it was dark, he made out a distant light and headed towards it. He came to a dilapidated shepherd's hut, but as he approached, the light went out. He was about to knock on the door, but then he heard a voice inside saying: "Did you hear something?"

"No," said another voice. "Not a thing."

"I'm sure I heard someone," said the first voice.

"Then go and take a look," said the other man. "And if you find someone, then blow out his light."

Laurenzo made himself scarce, watching from a safe distance as the door opened and a man came outside. However, he didn't seem to see anything suspicious and disappeared back into the hut, closing the door behind him. Then the light went on again.

Laurenzo was curious now and decided to go and take another look. He crept to the hut and peered in through a window. There were two men sitting on the floor with, between them, all kinds of gleaming objects – silver cups, gold spoons and a pile of coins. They were dividing them up between them. *Robbers!* thought Laurenzo.

The men shared out the money and the cups, but when they came to the gold spoons they started arguing.

"I'll take six spoons and you can have five," said the first man. "It was you who put one of the spoons in his bag."

"That's not fair!" said the other man. "If I hadn't done

that, we'd never have been safe. Now he's in prison for our theft – and no one will ever suspect us. That's all my doing, so I deserve six spoons."

"No!" said the first man. "You're the one who was so keen on being safe – and that's fine – but you have to be prepared to give up a spoon for that."

"How dare you say that?" yelled the other man. "You're benefitting from our safety too, aren't you? Who came up with the whole idea? Who gave him a cup of wine with a sleeping potion in it, so that we could borrow his tools and put some of the loot in his bag, without him waking up? I deserve that extra spoon!"

At that moment, a moth flew right into Laurenzo's dog's face. The dog jumped and started barking. Laurenzo was startled and held his dog's muzzle shut, but the men inside the hut were even more alarmed now.

"You see, I said there was someone out there!" shouted the first man.

"It's a ghost!" said the other one, with a shudder.

"Of course it's not! But it could be Jannos, the great master thief!"

"Let's get out of here," panted the second man. "We have to be in Talamura tomorrow morning. The lord is expecting us to join his hunting party."

"Fine. Then let's just hide the loot again. We'll get back to sharing it out tomorrow evening."

The men hid the treasure in a hole in the floor and left.

Laurenzo had retreated to a safe distance again, and he waited until they were gone. Then he went back to the hut. "Thieves," he said to himself. "And cowards too. It sounds like they made someone else pay for their theft." He went into the hut and knelt down beside the hole in the floor. Then he took everything out and had a good look at it. *So they're going to Talamura now*, he thought, *and they'll be back tomorrow night. I don't know what I'm going to do yet, but I'm taking one of these twelve silver cups. I might need it as proof.*

He put the smallest of the cups in his bag, returned the rest of the treasure to its hiding place, and then lay down on a pile of straw on the floor. He quickly fell asleep and dreamt once again of Jiacomo in a dark cellar and of the silver cups – all lined up on a shelf.

The next morning Laurenzo awoke before daybreak with a firm plan in his mind: he would go to Talamura. When he went outside, he saw that the fog had blown away and he set off, in sunshine and wind, following the tracks of the two thieves. He was much more cheerful than the day before, as he felt that he would soon hear some news of his brother. But suddenly a deep voice shouted: "Stop and give me your money, or I will take your life!"

He looked round in surprise and saw a big man on a black horse, with a bow in his hand, arrow at the ready.

"Who are you to order me about?" Laurenzo began indignantly, but the man interrupted him.

"Jiacomo! It's you!" he cried, throwing down his bow and bursting out laughing. He rode up to the young man, jumped off his horse, slapped him on the shoulder and said: "Thank goodness you're back in one piece! I was starting to worry, even though you hadn't sent your dog to me, which you said you'd do if you were in trouble. You know I was actually thinking of venturing into the lion's den to see what had happened to you? I couldn't believe you'd just abandon me."

Laurenzo realized that the man had mistaken him for his brother, but he did not correct him. He decided first to wait and see if this stranger was a friend or a foe. He was certainly a thief in any case – and it is wise not to place too much trust in a thief.

"Well?" said the man. "Why aren't you saying anything? Not going to greet your master?"

"Of course, master," said Laurenzo. "How are you?"

"Excellent, my boy. Come on, I'll just pick up my bow. And then we'll head home. But first tell me if you have the silver cup."

"The silver cup?" echoed Laurenzo.

"What's wrong with you? Why else did you go to Talamura?"

Talamura! thought Laurenzo.

"Answer me! Do you have the cup?"

"I do," said Laurenzo.

The other man slapped him on the shoulder again. "Bravo!" he shouted. "Go on, then! Show me!"

Laurenzo hesitated for a moment. Then he reached into his bag and took out the cup that he had stolen from the shepherd's hut. "You mean this one?" he asked.

The man took the cup. "Yes!" he cried. "Magnificent! Magnificent!" He stood as straight as he could, put on a solemn face and said: "You have acquitted yourself well and performed your task admirably. Now you are a master of our trade, free to go wherever you want and to steal from anyone you choose – except for me, of course."

He was about to pocket the cup, but Laurenzo said: "Can I have it back?"

"You want it back? But why?"

"It's stolen property," said Laurenzo.

The man burst out laughing again. "That's a good one!" he cried. "Stolen property! Of course it is! Now this cup belongs to me – and you have to tell me how you acquired it."

"Tell me first what right you have to this cup," said Laurenzo.

The other man stared at him in surprise. "You are behaving so strangely that I'm almost tempted to cuff you around the ears!" he said. "What right do I have to the cup? You stole it for me, didn't you? And now that you've succeeded, you can call yourself a master thief."

"I thought..." said Laurenzo. "I thought that... I intended never to steal again."

"I hope you've got over that nonsense now!" said the man. "Come and tell me about your adventures over a fine meal."

"Wait a moment," said Laurenzo. "That cup does not belong to you or to me. I don't know whose it is – and I won't know until you tell me. Oh, please don't be angry with me, sir. You see, I don't know you. This is the first time I've ever set eyes on you. But you are Jiacomo's master and, I hope, his friend."

"What on earth are you talking about? Of course I'm your master, and I'm also your friend."

"Then perhaps it is fortunate that I met you," said Laurenzo. "I'm not Jiacomo, you see. I'm his twin brother."

"His twin brother?" the master thief cried. "His twin brother! But you're the very image of him!"

"Indeed I am," said Laurenzo. "But truly, I am not Jiacomo. I fear he's in great danger. And you can help me to find him."

The man had still not entirely recovered from his shock.

"Twin brother..." he mumbled. "Yes, of course. Jiacomo told me himself that he had a twin brother. What's your name again?"

"Laurenzo."

"Laurenzo, yes. Jiacomo did talk about you. I'm Jannos, his master. But how did you get one of the cups from Talamura? And what's happened to Jiacomo?"

"I have no idea," said Laurenzo, answering only the last question. "My brother and I were supposed to meet at an agreed place, but he didn't turn up. Now I'm afraid that something happened to him. Can you tell me more about what he was up to?"

"I certainly can," said Jannos and he told him about the task he had set for Jiacomo.

"Then I shall go straight to Talamura!" cried Laurenzo. "I think Jiacomo has been imprisoned there for a crime he did not commit."

"Wait a moment!" said Jannos. "I want to help you. Besides, you still have to tell me how you came to have one of the silver cups in your possession."

Laurenzo hesitated. Jannos was a thief – could he trust him?

The man seemed to read his mind. "You probably don't have a high opinion of thieves," he said, "but you mustn't think I'd ever abandon an apprentice of mine."

So Laurenzo told him about the two men he had eavesdropped on.

"The villains!" cried Jannos. "Where is the hut where they hid their loot?"

"That will remain my secret," replied Laurenzo.

"You still don't trust me," said Jannos, "but even if you don't tell me, I'll still find that hut. If you go to Talamura, someone needs to keep an eye on the place, don't they? Just in case the thieves return before tonight."

"Fine," said Laurenzo, "keep an eye on the hut, but don't do anything until I'm back. If the thieves do come back, just make sure they don't escape again." He told Jannos where to find the hut and asked him the shortest way to Talamura.

"Shall I come with you?" asked Jannos.

Laurenzo shook his head. "Talamura is dangerous for you," he said. "I'd better go alone, as I have nothing to fear. And will you give me the cup back? I might need it."

Jannos gave him the cup and said: "Here, take my horse. You'll get there faster."

Laurenzo thanked him, climbed onto the horse and listened to Jannos's directions. But before he rode away, the thief stopped him.

"How many cups were there in the shepherd's hut?" he asked.

"Twelve," replied Laurenzo, "including this one."

"Then Jiacomo has the thirteenth," said Jannos. "Go now, twin brother! If you do not return soon, with Jiacomo, I will come and fetch you, even if the gallows awaits me in Talamura. Farewell!"

And so Laurenzo rode off to Talamura, deep in thought and with worry in his heart.

After he left the plain, a winding track led him through hills and pine forests. *The castle cannot be far now*, he thought.

Then he heard the sound of horns in the trees nearby. His dog pricked up his ears, began barking happily and ran down a narrow side path. Laurenzo followed, whistling for him to come back. The dog came running up and Laurenzo was just about to turn around and go on his way when a young man on horseback came riding down the path towards him. He gaped at Laurenzo, and then said: "However did you get here?"

Someone else who thinks I'm Jiacomo, thought Laurenzo.

"How did you escape?" the young man continued. "Stay there, do not move a muscle!"

But Laurenzo did not intend to obey. Once again, he heard horns somewhere close, and he worried that the young stranger belonged to a hunting party. So fleeing seemed to be the best plan. He urged on his horse and galloped off, as quickly as he could.

"Stop him! Stop him!" cried the young man. "Stop that thief! He's escaped!"

But Laurenzo rode faster than him and when, after a while, he looked back, there was no sign of pursuit.

"Come on," he said to his dog. "Let's go to the castle."

When he saw the stately castle ahead, he reined in his horse and hesitated for a moment. *If I'm not mistaken, Jiacomo's in there*, he thought, *but what kind of welcome am I going to get? Is asking for entrance the best way to help him? They'll let me in, I'm sure of that. They'll probably think I'm Jiacomo. Right then, I'm going inside. What can they do to me?*

He rode along the path up the hill and knocked at the castle gate.

Two guards opened the door.

"Good afternoon," said Laurenzo. "May I come in?"

The guards looked at him stupidly.

"How did you get here?" asked one of them.

"It's witchcraft!" cried the other.

"May I come in?" repeated Laurenzo.

"But I thought you were already inside – and that you'd be there for a while!" exclaimed the first guard.

"In the deepest dungeon," added the other.

Although Laurenzo had been expecting something like this, it still came as a shock.

"You can see that I'm standing here in front of you," he said. "Now let me in. I wish to talk to the lord of this castle."

The guards were still staring at him in astonishment, but they let him in.

"The master's out hunting," said one.

"But his wife is at home," said the other.

87

"Then take me to her," Laurenzo ordered them, "and quickly, please!"

The sound of horns rang through the pine forests. The Lord of Talamura rode through the trees, followed by his retinue, looking for wild animals, when he heard a breathless voice behind him: "Uncle! Uncle! He's escaped!"

The Lord of Talamura reined in his horse and looked around. His nephew Ricardo came galloping up.

"Jiacomo has escaped!" he cried. "I just saw him, near the big road."

"Nonsense!" said the Lord of Talamura. "That's impossible. Jiacomo is in the castle's deepest dungeon. He'll never be able to escape from there."

"I saw him," Ricardo insisted. "He fled and rode towards Talamura."

"Towards Talamura?" said his uncle. "If he's escaped, he should be going in the other direction!"

"I'm telling the truth, uncle!" cried Ricardo. "He was right there in front of me, and he had his dog with him."

"I'm baffled," said the lord, still not entirely convinced. "But, just to make certain, I'll go with you. Jiacomo must not be allowed to escape!"

So the Lord of Talamura, his nephew Ricardo and the whole hunting party returned to the castle. And they were most surprised when they reached the castle gate to hear that Jiacomo had entered the castle not long before.

"I don't understand how he could have escaped!" cried the lord. "But I understand even less why he came back!" And followed by his nephew and his servants, he hurried to the castle's great hall, where he knew his wife would be. When he got there, he froze in the doorway, because sitting next to his wife was... Jiacomo. (Or at least that's what he thought.)

"What is the meaning of this?" he said, stepping into the hall, followed by his men. "What is the meaning of this?" he repeated. "How did you get here?"

The young man stood up and gave him a bow. "Greetings, my lord," he said. "I have come here to put right something that is wrong." He looked at the lord and at his companions, his gaze resting on a couple of them for some seconds.

"How on earth did you manage to escape?" cried the Lord of Talamura. "And how dare you come back here? Go on, Josefus," he said to one of his servants. "Fetch the guards from the dungeon. They have not done their job, and they deserve to be punished."

"The guards will tell you that they have allowed no one to escape," said the young man. "They will say that the door of the dungeon is still locked and that the bars are still in place. And that is the truth!"

The Lady of Talamura approached her husband. "Let him finish," she said. "Do not be angry, but listen to what he has to say."

"It was you! You sent for him!" began the lord.

"I did not," his wife replied. "Speak... Jiacomo!"

"Thank you, noble lady," said the young man. Then he turned back to her husband and said: "Send for your guards. Perhaps your nephew Ricardo could fetch them."

"Fine," said the lord. "Be quick about it, Ricardo!" Ricardo disappeared in a hurry.

"Speak, Jiacomo! " said the Lord of Talamura. "I think you have finally seen the error of your ways – is that not so?"

The young man shook his head. "I want to tell you once again that I am innocent," he said. "And what's more, I can prove my innocence to you now, if you will not take my word for it." He paused before continuing: "You had me thrown into a dungeon because I had supposedly stolen from you – even though I was so grateful to you! And the real thieves are walking around free and have your trust. I was not far from Talamura when I was called back to be told that your cups had been stolen. So tell me, where could I have hidden them?"

"You refused to say," said the lord.

"If I had hidden them," the young man went on, "then it must have been in some place between the castle and the point where one of your servants stopped me and told me to return. Which servant was that again?"

"Josefus, I believe," said the lord.

"Yes, that's right! Josefus, you are my witness. Where was I when you came to tell me that the Lord of Talamura wanted to speak to me?"

"I don't remember," replied the servant reluctantly.

"Think about it," said the young man. "I'm sure you do remember."

"It's such a long time ago..." said Josefus.

"Near the first houses in the village?" asked the young man. "Or beyond?"

"Yes, near the houses," replied the servant. "It'll have been somewhere around there."

The young man quickly turned to the lord of the castle and said: "So I could have hidden the loot in a spot somewhere between the first houses in the village and the Castle of Talamura... or inside the castle itself."

"It definitely wasn't in the castle," said the lord. "I had it searched, every last inch."

"When?"

"On the day of the theft."

"Too late, in any case. One of the thieves had already taken out the treasure by then," said the young man. "And I know where the hiding place is! It's some way from the village. I never got that far!"

"You know where my precious belongings are hidden?"

said the lord, not quite knowing what to do with his face. "Tell me! Where?"

"Why don't you ask Josefus?" cried the young man. "And the man standing beside him! They are the thieves!"

The Lord of Talamura spun around and looked at the two servants.

"He's lying!" shouted Josefus. "He's just hidden the cups somewhere else, and he's trying to put the blame on us. He's a thief, not me!"

"Last night the two of them were arguing about the treasure they had stolen," said the young man, "while the innocent Jiacomo sat in the dungeon."

At that moment Ricardo came back, followed by the two men who had been guarding Jiacomo's dungeon.

"Look, there he is!" Ricardo cried. "But you both say he's downstairs in the dungeon!"

"There he is indeed!" said the bewildered guards. "And yet just now he was downstairs, behind thick walls and with us standing guard at the door!" They looked the young man up and down, and then one of them said: "Are you some kind of witch? Do you have the power of being in two places at once?"

"So you didn't let me escape?" said the young man.

"No!" replied the guards. "You've not set foot outside your cell!"

"What about last night? Was I in the dungeon last night?"

"Yes!" cried the guards. "You were!"

The Lord of Talamura was about to say something, but he did not get the chance. The young man walked over to the guards, looked at them seriously and said: "Would you be prepared to swear an oath?"

"Yes!" cried the guards. "You were in the dungeon all night!"

Now the young man turned back to the lord. "I was in the dungeon last night," he said. "Your servants will swear I did not leave the castle. And I had a dream last night, a strange dream. I was looking into a small shepherd's hut out on the plain and there were two thieves dividing up their loot: gleaming coins, golden spoons and silver cups. I heard them say that they had put the blame for the theft on me by hiding a golden spoon in my bag. Then they were startled by a noise and took to their heels and I... woke up. Wasn't that a strange dream?" He paused and then said: "But it wasn't a dream. It was true! Look, here's one of the silver cups!"

As he spoke, he took out a silver cup and held it up.

The servant who was standing beside Josefus shrieked: "But how do you know that?! How could you possibly know that?!" Josefus's face turned deathly pale.

The Lord of Talamura looked at the two servants. The guilt was written on their faces.

"You villains!" he roared. "You treacherous villains! It was you all along!"

The servants fell to their knees and begged for mercy.

"Take them prisoner," the lord of the castle commanded.

The lady went to the guards and said: "Quickly, go and fetch Jiacomo."

Her husband had not heard these words, and when the two thieves had been led away, he said in a voice full of self-reproach: "Jiacomo, you are free. Forgive me for what I have done to you!"

But the young man shook his head and said: "I am not Jiacomo, my lord! Jiacomo is still in the dungeon."

"But how...?" said the lord of the castle.

"This is Jiacomo's twin brother," replied his wife. "I'm sure Jiacomo won't be quite as blooming with health!"

The Lord of Talamura opened his mouth and then shut it. "So you're not Jiacomo?" he said finally. "And he's in the dungeon? Quick! Free him! Bring him here!"

"I've already taken care of that," said his wife.

"Jiacomo's twin brother?" said the Lord of Talamura.

"Yes, my lord," replied Laurenzo, as it was indeed him.

"I am so glad he came," said the lady. "Without him, Jiacomo would still be locked up."

"So he was innocent after all..." mumbled the lord.

"I'll show you where to find your treasure," said Laurenzo. "At the moment it's safe, being guarded by an acquaintance of mine." He looked longingly at the door and asked: "May I go and fetch Jiacomo?"

"Of course!" said the Lord of Talamura. "He must not remain locked up for a moment longer. I shall go with you."

"And so shall I," said his wife.

"As will we," said Ricardo of Pava and the servants.

So they all headed off to the dungeon to free Jiacomo. Halfway there, they met the guards coming back, with Jiacomo between them. He was pale and thin, but when he saw his brother, Jiacomo's face lit up. "Laurenzo!" he cried.

The twin brothers ran and threw their arms around each other. What a wonderful reunion! Everyone who saw them was very touched, and the lady of the castle even dabbed away a tear or two.

Finally the Lord of Talamura approached them. "You're free, Jiacomo!" he said. "Your innocence has been proven. You have your brother to thank for that. And as for me... Well, you will have to forgive me."

Forgiveness came very easily to Jiacomo. He was so happy to be free and to see his brother again that his sad time in the dungeon was almost forgotten.

Then they all went back to the great hall, where they sat together and were happy. The two brothers had the most to say – after all, they had to tell each other about all their adventures of the past year.

After a while, the lord took out two silver cups: the cup he had once given to Jiacomo, and the cup Laurenzo had brought with him. He intended to go and fetch the other eleven the following day.

"Look," he said. "Here is your cup, Jiacomo. You can have it back. I hope that when you look at it later, you will not harbour a grudge against me. And this cup is for Laurenzo, for coming to his brother's rescue in such a clever and skilful way." The twins thanked him warmly.

"Nonsense!" cried the lord, almost sounding annoyed. "I would like to give you much more. Is there any other wish I could grant you?"

"Yes," said Jiacomo. "Would you pardon the two actual thieves? I know they deserve to be punished, but I still sympathize with them, as I was a thief myself. And besides, I think it was me who gave them the idea!"

The next day, the brothers said goodbye to the Lord of Talamura and his wife. They had been invited to stay longer, but Laurenzo had to return to Bainu, and Jiacomo wanted nothing more than to go with him. However, they promised that they would visit Talamura again.

The Lord of Talamura and Ricardo rode with them. They were going to fetch the cups, the spoons and the coins from the hut on the plain. They found all of the treasure still in good condition, and in front of the hut a bearded beggar stood guard.

"But that's Jannos!" Jiacomo whispered to Laurenzo.

Then the lord and Ricardo said farewell to the brothers and rode back to Talamura. When they had disappeared from sight, the beggar took off his false beard and his ragged coat – and it was indeed Jannos!

"I didn't want to run the risk of being captured," he said. "The Lord of Talamura isn't very keen on me, you see!" He slapped the brothers on their shoulders, and gave Jiacomo a firm handshake. "It's so good to see you again!" he said. "Come back to my place with me. Today you will be my guests."

Later, after dinner, Jiacomo gave him the silver cup.

But the thief would not accept it. "No," he said, "you must keep it as a reminder. You certainly had to go through a lot to earn it. It's just a pity that you want to leave now, to go to Bainu and learn an honest trade. You really could become a very good thief!"

"No, thanks!" said Jiacomo, laughing. "Anyway, I don't agree. What kind of thief lets himself get locked up for a crime he didn't commit?"

The next morning, the brothers said goodbye to Jannos and promised to come back and visit him. Then they travelled across the Plain of Babina towards Bainu, happy to be together again. And their dogs, running and jumping around them, were just as happy.

At the fork in the road where they had said goodbye to each other over a year before, they met the old pedlar again and they told him all about their adventures. They showed him their silver cups and Laurenzo said: "Later, when I'm a smith, I'm going to make silver cups. And maybe I'll give a couple of them to the Lord of Talamura and his wife."

After the adventure with the silver cups, the twin brothers went back to Bainu. Master Philippo welcomed Laurenzo and his brother warmly, and he suggested that Jiacomo could also learn the trade of goldsmith. Laurenzo could teach him. Jiacomo was in favour of the idea and at first he worked very hard. But after a while he started to get bored, and eventually he said: "I love beautiful objects, but I don't have the talent or the patience to make them. So I'm going to look for other work instead."

When he had tried six different jobs and attempted to learn three trades, he sighed and said: "There is no job that is right for me and no trade that appeals to me."

"Nonsense," said Master Philippo. "It's you that's not right for any job – and you're too lazy for any trade. Why don't you want to work, like your brother does? He's going to be an excellent goldsmith, but you won't even be able to earn a dry crust."

Jiacomo hung his head, but Laurenzo said: "I'm sure my brother will find something that he's suitable for. And as long as he's not earning any money, I'll share what I have with him."

"No," said Jiacomo. "I don't want to live in your shadow and at your expense. I can't become a goldsmith and I don't want to be a thief. And I don't want to be a gardener either, or a cobbler, or a clerk or a soldier. The only thing I can do is go out into the big wide world and seek my fortune there."

"But then we must part again!" cried Laurenzo.

"There is nothing else for it," sighed Jiacomo. "I'm not getting anywhere here in Bainu. I shall go travelling again and try my luck far from here. But I shall return, sitting on a fine horse and carrying sacks filled with gold."

"Folly," said Master Philippo. "If you can't find anything here, then you won't find anything out in the big wide world either."

"Oh, but I will!" cried Jiacomo. "I can already feel that I'm going to be lucky!" And his eyes gleamed at the thought of his adventure.

Seeing the look on his brother's face, Laurenzo said: "If that's how you feel, then you must go," even though his heart was heavy at the thought of losing his brother again.

"Come with me," said Jiacomo.

But Laurenzo shook his head. "No," he said, "my work is here. As the old pedlar said: we should each go our own way."

"But we shall never forget that we belong together," said Jiacomo. "We'll always be good friends, no matter what happens. And I'll return soon to tell you about my adventures."

So the two brothers said goodbye for the second time, and Jiacomo left Bainu to seek his fortune.

The Knight of the Riddles

"Eat, I bid you, my guest. You are most welcome!"

ONE THOUSAND AND ONE NIGHTS: 'The Feast'

Jiacomo went on foot, but he had sturdy shoes and a big hunk of bread in his bag to keep him going. He had company too, as his dog went with him. He walked over hills and through valleys, saw strange towns and villages and made some money here and there, but he did not find a fortune. After a while, his clothes were becoming ragged and his shoes were wearing out, but he remained cheerful.

"At least I've become richer in experiences," he told himself, "and that counts for something."

One day, his wanderings took him to the Plain of Babina, where he hesitated, unable to decide which way to go. He could pay his old master, Jannos, a visit, but he would obviously try to persuade Jiacomo to steal again. Besides, he did not want to turn up in such a poor and shabby state. *I'll head south instead,* he thought. *That's where Pava is, the city Ricardo came from.*

No sooner had he set off than he met someone he knew. It was, in fact, none other than Ricardo of Pava, the man he had just been thinking about.

Ricardo looked very prosperous. He was sitting on a snow-white horse and was followed by three servants.

"Ah, it's one of the twin brothers!" he cried. "Which one are you? Laurenzo or Jiacomo? And where are you off to?"

"To wherever my fortune takes me," replied Jiacomo. "But I'm starting with Pava."

"It's a pity you didn't do so before," said Ricardo. "Then you could have been my guest. I've just left my home for a trip to Bainu."

"Which is where I'm from," said Jiacomo. "Give my best wishes to my brother, the goldsmith."

"Ah, so you're Jiacomo," said Ricardo. "I don't understand why you look so shabby. You should have been a wealthy man long ago, with all your intelligence and skill!"

"If I were a thief, I would be rich," replied Jiacomo. "But you know I don't want to be a thief any longer!"

"Poor Jiacomo," Ricardo taunted him. "How sad that thieves end up in jail. And stealing is your only talent!"

"That's not true!" Jiacomo cried. "I can do more than that! Just you wait and see. I'll be rich before long."

"How do you plan to achieve that?"

"I don't know yet. I'm waiting for some luck to come my way."

Ricardo shook his head. "Then you're a fool," he said. "Come and travel with me to Bainu."

"No," replied Jiacomo. "I don't want to go back yet."

"Then come with me to the nearest inn. You look like you could do with something to eat."

"Thank you, but I'm not hungry," said Jiacomo haughtily. "But I'll come with you for a while and you can tell me how you are and how your uncle and aunt, the Lord and Lady of Talamura, are doing."

Soon after that, he said goodbye to Ricardo, who left him with these words: "If you truly wish to seek your fortune in Pava, I have some advice. There's a knight there who once found a hoard of treasure in an abandoned castle. Reimond is his name, but they also call him the Knight of the Riddles. He's given away much of his money, but he's still the richest man in Pava, and no one is more hospitable to beggars than him. Go and pay him a visit: he will entertain you lavishly and, if he likes you, then maybe you can win a fortune from him!" And before Jiacomo could reply, Ricardo urged on his horse and rode away.

"Beggars!" muttered Jiacomo indignantly, as he walked onwards across the plain, towards Pava. "Who does he think he is? I'm not a beggar!"

The wind rose, making him shiver in his thin clothes. *This really is the kind of weather when a man might meet one of the Little Folk*, he thought. *If only! Although, if they make you rich, they always want something in return. Your immortal soul, for instance, and I wouldn't want to be without that.*

He did not see any of the Little Folk, but he did meet three robbers, who ordered him to hand over his money.

"All I have is three small coins," said Jiacomo. "You can have those."

But the robbers said angrily: "We're not beggars asking for alms! Keep your money. You're not worth the effort of robbing!"

"Well, well," sighed Jiacomo a little later, when he was resting in a small cave that he had found among some rocks, "soon Ricardo will be proved right, and I'll be able to call myself a beggar!" He made a small fire to warm himself by and shared his last piece of bread with his dog. "It's getting dark and we're going to sleep," he said. "Tomorrow we'll look for work in Pava, and then we shall dine on chicken and venison."

The next day, he continued his journey, and when it was midday, he saw the city lying ahead of him. "We're there," he said, and he sang:

> *"There is Pava, that beautiful town.*
> *Will my star rise? Or will it go down?*
> *Here I come with three coins to my name.*
> *Will I find fortune? Will I find fame?"*

At the city gate, he met three old beggars, who asked him for alms.

He took out his three coins and gave one to each of them. "It's not much," he said, "but I have nothing else to give."

The beggars thanked him warmly and said: "May good fortune await you in this city!"

"Let's hope so," said Jiacomo to himself, as he entered Pava. "I don't have a single coin left, and I'm so hungry that I feel faint."

Pava was smaller than Bainu, but very beautiful.

All of the houses were painted in bright and cheerful colours, and most of the people seemed wealthy. But there were also beggars walking around, who looked poor and were wearing ragged clothes.

Jiacomo came to an inn, where the scent of the most delicious food was wafting out, and he went in to ask the landlord if he could work for him in exchange for a meal. But the innkeeper just grunted that he had enough staff and told him to clear off. The same happened at the next inn too.

"I'm afraid I won't make my fortune here," said Jiacomo with a sigh. "This city is beautiful indeed, but the people are so unfriendly."

He went into a cobbler's shop and a baker's, but they had no need for his services there either. He asked some labourers who were carrying bricks if he could help them but they said he looked far too weak for such tough work. Finally he found himself wandering sadly down a street of elegant houses, feeling hungrier than ever.

Then he noticed that his dog had disappeared. He stopped and whistled a few times. The dog soon came running up, carrying a big bone in his mouth. Jiacomo looked at it enviously and said: "Where did you get that?"

The dog jumped around him and then dashed off. Jiacomo followed him and came to a big wall with a gate in it. The dog jumped up at the door in the gate and looked at his owner, wagging his tail.

Beside the gate, a man sat on the ground. He looked like a guard, but he did not seem to be doing much guarding. He was chewing on a blade of grass and sleepily humming a tune.

"Excuse me," said Jiacomo, "Who lives here?"

"You must be a stranger in Pava," replied the man, without taking the blade of grass out of his mouth. "Or you'd know this is the gate that leads into the garden of Sir Reimond, who has more riddles and riches than everyone else in this city put together."

Sir Reimond, the man Ricardo had told him about!

I'm going to go in and ask for his hospitality, thought Jiacomo. *I'm little more than a beggar now. My dog got a bone here, so I'm sure I won't be sent away empty-handed.*

He put his hand on the gate, but hesitated. He did not really want to become a beggar.

The man on the ground took the blade of grass out of his mouth and said: "The knight is very hospitable, but you can't just walk in there."

"Why not?" asked Jiacomo.

"Can you read?" asked the man.

"Yes," said Jiacomo, rather puzzled.

"Then you can't just walk in there," said the man. "Sir Reimond is very kind-hearted, but he will not tolerate his orders being disobeyed."

"What orders?" asked Jiacomo, who was becoming more and more baffled.

"You can't just walk in there," said the man.

Jiacomo pressed down the handle, and the door opened. "But it's open!" he cried.

The man was chewing his blade of grass again and did not reply. Jiacomo pushed the door open and found himself standing in front of a large sign that said the following:

Welcome to this garden, intrepid stranger!
Enter with no fear of danger.
But if you wish to improve your fate,
by setting foot through this gate:
YOU MAY NOT WALK UPON THE PATH!
YOU MAY NOT WALK BESIDE THE PATH!

Jiacomo looked at the lovely garden, which was full of plants and flowers. A winding path led to a big, beautiful house. Then he read the sign again and heard his stomach rumbling. "Now I understand," he muttered. "The knight is hospitable, but you can't just walk in here because you must not disobey his orders." Suddenly, though, he began to laugh and said to his dog: "Even though I can read, I shall go in there, but I will not walk on the path and I will not walk beside the path."

Standing on one leg, he hopped along, on the path and then beside the path. As he reached the house, a man came out. He was old with a long, grey beard, and was dressed in expensive robes.

"Hello there, young man!" he called to Jiacomo. "Why are you hopping so foolishly through my garden, like a child playing a game?"

Jiacomo stopped, balancing on one leg, and said: "Greetings, Sir Reimond. I am hopping because I am not permitted to walk, not on the path or beside it."

Sir Reimond, because it was indeed him, began to laugh. "You've solved my riddle well," he said. "Stand on both of your feet again and tell me why you have come here."

Jiacomo replied that he was from Bainu and that he was a stranger in the city, and he ended by asking for hospitality.

"You are welcome," said the old knight. "But first tell me your name, your trade and what you are seeking."

"My name is Jiacomo, at the moment I am no more than a beggar, and I am seeking my fortune."

"Then come inside, Jiacomo, and have a good meal with me. Whether you find a fortune or not will depend on you yourself."

Jiacomo followed Sir Reimond into the house; it was furnished very beautifully and expensively.

"As you have come a long way, perhaps you would like to freshen up first," said his host, leading him to a small room. "There is a bowl of water and a towel for you. Have a wash, and then come into the dining room next door." With those words, he left Jiacomo on his own.

The young man looked round in surprise. There were a few pieces of furniture in the room, but no sign of a bowl of water or a towel. The table his host had pointed at was empty. So he walked to the door that the knight had left through; he would just have to go to the dining room without washing. He found himself in a large room, where Sir Reimond was sitting at a big table.

"Ah! Come and join me, my guest!" he cried. "Have you freshened up?" Before Jiacomo could reply, he continued: "Now we shall eat. You're going to enjoy this meal – I have the best cook in town."

Jiacomo sat down and told him how grateful he was for the warm welcome.

"Nonsense!" his host cried. "Eating in company is always more pleasant than eating alone. I shall tell my staff to serve the food." He clapped his hands, looked at the door and said: "Bring in the meal."

No one appeared, but Sir Reimond nodded and said: "Thank you." Then he acted as if he were lifting the lid off a bowl. "Mm!" he said. "It smells delicious!" He turned to Jiacomo and asked: "Shall I serve your food, my guest?"

Jiacomo stared in bewilderment at his host and then at the table, which was polished to a beautiful shine but was completely empty!

"Yes, please... s-sir..." he stuttered, not knowing what else to say.

The knight acted as if he were filling two bowls to the brim, said he hoped Jiacomo would enjoy the food and then began to empty his imaginary bowl with an imaginary spoon.

"Please, do begin," he said to Jiacomo. "Soup is best when it's hot. Or would you like a little bread with it?" He clapped his hands again and ordered: "Servant, please bring us some bread."

Jiacomo saw neither servant nor bread appear, but the knight acted as if he were taking a bowl and holding it out to his guest. "What would you like?" he asked. "Wheat bread, barley or rye? I'd recommend this piece here. You'll find no finer or softer bread."

Jiacomo stared at him in surprise. There was no such thing as invisible bread, was there? Finally, he hesitantly pretended to take something from the invisible bowl. The knight did the same and went on eating his imaginary soup, smacking his lips and taking the occasional bite of his invisible bread.

"Don't be shy, guest," he said to Jiacomo. "Tuck in."

Jiacomo pretended to pick up a spoon as well and made eating movements. *What on earth is going on?* he thought. *He must be insane. Stark raving mad!* And as he pretended to eat, he tried to think of a way to escape his strange host as quickly as possible.

Sir Reimond put down his imaginary spoon, clapped his hands again and called for the next dish.

"Fried fish in celeriac sauce," he said, looking happily at the empty table. "That's my cook's speciality. Everyone's asked him for the recipe, but he keeps it secret and only makes this dish for me. Have a big portion, Jiacomo. You look like you could do with a little strength."

I'm not going to get any strength from this meal, thought the young man. He was even hungrier than before and looked enviously at his dog, who had at least been given a nice big bone and was now sleeping peacefully.

The knight served up the imaginary fish for himself and his guest and said: "Isn't it delicious?"

"I have never tasted anything quite like it," replied Jiacomo, chewing on something that was not there.

The knight did the same. He was acting as if he were enjoying the best meal he had ever eaten, but then he looked at Jiacomo – and Jiacomo was shocked to see his expression.

He isn't insane at all! he thought. *He's just making fun of me!* His first impulse was to stop this silly game, but he kept a grip on himself and pretended to go on eating. *Ricardo must have known about this*, he thought. *He sent me walking right into it! This hospitable Sir Reimond is a man who takes pleasure in tormenting people who are poor and hungry!*

He became furious at the thought. But still he stayed sitting calmly at the table. *I won't let him see my disappointment*, he thought to himself. *He obviously expects me to get angry, so that he can have a good laugh at me! No, I won't let him see that I'm starving and that my mouth starts watering whenever he talks about his imaginary food. I won't give him that pleasure. I will play his game and do it better than him!*

He pretended to put down his spoon, gave a sigh of satisfaction and said: "That was absolutely wonderful, sir!"

Sir Reimond clapped his hands again. "Look!" he cried. "Now we have roast goose, stuffed with nuts and plums, with raisins and candied peel, and basted with red wine. And a compote of pears and peaches from my own garden, with toasted bread and creamy butter." He insisted again that Jiacomo should have large portions and then acted as if he were slicing the tastiest parts of the goose and placing them on his guest's plate.

"How is it?" he kept asking.

"Exquisite!" said Jiacomo, whose jaws were beginning to ache from chewing without anything in his mouth.

"Bring more food!" ordered the knight. "Venison in cream sauce, chicken and apple purée, veal with mushrooms, omelettes with preserves!" Again he filled imaginary plates, but finally Jiacomo pretended to put down his spoon, and then he wiped his fingers and said: "Sir, this has been a marvellous meal, but now I have truly eaten enough."

"Really?" asked the knight.

"I couldn't eat another bite," said Jiacomo and he wondered if his host could hear his stomach rumbling.

"Fine," said Sir Reimond. "Then it's time for dessert." And he called for custard and fruits, for blancmange and honey cakes.

Jiacomo was exhausted and faint with hunger, but he still managed to pretend to enjoy the dessert, which was of course also imaginary. Then he got up from the table with a sigh and said: "Sir, I haven't eaten so well in ages. Thank you very much."

"No need to thank me!" cried the knight. "You're not leaving, are you? After such a fine meal, what's needed is a good drink. I'm sure you'd enjoy a cup of excellent wine!" He looked at Jiacomo, taunting him with his twinkling eyes.

Jiacomo matched his gaze. "Forgive me, sir," he said, "I rarely drink wine and I am not accustomed to it."

"Oh, go on," said the knight. "Drink a cup with me. It's fine wine and it will do you no harm." He walked over to a cabinet and brought out a bottle and two cups, which were just as imaginary as his meal. Then he pretended to fill the cups and offered Jiacomo one of them. "Try it," he said.

Jiacomo pretended to take the cup, to hold it up to the light, to admire the colour of the invisible wine and to breathe in the aroma with pleasure. Then he wished his host good health and pretended to empty the cup.

"Doesn't it taste like the nectar of the gods?" said the knight. "Let me pour you another one, my boy."

"Yes, please," replied Jiacomo. He had his imaginary cup refilled and then downed it in one.

This went on for a while, with the knight pretending to refill their cups and them both drinking and enjoying the invisible wine. Jiacomo played the game very well, so well that he pretended the wine was going to his head. He began swaying to and fro and singing, with a thick tongue, as he banged away on the empty table:

> *"Oh, I'm feeling mighty fine!*
> *It's the wine! Hey, it's the wine!"*

Then he swung his arm around
and gave his host such a whack
on the head that Sir Reimond fell
off his chair.

"Ow!" he said. "What was that for?"

Jiacomo just laughed and
raised his hand for another
whack.

"Have you gone mad?"
cried the knight, holding up
his arm to fend him off.

Jiacomo pretended to be startled and
suddenly to sober up. He knelt down and said:
"Oh, Sir Reimond, please forgive me! You gave me wine even
though I am not accustomed to it, and that is why I forgot
my manners and behaved so ungratefully. Forgive me, that
was truly not my intention!"

The knight was still sitting on the floor and staring at
him, but instead of becoming even angrier, as Jiacomo had
expected, he burst out laughing.

"Good for you, my son!" he cried. "You have beaten me, in
both senses of the word!" And when he had stopped laughing,
he added: "I like you. You went along with my joke and, without becoming impatient, you played it to the end – outdoing
even me. Now help me up, and you'll get to enjoy the fantasy
meal for real."

When Jiacomo had helped him to his feet, Sir Reimond
clapped his hands again, but this time twice. Now a real
servant appeared, who also brought a real meal to the table.
Needless to say, Jiacomo certainly did it justice!

"Don't take offence at my joke," said Sir Reimond. "I sometimes do that when someone who is young and strong turns up as a beggar at my gate. See it as a test. I now know that you can remain in good spirits even when things don't go as you'd expected, and that you have enough ingenuity to turn an unpleasant situation to your own advantage. Those qualities are more valuable than the fortune that you hope to find. Why do you want to find a fortune anyway? You could earn a living in all kinds of different ways."

Jiacomo told his host more about himself as he ate until he could eat no more.

"Right," said the knight finally. "Now we'll drink one more cup of wine and I'll show you to your room. Tonight you will be my guest and tomorrow too. And there's no need to worry that you'll have to sleep in an imaginary bed!"

And so Jiacomo slept in a soft bed again for the first time in many days, with his dog lying on the rug beside it.

The next morning, two servants woke him up. One of them brought him a bowl of water and some towels, and the other a set of new clothes, with a message that the knight wanted him to put them on.

I feel like a prince, thought Jiacomo, when he entered the dining room, washed and dressed in fresh clothes. Breakfast was ready, but his host was not there. A servant told Jiacomo that he was in the garden.

"Then I shall go there and wish him good morning," said the young man, heading to the garden, followed by his dog.

As the knight came to meet him, he called out: "Isn't the weather magnificent?"

Jiacomo started to thank him for all that he had given him, but his host silenced him. "Come with me and look at my garden," he said. "I was working there early this morning. Walk with me – and keep your eyes open!" As he spoke those last words, he gave Jiacomo a mysterious look.

When the young man had admired the garden, they went into the house together for breakfast. And as they were eating, the knight said: "So you're seeking your fortune."

"Yes, sir," replied Jiacomo.

"You know that I am rich," said the knight. "And every now and then I give money away. But I never give it to just anyone. If I give something, it is not charity, but honestly earned – and not easily!" He took a bite of bread and a drink of milk and continued: "They call me the Knight of the Riddles, because I like nothing more than setting and solving puzzles. You have already solved one of them – the one on the sign by the garden gate – and now I shall give you another."

"I'm ready, sir," said Jiacomo, full of anticipation.

"There is a box buried in my garden, a chest with gold pieces inside. You can't see where, as flowers are growing over it. This morning I was working in my garden, plucking dead flowers and cutting dead twigs. Now listen carefully, Jiacomo!

> *"Where the treasure was buried is where I got it.*
> *It was in my hand but I could not find it.*
> *The more I sought it, the more it vexed me.*
> *And when I had found it, I threw it away.*

"Now can you tell me where I buried that chest?"

Jiacomo frowned as he thought about it. Then his face lit up. "I know!" he cried. "By the rose bushes!"

"Why do you think that?" asked the knight.

"They are the only plants in your garden that have thorns. Because what you were talking about has to be a little thorn."

"Bravo!" cried the knight. "That's the right answer." He placed his hand on Jiacomo's shoulder and said: "Young man, that chest in my garden is yours – on one condition. It involves another riddle."

"I have to solve another riddle?" asked Jiacomo, his eyes gleaming.

"No," said the knight, "this is more difficult. You have to give me a riddle. You will be my guest for a week and in that time you can ask me as many riddles as you like. If there is one that I cannot solve, then the chest belongs to you. Do not imagine that it will be easy though. I am known as the Knight of the Riddles for good reason." He smiled at Jiacomo. "Well then," he said, "are you up for it? You have the chance to win a small fortune!"

"I most certainly am!" cried Jiacomo. "Of course I'll give it a try!"

"Excellent," said his host, rising from the table. "This morning I have to leave you, but here are three gold pieces. Go into town and buy yourself something. I expect you back here this afternoon. Can you play chess?"

"No, sir," replied Jiacomo.

"Then I shall teach you, because I would like to play. And you can give me some riddles. Farewell, Jiacomo, until later!"

When his host had left, Jiacomo went into town, trying to come up with a difficult riddle. But there was so much to see

116

in the streets that he stopped thinking about it for a while. He came to the market square and walked past the colourful stalls, where the traders were praising their wares. He reached for the three gold pieces that the knight had given him and thought about what he might spend them on.

Then he suddenly heard a voice behind him: "I see you have indeed found good fortune in this city." He looked round and saw the three beggars, the ones he had given his last few coins yesterday.

"You look well," continued the one who had spoken, "and you're wearing fine new clothes. How did that happen?"

"Thanks to your blessing," replied Jiacomo cheerfully. He walked with the beggars and sat down with them on a wall at the edge of the market square. Then he told them everything that had happened to him, all about Sir Reimond's meal and the riddles.

"We wish you good luck," said the beggars. "And we hope you can come up with a riddle that the knight cannot solve."

"Thank you," replied Jiacomo. "And here is something for you, so that you can share in my good fortune." And he gave them the three gold coins.

The beggars gratefully accepted the coins, and one of them said: "This is the second time you have given us what is yours. In return, I will tell you a riddle and its answer." He leant over to Jiacomo and whispered in his ear.

"And if the knight already knows that riddle, I have another one for you," said the second beggar, and he also told Jiacomo a riddle and the answer.

"I don't want to be left out," said the third beggar. "I will also give you a riddle just in case the knight solves the other two."

Then the three beggars wished Jiacomo a good day and, once again, good fortune, and they disappeared into the hustle and bustle of the city.

The young man returned to Sir Reimond's house and waited for his host to come home. He spent the afternoon learning how to play chess, and his teacher was very pleased with him.

"You're doing well," he said. "Even though I've checkmated you."

"May I ask you a riddle now?" asked Jiacomo, when his host had put away the chessboard and the pieces.

"Go on then, my boy," said the knight.

"What sounds louder than the horn?
And what stings sharper than the thorn?"

"That's two in one," said the knight with a smile. "But I'll give you the answer:

> *"Thunder sounds louder than the horn.*
> *Hunger stings sharper than the thorn."*

"You guessed it!" said Jiacomo, full of admiration but also rather disappointed.

When they were eating their dinner, which was very big and not at all imaginary, the young man tried his second riddle.

> *"What weighs heavier than lead?*
> *And what fills you up more than bread?"*

"That's easy to answer," said the knight.

> *"Sadness weighs heavier than lead.*
> *God's blessing fills you more than bread."*

"Hmm, you're very clever," said Jiacomo. He was beginning to realize that it was not going to be easy to get his hands on the chest of gold.

After dinner, they played a few more games of chess. Jiacomo lost three times, but he won once, so he was making good progress.

"Right, then," said the knight, "now it's time for bed."

"I have another riddle for you," said Jiacomo.

"Excellent," replied the knight. "How does it go?"

> *"What is busier than a bee?*
> *And what is deeper than the sea?"*

"Two in one again," said the knight. "And here's the answer:

"A town is busier than a bee.
And love is deeper than the sea."

"You guessed it again!" cried Jiacomo.

"I'm sorry," said Sir Reimond. "Do you have another one for me?"

"Not right now," said Jiacomo. "But I hope to have a very tricky one for you tomorrow."

That night he did not get to sleep until late. He considered all the riddles he had ever heard and tried to come up with new ones, but he didn't like any of them. "If I know the answer, the knight is sure to know it too," he finally said with a sigh. "I shall try to go to sleep. I can do some more thinking tomorrow."

The next morning began just as the previous one had. First he went for a walk around the garden with his host, and then they had breakfast together. After breakfast, the knight had work to do, so Jiacomo had to keep himself busy again. He wandered into the garden, followed by his dog, who barked away happily, hoping that his owner would play with him. But Jiacomo paid no attention to him, because he was coming up with riddles.

"I only know a couple of easy ones," he finally said to himself. "But something is better than nothing. I'll go into town; maybe I'll meet those beggars again and they'll have another riddle for me."

However, he did not find the beggars and after a while he came back. He had seen all kinds of things and had quite a good time, but he still did not have a new riddle. The guard sat by the garden gate, humming and chewing a blade of grass, but when he saw Jiacomo, he took the grass out of his mouth and asked: "How are you doing? You got a riddle yet?"

"Not a good one," replied Jiacomo.

"Don't go thinking you'll get that chest of gold," said the guard. "You're not the first one who's tried to ask Sir Reimond a question he doesn't know the answer to! We've asked him how long a second of eternity lasts, and what's hotter than fire, and what's colder than ice, and how many stars there are in the sky. The strangest questions you could imagine, but he had an answer for everything. Do you know that even the king visited him once to put him to the test?"

"Then I have no chance," said Jiacomo. "Unless I can find a riddle he's never heard before."

"He has heard every riddle that there is," said the guard. "All you can do is come up with a new one yourself. And even then he'll have an answer. I bet he could even tell the difference between two drops of water."

Jiacomo stared at him. "I know!" he exclaimed. "I have a riddle, a question he has never been asked before! It's the perfect puzzle!" He took the guard's hand and gave it a good shake. "And it was you who gave me the idea!" he cried. "Now I need to go quickly to see Sir Reimond."

He ran into the garden and to the house, as the guard watched him in surprise.

The knight was in the dining room. When Jiacomo came racing in, he looked at him cheerfully and said: "Ah, my boy, so you're back, are you? I'm ready for another game of chess."

Jiacomo greeted him and said: "I've got a riddle for you!"

"Marvellous," replied the knight. "Out with it."

"My riddle isn't here though," said Jiacomo. "I need to go and fetch it."

"I see," said the knight, "this must be a very special riddle. Where do you have to go to fetch it?"

"Bainu," replied Jiacomo. "And I would like to ask you, sir, if I might borrow a horse. If I ride quickly, I can be back within the week."

"What goes faster than a horse?" asked the knight.

"The wind."

"And what goes faster than the wind?"

"Thoughts."

"Excellent!" cried the knight. "You may borrow a horse from me. But first have a bite to eat. Otherwise you'll soon become tired."

Before long, Jiacomo rode away, as he had said, to go and fetch his riddle from Bainu, and Sir Reimond ate his meals alone again, wondering what kind of question the boy would return with.

Four days later, the guard at the gate stared in amazement – and then rushed to tell his master that Jiacomo had returned.

The knight was reading in his study. "Ah, jolly good," he said, when he heard the news. "Let him in, then."

"He's not alone," replied the guard.

"His friends are welcome too," replied the knight. "Don't make them wait. They've arrived just at the right moment. It's almost time to eat!"

The guard went to fetch the guests. "Oh, oh, oh," he mumbled to himself, "what I wouldn't give to be present at this meeting!"

Sir Reimond closed his book and stood up to welcome his guests. The door swung open and two young men stepped inside. The knight froze and looked at them in astonishment. He had been expected Jiacomo and some friends, but now he saw that there were two Jiacomos standing before him! They looked exactly alike. The same face, the same size, the same clothes! Even the dogs with them were the same.

"What is this?" he cried. "Have you split yourself in two?"

The young men bowed and greeted him. Then they spoke, as if with one mouth: "Here is your riddle, Sir Reimond. Which one of us is Jiacomo?"

The knight looked at one, then the other, and burst out laughing. "No one has ever presented me with a question like this before," he said. "And it's such a tricky one! I've never seen two different people who were so alike. Are you brothers?"

"Yes, sir," replied the young men.

"One is the very image of the other. But how can I guess which one is Jiacomo? I can point at one of you and have a chance of getting it right, but then I won't have solved it as I did all those other times. Then I was able to find the solution with my own common sense, but now it can only be guesswork. I might be known as the Knight of the Riddles, but I have never relied on guesswork!"

The twin brothers said nothing. They just looked at him and smiled.

"Even your smile is the same!" cried Sir Reimond. "And yet there must be another difference, as no two people are the same. But how can I judge your characters when I've never met one of you before and have known the other for only two days?"

He looked thoughtfully at the brothers.

"Say something," he asked them.

"What do you want us to say?" asked the brothers.

"Even their voices are the same," said the knight with a sigh. "And they are being careful not to say too much! Ah, but I taught Jiacomo how to play chess. Would each of you like to play a game with me?"

"Then you must explain the game to both of us again," said the brothers, "as Jiacomo will pretend he does not know how."

"Of course," said the knight. "I should have known. What now? It's never taken me this long to give the answer to a riddle before. Let me try..." He looked again at one, then the other and said: "I'm just guessing. I can't be certain! And I only want to give an answer if I'm absolutely sure. And I can't do that, so I have no answer for you. I just don't know! Jiacomo may have his chest of gold."

"Hurrah!" cried the brothers happily and they thanked Sir Reimond enthusiastically.

"There's no need to thank me," said the knight. "I'm glad to give you the gold. But I still don't know which one's Jiacomo. So which one of you is the lucky winner?"

"We both are," replied one of the young men. "What belongs to one of us belongs to the other one too."

"You earned it," said his brother. "So you must keep it for yourself."

"Not a chance!" cried the other one. "The two of us share everything."

"So now I know which one is Jiacomo," said the knight. "And what about you, Jiacomo's brother, what's your name?"

"Laurenzo, sir."

"Welcome, Laurenzo! And you, Jiacomo, may go and dig up that chest. Now you have a small fortune and you can do whatever you like with it. I don't need to give you wise advice, as I already know that you have a clever head and a good heart. And if I am not mistaken, your brother is the same."

The knight clapped his hands twice and ordered the servant who appeared to put food on the table. "Come with me," he said then. "Let's go and enjoy a good meal." He looked at them, shaking his head. "Now I've forgotten again who is who," he said. "This was a difficult riddle indeed! I am glad Jiacomo earned his money, as there is no one I would rather give it to. But I am going to study the two of you very closely, so that by the end of the evening I will be able to say with ease who is Jiacomo and who is Laurenzo. This riddle will not remain a mystery to me!"

The twin brothers returned to Bainu with plenty of money. Laurenzo went back to working hard to hone his skills as a goldsmith, while Jiacomo led a varied life, sometimes working, but more often lazing about. They still lived with Master Philippo and he was fond of them both, but he often shook his head at Jiacomo. "Laurenzo is going to become a good goldsmith," he would say, "but you'll never achieve anything, even though you have a good head on your shoulders. You're too lazy!"

Jiacomo just laughed. "Why should I work when I don't feel like it?" he said. "I'm not bothering anyone, am I? Laurenzo will become a famous goldsmith one day, but I'm happy to play my lute and wander the streets of Bainu and earn a little here and there, now and then. Besides, I have a stack of gold. When that runs out, I'll just see what happens next."

And Laurenzo agreed. "I enjoy my work," he said. "But Jiacomo is different, even though we look as alike as two drops of water. And he isn't lazy, my brother, even though it might sometimes seem like it."

Then the goldsmith smiled and said: "I'm not sure you're right, but I wouldn't like to be without either of you. You bring happiness into my home."

Yes, the brothers enjoyed their life in Bainu. Sometimes they went travelling together as they had done before, and they had lots of adventures. One time they travelled to Sfaza to sell some objects that Master Philippo had made, and on the way back they met a man called Teodu.

Here is the tale of that meeting, which Teodu later told his children and his grandchildren many, many times.

The Mystery of the Disappearing Sacks of Flour

"Keep your eyes open and your wits about you."

A piece of good advice

A poor man called Teodu was walking along one of the roads across the low hills to the west of Bainu. It was a warm summer's day; as he walked, he sighed many times, and it was not only because of the heat. He kept stopping to look around, putting his hands up to his mouth and shouting. Sometimes he left the road to climb a small hill and take a better look at the area, only to trudge back down, sighing even more deeply. But then he spotted something ahead of him that made him walk faster. Two horses were grazing at the side of the road and two young men were sitting on the ground nearby, talking and eating, with two dogs begging for food beside them. They were, of course, Laurenzo and Jiacomo, the twin brothers, who were on their way back to Bainu.

Teodu greeted them and asked: "Have you by any chance seen my horse come this way?"

The brothers did not answer at first. Both of them looked at Teodu and then turned their eyes to the road.

"Have you seen my horse?" repeated Teodu. "It ran away and I've been searching for it all morning."

"What does your horse look like?" asked Laurenzo. "Is it lame in one leg?"

"Yes!" said Teodu. "So you've seen it?"

"And is it blind in its left eye?" asked Jiacomo.

"Yes!" cried Teodu delightedly. "So it came this way, did it?"

"It came this way," replied Jiacomo.

"Then I'm on the right path," said Teodu. "Thank you!" And he walked on, much happier and with faster steps than before.

After a while, he came to a big windmill. The miller was standing in the doorway.

"Good afternoon," said Teodu. "Have you seen my horse by any chance? It's blind in one eye and lame in one leg."

"I certainly have," said the miller. "It wandered past not long ago. If you carry on down the road for a way, you're sure to find it."

Teodu thanked the miller, walked on for a while and – yes, there was his horse! But instead of lighting up, his face clouded over, and when he had reached the animal, he let out a wail. "Woe is me!" he cried. "My sacks of flour have gone! I've been robbed! Why did you do that to me?" he yelled at his horse. "Why did you have to run away and get my food stolen?"

The horse stared at him reproachfully from its one good eye, as if it wanted to say: "Why didn't you tie me up, master, and take better care of me?"

Teodu took the horse by the reins and walked back to the mill, where the miller was still standing in the doorway.

"Ah," said the miller, "I see you've found it."

"I've found my horse, yes," Teodu replied sadly. "But it was carrying two sacks of flour before – and now they're gone.

I don't know what to do, because I'm poor and can't buy any new ones."

"That's a shame," said the miller. "But it's what happens when you don't keep an eye on your belongings."

"What good are your words to me?" shouted Teodu. "They won't bring back my flour!" And again he began to bemoan his fate. "Tell me," he said to the miller finally, "was my horse still carrying the sacks when you saw it?"

"What are you saying?" said the miller angrily. "Of course not! You seem to think I stole them – me, with my shed full of sacks of flour! If you let your nag run around unattended, any vagabond can steal its load."

"Please don't be angry!" said Teodu. "It's just that this is such a blow. I had to work a long time for that flour and now I've gone and lost it."

"If I were you," said the miller, "I'd go back along the road you came down and try to find out who took the sacks from your horse."

"I'll do that," said Teodu. "I met two young men back there, who also saw my horse. Maybe they can tell me more."

"Then hurry," said the miller. "Who knows? They could be the thieves! There are lots of bad people along this road." And with those words he went back into his mill.

Teodu climbed onto his horse and rode slowly back to the place where he had met the twin brothers.

Laurenzo and Jiacomo had just stood up and were preparing to continue their journey.

"Look," said Laurenzo, "we were right. There's the man again, on his horse this time. So he obviously found it."

"I'm glad you got your horse back," said Jiacomo to Teodu, as he came closer.

"Only my horse though," replied Teodu gloomily. "Tell me, when you saw it, was it carrying a load?"

"A load?" said Jiacomo. "I don't know. I didn't actually see your horse."

"What do you mean?" asked Teodu, who was completely baffled.

"My brother's telling the truth," said Laurenzo. "This is the first time we've seen your horse."

"That's not true!" shouted Teodu. "You told me yourself that it came past here, my half-blind, lame horse – and it was loaded with two full sacks."

"We knew your horse had only one eye," said Laurenzo.

"And we also knew it was lame," said Jiacomo.

"But we didn't know it was carrying two sacks," they both said at the same time.

"We hadn't seen it at that point," said Laurenzo.

"That's a lie!" cried Teodu. "Then how did you know what it looked like? You're trying to make a fool out of me! You're cheating me! Oh, and you're probably the ones who stole my sacks of flour!"

"Sacks of flour?!" exclaimed Jiacomo. "We didn't see your horse come by, let alone steal anything off its back!"

"Don't be angry," said Laurenzo to Teodu. "I shall tell you how we knew what your horse looked like without having seen it. When you came past the first time, my brother and I were just talking about the tracks on the road. Take a look."

Teodu looked. "I don't see anything unusual," he said grumpily.

"We saw your horse's hoof prints," Laurenzo continued.

"One of them was not as deep as the three others. So we knew the horse that had made them must be lame in one leg."

"And we noticed that clumps of grass had been eaten along the right-hand side of the road," said Jiacomo, "and not on the left. So the horse hadn't seen anything on the left. Which meant it must be blind in that eye."

Teodu gaped at them. He could not argue with their reasoning. "Well, that was very clever of you," he said. "But it's no good to me, because you can't know anything about my sacks of flour."

"Why don't you tell us what happened?" said Laurenzo.

"I was on my way home," replied Teodu, "with two sacks of flour that I'd just bought. On the way, I started to feel tired, so I stopped for a quick rest. I didn't tie up my horse, as I wanted to be on my way before too long, and I'd be able to keep an eye on it for just those few minutes. But I fell asleep and when I woke up, the horse and the flour had disappeared." Then he told them that he had found his horse close to the mill, but that its load was gone.

"Did you see anyone else apart from us and the miller?" asked Laurenzo.

"No one. But what does that matter? My flour is gone and I'm sure I'll never get it back. This is such a loss for me. Such a great loss!"

The brothers looked at each other. Then they turned back to Teodu, and Jiacomo said: "Don't be sad until you're sure you have good reason to be sad. We want to help you. Maybe we'll be able to track down your sacks of flour."

"That's very kind of you," said Teodu. "Do you think there's any chance of finding them?"

"We can try," said Laurenzo.

Teodu was already looking a little less miserable when he said: "I can see that the two of you are wise young men. If anyone can help me, I'm sure it's you."

"Then let's go to the mill," said Laurenzo, "to the place where you found your horse. We'll walk and take a good look at the tracks on the road."

And the three of them headed off, leading their horses by the reins, and peering down at the ground.

"Do you see the hoof prints your horse made the first time it came past?" Laurenzo asked Teodu. "They've faded here and there, but you can still see them."

"And do you see that there are still clumps of grass to the left of the road, while a lot of grass on the right has been eaten?" asked Jiacomo.

"Yes, I can see that," said Teodu. "But if you hadn't told me, I'd never have noticed."

Without meeting anyone else, they came to the mill.

There was no sign of the miller.

"So where was your horse?" asked Laurenzo.

Teodu pointed. "There, where the road makes a bend," he replied.

"Wait a moment," said Jiacomo. He knelt down on the ground and closely studied the hoof prints. Then he stood up, walked on for a bit, and took another look. Returning to the others, he said, "Let's leave, so that the miller doesn't see us when he comes outside."

They retreated to a safe distance from the mill and Teodu said, "What's going on?"

"I've looked at the tracks," replied Jiacomo. "And just before the mill, they suddenly become less deep."

"So what does that mean?" asked Teodu.

"Your horse was carrying a load," said Laurenzo. "If its hoof prints suddenly become less deep, that means it has become lighter. Which could only have happened if the sacks of flour were taken off its back."

"I see," said Teodu. "Do you... Do you think the miller did it?"

"Most likely," said Jiacomo. "Look, here are some tracks that weren't made by us or by our horses – and they lead to the mill. There aren't any other tracks, and we didn't meet anyone else."

"The cheat! The liar!" shouted Teodu. "He has a whole shed full of flour!" Then his face clouded over and he said: "Even if he is the thief, there's nothing we can do about it. After all, he's got so many sacks of flour – how can we prove that two of them don't belong to him? My sacks look the same as any other sack. They're not marked in any way."

"It's going to be tricky," said Laurenzo. "If he really is the thief, then we'll have to use our cunning to unmask him and find a way to make him confess."

"So let's come up with a nice trap for him," said Jiacomo.

"Two sacks of flour among a hundred others," said Laurenzo thoughtfully.

The brothers fell silent and thought for a while. Teodu looked expectantly from one to the other.

"If he is the thief, then he'll be feeling guilty," said Jiacomo after some time.

"We need to make use of that," said Laurenzo.

Again they fell silent.

"If the sacks had been marked..." muttered Laurenzo.

"Yes, that's it!" cried Jiacomo.

"Ah, I see where you're going," said Laurenzo.

They looked at each other, their eyes gleaming. Then Jiacomo turned to Teodu.

"Listen," he said. "Go and wait somewhere nearby for a while. We'll head to the mill. In about half an hour, follow us there and ask the miller again if he's seen your sacks of flour. When you see us, accuse us of the theft."

Teodu stared at him in surprise. "But why?" he asked.

"We'll tell you later," replied Jiacomo. "So you need to accuse us of theft, and it has to be in front of the miller. Can you do that?"

"Fine. If that's what you say it will take."

"We'll say it wasn't us. And then you'll say that you'll track down your belongings anyway, because your sacks are marked with a black cross."

"But that's not true!" cried Teodu.

"That doesn't matter. But make sure you don't forget to say exactly that! Then we'll calm you down, and finally you'll have to make peace with us and let us persuade you to have a cup of wine with us and the miller. Can you do exactly what I have said?"

"I'll do it," said Teodu. "Even though I don't understand a thing. But I'm sure it'll all be fine."

"So that's agreed," said Jiacomo.

Teodu climbed onto his horse and rode away, and the twin brothers headed to the mill.

"I see what you're planning," said Laurenzo.

"I hope it works," said Jiacomo. "Now let's agree exactly what we're going to do."

A little later, they knocked on the door of the mill. The miller came out and asked what they wanted.

"We are travellers," replied Laurenzo, "and we would like to request your hospitality for an hour or two. May we rest here for a while? It's very hot today, and we're weary."

"It won't have to cost you anything," Jiacomo added. "We have food with us. And we'd like to invite you to have a drink with us. There's some wine in our knapsacks."

"Come on in!" said the miller. "I've never seen two young men who were so alike. I enjoy a chat – and I wouldn't say no to a cup of wine either."

"May I tie up our horses while we're inside?" asked Laurenzo. "There's some space behind the mill, isn't there?"

"Just put them next to the shed," replied the miller. Laurenzo walked off with the horses while Jiacomo followed the miller inside.

"Where have you ridden from?" the miller asked.

"We came from Sfaza and we're on our way to Bainu, our hometown," replied Jiacomo. He took out a bottle of wine and said: "If you have cups, I'll fill them."

"You're my kind of guest," said the miller, placing three cups on the table.

Then they sat down. The miller asked if there was any news from Sfaza and Bainu, and Jiacomo told him what he knew. After about five minutes, Laurenzo returned, gave his brother a wink and joined them. They sat for a while, drinking wine and talking together.

The bottle was half-empty by the time there was a knock at the door. It was Teodu.

"You again?" said the miller.

"Yes, I-I just wanted to ask you once more if you know anything about my sacks of flour," stuttered Teodu. "And about my horse, the one you saw..."

"Oh, it's the man who was looking for his horse!" Jiacomo exclaimed.

Teodu looked at the brothers. "You stole them!" he cried. "It was you who stole my good sacks of flour!"

"What? Wherever did you get that idea from?" shouted the brothers, looking very indignant.

The miller looked at Teodu and then at the brothers and said: "I think you should continue your argument elsewhere."

"My sacks of flour are gone – and I want them back!" shouted Teodu, who was really getting into the spirit of things now. "Do you know where they are?"

"No," replied the brothers. "We've no idea!"

"I'd recognize them anywhere!" said Teodu. "They're marked with a black cross!"

"We truly haven't seen them," said Laurenzo, "but if they're marked, you're sure to find them. Did you keep your eyes open as you came along the road? They could easily have fallen off your horse's back."

"Ah, but before you go and look, you must sit down and have a cup of wine with us," said Jiacomo. "At least if the miller has no objections."

"It's fine by me," said the miller. "The wine might put you in a more cheerful mood. And then I'll help you to look for your sacks."

Teodu sat down, and the miller poured him a cup of wine.

"I don't want to drink all your wine," the miller said to the brothers. "Wait a minute, and I'll fetch one of my own bottles." He hurried off through a back door.

"What now?" whispered Teodu.

"Don't drink too much and just act normally," whispered Laurenzo.

It was some time before the miller came back, a little red in the face, as if he had been running. "Here's some of my wine," he said. "I'm sure you'd like a drop more, wouldn't you?"

"Just one more cup," replied Jiacomo. "We need to be on our way soon." All four of them drank silently, looking at one another.

"But I really would like to know where that flour of yours has got to," said Jiacomo to Teodu, putting down his cup.

"And I wish you knew!" Teodu replied.

"Feel free to take a look inside our bags," said Jiacomo. "You'll see that we don't have it. Two bags full of flour aren't easy to hide." He turned to his brother and said: "Where would you hide a sack of flour?"

Laurenzo pretended to think deeply about this question. "In a shed full of sacks of flour," he said finally.

The miller's face turned red. "I'm not having that!" he cried. "You're suggesting it was me!"

"No, no, not at all," said Laurenzo. "Please don't be angry!"

"I have enough flour of my own," said the miller. "I don't need any more!"

"Oh, but the sacks weren't necessarily stolen!" cried Jiacomo. "Maybe they fell off the horse. Whoever found them didn't know whose they were and so he kept them, planning to return them as soon as someone came to ask for them."

"Maybe he wouldn't dare at first," added Laurenzo, "as he was afraid of being accused of theft. But if he knew how happy he'd make the owner, I'm sure he'd do it!"

The brothers looked at the miller expectantly.

"You still seem to think I have them!" he said. "But I don't. I haven't stolen any sacks of flour, and I haven't found any either. Take a look in my shed if you don't believe me!"

Jiacomo stood up. "Yes, why don't we do that?" he said. "Not because we don't trust you, but to clear you of any suspicion. Go and look," he said to Teodu, "and then at least you'll know where your property isn't."

"Come with me," said the miller with a frown. He stood up and led Teodu and the brothers to the shed.

It was indeed full of sacks of flour. "They're all mine," said the miller. "Take a good look. You had sacks with a black cross on them, didn't you? Well, you won't find them here."

"You're right," said Teodu. "I'm sorry. Thank you. Let's just leave."

"Wait a moment," said Jiacomo. "This is a fine shed, but it's not very tidy. Look, there's flour on the ground."

"So what?" asked the miller angrily.

"Flour in a flour shed is nothing out of the ordinary," replied Jiacomo, "but there's something strange about this flour... the way it's in a line. It's a trail! See, I can follow it to the door. I'm just going to see where it leads."

"This is ridiculous!" cried the miller.

Jiacomo paid no attention to him, but followed the trail of flour out of the shed and into the yard. Laurenzo and Teodu went with him.

The miller stood there for a moment, then ran after them

and said: "Why are you so interested in that trail? Why don't you mind your own business?"

"I just want to take a look," Jiacomo replied with a smile. "If your conscience is clear, then you have nothing to worry about."

The miller turned as white as his flour and fell silent. But when the trail ended at a big tree at the back of the yard, he spoke up. "Do you see now that it doesn't lead anywhere?"

"Ah, but there's a hatch in the ground!" said Laurenzo.

"The trail stops here," said Jiacomo. "Let's just open this hatch, shall we?"

"No!" shouted the miller. "I won't let you!"

The brothers paid no attention to him, but lifted the hatch together. Beneath it was a shallow space, with two sacks inside, both marked with a black cross.

"Fine, yes, it was me!" cried the miller. "But I was going to give them back. I swear!"

"There's your stolen flour," said Jiacomo to Teodu. "And the thief is standing right beside you."

"Have mercy!" cried the miller. "I didn't really mean to steal them. I'll give them back, right now! Don't have me thrown into jail!"

"That's something you need to decide," said Laurenzo to Teodu, who was looking at the sacks with a mixture of surprise and joy. "This man stole your flour, even though he already had a shed full of flour. What do you think should happen to him?"

"Oh..." said Teodu. "I'm just happy to have them back."

"You need to give him a new sack at any rate," Laurenzo said to the miller, "because there's a hole in one of these sacks. That's where all the flour came out."

"I'll do it!" wailed the miller. "But please don't report me!"

The brothers looked at him, with very serious expressions on their faces.

"You should be ashamed of yourself!" said Laurenzo. "Stealing from someone who is poor and can't spare it, while you yourself have more than enough."

The miller hung his head. "I'm sorry," he mumbled.

"Just being sorry is not enough," said Jiacomo. "Why not try to put things right? Give this man two extra sacks of flour – so that he has more than you took from him."

"I'll do that," said the miller. "I really am sorry. Just don't have me locked up!"

"As long as you do as you have said, we'll leave you in peace," said Laurenzo. "And don't steal in future!"

"At least not like this," said Jiacomo, "not from someone who is poor. This theft was a really bad job. Anyone can steal two sacks off a horse's back!"

And so it happened that Teodu not only found his two sacks of flour, but also got two extra ones, and Laurenzo and Jiacomo each had to load one sack onto their own horses, as the lame horse could not carry all four.

As Teodu, accompanied by the brothers, headed home, he thanked them many times. But he also had something to ask.

"The miller confessed that he stole my flour," he said. "But I still don't quite understand. My sacks weren't marked with a black cross, but these ones are!"

"It's really simple," replied Jiacomo. "Before you got there, Laurenzo sneaked into the shed and drew a black cross on two of the sacks. Then, just as we had told you to do, you said that

your sacks were marked. If the miller had been innocent, he wouldn't have cared about that, but as he was guilty, it gave him a fright. He obviously hadn't seen any black crosses and as soon as he got the chance, he ran to the shed, where he did indeed find two sacks marked with crosses. So he thought they must have been the stolen sacks, and he quickly hid them somewhere else."

"I'd also made a hole in one of the two sacks," Laurenzo explained. "So all we had to do was follow the trail of flour to find them."

"How clever of you!" cried Teodu, full of admiration. "And I'd like to thank both of you again."

The brothers smiled and said: "We're just happy that we could help you."

"Heaven bless you," said Teodu. "And you must come to my house and eat the cakes that my wife will make with the flour."

"We'd be glad to," said the brothers.

When Laurenzo's apprenticeship was over and he was allowed to go into business as an independent goldsmith, Master Philippo asked him to stay and work with him. "I am old," he said, "and I have no children. You can continue our work when I'm gone."

Laurenzo liked that idea, and so he stayed with the old goldsmith. Jiacomo stayed too, as he did not want to be separated from his brother. Besides, he had found a job he enjoyed: he would sell the objects that Laurenzo made. That meant he would have to travel now and then, which suited him perfectly.

One day a messenger came with a letter for the twin brothers. The Lord of Talamura was inviting them to spend the summer with him. His nephew Ricardo would be there, and so would his sister, and the lord thought it would be entertaining if some other young people came to join them. The brothers gratefully accepted this invitation. Laurenzo bought some silver with the money that Jiacomo had received from Sir Reimond, and he then used the silver to make two beautiful cups. "We shall present them as a gift to the lord and his wife," he said.

When summer came, the young men said goodbye to Master Philippo and set off for the region of woods and mountains where Talamura was located. The lord and his wife welcomed them warmly and were most grateful for the silver cups that Laurenzo had made. The brothers renewed their acquaintance with Ricardo of Pava and met his sister, Margerita, for the first time. Yes, it seemed as if they would have a fine time at the Castle of Talamura, and in many respects they did. However, it was also during this stay that Laurenzo and Jiacomo fell out with each other for the very first time.

The Diamond Candlestick

He thought she was so beautiful that he could not help falling in love with her at first sight. "It certainly cannot be true," he said, "that she is a wicked witch."

ANDERSEN: 'The Travelling Companion'

The Lord of Talamura said to his wife: "It will be a happy summer, with all these young people in our castle. Our nephew Ricardo and his sister Margerita, and Laurenzo and Jiacomo, the twin brothers. These old walls will resound with their laughter!"

But would it turn out as he expected?

Laurenzo and Jiacomo both fell in love at the same time. Now that in itself is not a bad thing, but what was not good was that they both fell in love with the same girl. Margerita of Pava was beautiful and charming, and she had only to look at them once to capture their hearts.

Yes, Margerita was beautiful, but she was also very proud, spoilt and moody. She had left many admirers in Pava – two for every finger on both hands – and they had all been at her beck and call. She thought it only natural that Laurenzo and Jiacomo should fall in love with her. After all, she had more important admirers than them. One of them was even a prince! There was something special about these brothers though, as they were so alike. So she began by being friendly towards them, and before long she had turned them into two faithful pages who never left her side.

Laurenzo and Jiacomo had always been good friends and they remained so at first, but it is hard to remain on good terms when you both love the same lady.

"Who wants to do something for me?" Margerita would ask.

"Me!" the brothers would cry at the same moment.

"Who will dance with me?" asked Margerita. "Who will come out for a ride with me?"

"Me! Me!" cried the brothers.

And that, of course, was not pleasant.

Besides, Margerita never knew which one was Laurenzo and which was Jiacomo, and neither of them liked that, as they both wanted to be the only man for Margerita.

And Margerita smiled. She smiled when, because of her, the two brothers glared at each other, and she even found pleasure in setting them against each other. One time she would be friendly to Laurenzo, and another time to Jiacomo, but she never showed a preference for either of them.

"Margerita doesn't have a favourite," said Ricardo, her brother. "She may be my sister, but I have to admit that she has no heart. She makes men into her slaves and when she tires of them she sends them away. She asks for so much, but she gives nothing in return." And he said to the brothers: "Let me give you some good advice. Return to your hometown, as quickly as you can. Even if you were kings or emperors, Margerita would still think herself too good

147

for you. Someone really should teach her a lesson, but no one dares."

Laurenzo and Jiacomo were annoyed by Ricardo's words and obviously they did not even consider following his advice.

A day or two after that, it so happened that Laurenzo met Margerita on his own for once.

"I've heard that there are flowers up on top of the mountains," she said, "beautiful white flowers. I would so love to have a few of them."

"Then I shall fetch some for you," said Laurenzo.

"But it's so dangerous," replied Margerita.

"What do I care about danger?" cried Laurenzo, and he immediately set off.

He climbed steep slopes, leapt over rushing streams and ventured into places that even the mountain goats avoided, risking his life to pick a bunch of flowers for Margerita.

However, when he triumphantly returned to give them to her, his face clouded over, because there was Jiacomo – with a bouquet of the same flowers.

"I'm giving them to her," he growled. "She asked me for them."

"Me too!" said Jiacomo.

Margerita laughed. "Don't argue, boys," she said. "Or you'll both forget to give them to me." She accepted the flowers, a bunch in each hand. "Thank you, Laurenzo and Jiacomo," she said. The brothers looked at her, their faces serious.

"Margerita," said Laurenzo, "did you ask my brother for flowers too?"

"Why shouldn't I?" replied Margerita. "I wanted to know which one of you was prepared to go to the greatest lengths for me, but I might have guessed you would be the same in that respect too."

"We are two different people," said Laurenzo. "Can't you even tell which one is which?"

"No," said Margerita. "You are so alike that I could not say."

"But we're completely different," said Jiacomo. "My brother is a goldsmith and I—"

"You? You're nothing," said Laurenzo, interrupting him.

"Shut up!" shouted Jiacomo. "You can use a forge, but I can do so much more! I can write poetry, for instance. Poetry for you, Margerita."

"I can make a gold ring for you," said Laurenzo.

"Why should she want a ring from you?" yelled Jiacomo.

Margerita frowned and then said: "If the two of you are going to argue, I'm leaving." With those words, she turned around and left them on their own.

The brothers were indeed arguing – for the first time in their lives – and when they sat at the dinner table that night with the lord, his wife and Margerita and Ricardo, they were gloomy and silent.

After the meal, the Lord of Talamura took them aside and said: "Young men, listen to me. Don't let anything come between you! Leave now and repair your friendship."

And the lady of the castle gave Margerita a good telling-off. "Stop playing with those boys' feelings!" she said. "You're making them miserable, and I'm sure you don't even love either of them."

Later that evening, when the brothers were together in their room, Laurenzo said to Jiacomo: "This can't continue. One of us has to leave."

"Then you should go," said Jiacomo.

"Why not you?"

"Which of us does Margerita like best?" They looked at each other in dismay. They didn't know!

"I have an idea," said Jiacomo after a while. "Let's leave it to chance. I have a silver coin here. We'll toss it, heads or tails. Whoever wins will stay here, and the other has to leave." But Laurenzo was not so keen on that suggestion.

"Then let's agree this instead," said Jiacomo. "The loser only has to go away for two weeks. Then he can come back and have his turn at trying his luck."

Laurenzo thought about this. "Fine," he said then. "It's the only solution."

Jiacomo threw the coin into the air. "Heads!" he called.

"Tails!" said Laurenzo.

The silver coin fell tinkling onto the floor. It was tails.

"I won!" cried Laurenzo happily.

Jiacomo gave a deep sigh. "It can't be helped," he said. "I have to go. But in two weeks I'll be back here, not an hour... No, not a minute later!"

"Then go to Bainu," said Laurenzo, "and tell Master Philippo that I'm staying a little longer."

"What would I want in Bainu?" said Jiacomo. "I am going in search of solitude. I intend to become a voluntary exile, a man disappointed in love."

The next day, he sadly said farewell to all who were staying at the Castle of Talamura and explained that he was sorry but urgent business was calling him away. Then he rode off and sought out the loneliest paths across the plain. As he rode, he tried to compose sad love songs. Eventually, though, he grew tired of the loneliness and so he went back to Bainu after all, to wait until he could return to Talamura.

Laurenzo now had Margerita to himself, but that did not make him any happier, as he still did not know if she loved him. One day she would be friendly, the next as cold as an iceberg, but no matter how she behaved, she remained ravishingly beautiful and he fell more and more in love with her every day. *Ah, but she is a young lady of distinction*, he thought sadly, *and I am just a simple goldsmith.*

One day he went to Ricardo and asked him: "What would you say if I asked your sister to marry me?"

"Well, you can always ask," replied Ricardo. "As many have done before. But you mark my words, she'll ask you for something too."

"What do you mean?" said Laurenzo. But Ricardo did not reply.

Then, one morning, Laurenzo went for a walk with Margerita in the castle garden. The flowers were blossoming, birds were singing and the butterflies were dancing through the air. Margerita was more beautiful than ever and in a pleasant mood, and Laurenzo plucked up the courage to make his marriage proposal.

Margerita looked at him in surprise and said: "Marriage?"

"I-I know I'm not good enough for you," stammered Laurenzo. "But I love you, Margerita!"

"I don't care if a man is a prince or a beggar," said Margerita. "As long as he loves me."

"I do! I do!" cried Laurenzo.

"And as long as he is willing to win my love," Margerita continued.

"I'll do anything!" shouted Laurenzo.

"I don't know what answer to give you," said Margerita. "Your proposal took me by surprise. Would you do something for me, Laurenzo?"

"Anything," whispered Laurenzo.

"You're a goldsmith, aren't you? Could you make a candlestick for me? I've always longed to own a candlestick – a diamond candlestick that glitters and sparkles as the candle burns.

Oh, and it doesn't have to be made entirely of diamonds. It could be made of silver and studded with diamonds." Margerita looked at Laurenzo with a smile. "Make that candlestick for me," she said. "And perhaps then the flame of love will be lit inside my heart."

Laurenzo took her hand and kissed her fingers. "I shall make one, Margerita," he said. "Wait for me. I will bring it to you within a week."

That same day, he left Talamura and rode at full speed across the plain and back to Bainu. When he got there, Master Philippo and his brother welcomed him, one with great joy and the other with great surprise, but he did not remain in their company for long. Shutting himself away in his workshop, he began to make the candlestick. He worked day and night, making one candlestick after another until he had it just right, and spent all the money he had on silver and diamonds. Then he ran out of money, but he still did not have enough diamonds. He knew Jiacomo still had some money, but he did not want to ask him for a loan. So he went to an unscrupulous moneylender and borrowed the money from him. He started work again and, three days later, the candlestick was finished. It was magnificent, entirely made of silver and studded with sparkling diamonds. Laurenzo went to Master Philippo and his brother, showed them his work and said: "This is for Margerita."

"It's absolutely beautiful," said Master Philippo, "and very well made. But it seems a pity just to give it away."

"She asked me for it!" cried Laurenzo. "And I want to marry her!"

The old goldsmith shook his head and said: "You are going to ruin yourself. No woman is worth such a gift."

"Margerita is," said Laurenzo angrily.

Jiacomo said nothing, but just gave a deep sigh.

"Then go and take her this candlestick," said Master Philippo. "Marry her, if she so wishes, and bring her here. Perhaps then you will become a little calmer and more level-headed."

And so, in good spirits, Laurenzo returned to Talamura to offer Margerita his gift. Jiacomo stayed behind in Bainu and thought sadly to himself: *I've lost my chance. Why did I ever come up with the idea of tossing that coin?*

The next day, a visitor came to Master Philippo's workshop. When he saw Jiacomo, he said: "I've come for my money. I need you to pay me at once, with the interest added!"

"Money?" asked Jiacomo. "What money?"

"The money you borrowed from me, of course! Here's the agreement we signed. I must have it now, because I need the money myself."

Jiacomo looked at the agreement. *I see*, he thought, *so Laurenzo borrowed some money. I had no idea the candlestick was that valuable.* Then he turned to the moneylender and said: "I'm sorry, sir, but you'll have to wait a little longer."

"You must pay me immediately!" cried the moneylender. "Or I shall lodge a complaint and have you prosecuted!"

"Be patient," said Jiacomo.

"When will you pay me?" asked the man.

Jiacomo answered with a rhyme:

> *"Please be patient! Please take it slow!*
> *I'll pluck the stars from heaven*

154

to pay back what I owe!
But the moon so fine
with its silvery shine
I shall give to my
sweet Margerita!

"Anyway," he added, "it's not me you want. It's my brother."

"You're trying to make a fool of me!" the moneylender shouted angrily.

"Not at all," replied Jiacomo. "But yes, I shall pay you. I always used to say that whatever belongs to me also belongs to my brother. And even though I no longer feel quite the same way, I shall still give you your money."

He paid the moneylender, who went away, convinced that Laurenzo (because he still thought Jiacomo was Laurenzo) was not entirely in his right mind.

And Jiacomo thought to himself: *Now I have a good reason to go to Talamura. I have to tell Laurenzo that I've paid off his debt!*

And so, one day after his brother, he too set off for Talamura. And Master Philippo stayed behind alone in his workshop, shaking his head at so much foolishness.

"But the moon so fine, with its silvery shine, I shall give to my sweet Margerita," Jiacomo had said, and he was not far wrong: Margerita would indeed have been capable of asking for the moon. When Laurenzo happily returned to her and presented the candlestick, she thanked him warmly and praised him for his fine work. But when Laurenzo repeated his proposal of marriage, she said: "First there have to be two!"

"What do you mean?" asked Laurenzo.

Margerita looked at him through her long eyelashes. "Only one candle can shine in this candlestick," she replied. "That's *your* heart. But there needs to be a second candlestick, for *mine*. Make me another candlestick, Laurenzo, exactly the same as this one, and then I shall consider your proposal."

Laurenzo stared at her and said nothing.

"You'll do that for me, won't you?" asked Margerita. "Or don't you love me any longer?"

Laurenzo turned and walked away.

"Hey!" called the lord, who happened to be by the castle gate. "You only just came and now you're going away again?"

"I need to be alone for a moment," said Laurenzo, heading for the path that led downhill and away from the castle.

The Lord of Talamura went to his wife and said: "Whatever is going on now? There's always something with these young lovers! We should just send Margerita back to Pava."

Laurenzo spent all day wandering over the mountains and through the woods around Talamura. When evening came, he returned to the castle – and who did he meet at the gate? Jiacomo!

"I got here quickly," said Jiacomo. "I rode fast and barely rested." Giving Laurenzo a searching look, he asked: "Why do you look so gloomy?" Laurenzo did not reply.

"Was Margerita happy with the candlestick that cost all your money – and mine too?"

"She wants another one," said Laurenzo.

"Another one?" cried Jiacomo in surprise. "And how do you intend to manage that?"

"You know very well that I can't," replied Laurenzo. "And so does she! You got here just in time, as I'm leaving tomorrow."

The brothers went into the castle together and had their presence announced to Lord Talamura and his wife. Laurenzo told them that he wanted to go back to Bainu the following day, and Jiacomo asked if he could stay in his brother's place.

"Yes, that's fine," said the lady of the castle, "but Ricardo and Margerita have just decided that they will leave tomorrow. So you will have to do without their company."

That evening a fine meal was served, as most of the guests would be leaving soon. But in spite of the delicious food and the wine, which was served in fine goblets, the mood was sombre. Laurenzo did not speak a word and gazed miserably at Margerita. Jiacomo, too, was silent, and he kept looking at the young lady as well. His eyes were not sad though, but gleaming with excitement.

After the meal, Jiacomo managed to speak to Margerita on her own for a moment. "Are you glad that I have returned?" he asked.

"So you are Jiacomo," she replied. "I was watching the two of you and wondering which one was Laurenzo and which was you."

"Did you know I was Jiacomo?"

"I thought you were."

"Why?"

"Laurenzo looked sad," replied Margerita. "You didn't."

"It's your fault that Laurenzo looks sad," said Jiacomo.

"It's his own fault! I can't help it."

"And soon it will be my turn to look sad," said Jiacomo. "Is that not so, cruel Margerita?"

"How should I know?"

"My brother is leaving," said Jiacomo, "because he cannot make another candlestick for you. But what would you say if I could get one for you?"

Margerita smiled. "That would be very kind of you," she said.

"I am not capable of making one," said Jiacomo. "So I shall have to get one some other way. Would you object?"

"Absolutely not," said Margerita.

"Even if I steal it for you?"

Margerita laughed. "That would be amusing," she said. "I've never received a stolen gift before!"

"What's all this about stealing?" said the lord of the castle, who was just walking past. "Come and sit with us, as this is the last evening when we shall all be together."

The next morning, the weather was dreadful. The rain poured down and the wind howled around the castle.

"This is not good weather for travelling," said Jiacomo to Laurenzo. "You'll have to stay another day."

"It's raining," Margerita said to Ricardo. "We can't travel today."

"We're in no hurry," her brother said, and then he added: "Look, there's one of the twins. I don't know which one. But that doesn't matter. They're both fools for letting you bully them! I still wish you'd treat them better though."

Margerita shrugged her shoulders and turned to the young man who was coming towards her.

"Good morning, Margerita," he said. "If you don't know who I am, I shall tell you. Jiacomo at your service! And I've come to bring you a gift."

He stared at Ricardo, hoping he would take the hint and leave, but he did not.

"Here is something you would like to have," he continued. "But don't ask me how I got it!"

"Oh," whispered Margerita, "that's really very kind of you, Jiacomo!"

"Do you love me?" asked Jiacomo, holding the present behind his back.

"Oh, let me see it," wheedled Margerita, as if she had not heard his question.

> *"Oh, fair maiden, look here, quick!*
> *I bring for you a candlestick,"*

rhymed Jiacomo and he gave her his gift.

Margerita let out a cry of delight. "Oh!" she exclaimed. "It's identical to the other one! Oh Jiacomo, thank you so much!"

"Put them next to each other," said Jiacomo. "Then you'll have a reminder of us."

"I shall do it at once," said Margerita. "Look, Ricardo! Isn't it beautiful?" She walked over to the table where she had put Laurenzo's candlestick and then stopped and stared in astonishment. It was no longer there!

"Where has Laurenzo's candlestick gone?" she cried. "Ricardo, do you know?"

"You're holding it," said Jiacomo. "You didn't care how I got hold of a candlestick, did you? You even said I could steal it. So I stole this one last night, and then it belonged to me. And now I have given it to you."

Margerita almost dropped the candlestick. Ricardo quickly snatched it from her and put it down on the table.

"How dare you...?" the young lady began angrily.

"You gave me your per-mission," said Jiacomo. "You said you thought it would be amusing to receive a stolen gift, didn't you? So last night I risked my life to climb the castle walls for it – and in the rain too. Shouldn't you be thanking me?"

"Go away!" shouted Margerita. "You cheat! You thief! I'm never going to speak another word to you!"

Jiacomo left and Margerita sat down and cried bitter tears of fury. But Ricardo could not help but smile a little.

The bad weather continued and kept all the guests of Talamura inside the castle. Margerita strode around like an outraged princess and completely ignored the twin brothers. She could not say anything to either of them, as she really did not know which one was Jiacomo. The brothers took it calmly, but the lord and lady had finally had enough of her behaviour.

"Stop making such an awful fuss!" cried the Lord of Talamura. "Let's at least keep everything warm and friendly inside the castle!"

"I'm sorry, uncle," replied Margerita, "but I have sworn never to speak to Jiacomo again. He insulted me."

"It's your own doing, sister," said Ricardo, "and besides, you're not talking to Laurenzo any more either, even though he never insulted you. Quite the opposite, in fact. He made a beautiful candlestick for you."

"I don't know which one of the two is Laurenzo," said Margerita. "And even if I did know, then I wouldn't say a word to either of them! They are far too alike – and they both look equally amused."

"What nonsense!" said the Lord of Talamura, frowning angrily.

But Jiacomo laughed and said quickly: "It doesn't matter! Sooner or later she's bound to forget and say something to us."

Margerita turned away and said to the Lady of Talamura: "I'm sorry, aunt, but I will absolutely never, ever speak another word to either of them. And I shan't forget!"

161

The Lord of Talamura looked even angrier, but this time it was Laurenzo who calmed the situation. "Come on," he said, "let's be happy. Let's sit together and entertain each other. And Lady Margerita may keep silent – until she forgets."

"Yes, let's sit down together and have some fun," Jiacomo agreed. "And, Laurenzo, I would be willing to bet a silver coin that Margerita will say something to us within the hour." Margerita just gave him a haughty look and remained silent.

"Yes, let's enjoy ourselves," said Ricardo. "Pick up your lute, Jiacomo, and sing for us!"

"I don't know any songs," replied Jiacomo.

"Then tell us a story," said Laurenzo. "You know plenty of those." Everyone, except for Margerita, agreed with him.

"Fine," said Jiacomo, giving his brother a wink. "I shall tell a story. Listen carefully, Laurenzo, because this story is specially for you."

And he began, while outside the rain clashed down and the wind whistled through the pine trees.

"Long ago, three travellers met upon the Plain of Babina. And as the plain back then was an even wilder place than it is now, with robbers lurking in every hiding place, they decided to travel on together, as three are stronger than one.

"The first was a woodcarver from Pava, the second was a tailor from Forpa and the third was a pilgrim back from the Holy Land. Their destination was Bainu. So they travelled on together, and they got along well and became friends.

"When evening came, each of the men put up his tent, and as they were still in dangerous territory, they decided to take it in turns to keep watch.

162

"The woodcarver took the first turn; he sat by the fire, with a stick in his hand, but he was very tired, and had trouble keeping his eyes open. Then he spotted a tree trunk lying on the ground nearby and he thought he might spend his time making something out of it, and that would keep sleep at bay. So he took out his tools and began carving and the time flew by, so much so that he was almost late in waking the tailor, who was to keep watch after him. When the tailor saw what his travelling companion had made, he was so full of admiration that he was immediately wide awake. It was a figure of a young woman, more beautiful than any woman alive. He decided to use his skill to make it even more beautiful and to while away his time on watch. So he took his needle and thread and the expensive fabrics he had with him, and he made magnificent clothes to dress the statue in. When he was finished, he woke the pilgrim and showed him what he and the carver had made. The pilgrim praised the beautiful work of art and, when it was his turn to sit by the fire and keep watch, he could not keep his eyes off it.

"*It is such a shame*, he thought, *that I have no craft and cannot make anything. This statue is so beautiful. All that it is lacking is life.*

"Time passed and he kept thinking: *If only the statue lived and breathed...*

"Now he was a very religious man and he began to pray. 'Oh, Almighty God,' he said, 'bring this statue to life, so that it may praise your name. Let a miracle happen, so that people may see your power. Breathe your breath into this statue, but only if it be your wish. Your will be done.'

"When he had finished praying, he opened his eyes and right at that moment the sun came up and touched the statue with its beams of golden red. And the statue began to breathe and to move and it changed into a living young woman, more beautiful than any other.

"The pilgrim was delighted and thanked God. Then he took the young lady by the hand and woke his friends. They could not believe their eyes, but they had to believe it when they saw her smile at them."

Jiacomo paused for a moment and looked at Margerita, who had been listening attentively, even though she had tried not to let it show. Then he continued: "And all three of them fell in love with her, the woodcarver, the tailor and the pilgrim. And all three of them declared their love and asked her to marry them. But the young woman only smiled and did not reply.

"'She must become my wife,' said the carver, 'because I made her out of a tree trunk.'

"'No!' cried the tailor. 'I made beautiful clothes for her, so I'm the one who should marry her.'

"'Absolutely not,' said the pilgrim. 'If I had not been here, she would not be alive. She belongs to me.'

"'No!' cried the woodcarver.

"'That's out of the question!' cried the tailor. And then they started to quarrel."

Jiacomo stopped at this point and turned to Laurenzo. "Tell me," he said, "which of the three do you think had most right to marry the lady?"

Laurenzo looked at his brother and an almost imperceptible smile appeared on his face. "The tailor," he replied.

Margerita exploded. "The tailor? Of course not, you fool!" she said indignantly to Laurenzo. "It was the pilgrim who had most right! Without him, she would never have come to life!"

"Hurrah!" cried Jiacomo. "You forgot! You said something to Laurenzo."

Margerita blushed and bit her bottom lip. The Lord of Talamura began to laugh, and so did Ricardo.

"Fair's fair," said Ricardo. "You forgot that you weren't going to say anything to the brothers, and now you might as well start behaving normally again."

"Oh, well, you tricked me into it," said Margerita angrily. "But I will talk to Laurenzo now, if he really wants me to."

"If you're not speaking to Jiacomo, then don't bother speaking to me either," said Laurenzo.

"Fine, then I shall speak to both of you," said Margerita. "But they don't have to be kind words."

"We're just happy to hear you saying something," said Jiacomo.

Margerita stood up from her chair and said: "I'm tired. I'm going to my room. Good night, everyone." And haughtily she strode off.

The next morning the sun was shining again, and both the twin brothers and Margerita and Ricardo decided to return to their homes. They sat together to eat for the last time, and then they would say farewell to Talamura and to their kind hosts.

Margerita's bad mood seemed to have disappeared, but she was still not very talkative. She did ask the brothers if they would accompany her to Pava though. Laurenzo and Jiacomo politely refused. "We'll ride some of the way across the plain with you," they said. "But then we really need to go home to Bainu. We've already stayed away too long. It's time we were going."

Margerita was silent. She did not even mention that the brothers had come from Bainu to Talamura only two days before. But Ricardo said to Laurenzo: "Jiacomo, I don't want to say farewell to you before you tell us how your story ends."

"I'm not Jiacomo," replied Laurenzo. "But even so, I think I can tell you the rest of the story."

"Then please do so," said the Lord of Talamura.

"Yes, I'd like to hear it as well," his wife said.

"Me too," said Jiacomo.

And so Laurenzo told them.

"The three men – the woodcarver, the tailor and the pilgrim – were arguing about the beautiful young woman, and finally they came to blows. But that did not help, as it did not result in agreement either.

"Then an old man came by, who stopped and said: 'Shame on you for fighting like this! Tell me the reason for your disagreement, and maybe I can help you to solve it.'

"'We'd be happy to,' said the three travelling companions. 'You can give us an impartial opinion.' And they told him what had happened.

"The old man could hardly believe their story, but the travellers managed to convince him, and they pointed out the young woman, who had been watching it all from a distance.

"'Fine,' the old man said finally. 'Then listen and hear what I think. All three of you love her – the one who carved her out of wood, the one who dressed her in beautiful clothes and the one to whom she owes her life. If I were now to declare one of you her rightful husband, the others would immediately become angry and dispute his right. Is that not true?'

"'I think she should marry me!' all three travelling companions replied in unison.

"'Then I shall give you different advice,' said the old man. 'Ask her which one of you she would prefer to marry – and then accept her decision.'

"The travellers thought this was wise advice, and each of them in turn went to the young woman, declared his love and pleaded his case.

"She listened to all of them, but she said nothing. Not to the woodcarver, not to the tailor, not to the pilgrim.

"Then the old man went to her and said: 'So now you know how things stand. These three men love you. Which of them would you prefer to marry?'

"But the young woman merely smiled and did not reply.

"'She won't say,' said the disappointed old man.

"'She doesn't know,' said the pilgrim. 'So it will have to be decided in another manner. I will marry her!'

"'No!' cried the woodcarver.

"'Not a hope!' shouted the tailor, and they started quarrelling and fighting again.

"The old man intervened. 'Stop it, you fools!' he yelled. 'Look at her! What are you actually fighting about?'

"The three travellers looked, and they were shocked. Because – lo and behold! – the young lady stood there, still and stiff. She had turned back into a wooden statue!

"And when they saw that she was only a piece of sculpted wood, which had no heart and so could not feel love, their infatuation melted away. And they travelled onwards as good friends again, and everything that had happened seemed just like a strange dream."

"That was a good story," said the Lord of Talamura.

"The ending was not quite what I expected," said Ricardo.

Margerita said nothing, but when she said goodbye to her aunt a little later, she asked her: "Do you think the twins intended that story to have some kind of meaning for me? Do you think I'm like a statue, a statue without a heart?"

"You sometimes behave that way," replied the lady of the castle, "but I'm sure you have a heart. You just need to show that you have one!"

Margerita went to the brothers and said: "I still have the diamond candlestick that the two of you gave me. Maybe you would rather have it back."

"No, you can keep it," the brothers said, "so that you'll have a reminder of us."

Then everyone said goodbye, and Margerita and Ricardo rode off to Pava and the twin brothers to Bainu.

"The summer is over," said the Lord of Talamura to his wife, "and it didn't go as I had imagined. I'm sorry that Laurenzo and Jiacomo were unlucky with their first love, but I don't imagine they'll spend a long time moping. And as well as a candlestick, Margerita has received a lesson that might do her some good!"

After their stay in Talamura, the twin brothers travelled back to Bainu, feeling happy and sad at the same time.

In Bainu they went on with their normal lives. They lived with Master Philippo, the old goldsmith, who treated them as if they were his sons or grandsons. Laurenzo still learnt a great deal from him, even though he was no longer an apprentice but a goldsmith in his own right. Jiacomo sold the work that his brother made, not only in the city of Bainu, but also beyond. He travelled throughout the whole of Babina and when he returned he always had a lot of stories to tell.

He often visited his old friends when he was on his travels: the Knight of the Riddles, the pedlar at the fork in the road, Teodu and the Lord and Lady of Talamura. But he never visited Margerita of Pava. He also once went to the place where his former master had lived, Jannos the thief. But the house on the plain was empty and abandoned. Maybe Jannos had found a new hunting ground or perhaps he had finally chosen to lead an honest life.

Time passed and the twin brothers were very contented with their lives, as they were both doing work that they enjoyed. But that was certainly not the end of their adventures!

THE EIGHTH TALE

The Inn of Elvenghest

But he wondered what sort of people he had found himself amongst, who lived so far from anywhere and had work to do at night.

LI FU YEN: 'A Lodging for the Night'

I   A GHOSTLY ENCOUNTER

The Plain of Babina is desolate, and its landscape is monotonous. Nothing grows on the plain but yellowish grass and the occasional crooked tree and, here and there, like sinister figures, dark boulders rise up. Often there are storms, and then the witches make merry and dance in a secret grove. Often there is a thick fog, and then the will-o'-the-wisps wander around and lure people away from the road.

That is how it was at the time when Laurenzo and Jiacomo lived in Babina and maybe it is still the same now, even though most people claim that they do not believe in witches and fairies and will-o'-the-wisps. There were travellers who said they had seen sprites dancing in the shifting mists; others who said they had heard strange music, which could not have been made by any mortal being. And those who crossed the plain on their travels made sure not to leave the road, because away from that road a person might encounter the strangest things.

One morning the goldsmiths Laurenzo and Philippo were working away together. Laurenzo's brother Jiacomo was sitting on a table, watching them work and telling them the latest news.

"Now you must be quiet for a while," said Master Philippo after some time. "I'm starting a very precise piece of work and I don't want to be distracted."

"Fine," said Jiacomo, "then I'll just go and take the dogs for a walk. And I'll leave the two of you to work busily, quickly and without any disturbance."

But there would be no walking that morning, and no working either. No sooner had Jiacomo jumped down from the table than there was a knock at the door, and a man entered the workshop. He greeted Master Philippo and the two brothers and said: "I am Konrad, a merchant by trade. Could whichever one of you is a goldsmith perhaps help me?"

"Certainly," replied Laurenzo.

"You don't have to make anything for me," said the merchant. "I just want to show you something and to ask your opinion about it." He took out a package, unwrapped it and showed them a small bowl made of gleaming metal.

"What do you think of it?" he asked.

Laurenzo took the bowl from him and studied it. "It's fine work," he said.

"Is it made of gold?" asked the merchant.

"It is indeed, sir," replied Laurenzo. "A precious object."

"Really?" asked the merchant. "Real, solid gold?"

Laurenzo tapped it with his finger. "Real, solid gold," he said.

Master Philippo joined them and said: "A golden bowl. Where did you get it?"

The merchant frowned and looked at one goldsmith and then the other. "So the thing is valuable," he said.

"Certainly," replied Master Philippo. "Do you wish to sell it?"

"No..." said the merchant hesitantly. "I only just... got the bowl." And again he asked: "And it's really solid gold? Truly?"

"Let me give it a little tap," said Jiacomo, laughing. "Do I hear the sound of gold? Yes! And if that's not enough, let me blow upon it. Has it disappeared? No! It's still there, and so it is truly solid and real. There's no magic involved!"

"Magic? Whatever gave you that idea?" cried the merchant. "Did you think there might be something magical about this bowl? And if so, how can you tell?"

"I just told you that this bowl is exactly as it should be," replied Jiacomo seriously. "If that weren't the case, I'd have had a strange feeling, here in my stomach."

"Oh Jiacomo, stop talking nonsense!" cried Laurenzo. Then he turned to the merchant and said: "Don't worry, sir! My brother's just teasing you. This is an ordinary golden bowl – and a precious possession."

"Oh, but you don't know where this bowl came from!" cried the merchant. "What would you say if I told you that not so long ago all of the money in my purse had turned into sand and stones?" Master Philippo and the brothers stared at him in surprise.

"I wouldn't believe a word of it," said Laurenzo.

"I would," said Jiacomo. "A thief stole your money and then filled your purse with sand. Perfectly simple."

The merchant shook his head. "If only that were true!" he said. "Then at least I would understand. You look puzzled but you'd be amazed if you heard what happened to me."

"So what happened to you?" asked Jiacomo.

"I shall tell you," replied the merchant. "It's a long and eerie tale." He sat down and wiped his forehead. "Listen," he said, "and you shall hear how this bowl came into my possession." And the merchant began to tell his story.

"I travel a great deal and am just back from Forpa. I came across the Plain of Babina, of course, but that was the last time for me. From now on, I'll go the long way round!

"Anyway, I was travelling across the plain, even though my friends had warned me not to."

"Why?" asked Jiacomo. "Were they scared of robbers?"

"Robbers?" said the merchant. "Do you think I'd let a bunch of robbers scare me off? They're just ordinary people like you and me, no matter how wicked they might be. No, my friends had warned me about the Little Folk – about elves and fairies and will-o'-the-wisps and spirits and whatever you want to call them. Oh yes, you're laughing," he went on, "and I did at the time too. One of my friends, a merchant like me, told me that strange things had been happening recently on the plain and he begged me, whatever I did, not to leave the road.

"Well, I set off on my travels. At first the weather was good, but when I was just a day's journey from Bainu, clouds filled the sky and the wind rose. It was getting late too. Within an hour or so, it would be dark. I was warmly dressed but even so I grew cold and, like many a time before, I regretted that there was no inn on the plain where travellers could rest.

"No sooner had I thought that than I saw a signpost to the right of the road, beside a small, crooked tree, and written upon it were the words: *The Inn of Elvenghest*.

"I was surprised, as I had never heard of this inn and I had never seen the signpost before, even though it was not the first time I had travelled across the plain. Then I remembered something that one of my concerned friends had told me. There was a story that, somewhere on the Plain of Babina, there was an inn where things were not as they should be. Only a few people had been there, and anyone who went looking for it could not find it. I wondered whether this might be the place. But whether it was as it should be or not, I decided to go and take a look.

"So I turned my horse, left the road, and rode in the direction the sign was pointing. After about ten minutes though, I still hadn't arrived anywhere, and I was beginning to doubt that the inn really existed. *No respectable inn would ever be so far from the road*, I thought, and I remembered my friends' warnings. Had I been foolish to leave the road, particularly when it would soon be dark? 'I'll ride on for a short way,' I said to myself, 'and then I'll turn around.'

"A large boulder was blocking my way, but when I rode around it, I saw the inn in front of me. It was a small stone building with a thatched roof and above the front door hung a sign with, written in big letters, the words *The Inn of Elvenghest*.

"Well, my vague fear immediately vanished, as the building did not look terrifying in the slightest. Besides, I noticed again just how cold it was, and so I was happy at the prospect of a warm room, a good meal and then a soft bed for the night.

"I climbed off my horse and knocked on the door. When no one answered, I left my horse and went inside. I came into a room that was neat and tidy, quite attractive even. A young man with blond hair and a pale complexion was sweeping the floor, and he looked up in surprise when he saw me.

"'Good evening,' I said.

"The young man stopped sweeping, but he said nothing.

"'Good evening,' I repeated. 'Can I get a meal here and lodging for the night?'

"'Good evening,' replied the young man, leaning the broom against the wall. 'We weren't actually expecting any guests, but you are welcome.'

"'It's a strange inn that doesn't expect any guests,' I said irritably. 'Or are there already so many guests that there is no room left for me?'

"'There's enough room,' replied the young man. 'Sit down and make yourself comfortable.'

"I told him that my horse was still outside and asked him if there was a stable.

"'I shall take care of your horse,' he said. He walked past me and headed outside, closing the door behind him.

"I took off my cloak and walked over to the hearth, where a cheerful fire was burning away. There was a copper pot hanging over it, which was filled with soup. When I had warmed myself, I sat down on one of the chairs and looked around the room. I already mentioned that it was neat and tidy. The walls were painted white, and here and there were small windows with green glass. Chandeliers of gleaming metal hung from the ceiling. The floor was made of coloured stones, all in different shapes, which had been joined together to make irregular designs. On the bar, which the landlord should have been standing behind, I saw, instead of ordinary pitchers and bottles, jugs that appeared to be made of silver, and there were beautiful cups and flagons on the shelves on the wall. The furniture, though, was perfectly ordinary: wooden tables, chairs and benches, a big cupboard and three iron-bound chests.

"When I had been sitting there for a while, I started to feel hungry and I wondered why no one had come to take my order. The young man who was going to take care of my horse had been gone for a really long time.

"If this is how they treat their guests, they'll never get rich, I thought. I could, of course, have shouted until someone came, but something was stopping me. It was very quiet in the inn, a silence I didn't dare to break. But then I thought I heard the sound of footsteps somewhere and whispering and quiet laughter. A little later, a door at the back of the room opened, and the young man with the blond hair came back in. I stared at him in surprise, as he looked very different from before. He had changed his simple clothes for the attire of a nobleman, and was now dressed in velvet leggings and a jacket trimmed with expensive fur. Around his neck was a chain that glittered and gleamed, fit to be worn by a prince... at least if it was genuine.

"He appeared not to notice my surprise and asked politely what I would like. 'I've, um, been waiting for some time,' I said, not knowing quite how to talk to him now. 'Is the landlord of the inn here or not?'

"'He is always here, sir,' he replied.

"'Are you a guest too?'

"'No, sir,' he said.

"'Then are you the landlord?' I asked.

"'No, sir,' he replied. 'I am his servant.'

"This surprised me even more. What kind of inn was this, where an ordinary servant looked like a nobleman?

"'Well,' I said finally, 'I'm hungry. Please give me some of the soup that's hanging over the fire. And I would like a room for the night.'

"The young man looked at the copper pot and paused before replying: 'I don't know if you'll like the soup.'

"'I should certainly like something to eat,' I said angrily. 'That's not asking too much at an inn, is it?'

"'As you wish, sir,' he replied. 'Would you also like something to drink?'

"'Yes, please,' I said.

"He brought me a cup and filled it from a silver jug. It was spiced wine and it tasted delicious.

"By then it was dark and the servant dressed as a nobleman lit the candles. Then he picked up a cloth and began to wipe the tables. Now and then he interrupted his work to stir the soup, but whatever he did, he did not speak a word. I watched him, slowly drinking my wine.

"'Where is the landlord?' I asked after a while.

"'Here in the inn, sir,' he replied. 'That's where he always is.'

"So I wondered again why he was not behind the bar.

"Outside, the wind had grown in strength, but I still thought I could hear noise somewhere in the inn. And I had the feeling that I was being spied on, not by the young man, but by someone else. I was annoyed with myself for thinking such foolish thoughts, and so I asked for some more wine. The young man filled my cup once more and laid my table.

"'I don't imagine many guests come here,' I said.

"'Only those who know how to find the way,' he replied, and then he added: 'I'm surprised you found the way here.'

"'If you depend on those rare guests who happen to find this place, then business can't be going well!' I exclaimed.

"The servant stroked the chain around his neck and said: 'Ah, we can't complain. We have our regulars.' With those words, he turned around, walked over to the hearth and stirred the soup again.

"The longer I stayed there, the more uneasy I felt. What kind of inn was this? Was it indeed not as it should be? I fidgeted in my seat and wondered if I had better leave after my meal. But then I heard the wind howling and the rain rattling on the windows, and I decided to stay.

"The servant brought me a bowl of soup and a plate of bread and said he hoped I'd enjoy it. The soup was indeed very good and, as I ate, my fear disappeared.

"The servant stayed for a while, leaning on the bar. Then he went to the table next to mine and began to lay it. First he put a white tablecloth on it and then he fetched plates and bowls from the cupboard. Very carefully, he placed everything on the table, and I watched in astonishment as he put down a silver dish and then a spoon that seemed to be made of gold. The plates and bowls appeared to be made of gold too, and the cup next to the dish was decorated with stones that sparkled red and green in the candlelight. He appeared to be expecting another guest. What kind of guest must it be, whose table was laid with such precious objects? And how did those treasures find their way to such a small and unfrequented inn as this one?

"The servant regarded his work with satisfaction, moved a few things a little this way or that, dusted off the chair by the table and then came over to me and asked if I would like some more soup. He ladled some more into my dish and filled my cup again. I thanked him and asked: 'Are you expecting another guest?'

"'Yes, sir,' he said. He cast a glance at the door, and then looked at me with a serious expression, and whispered: 'Don't ask any more questions, stranger! You have found the Inn of Elvenghest and so you are welcome. But you must not ask any questions.'

"I didn't know what to say, but he did not wait for an answer anyway, and went back to stand at the bar. He took a pack of cards from his pocket and began playing a mysterious game with himself. Then I heard music in the distance, a quiet and melancholy melody.

"'Can you hear that?' I said.

"The young man just frowned at me and did not reply. The music faded away and I didn't know if I had really heard it or if I had just imagined it. I didn't dare to say anything else and just went on eating, even though my appetite had disappeared.

"Suddenly there was a loud knock at the door. I was so startled that I dropped the spoon. Then the door flew open, a cold and wet gust of air blew in, and half of the candles went out.

"The young man came out from behind the bar, walked calmly to the door and shut it. Then he gave a deep bow, which surprised me, as no one had entered. He held up his hands as if taking hold of something and placing it on a chair. Then he walked over to the table he had laid, bowed again and smiled, and pulled out the chair. At first I didn't understand his strange behaviour, but then I realized that he was acting as if someone had come in and he was welcoming them and seating them at the table.

"But there was no sign of anyone! It was just the two of us in the room. Had the peculiar servant gone insane? He bowed for the third time, picked up a jug and filled the sparkling cup. He ladled soup into the silver dish and placed some bread on a golden plate. He acted as if he were listening to some order I could not hear and nodded politely in reply. Then he began to light the candles that had blown out.

"And the laid table stood there with its gleaming load, the cup of wine sparkling away and the soup steaming in the silver dish – but there was no one sitting at the table!

"The servant had lit the candles and went and stood behind the empty chair, as straight as a pillar. I broke out in a cold sweat. Had someone actually come in when the door flew open? Were there three of us in the room – and was the new guest invisible to mortal eyes?

"I was sure I was witnessing something that had to do with ghosts, magic or the dark arts. Unable to move or speak, I sat perfectly still. Then the servant left his place behind the chair and came over to me.

"'Sir,' he said, 'your room is ready. Wouldn't you like to go to bed now?'

"I stood up, my knees trembling, glad to leave the room. The servant picked up a candle, opened the door beside the bar and led me down a short and narrow hallway and up a steep flight of stairs. At the top was a small landing with a number of doors leading off it. I wondered if I should run downstairs and leave the inn, but my legs were still shaking so much that I didn't dare to trust them. Besides, at that moment, one of the doors opened and a very big, dark man appeared. He nodded at us and went downstairs.

"'That's the landlord,' whispered the servant.

"The big man stopped at the foot of the stairs and glanced up at us. He did not speak a word, but he looked terrifying. The servant opened another door and said: 'Go on in.'

"I abandoned my escape plans and did as I was told. The room I entered was small, but it looked peaceful and clean. The first thing I saw was a big bed with colourful blankets and bright white sheets. The young man lit a candle on a table beside the bed and wished me a good night. At the door, he paused and said in a mysterious tone: 'Don't be startled if you hear some noise later. We sometimes have a lot of work to do at night.' Then he left, closing the door behind him.

"I immediately turned the key, then checked to see if the window was properly closed and searched the entire room. But there was no one under the bed, no one in the wardrobe, no one behind the curtain. In short, there was no one in the room except me. All I took off was my jacket and shoes, and then I got into bed. But I didn't dare to sleep. Full of nerves, I lay there, looking at the shadows in the corners of the room and straining my ears to see if I could hear anything suspicious. The wind was howling outside, but otherwise all was silent.

"Then I heard voices downstairs, probably in the dining room. I could hear music and ghostly laughter too. Startled, I sat up in bed. There was a sound of clattering and the clashing of metal, of loud banging and shrill whistling. And then I heard a scream that made even the wind hold its breath for a moment. It was such a dreadful noise!

"Shaking all over, I huddled deep under the covers. Then, just as suddenly as it had begun, the noise stopped. Cautiously, I put my head back up out of the covers and lay there waiting for it to start again. I don't remember anything else, so I must have fallen asleep."

The merchant fell silent and took a deep breath.

"And then? What happened next?" his listeners asked excitedly.

"The strangest thing is yet to come," said the merchant and he went on with his story: "It was the cold that woke me up. I went to pull the covers over myself, but I couldn't find them. And my bed was suddenly hard as stone and the daylight was shining in my eyes. I rolled over and tried to go back to sleep, but the cold and damp, the chirping of the birds and the whinnying of a horse were preventing me. I sat up and rubbed my eyes... and then rubbed them again, not believing what I saw! Because I was outside, on the ground, and I could see the signpost with *The Inn of Elvenghest* written on it! Nearby, tied to the small crooked tree, was my horse. My bag was beside me, and I was fully dressed with my shoes on and my cloak over my knees.

"I looked around, not knowing if I was dreaming or if I'd just woken from a dream. Had I been at the Inn of Elvenghest or not? And if so, how did I get here? I realized that I might have been robbed and opened my bag to see if my belongings were still in there. Everything was still there – and there was something else in there too. To my surprise, I found a small golden bowl, the same one you just looked at. I recognized it, as it had been on the table the night before. So I hadn't been dreaming. Then I looked in my pockets for my purse. That was there too, but the money that had been inside had all changed into sand and pebbles!

"I didn't have a clue what was going on and if it hadn't been broad daylight, I might have leapt up and run away. But instead I decided to go back to the inn and to ask why they had treated me so badly. So I climbed onto my horse and, for the second time, I rode in the direction that the sign pointed. The weather was fine; the sky was a little misty, but the wind had calmed and there was no sign of anything resembling magic.

"I rode for some time, but saw no sign of the inn. So I rode on further, but there was absolutely no trace of it. I must have ridden for an hour, but still I didn't find the inn!

"I was becoming increasingly uneasy, as I feared I'd lost my way. So I turned around and headed back the way I'd come, and after a while I came to the signpost, but still without finding the inn. But I knew for certain that I had left the road at the signpost the night before and had seen the inn after riding for quarter of an hour.

"That was when I realized it had been no ordinary inn, not a lodging for mortal beings, but a magic inn, which was meant for the Little Folk. I should have known at once. The name gave it away: *the Inn of Elvenghest*! Yes, it was an inn for elves and spirits and maybe even for the servants of the devil himself! And I ate there, drank there and slept there. And it was no dream – the golden bowl is proof of that!

"I made the sign of the cross and rode as quickly as I could to Bainu, without leaving the road for a second.

"So that is my story. I stayed at the Inn of Elvenghest, which vanished overnight, without leaving a trace, and I have not made up one single detail about what I experienced there."

"That was a fine story," said Jiacomo, when the merchant had finished.

"A fine story?" he exclaimed. "It's a dreadful story! A ghostly encounter!"

"I wish it had happened to me," said Jiacomo.

"That's easy for you to say!" cried the merchant, sounding quite angry.

"You survived in one piece, didn't you?" said Jiacomo. "You even came out of it with a golden bowl. It's just your money that's missing. Was it much?"

"Yes," replied the merchant. "It was quite a lot."

Jiacomo gave a quiet whistle and looked pensively into the middle distance.

"A strange story indeed," said Master Philippo thoughtfully.

Laurenzo picked up the bowl and took another look at it.

"You believe me, don't you?" asked the merchant.

"I don't know what to believe," replied the old goldsmith, as he examined the bowl. "You don't seem like a liar, but your story is strange, very strange indeed."

"The bowl is real and doesn't look as if it might suddenly vanish," said Laurenzo. "If you didn't have the bowl, I'd think you'd dreamt it all."

"But I do have the bowl!" cried the merchant. "And I'm sure I didn't dream it. Besides, I've recently heard that other people have had similar experiences out on the plain."

"Not me," said Jiacomo. "I lived there for almost a year, and I know my way around the plain better than most people, but I've never seen this inn... not even the signpost. I've never seen any elves dancing out there. I sometimes thought I might, when the mist was swirling in the moonlight, but even though I took a good look around, I didn't see anything. I haven't come across any ghostly horsemen, no witches on broomsticks, no evil spirits, no talking animals, nothing... although I certainly tried. And then you pay the occasional visit to the plain and this happens to you!"

"There's really no need to envy me," said the merchant. "If you'd experienced it for yourself, you'd be speaking very differently."

"Ah, but I hope that I do experience it for myself," replied Jiacomo. "And so I'm planning to pay a visit to this inn."

"You must be mad!" cried the merchant. "You can't go there!"

"Why not?" said Jiacomo. "I'm already looking forward to it! Tell me, who are the others who have experienced something similar, and when did it happen?"

"Stefano, a student, once saw a horrible creature there that was not a human and not an animal," replied the merchant. "And there's a pedlar – I can't remember his name – who also visited the inn. He came back with terrifying memories and a golden ring. He too woke up at the side of the road and couldn't find the inn."

"When did this happen?" asked Laurenzo.

"Less than a month ago," replied the merchant. "And Sebastiano, a friend of a friend of mine in Forpa, has a brother who experienced the same thing. Oh, there are plenty of people who have been to that inn."

"The plain is large," said Jiacomo. "Whereabouts was this signpost?"

"If you're coming from Forpa, it's on the right-hand side of the road," replied the merchant and after some thought he added: "It was past the side road to Pava."

"I see. In that boring region," said Jiacomo, "where the road meanders and the landscape is so dull."

"And I shall never go there again," said the merchant, shivering.

"So what do the goldsmiths say?" asked Jiacomo. "Was the golden bowl made deep in the earth in dwarven caverns?"

"Humans can make such objects too," said Laurenzo.

"Oh, but who knows what magical powers it might possess?" cried Jiacomo. "So you don't think the dark arts are involved, Laurenzo?"

"No dark arts," said Master Philippo, looking at the bowl with a frown, "and I know that for certain." It looked as if he wanted to say more, but he changed his mind and fell silent.

"I should like to visit that inn too," said Laurenzo.

"Then we shall go together," said Jiacomo cheerfully. "We'll cross our fingers and carry silver coins over our hearts for protection. And we won't take any money, as it might turn into sand." And he asked the merchant: "These other people who visited the inn, did their money turn into sand too?"

"The pedlar's did," replied the merchant, "but I'm not sure about my friend's friend's brother."

"So you didn't pay for your accommodation," said Laurenzo.

"Pay for it?" cried the merchant. "I lost all the money I had with me. And I'd really rather not have that magical golden object at all!"

"Give it to us," said Jiacomo, "and we'll return it to the innkeeper."

"So you're sticking with your plan?" asked
"You're going to pay a visit to the Inn of Elve.

"Indeed we are," replied the brothers.

The merchant gasped in horror. "Both of you?"

"Of course," said Laurenzo. He turned to the old goldsmith and asked: "Are you coming too, Master Philippo?"

"No," Master Philippo replied, "I'm too old for such adventures. And besides I'm not really one for ghosts." He looked at one brother and then the other before adding: "But you can ask the landlord a question on my behalf."

"What do you want to know?" asked Laurenzo.

"I should like to know how he came by this bowl," replied the goldsmith. "I know for certain that it was not made by supernatural powers, because I made it myself. It was some time ago now, almost twenty years, but I don't believe that I'm mistaken."

The others stared at him in surprise.

"How strange," said Laurenzo.

"How funny," said Jiacomo.

But the merchant exclaimed: "How can you remember something you made twenty years ago? There are so many bowls that look alike!"

"I understand your doubts," said Master Philippo. "And I hesitated before telling you that I was the one who made that bowl. But I'm sure of it. I made six like it at the time, decorated on the inside with patterns of my own design, and I was very proud of them."

"Who did you make them for?" asked Laurenzo.

"I made them for my own pleasure. Then later I sold them, but I can't remember who bought them."

"In twenty years, they might have changed hands several times," said Laurenzo thoughtfully.

"Finally ending up in a haunted inn," said Jiacomo. "Now I'm even more keen to go there."

He turned to the merchant. "Drink a cup of wine with us," he proposed. "And then you must tell us your story again, because we all want to know everything that there is to know about the Inn of Elvenghest."

2   THE TWO BROTHERS VISIT THE INN

Across the Plain of Babina rode two young men on horses. They were as alike as two drops of water, as were the dogs that were following them. Laurenzo and Jiacomo were on their way to the Inn of Elvenghest.

"The sun is shining," said Laurenzo. "It should really be windy or rainy, now that we're going to this mysterious inn."

"There's still time for that to happen," said Jiacomo cheerfully. "And happen it will, as the sun never shines for long on the plain."

An hour later, Laurenzo said: "You see, it's starting to get misty now, and chilly too."

"We should be about there," said Jiacomo, "but I still don't see anything resembling a signpost, even though we must be near the side road to Pava."

"Look!" cried Laurenzo. "Over there! I see something!"

"Yes!" exclaimed Jiacomo. "A post. It's the sign, you're right!"

The brothers urged their horses into a gallop and before long they had reached the signpost.

"Next to a small, crooked tree," said Jiacomo "...
are the words: *The Inn of Elvenghest*. Let's hope ...
the inn now and that it hasn't been spirited away by m...

"Do you believe in inns being spirited away?" asked Laurenzo.

"I'd like to," replied Jiacomo, "because that really would be quite amazing. But sadly it's hard to believe that a building really can vanish overnight – particularly if there's a better explanation."

"And do you have a better explanation?" asked Laurenzo.

Jiacomo looked closely at the signpost. "I think so," he replied. "And what are your thoughts on the subject?"

"I don't think the inn moved. I think it was the signpost that moved!"

"I had exactly the same thought!" cried Jiacomo. "It's easier to move a signpost than a whole building. You just pull it out of the ground and plant it again a bit further along."

"Next to another crooked tree," said Laurenzo.

"Next to another crooked tree," agreed Jiacomo. "The landscape here is monotonous, and everywhere looks like everywhere else."

"So that's how it happened," said Laurenzo. "While he was sleeping, Konrad the merchant was deposited somewhere by the side of the road, some distance from the inn. The signpost was put next to him. When he woke up and went in search of the inn, he didn't find it, because the signpost was in a different place. But why would the people at the inn treat their guests in such a manner?"

"They give them a golden bowl as a souvenir," said Jiacomo, "but they change their money into sand and stones."

"Do you have an explanation for that?" asked Laurenzo.

191

"Perhaps," said Jiacomo. "But first I'd like to go to the inn."

The two brothers rode in the direction the signpost was pointing, just as Konrad the merchant had recently done.

"It's getting dark," said Laurenzo.

A little later they saw the inn ahead of them: a stone building with a thatched roof.

"Luckily it's not been spirited away," said Laurenzo with a smile.

They rode towards the inn, but then Jiacomo stopped his brother and said: "The folk at that inn have given a number of travellers the fright of their lives. So how about we play a trick on them? Only one of us will go inside, while the other rides around the back to the stables. They might have invisible guests, but I'm sure they've never had a guest who can be in two places at once!"

Laurenzo understood what his brother was planning, and he chuckled. Then Jiacomo went to the front door and Laurenzo rode around the back to where the stables should be.

Jiacomo opened the door and stepped inside. The room looked just as the merchant had told him. There was no sign of anyone there.

"Good evening!" he called. "You have a customer!"

A door opened at the back of the room and the young man with blond hair appeared. "Good evening," he said. "What can I do for you?"

"A meal and lodging for the night," replied Jiacomo.

"I wasn't expecting anyone to come," said the young man, "but now that you've found the way here, you can stay."

"That's nice," said Jiacomo. "Very hospitable. Are you the landlord?"

"No, sir. I am the servant."

"I came on my horse," said Jiacomo. "Where's the st..."

"I shall take care of your horse," said the servant.

"Ah, there's no need," replied Jiacomo. "I've already found it. I just took my horse in there. At this very moment, I'm tying him up by the hay rack."

The servant gave him a very puzzled stare. "I'll go and take a look," he said, disappearing through the back door.

Jiacomo walked around the room, taking a good look at everything. He spent a while studying the iron-bound chests.

Meanwhile the servant had reached the stable. To his surprise, he met the new guest there again – or at least he thought he did. "How did you get here so quickly?" he asked.

Laurenzo, because that is of course who it was, gave him a friendly smile. "I told you I'd take care of my horse myself," he replied. "There's no need to be surprised. I can do everything twice as fast as ordinary people. I can do two things at the same time, you see."

"But how...?" began the servant.

"I thought you'd understand," said Laurenzo. "You're a servant at the Inn of Elvenghest, after all. I'm looking after my horse here, and I'm sitting in the dining room over there. Oh, would you please bring me a cup of wine?"

The pale young man became even paler and hurried back inside. The new guest was sitting comfortably in a chair, as if he had never been away. (Which, of course, he had not.)

"S-sir...!" stammered the servant.

"Yes?" said Jiacomo with a smile. "Oh, and where's my wine?"

The servant gave a trembling sigh and reached for a jug with shaking fingers. "I don't understand this at all," he said. "How can you be in two places at once?"

"Now you're getting it!" cried Jiacomo. "In two places at once. It's very simple! I thought you'd be used to such things."

The servant poured a cup of wine, spilling a little, and placed it on the table in front of Jiacomo.

"Yes, it's very simple," Jiacomo repeated. "Shall I show you how I do it? Go and stand by the door, take a good look at me, count to three, turn your back, open the door and look outside. Then I'll come walking towards you."

The servant hesitated, but then did what Jiacomo had said. He looked, counted, opened the door... and saw Laurenzo coming. Stifling a cry, he looked round and saw Jiacomo, who was sitting calmly in his chair and drinking wine.

"Two places at once!" he said cheerfully, raising his cup.

Then it dawned on the servant. "Oh!" he cried. "You're two... I mean... There are two... two different..."

"Exactly," said Laurenzo, who had come closer. "Twins."

The young man looked at one brother and then the other, with a mixture of annoyance and relief.

"Now you just need to take care of my horse," said Jiacomo. "It's over by that boulder, opposite the inn."

The servant pulled a sour face and disappeared. The brothers had a good laugh. Laurenzo sat down across from Jiacomo and said: "He's just annoyed because we frightened him instead of him frightening us."

"He might turn the tables before long," replied Jiacomo. "Wait, I'll get a cup and pour some wine for you too."

When he had done so, he leant towards his brother and whispered: "I know who the owner of this inn is!"

"Who?" asked Laurenzo.

"The landlord of this inn is not an elf, not a giant, not a spirit, but Jannos, the master thief and highwayman, my former teacher!"

"But how do you know that?" said Laurenzo. "Have you seen him?"

"I didn't see him, but I know those chests. They belong to Jannos. The landlord is a big, dark man: Jannos!"

"Oh," said Laurenzo. "Now I understand how all those precious things got here, the silver jugs, the golden plates. They're all stolen property!"

"Jannos the innkeeper," said Jiacomo. "What do you think of that?"

"He's certainly no ordinary innkeeper, that's for sure," replied Laurenzo. "Do you think he's still a thief?"

"Hush!" whispered Jiacomo. "I can hear something."

The brothers fell silent and listened. They could hear quiet footsteps outside. Then the door by the bar opened a crack. But it shut again just as quickly and the footsteps left and faded away.

"That might have been Jannos," said Laurenzo.

Jiacomo stood up. "I'm going to take a look," he said. But before he reached the door, it opened again, all the way this time. The young servant came into the room. He was dressed in a velvet suit with wide sleeves and around his neck he had the sparkling chain that the merchant had mentioned. He bowed to the twin brothers and said: "Your horses have been taken care of."

"Well," said Jiacomo, "don't you look fine? I almost didn't recognize you."

The servant bowed again and asked if the gentlemen would like something to eat.

"Yes, please," said Laurenzo. "Is that in honour of our visit?"

"What do you mean?" asked the servant.

"Those fine clothes."

The servant frowned and, after a little hesitation, replied: "Do not ask me any questions, sir! Questions are not permitted at this inn."

"How strange!" said Jiacomo. He looked around and pretended to shiver. "How terribly strange! There is something ghostly about this inn." And he asked: "Is it... not as it should be?"

The servant did not seem to know quite how to answer. "You are welcome here," he said finally, "as long as you do not ask any questions." He walked over to the fire and stirred the pot. Then he lit the candles, as it was getting dark.

Jiacomo went and sat back down with Laurenzo at the table. "There's just one thing missing," he whispered to him. "The wind howling outside." Laurenzo laughed.

The servant gave them a suspicious look, but he said nothing. He laid their table and stirred the soup again. Then from somewhere, in the inn or outside, came the sound of quiet, mysterious music.

"Someone's playing a flute," said Jiacomo.

The servant looked at him in surprise and said: "What's that you say?"

"Music," said Laurenzo.

The servant raised his eyebrows and said: "I can't hear anything."

"I can," said Jiacomo. "Listen!" He hummed along quietly and then continued: "I could sing a song to that tune. Like this:

"What lurks out there in the darkness
while we search for somewhere to rest?
Who rides so late to that eerie place,
the Inn of Elvenghest?

In dim mists the fairies dance.
I thought I saw them play.
But I never found them anywhere,
in the bright sunlight of day."

The music died away. The servant shrugged his shoulders and went to see if the soup was hot enough. Then he ladled out a dish of soup for each of the brothers. When Laurenzo asked him if he had anything for the dogs, he put some meat on a plate and placed it on the floor. Then he began to lay another table with a silver dish, some golden plates and bowls, and a cup studded with precious stones. He did it slowly and solemnly, as if it were work of great importance.

"That's for the invisible guest," whispered Laurenzo.

But Jiacomo said loudly: "I would like to sit at that table!" The servant glared at him.

Jiacomo asked: "Are you laying that table for yourself, for the innkeeper or for a guest?"

"For a guest," replied the servant.

"Then we would like to sit there," said Jiacomo.

"I'm sorry, sir," said the young man, "but that won't be possible."

"Why not?" asked Jiacomo. "All guests are equal. Besides, we were here first. And we would like to eat from silver dishes too." He stood up and walked over to the table.

The servant blocked his way and cried: "Don't do it, sir! You'll regret it!"

"It's not fair to treat one guest better than the others," said Jiacomo. "Who is the guest you are expecting?"

"I can't tell you," replied the servant. "But this table is not for you."

"I am a guest too and no less important than anyone else!" cried Jiacomo. "Even if it were the king of the fairies or the devil himself! What do you say, Laurenzo?"

"I agree," his brother replied.

"Gentlemen," said the servant, "you are playing a dangerous game! Sit at this table if you so wish, but you will come to regret it." He turned around and left the room.

"A man could almost start to believe in ghosts," said Jiacomo, sitting down at the lavishly set table. "Come and join me, Laurenzo."

Laurenzo did so. "He's gone to ask the landlord what to do," he said.

And indeed they could hear the murmur of voices elsewhere in the inn. The brothers looked at each other and smiled.

"We need another dish," said Jiacomo.

"I shall give you one," said the servant, coming back into the room.

"A silver dish," said Laurenzo.

"Would you like some more wine?" asked the servant.

"Yes, please," replied the brothers.

The servant fetched a dish and a cup and served them both before returning to stand behind the bar.

The brothers ate and pretended to drink. But they secretly poured their wine under the table.

Then there came a knock at the front door.

"Now you're for it!" said the servant, glaring at the brothers. Slowly he walked to the door and opened it. At once he uttered a loud cry, stumbling backwards and crying, "Mercy!"

"What's wrong?" exclaimed the brothers.

No one had come in, but the servant backed away until he bumped into the bar, where he remained, with his hands over his eyes.

"Yet more theatrics," whispered Jiacomo to Laurenzo. But both he and his brother stood up, walked to the open door and looked outside.

It was dark and so misty that there was not a star to be seen. But on the ground, tiny flickering lights were moving all around. It was as if a bunch of candles had gone out for a walk.

The brothers stared in surprise at this wondrous apparition. They weren't dreaming, were they? No, they could really see them: lots of little lights moving slowly around one another. Without thinking, they both grabbed onto each other and their hearts began to beat faster.

Something brushed past their legs. They jumped, but it was just their dogs, who also stood watching the walking flames and then, loudly barking, ran at them. This broke the enchantment... and chased away the brothers' fear.

"Come on," said Laurenzo. "If it really was something supernatural, our dogs wouldn't go running after them."

So they walked towards the lights.

"It really is just a candle!" cried Jiacomo, when he reached one of them. They bent down to see. As they looked more closely, they realized what it was: a little crab with a candle stuck to its back.

"Now that's a good idea!" said Jiacomo, pulling the candle off the creature.

The dogs were still barking and jumping from one light to another, without daring to touch them though.

"We nearly fell for it," said Laurenzo. "Crabs with candles on their backs!"

"I should have known," said Jiacomo.

Laurenzo went up to each of the lights, put them out and took the candles off the crabs' backs. "I'm sure these little creatures don't think it's much fun though," he said.

When the brothers went back inside, the servant gave them a look of disappointment.

"What kind of inn is this?" asked Laurenzo. "Is it the custom here to terrify your guests? Then you'll have to think up something scarier than that for us."

The servant shuffled his feet and did not reply.

The brothers sat back down and Jiacomo filled their cups again. "Bring us two more cups," he said to the servant, "and some more wine."

The young man looked at them with a question on his face.

"Those two cups are for you and the landlord," said Jiacomo.

"Yes," Laurenzo added. "We'd like to have a drink together, the four of us."

"I'll have a drink with you," replied the servant, "but I don't know if the landlord will come down."

"What kind of innkeeper does not want to drink with his guests?" cried Laurenzo.

"Go and tell him to come here," ordered Jiacomo. "We're old friends of his – as he knows very well, because I'm sure he's been spying on us."

The servant looked at one, then the other, not quite knowing what to do. Then he took out a bottle and two cups and put them on the brothers' table before quickly disappearing.

No sooner had he left than Jiacomo poured the contents of his and his brother's cups into the new ones. He filled their own cups from the bottle that the servant had just put down.

"Look," he whispered, "if there's a sleeping potion in our wine, they'll be the ones to drink it."

"Very clever," whispered Laurenzo.

The door next to the bar opened. The servant appeared in the doorway and said: "My master, the landlord of this inn, would be pleased to meet you." He stepped forward and made way for the landlord, a big, dark man.

It was indeed Jannos.

"I guessed right!" cried Jiacomo, jumping to his feet. "Jannos the thief, my old master!"

"No longer a thief," said Jannos, "but an innkeeper. My dear Jiacomo, how are you faring? And you, Laurenzo, how are you?" He enthusiastically shook the brothers' hands and sat down with them at the table. "Come and join us, Joris!" he called to the servant. "And hear the names of our guests: Jiacomo and Laurenzo, twin brothers! You need to watch out for these two!"

Then he turned to the brothers and asked: "How did you know I was the landlord of this inn?"

"I recognized the chests," replied Jiacomo. "They belonged to you. And when I saw the crabs walking around outside with candles on their backs, I was sure that it was you who had come up with the idea. You once told me a story about a thief who stole from a church when both the priest and the verger were there. He stuck candles onto crayfish and released them in the churchyard, so they thought the Day of Judgement had arrived. Do you remember?"

"I should have done!" cried Jannos. "No wonder you didn't fall for it. All my other guests think my inn's haunted."

"An inn visited by invisible guests," said Laurenzo, "an inn that can disappear overnight."

"Don't you believe the stories?" asked Jannos.

"Not if you're involved, no," said Jiacomo, and he told his former master what he thought about his inn.

Jannos took a swig of wine and said to the servant: "What do you say, Joris? All your hard work tonight has been in vain."

"A complete waste of effort," replied Joris. He emptied his cup and added: "I had no idea these brothers were acquaintances of yours."

"We didn't manage to fool the two of you," said Jannos to the brothers. "So I shall now tell you why I treat my guests this way. A year ago, I stopped robbing and stealing in order to lead an honest life. I rebuilt an old sheep pen to make this inn and then I became a respectable innkeeper. But I still had lots of valuables – all of them stolen – and I wanted to get rid of them.

"Jewels, bowls, spoons and such things were no good to me. I needed money, so that I could live as a rich man. But unfortunately lots of people were after me, and I didn't want to venture away from the plain to sell my loot. And it wouldn't have been easy to offload the stolen goods.

"So I came up with an idea. I had this little inn, and I knew that would help me. Whenever a guest came, he was given a spooky welcome by my manservant Joris. Joris is an excellent actor."

"Yes," said Joris, "I'd like to go on the stage." Then he yawned and sighed: "Why on earth am I so sleepy?"

"It's all the hard work," said Jannos and he continued: "We scared our guests in many different ways. Joris would pretend to let in an invisible visitor and serve him. I don't need to tell the two of you that he wasn't really serving anyone. He was just play-acting! When the guest was convinced that the place was haunted, he was taken to his bedroom. We made sure that he got a sleeping potion in his wine, so that he would sleep soundly until the next morning. Then, when he was in bed, we would make some noise to scare him even more. As soon as he was asleep, we'd creep into his room, take the money from his purse and fill it with sand and stones. In return for the money, I'd put one of my treasures in his knapsack, something big if he had a lot of money, something small if he didn't have much. And that was an easy way to sell my stolen objects."

"To sell them?" cried Laurenzo. "I'm sure your guests would have a different opinion about that if they knew."

"Ah, but they don't know, do they?" said Jannos with a contented smile. "And then we would load the sleeping guest onto his horse and lead him some distance away from the inn. We'd deposit him at the side of the road and put the signpost next to him. When he woke up and couldn't find the inn, he'd make sure he got away from here as quickly as he could. He'd be so certain that he'd seen ghosts that he'd never come back and bother us again. As soon as he was well out of the way, we put the signpost back in the right place and waited for our next visitor."

He took a couple more swigs of the wine and said: "So now you know the whole story. And what do you think of it?"

"I admire your... ingenuity," said Jiacomo. "But I feel sorry for your guests."

"Sorry?" said Jannos, yawning. "They shouldn't be so stupid, should they? You two didn't fall for it, eh?" He gave the brothers a mocking look. "Sometimes it's good," he continued, "to give people a scare. Then at least they'll have an adventure to tell their friends about."

"That's true enough," said Laurenzo, laughing, and he told him about the merchant who had been to show him his golden bowl.

"I once stole that bowl from a bishop," said Jannos. "I've got a few more of them. Would you like to buy one?" He looked at the servant and cried in surprise: "What? Joris has fallen asleep! Hey, lazybones, wake up!"

The young man went on sleeping.

"That's odd," said Jannos and he asked the two brothers: "Aren't the two of you feeling at all sleepy?"

"Terribly," replied Jiacomo. "I've never been so sleepy before." And he yawned loudly.

"Me neither," said Laurenzo, also yawning. "I can hardly keep my eyes open."

"I'm really tired too," said Jannos, "but I don't know why." He fell forward onto the table and before long he was snoring away.

And the brothers' sleepiness instantly vanished without a trace.

"Look at the two of them," said Jiacomo. "Now they're the ones who have fallen for it!"

"Because they drank our wine," said Laurenzo.

"Shall we give them the same treatment they gave their guests?" said Jiacomo. "Shall we leave them by the side of the road, in the cold and in the wet?"

"Yes," said Laurenzo, "it'll do them some good!"

The brothers set to work. They loaded the two sleeping men onto horses. Jannos was so big that it wasn't an easy task, but eventually they managed. They led the horses some way from the inn and deposited their sleeping loads beside the road. Then Jiacomo fetched the signpost and planted it next to them in the ground.

"There you go," he said. "Sleep tight."

Then the brothers returned to the inn, took the horses to the stables and went back inside.

"Shall we go to bed?" asked Laurenzo.

"Wait a moment," said Jiacomo. "Let's just take a look inside the chests, shall we?"

"Right," said Laurenzo. "Open them up."

All three of the chests were locked, but Jiacomo still managed to get them open. The first one contained clothes and thieves' tools, the second had jewels and other treasure, and in the third were lots of bags of money. The brothers emptied the last two chests and filled them again with sand and stones. Then they took the money and the treasure and headed upstairs and into one of the bedrooms.

They actually were tired by that point, so they climbed into bed and were soon asleep.

The next morning they were awoken by voices outside. Laurenzo stood up and peered through the window.

"They're coming back," he whispered. "And I bet they're angry!"

"They'll be even angrier soon," said Jiacomo. "When they've looked inside the chests."

He was shortly proved right when they heard them banging about in the dining room and Jannos cursing loudly. Chuckling to themselves, the brothers got dressed and went downstairs.

Jannos and Joris were standing by the empty chests, and their jaws dropped when they saw the brothers coming in.

"Good morning," said the twins with friendly smiles.

"How dare you?" cried Jannos. "First sending us to sleep and dumping us by the roadside, then stealing our belongings – and now you have the cheek to wish us good morning? That's the most outrageous thing of all! So tell me, what have you done with my belongings?"

Jiacomo looked inside the chests and pretended to be shocked. "My goodness me!" he said. "They've been turned into sand and stones!"

Jannos wanted to look even angrier, but instead he burst out laughing. The servant smiled feebly.

"Well, you've certainly made a fool of me now!" cried the thief. "Congratulations, boys! But..." he continued, "I do still want my property back."

"We'll give you the money," said Jiacomo. "But not the rest – it's stolen goods."

"Maybe we can track down the rightful owners," added Laurenzo.

"That won't be easy," said Jannos. "Well, I'm not happy about it, but I suppose I'll have to agree. You've outsmarted me. And I'd have fooled you if you'd drunk that wine. Keep the treasure and do something good with it. The money's enough for me."

Then they enjoyed a nice breakfast together.

"What are you planning to do now?" Jiacomo asked his former master. "Are you going to go on frightening your guests and scaring them away?"

"No," said Jannos, "I've had enough of that. After tonight the fun's gone out of it. I'm going to become an honest, respectable innkeeper. I'm getting too old for stealing and playing pranks anyway." He stood up and solemnly declared: "Jannos the master thief will henceforth cease to exist, and so will the Inn of Elvenghest. In their place will be Jannos the innkeeper and an inn that shall be known as the Two Brothers!"

Laurenzo and Jiacomo clapped their hands. But Joris looked sour, because now he'd have to be an ordinary servant. Jannos gave him a wink though and said: "We'll still allow ourselves a little joke now and then!"

And that is the end of the story of the Inn of Elvenghest.

The inn itself continued to exist for many years under the name of the Two Brothers. Many travellers stayed the night, but no more strange things ever happened there again. Laurenzo and Jiacomo also visited sometimes and smiled at the sign with their portrait painted on it. There was a servant at the inn too, but it was no longer Joris, the blond young man, as he had left for Bainu, where he became a famous actor.

And that was how the travellers who crossed the plain came to have a safe inn where they could rest. And yet there were those who continued to claim that they had seen elves and ghosts. But that can't have been anywhere near the inn. After all, elves, ghosts, goblins and such creatures only live in places where no one ever goes.

One day, Jiacomo said to Laurenzo: "I have been to Forpa and to Sfaza, to Puna, Pava and Miranja. I have travelled across the plain many times and know Babina from north to south and from east to west. Now I feel like going on a longer journey. I wish to go to the south, and cross the land of Ibuna until I reach the coast and then sail upon the sea, which I have never seen before. They say there are beautiful lands on the other side of the ocean. I have spoken to merchants who have been there and they tell me there is much to sell and much to buy in those lands."

"If it is what you wish, then you must go," said his twin brother, "although I will miss you, and it worries me to think of the dangers that will threaten you at sea and in the unknown lands far from here."

"No more dangers than here," said Jiacomo. "Wouldn't you like to see the sea too, and to sail upon it? A caravan of merchants is leaving Bainu next week, and we can travel with them."

"We?" said Laurenzo.

"Yes, of course. You have to come as well. Don't you want the two of us to travel into the world and have adventures, like we used to? We can take some of your work with us to sell and you will have new skills to learn too, as they say there are very good goldsmiths in those parts."

Laurenzo thought about it. He did want to go, and not only for the opportunity to learn. The adventure itself was tempting him.

"Come with me!" cried Jiacomo. "We'll be back in Bainu in a year's time."

"But my work..." Laurenzo began hesitantly.

"You've always worked so hard. You can afford to take a break. We'll earn money on the way by trading."

"Fine, then," said Laurenzo. "I'll come with you."

"Hurrah!" cried Jiacomo and he added: "I wouldn't have gone on my own, but now that we are going together, I know we'll have a wonderful time."

Master Philippo, the old goldsmith, shook his head at the brothers' travel plans. But he did not try to stop them. "Young people don't always want to stay at home, and that's the way of the world," he said. "So I shall simply wish the two of you a good journey. And may Saint Christopher protect you!"

The King of Tirania

*"And suddenly a terrible gust of wind lifted up all
the sea and cast it onto the ship, shattering it on
every side and washing away all the passengers,
including the captain and the sailors and me."*

ONE THOUSAND AND ONE NIGHTS: 'Sinbad the Sailor'

I THE ADVENTURES OF LAURENZO

So the twin brothers set off into the world again, but this
time they left Babina behind and travelled through the land
of Ibuna to the coast. Before them lay the sea, which they had
never seen before: a vast pool under a clear blue sky. They
boarded the ship and happily sailed across the calm water to
far-off unknown lands. But the sea did not remain calm. After
a week's sailing, it showed its vicious side. A storm rose, with
the sky becoming as black as ink, and the waves rearing up
like furious dragons with foam-crested heads.

The ship was tossed to and fro, the sails were ripped to
shreds, the masts snapped and finally it took on water, capsized
and sank. Then the sea was satisfied and became calm once
more. But everyone on board had already drowned. At least,
almost everyone.

On a beach on a strange coast, one soul had washed ashore. That person slowly sat up and looked around. It was Laurenzo. There he was, all alone. He had survived the shipwreck, but where were his travelling companions? And most importantly, where was Jiacomo?

He got to his feet and began walking along the shore, calling: "Jiacomo! Jiacomo!"

No one replied. There was just the soft murmur of the sea. The beach was deserted, and the hills were silent. Distraught, Laurenzo repeated his cry: "Jiacomo!"

Finally, he sank down onto the sand in despair. He had escaped with his life, but how could he feel joy if Jiacomo was not there?

He had no idea how long he had been lying on the beach, soaking wet and filled with grief, when he heard someone calling. He looked up and saw three men approaching across the hills.

They ran up to Laurenzo, stood around him and started speaking to him, but he did not understand their language. Standing up, he said: "My ship was wrecked. Do you know if any other people have been washed ashore?"

But the men did not understand what he said.

Laurenzo pointed at the sea and told them with hand gestures that he had come from there. The men nodded in sympathy. Then one of them said something, and the others looked excited. The first man raised a finger in the air and ran off, while the others looked Laurenzo up and down, touching him gently and asking him questions he did not understand. A little later, the one who had run away came back, followed by two more men, who were carrying a litter. In this litter there sat a thin, important-looking man with a turban on his head. He stepped out, walked up to Laurenzo and bowed deeply to him, saying something in a solemn voice.

Laurenzo indicated once again that he had been in a shipwreck. Then the thin man nodded and asked with a gesture: "Where are you from?"

"Babina," replied Laurenzo.

To his surprise, the man answered him in his own language. "Welcome, stranger," he said and he added: "I can speak with you and understand you, because I once lived in your country for a time. I understand that your ship was wrecked and that you were thrown out onto the beach. But be glad that you made it out alive."

"I am not glad!" cried Laurenzo. "Tell me, did no one else wash ashore?"

"Not as far as I know. It was sadly a very fierce storm."

Laurenzo bowed his head. "My brother was with me," he said. "We had both grabbed a plank to keep us afloat, but a wave separated us and I haven't seen him since then. I can't believe he has drowned. We were born on the same day and I always imagined we would die on the same day."

The man looked at him sadly. "I fear that he is dead," he said. "But just to make certain, I'll instruct my servants to search along the shoreline for other survivors." He gave an order in his own language and the three men who had found Laurenzo hurried away. Then he spoke to Laurenzo in Babinian: "Come with me. Climb into my litter, and we shall go to my home." Laurenzo did not move.

"Come along," said the man, taking him by the hand. "You can't stay here. You still don't know what land you have found yourself in. This is Tirania."

Laurenzo did not care if he had washed up in Tirania or some other land, but he let the man help him into the litter without protest. The thin man sat down opposite him and then they set off, away from the shore and the sea. Laurenzo was silent, absorbed in his sorrow, and the man opposite him was also silent. But then, after some time, he spoke and said: "If you look outside, you will see our city: Baharan, the place where the king lives."

Laurenzo looked and saw the city, bounded on one side by the sea and on the other sides by mountains. It looked cheerful in the sunshine, with its white and pink houses with flat roofs, towers – some pointed and others topped with onion-shaped domes – and dark green palm trees.

"Welcome to Baharan," said his travelling companion, drawing the curtains of the litter.

Laurenzo leant back in exhaustion, but was suddenly startled by loud shouting and the clashing of weapons. The man opposite him peeped through the curtains but did not seem too concerned. Shortly after that, the litter stopped and Laurenzo and his companion stepped out in front of a big, white house.

"Welcome to my home," the man said. "My name is Asmian."

"I am Laurenzo."

"Welcome, Laurenzo from Babina," said Asmian. He took the young man by the arm and led him into his home.

It was very beautiful, with tiled floors, couches with silk cushions and pots with strange plants in them. Asmian clapped his hands and immediately servants appeared, who took Laurenzo with them, ran a bath for him, gave him a new robe to wear and finally placed a delicious meal before him. Then they led him to a room where a soft bed was waiting, and they left.

Laurenzo did not feel at all like sleeping, but he was glad to be alone. He lay down on the bed and sighed for Jiacomo, but he was more tired than he thought and was asleep before he knew it.

When he awoke, he lay there for a while, wondering what to do next. His thoughts were interrupted by the entrance of four servants. One of them was carrying a silver washbasin, the second had towels and the others brought more new clothes, including a turban of red silk. Laurenzo washed and dressed himself and when he was ready, the servants bowed respectfully and indicated that he should follow them.

They took him to the garden, which was beautiful, with ornamental trees and a gurgling fountain. Then they bowed again and left him on his own. A little later, his host appeared, followed by a boy carrying a tray full of fruits.

"I hope you feel a little better now," said Asmian with a bow.

"As far as my body is concerned, yes, thank you," replied Laurenzo, "but my soul is still filled with sorrow."

"I cannot take away your sorrow," said Asmian. "All I can advise is that you accept your loss and console yourself with the thought that no man goes before his time. At this moment, life might feel worthless to you, but when some time has passed you will feel glad that you still have it, particularly now that you have the opportunity to do such good work."

He turned to the boy and told him to offer the fruits to Laurenzo.

Out of politeness, Laurenzo took one from the tray, a strange fruit that he did not recognize, but which tasted good. Then he asked his host if any other victims of the shipwreck had been found on the coast.

"I am sorry to tell you that no one has washed ashore," replied Asmian. "Otherwise I would have let you know at once."

Laurenzo turned away and sighed.

"Come," said Asmian. "Walk with me through the garden. Then I shall tell you a little about Tirania, the country you may now consider your own."

So Laurenzo walked around the garden with his host and listened to what he told him about his country.

"Tirania is an island," said Asmian. "It is small, but it contains everything its inhabitants need. We cultivate grain, grow an abundance of fruits and the mountains contain copper, tin and gold. We could all be happy here, but sadly, even though there is enough for everyone, and even though we have no enemies, I believe that there is more fighting in Tirania than anywhere else in the world. Baharan echoes every day with the clash of weapons and even the children fight in the streets. No one goes outside after sunset unless they have at least a strong stick, and preferably a couple of armed friends. In short, Tirania is a land of strife and discord." He fell silent for a moment and then said to Laurenzo: "It is not like the land that you come from."

Babina... thought Laurenzo, *Babina... To be back there, together with Jiacomo!*

"Do you not think it bad," said Asmian, "for people from the same land to keep fighting and quarrelling? It is as if brothers were at each other's throats!"

Brothers!

Laurenzo thought about Jiacomo and stopped paying attention to what his host was saying.

But then a man came running into the garden.

His clothes were torn and he had a black eye.

"What happened?" asked Asmian.

"I've been fighting, my lord," replied the man, "with the servants of Dasuf. They wanted to know who your guest is and when I said I didn't know, they attacked me."

"I see," said Asmian. "Go and change your clothes and wash your face. We shall have to teach Dasuf's servants a lesson!"

When the man left, Asmian said to Laurenzo: "Now you have seen it for yourself! Dasuf belongs to the other party, and our hostility extends even to our servants. Long ago, Tirania was ruled by wise and sensible men, and peace reigned throughout the land. But then people came along who had something to say about everything and who thought they could do everything better themselves. Since then, there have been two parties in this land, known as the First Party and the Last Party. I am the head of the First Party and Dasuf is the leader of the Last Party. Every citizen of Tirania belongs to one of the two parties and hates the other one. I have tried many times to make peace between the two, but the Last Party refuses to listen. They reject every measure that is planned in the interests of our country."

Asmian fell silent and looked at Laurenzo. He realized that Asmian was waiting for an answer.

"That sounds very difficult," he said. "Is there really nothing that can be done about the situation?"

"Only the king is above the two parties," said Asmian. "At least, that is how it should be. He is chosen from one of the prominent families, but you will understand that this causes many problems. Every family here belongs to either the First Party or the Last Party, and so the king is always more in favour of one or the other. He is never truly impartial. Over the past three years, we have had eleven kings. One after another has been dethroned, driven away or murdered, as there was always one party or the other that did not agree with his rule."

He stopped at a bench and said: "Please sit down, noble sir, and listen closely to me. I shall tell you why Tirania is so delighted to welcome you. The shipwreck, which was a disaster for you, will prove a blessing for us."

Very puzzled, Laurenzo sat down. Asmian stood before him and said: "The situation in our country was so grave that not only our party but also the other one recognized that it could not continue. And so Dasuf and I went (separately, as we are no longer on speaking terms) to a wise old hermit, who lives in a cave nearby. He is the only man who does not participate in the disputes, but he will not leave his cave, as he is afraid that he will somehow end up getting involved. We asked the hermit for advice and this was his reply: 'The king who rules

Tirania must be impartial and stand above all disagreements. And as such a man cannot be found here, you must place the red turban on the head of the first stranger who comes to this land and proclaim him your ruler.'"

Asmian made a bow and continued: "Both parties decided to follow this advice and swore to obey the orders of the future king. You, a castaway from Babina, are the first stranger since then to set foot on our soil and so you will be our king and rule us from the great palace in Baharan."

Laurenzo stared at him in amazement. "What a preposterous notion!" he said finally. "I don't want to be a king!"

"Oh, my lord!" cried Asmian. "Do not disappoint us! I know that you are sad and that our land is strange to you, but there is no better remedy for sorrow than working hard for a good cause, and Tirania will not remain strange to you for long."

"I am sorry for you and your nation," said Laurenzo, standing up, "but I really do not want to be king. I wouldn't even know how to rule. I'm just a simple goldsmith. Let me return to Babina."

"I will teach you how to rule," said Asmian. "I'll help you at first, of course. You cannot return to your own land for the time being anyway, as we have no ships at our disposal. Do not abandon us. Be ready to help when you are called upon. You are alone, with no ties to bind you. So what is there to prevent you from staying here?"

Laurenzo thought about Master Philippo, who would be waiting for him in Bainu, but Bainu seemed so far away and unwelcoming, now that Jiacomo would no longer be there. He really did not care where he was and what he did. He might as well remain in Tirania as go anywhere else.

"I shall stay here for a while," he said, "and I will be of service to you. But not as king."

"You can only be of service to us as king," said Asmian. "Just try it! I beg of you!"

"Fine, then I shall try," said Laurenzo. "But don't blame me if I am a bad ruler."

Asmian's face lit up. He bowed deeply before Laurenzo and said: "Lord and master, allow me to lead you into my home and introduce you to my family and friends. Soon I shall announce your arrival and your acceptance of the crown and have the royal palace prepared for you to take up residence."

"Thank you," said Laurenzo. "But do not bow too deeply to me. I am just a poor castaway who has nothing left."

"Now you have an entire land!" cried Asmian. "There is one more thing I wish to say to you: at first you will need advice from someone who knows this country. I am prepared to give you that advice. You will have to appoint ministers, so make me your prime minister."

"Can I do that? Just like that?" asked Laurenzo.

"Of course, sire. The king's will is law."

"Good. Then I shall begin by appointing you my prime minister."

"Thank you, sire," said Asmian. "I shall explain to you later how you should solemnly swear me in. But first you need to be crowned yourself."

"How many ministers do there have to be?"

"Seven. I shall introduce you to all of the capable men, sire."

Laurenzo shook his head. "This is madness," he muttered. "King of Tirania! Jiacomo would have found this hilarious!"

"There's one thing I can already start with," he said to Asmian. "I shall learn the language of your country, so that at least I can understand my subjects."

"I am happy to be your interpreter," said Asmian.

"No, that's too roundabout. I wish to be able to speak myself. Perhaps you could find me a teacher though."

"As you wish," said Asmian.

"Then lead me into your house," said Laurenzo.

2 THE ADVENTURES OF JIACOMO

"Perchance he is not drown'd. What think you, sailors?"
"It is perchance that you yourself were saved."
"O, my poor brother! And so perchance may he be."

SHAKESPEARE: *Twelfth Night*

No other victims of the shipwreck had been washed up on the coast of Tirania, but Jiacomo had not drowned. After a long time floating around in the sea and clutching onto a plank, he had been fished out by a pirate ship. Like Laurenzo, he was filled with sadness about his brother's fate, as he feared he must have drowned. And he reproached himself bitterly for ever having suggested going on a journey. If he had not done so, he and his brother would still be living peacefully in Bainu, and Laurenzo would still be alive.

He asked the captain of the pirate ship if there was land nearby. Perhaps his brother had been washed ashore.

"There is land," replied the captain, "but I don't think you'll find your brother there. You can see for yourself though,

223

because I have to go there to repair the damage that I suffered in the storm."

"If you could drop me off on land, I would appreciate it," said Jiacomo. "Which country will that be?"

"Tirania. If you hope to find your brother somewhere, that's where you need to be. I suspect he's dead, but you never know. I'll put you ashore. We'll sail to a lonely bay where no one ever goes, because I don't want to run the risk of being caught and hanged for piracy. When my ship's repaired, I'll be straight back out to sea. I'm none too fond of Tirania."

"Why's that?" asked Jiacomo.

"It's a tiresome place," said the captain. "It's full of people who do nothing but argue and fight. There are two parties in the country and they're constantly at odds, even though no one can remember why. I used to go there often, and whenever I got caught, I'd figure out which party the man who had hauled me in belonged to. Then I'd pretend to be an enemy of the other party, and he'd immediately let me go. But eventually both parties realized I was tricking them, and since then I usually go out of my way to avoid Tirania."

The pirate ship sailed to the bay that the captain had mentioned, a quiet place surrounded by high rocks.

"Do you really want to stay here?" the sailors asked Jiacomo. "You're better off sailing with pirates than living in Tirania."

"I want to stay here," replied Jiacomo. "I need to know if any survivors of the shipwreck washed ashore."

The captain said he would show him the way. "You'll never find the road to Baharan by yourself," he said. "That's the only city here, you see. And you'll be sure to meet people there who can tell you if anyone came ashore."

They set off along secret paths through the rocks, and across the beach, until the captain stopped and said: "You can't go wrong from here. I'll get back to my ship – I'm too fond of my freedom to go any closer to Baharan."

Jiacomo thanked him and wished him a safe journey.

But right at that moment, a group of what must have been twenty soldiers appeared from between the rocks, with a fat, important-looking man at their centre. As soon as he saw them, the leader cried out: "It's that pirate! Catch him!"

The captain turned and ran, but he had sea legs so he couldn't go too quickly and the soldiers had no trouble catching him. Then they captured Jiacomo too and took both of them to the fat, important-looking man.

"Well," the fat man said to the captain, "you've got some nerve, daring to set foot on land here!"

Jiacomo did not understand the words he spoke, but he still cried out: "This man has done nothing wrong. All he did was help me!"

The fat man looked at him now, and his jaw dropped.

"Who are you?" he then asked in the language of the beautiful land of Babina.

"He is under my protection," said the pirate captain. "You must let him go, as he has done nothing wrong. This is the first time he has ever set foot in this land."

"Please let the captain go too," said Jiacomo. "He only came to show me the way. Don't let his kindness prove his downfall!"

The man studied him and then told his soldiers to withdraw.

"Are you a pirate too?" he asked Jiacomo.

"No, sir," replied the young man.

"Did you sail on board his ship?"

225

"I did."

"Then you are a pirate!"

"He was my passenger!" cried the captain.

"Anyone who sails on a pirate ship is a pirate," said the fat man and he went on with his interrogation. "Judging by your language, you are from Babina. Is that correct?"

"Yes, sir," replied Jiacomo.

"Why are you asking all these questions?" cried the captain. "The young man has done nothing wrong. He is—"

"Silence!" the fat man interrupted him. "Or I shall have you hanged at once!" He turned back to Jiacomo and asked: "So you've never been to Tirania before?"

"Never."

"And you only just arrived here?"

"Yes, sir."

"Good," said the man with a smile. "So you are a stranger and a pirate. Your friend there is the most dangerous pirate of all. And you should both hang. But I will spare the two of you if you, stranger, will do something for me."

"If I can help, then I will," replied Jiacomo.

"Your friend is free to go, as long as he makes sure to leave this land. But you, stranger, must remain in Tirania. Tirania, the most beautiful place on Earth, and yet so sadly tested by strife and discord. You will be the one to bring peace and order to our people."

Jiacomo looked at the fat man in surprise.

"Our nation is plagued by rulers who cannot rule," the man continued. "And we have recently gained a king who is so unjust that he beats the lot. That king must go!" He paused for a moment and then said solemnly: "You, stranger, are a simple pirate – and yet you resemble that king as one drop of water resembles another!"

Jiacomo flushed. "How long has this king been ruling here?" he asked.

"Three days."

"Why all this talk about kings?" cried the captain. "We're not interested in your politics! Just tell us what you want!"

Jiacomo hushed him by laying a hand on his arm. The captain frowned, but then his face lit up and he smiled. He was wise enough not to say anything.

"Do you know the king of Tirania?" the fat man asked Jiacomo.

"I have no kings among my acquaintances," Jiacomo replied.

"He comes from Babina, just like you."

"Many people live in Babina," said Jiacomo. "But now tell me, sir, what exactly it is that you want from me."

"Are you fearless, are you able to act and, above all, are you prepared to kill a man who is a villain?"

"If he is truly a villain, then yes," replied Jiacomo. "And as for your other questions, I believe I can also answer them in the affirmative."

The fat man gave him a penetrating stare. "I hope I can trust you," he said. "Tell me, do you have any other family? Cousins? Brothers?"

"No," said Jiacomo, after a moment's hesitation. "I am alone in the world."

"Wonderful!" cried the fat man. "Now the captain can go, as long as he makes sure he's back out at sea by tomorrow. You, stranger, are coming with me to Baharan."

"What do you want from him?" asked the captain.

But Jiacomo reassured him. "I am happy to go," he said. "I wanted to see Tirania, didn't I? Leave in peace, captain. There's no need to worry about me." He gave the captain a wink, thanked him again for his help and shook his hand.

Then they both went their separate ways; the captain back to the bay and Jiacomo to Baharan with the fat, important-looking man and his soldiers.

Behind the rocks, a litter was waiting for the fat man. He invited Jiacomo to sit with him inside the litter, and then four soldiers lifted it and, puffing and panting, started to carry it along.

"Let me tell you who I am," said the fat man. "My name is Dasuf. If you knew Tirania, you would know my name too. I am the leader of the Last Party."

Jiacomo bowed his head and muttered something vague, but polite-sounding.

"My friends and I wish to serve our country," Dasuf continued. "We want to bring peace and prosperity to the land, but the members of the other party, who call themselves the First Party, oppose us in every matter. Now they have succeeded in making the new king appoint only members of their party as ministers. Such a government will prove the downfall of Tirania!"

"Who is the king who rules here?" asked Jiacomo.

"He is a stranger who washed up on the shore. Asmian, the leader of the First Party, found him and welcomed him as an honoured guest. So now, of course, the king dances to his tune!"

"How strange," said Jiacomo.

"Do you know him?" asked Dasuf.

"You've already asked me that. No, I don't know him."

"You look so much like him that you could be his brother," said Dasuf.

Jiacomo was glad that the curtains were closed and so it was rather dark inside the litter. Otherwise Dasuf would certainly have seen his hope and his happiness. This king must be Laurenzo, no matter how strange it seemed. But he did not want to say that he knew him, as he had no idea what kind of man Dasuf was or what he wanted from him. So he just said: "People often resemble one another without being related."

"Hmm. Now listen carefully," said Dasuf. "There are two parties in this land, but the Last Party is the best party. My party, however, is powerless as long as the king only appoints ministers from the other party. I have already considered proclaiming a new king, but that will get us nowhere. It will only increase the discord. One king must rule Tirania, an impartial king, as is proper. And now that our enemies have won over the king, we must make sure that he disappears. Yes, the king must disappear and you must replace him!"

"Me? Replace the king?" cried Jiacomo.

"Shhh! Yes, stranger. The two of you are so similar that no one will notice that you are a different man. But, unlike him, you will be a just and fair ruler."

"That's ridiculous," said Jiacomo.

"How dare you?" said Dasuf. "It is a noble thing that you will be doing! I shall get you into the palace, and then you will kill the king and take his place."

When Jiacomo did not reply, he said: "You're not afraid, are you?"

"No. I'm just stunned," replied Jiacomo. "Murdering the real king and taking his place? I've never heard anything so preposterous!"

"The king who is now on the throne is false and unjust!"

I don't believe a word of it, thought Jiacomo. *At least if it really is Laurenzo. How can this Dasuf decide that, when the king has only been on the throne for three days?* But he said: "I will do as you ask, even though I do not yet understand why."

"Good," replied Dasuf. "And now I shall tell you why it is that we in Tirania want a foreigner as a king." He told Jiacomo what Asmian had told Laurenzo, but he said that the Last Party was good and noble and the First Party was wicked and evil.

"Now I understand," said Jiacomo when Dasuf had finished. "Although I still think it's ridiculous. Me as a king – or more like a fraud. It's too foolish for words!"

"You're not a fraud," said Dasuf, "but a benefactor! We need an impartial king – and an impartial king we shall have! And I can teach you how to rule."

"Thank you," said Jiacomo. "Now tell me something about my country and about the king I have to dethrone. And tell me how I can rule better than him. I'll have to appoint my ministers from both parties, of course."

"The right man in the right place," said Dasuf solemnly. "I shall tell you which men to appoint. And you must make me your prime minister."

3   THE REIGN OF SUTAN THE FOUR HUNDRED AND SIXTY-SEVENTH

"Rebellious subjects, enemies to peace!"

SHAKESPEARE: *Romeo and Juliet*

Laurenzo was now the king of Tirania. He had been made to take the same name as all his predecessors and so he was known as Sutan the four hundred and sixty-seventh. He wore the royal red turban on his head, and seven ministers helped him to rule the land.

One morning he was sitting on his throne, watching his seven ministers with a disgruntled face as they discussed affairs of state. Finally, Asmian came to him with a large sheet of parchment and asked him to sign it.

"I shall read it," said the king, "and decide if I shall approve it."

"You already know what it's about, sire," said Asmian. "Would you be so good as to sign it?"

"No, Prime Minister," said Laurenzo. "I wish to take some time to study it first, with the help of a dictionary."

"Do you not trust your prime minister, sire?" asked Asmian.

"Of course I trust you," replied Laurenzo. "But I know that I am still inexperienced and so I do not wish to hurry when making my decisions." He rolled up the parchment and rose from his throne. "The meeting is over," he said. "You may all leave. I would like Asmian to report to me this evening."

The ministers bowed. One of them stepped forward and spoke.

"One last request for Your Majesty," said Asmian, translating. "There is a prisoner. We would appreciate it if you would pass judgment on him."

"A prisoner?" said Laurenzo. "What did he do?"

"He is one of your most rebellious subjects," replied Asmian. "A member of the Last Party. He disturbed the peace on the market square yesterday and caused a fight."

"Bring him here," said Laurenzo, sitting back down on his throne.

A few minutes later, his servants brought in a man in chains. Kalaf, one of the ministers, began the questioning. Then Asmian told the king about the prisoner's crime.

"Sire," he said, "this man is a baker and he engaged in unfair competition with his fellow bakers. He was selling bread at the market without a permit. When they tried to make him leave, he started swearing and then fighting."

"Why do you need a permit to sell bread here?" asked Laurenzo.

"It's in our laws," replied Asmian. "Yesterday was Tuesday – and only members of the First Party are allowed to sell at the market on Tuesdays."

The prisoner looked at Asmian and then at the king and began talking loudly and angrily. After a while, Kalaf ordered him to be silent, and Asmian said to Laurenzo: "Sire, he says that he does not care about the law and that he will sell his bread whenever he wants. He says he will cut the throats of the members of the First Party if they interfere with his business. And he says... forgive me, sire, he says that the king is false and unjust!"

"What else did he say?" asked Laurenzo.

"Nothing else, sire. Isn't that enough?"

"I think he said more than that," said Laurenzo. "He was speaking quickly, and I don't understand your language very well yet. But I think he also said that Tuesday has always been the Last Party's market day. I think he said that it's the *new* law he doesn't care about. He also said that the king is allowing his ministers to make a fool of him! What is this new law, Asmian, and how long has it been in existence?"

Asmian turned pale. "Since yesterday, sire," he replied.

"Why don't I know anything about it?"

"Oh, sire!" cried Asmian. "We can't bother you with such trivial matters!"

Laurenzo frowned and said angrily: "I do not find new laws trivial, Prime Minister!"

The prisoner now turned to him and said: "King Sutan, it's like this. On Monday, Wednesday and Friday, the members of the First Party can sell their goods at the market. Tuesday, Thursday and Saturday have always been our party's days. But now it has suddenly changed. From now on, we can only sell on Thursdays, and all the other days are for the First Party!"

"This was decided in the interests of our entire people!" cried Asmian. "The members of the Last Party can't bake good bread. They'd give everyone stomach ache!"

The prisoner looked even angrier and he opened his mouth to answer the prime minister. But Laurenzo ordered him to be silent and said: "So can't the Last Party make cheese or sausages, or grow fruit or brew beer? Can't they weave fabrics, make pottery or baskets, or any of the other things that are sold at the market?"

"They try, but the results are no good," replied Asmian. "All they can do is catch fish. So an exception was made for the fishermen."

"Heavens above!" cried Laurenzo. "I don't know whether to be angry or to laugh at you!" And he continued in the language of Tirania: "Hear my command! I declare the new law invalid. Everything will remain as it was until I have examined the matter more closely. Now remove this man's chains and set him free."

When the prisoner had left, Laurenzo turned to Asmian. "Prime Minister," he said sternly, "do not make any new laws from now on without consulting me! But the old law is also wrongheaded. Why can't everyone sell their goods on the days they want to? Why does there have to be this division between the two parties?"

"Necessity, sire," replied Asmian sadly. "Now everyone buys their goods from members of their own party. If merchants from both parties were at the market at the same time, and all trying to outsell one another, the result would be murder and mayhem. King Sutan the four hundred and thirty-third introduced this law, and since then there has been a lot less fighting at the market."

Laurenzo sighed. "Right, you may all leave," he said. "I'm withdrawing to study your books of law. This afternoon I shall go for a ride around Baharan and this evening I shall convene another meeting. Goodbye!"

When he was alone in his rooms, he took out a law book and lay down with it upon a couch. He tried to read, but his mind kept wandering.

"I wish I'd never got involved," he said to himself. "I don't like being king of this ridiculous little country, where everything is divided into two camps! And I don't trust my ministers at all! What I really want to do is leave. If I stay here, though, I must try to be a just king."

He stood up and paced back and forth. There was a knock at the door, but he paid no attention. When the knocking continued, however, he stopped pacing and called: "Come in!"

A young man appeared in the doorway... a young man in a fine robe, with a red turban on his head.

It felt like he was looking in the mirror.

"Jiacomo!" he whispered.

"Laurenzo!" said Jiacomo. "I knew you had to be Laurenzo!" He slapped his brother on the shoulders. "Don't be startled," he added. "I'm not a ghost arisen from the sea."

The two brothers hugged, full of joy at their reunion.

"I thought you'd drowned," Laurenzo said finally.

Jiacomo closed the door and turned the key. "I'm made of sturdier stuff," he said. "I was afraid that you were dead too, until I heard about a brand new king who looked a lot like me."

They sat down together on the couch and looked at each other, their eyes gleaming. Then they told each other all about their adventures.

A servant knocked to ask when the king wanted to go out for his ride, but Laurenzo put his head around the door and said that important affairs of state were preventing him from going out.

"What shall we do now?" asked Jiacomo, when they had told each other everything. "Shall we try to get away from this ridiculous country? Maybe the pirate's ship is still in the bay. I'm sure he'll let us sail with him. I don't think escaping from Baharan will be easy though. Or we could always stay here for a while, of course, and see how things go."

"Now that we're together, everything's fine by me," replied Laurenzo. "You're right – leaving this country won't be easy. Both parties are determined to have one of us as king."

"Your time as king is up," said Jiacomo, laughing. "I'm supposed to get rid of you and take your place. At least that's what Dasuf wants."

"How did you get into the palace?" asked Laurenzo. "You still haven't told me."

"Over the wall. Once I was inside, I had nothing to fear, because everyone thought I was the king. I just walked calmly around the palace until I found you. And everyone bowed as I went by! But of course you're used to that by now."

Jiacomo gave his brother a mocking bow and continued: "What shall we do? If we stay here, we can learn something about a foreign country and foreign people – and we'll also have a good story to tell when we get home to Bainu."

"You want to stay," said Laurenzo. "I can see that."

"Yes, I want to replace you and reign as an impartial ruler. And I might just make Dasuf my prime minister!"

"You have no idea how heavily that red turban weighs on your head once you've worn it for longer than a day. It's not easy to rule a country, not even a small one! But I'd still like to stay here for a while too."

"Good," said Jiacomo. "Then I shall take the heavy burden from you and rule Tirania wisely. Dasuf will help me as my prime minister."

"Do you call that impartial, making Dasuf your prime minister?"

"Well, you appointed Asmian. Is that impartial?" The two brothers burst out laughing.

"Which party do you belong to?" asked Jiacomo.

"I'm above parties!" replied Laurenzo. "But I have heard that the First Party is everything and the Last Party is nothing."

"While I have heard exactly the opposite. The Last Party is the best, and the First Party is worthless."

"The question is," said Laurenzo, "which of the two is right?"

"One of them? Or neither?" Jiacomo pondered.

"The land of strife and discord," said Laurenzo. "It needs a good ruler for once."

"Exactly," said Jiacomo. "So which of us should do it?"

"Both of us!"

"Fine," said Jiacomo. "But how shall we go about it?"

"First we need to know the differences between the two parties," said Laurenzo. "We have to reach a point where there will be no more strife and discord."

"A bit of strife and discord is bearable," said Jiacomo, "but they really do take it too far here. Let's start by making Dasuf the prime minister. Asmian has already done it for a few days. Besides, Dasuf mustn't become suspicious. He knows that there are two of us, although he doesn't know we're brothers."

"So Dasuf needs to think that one king rules Tirania."

"And so does Asmian – and everyone else. Just one Sutan the four hundred and sixty-seventh."

"You're wrong," said Laurenzo. "The true name of Tirania's king is Laucomo!"

His Majesty Sutan the four hundred and sixty-seventh had spent all afternoon studying affairs of state, and no one had been allowed to disturb him, not even Asmian, the prime minister. Then he had sent for a large meal and, to his servants' amazement and his cook's delight, he had eaten it all.

Then he had gone to the council chamber and called for Asmian.

"Prime Minister," he said, "I have a task for you. I would like to be a good king, but I know nothing about my own country, except for what you have told me. So I would like to take a journey through Tirania and see it all for myself. But I do not want to go as the king, as no one dares to be themselves when they meet a king."

Asmian looked at him gloomily. "You want to go as an ordinary person," he said. "Incognito."

"Exactly, Asmian. And you will be my guide."

The minister's face brightened up. "What an excellent idea, sire," he said. "I am at your disposal."

"We shall leave early tomorrow morning," said the king. "In secret, of course. Kalaf, Yusaf and Halia will run the country in the meantime, together with three other men, whom I shall appoint soon."

"You're going to appoint new ministers?" cried Asmian. "But what about Yadi, Bidin and Paharani?"

"I'm going to send them on an inspection trip," replied the king.

"Don't they satisfy you, sire?"

"Certainly, but I've also heard a lot about the men whom I shall now appoint. Not much good, I have to say, but that's exactly why I want to get to know them. They are Amet, Ymar and Harabad."

"Your Majesty!" exclaimed Asmian, deeply shocked. "Those three men all belong to the Last Party!"

"So I should not appoint them? You told me yourself that I am supposed to be above the parties."

"But they aren't suitable to be ministers, sire!"

"How do you know that, Asmian?"

"Sire, I know these men better than you. Take my advice and abandon this plan!"

"Be silent, Asmian!" ordered the king. "You told me yourself that my will is law in Tirania. So go and prepare everything for our journey, without speaking to anyone about it. And tell the other ministers to report to me."

Asmian bowed and left, with a face like thunder.

Not long after that, the other six ministers arrived. The king told them that he was going to make a journey around the country in the utmost secrecy. Kalaf, Yusaf and Halia would take care of the government in the meantime, together with Amet, Ymar and Harabad from the other party.

A storm of protests was unleashed. "We can't work with those villains and we don't want to!"

"Silence!" roared the king. "You will work together or you can go home. Anyone I am unhappy with at the end of the week will be dismissed. Those who work hard and do their best will remain ministers."

Then he sent Kalaf, Yusaf and Halia away. They left feeling miserable and dissatisfied but they consoled one another by saying that of course the members of the Last Party would soon prove themselves unsuited to such a difficult role as minister. It was a certainty that the king would dismiss them at the end of the week!

"Do not think that I am dissatisfied with you," the king said to Yadi, Bidin and Paharani. "I had to appoint some ministers from the other party to avoid an uprising in my kingdom. You, however, will be given a different and honourable assignment. The three of you are going on a trip to inspect the fishing and shipping industries in our land."

The three men gasped and looked at one another in horror.

"Your Majesty," said Yadi, "that's impossible."

"Why?"

"The First Party has never been involved with fishing or shipping in any way. Our party has an extreme dislike of the sea."

"Then it is high time that changed," said the king. "You must go and look at the harbour of Baharan, visit the fishing villages and then take a trip out to sea on a ship."

"Oh, sire, please, no!" cried Paharani. "The sea is dangerous. No one knows that better than you!"

"Shame on you!" said the king sternly. "Fancy being afraid of something you don't know! It is shocking that no one from the First Party has ever bothered with the sea before."

"The Last Party does that, sire," said Yadi. "We're responsible for agriculture."

"You are going to see how things are at sea," said the king. "That is my order. You must leave at once. Pay close attention to everything you see – and bring me a detailed report in a week's time. Farewell!"

Yadi, Bidin and Paharani filed out, each looking more miserable than the last.

"Good," sighed the king. "That's all settled. Now I must prepare for my journey."

An hour later, various people headed out through the palace gate. First Yadi, Bidin and Paharani, dragging their feet, set off on their way to the sea, then, a few minutes later, the king and Asmian left to go and explore Tirania.

No sooner had the travellers departed than seven men appeared at the gate, asking to be admitted immediately to see His Majesty. And although Sutan the four hundred and sixty-seventh had just left on a journey, he was still at home to welcome the seven men, and he received them in his own rooms. The leader of the visitors was none other than Dasuf, and he greeted the king very cheerfully.

"Here I am, sire," he said, "along with my friends: Amet, Ymar and Harabad, Husan, Siwat and Burudin." He leant over to the king and whispered: "Our trick worked wonderfully! It's as if I'm seeing the king himself before me!"

"I *am* the king," said Sutan the four hundred and sixty-seventh, reprimanding him. "The king you were so keen to have. And now you are obliged to show me respect."

"Well, well!" said Dasuf in surprise.

"I mean what I said, Prime Minister!"

Dasuf bowed. "You are right, sire. As your prime minister, I shall be your most faithful servant."

"Thank you," said the king. "I would also like to appoint these gentlemen, Amet, Ymar and Harabad, as ministers. They will work together with Kalaf, Yusaf and Halia."

Amet, Ymar and Harabad declared as one that it was impossible for them to work together with members of the First Party.

"Don't be so stupid!" cried the king. "You surely understand that I can't immediately fire all of my former ministers, don't you? I shall replace them gradually."

"I understand," said Dasuf. "You're afraid of a revolt."

"Exactly," replied the king. "I do not wish to make an enemy of the First Party."

"Very cautious," said Dasuf. "And perhaps a wise decision." He turned to the newly appointed ministers. "Obey your king," he ordered. "And remember that our party has the advantage, as I am the prime minister."

Amet, Ymar and Harabad bowed and swore obedience.

"Good," said the king. "So that's settled. Husan, Siwat and Burudin, you will go on a tour of inspection of all the farms in Tirania. You must report back to me in a week's time."

Again there were protests. "The Last Party does not like farmers and does not know anything about farms!"

"Then try to learn something," said the king. "How can you rule subjects when you know nothing about them?" Then he sent them all away except for Dasuf.

"Now you need to tell me," said Dasuf, "how did you manage to get rid of the other king?"

"We shall not speak of that matter, Prime Minister," replied the king. "But I assure you that you will have no trouble from him."

Dasuf bowed. "Sire," he said, "I thank you!"

"You're welcome," said the king. "Now listen carefully, Prime Minister. I want to go on a journey around Tirania in the utmost secrecy, in order to get to know my land and my people. I shall not go as a king, but as a simple merchant. And you must be my guide."

"Sire," said Dasuf, "that is a marvellous plan. When do you wish to leave?"

"At once," replied the king.

And so His Majesty Sutan the four hundred and sixty-seventh left his palace for the second time that day, this time accompanied by Dasuf.

Six ministers remained behind to run the country: Kalaf, Yusaf and Halia from the First Party, and Amet, Ymar and Harabad from the Last Party. It was going to be a difficult week.

A week later, the travellers returned. The gatekeepers later argued about which palace gate they had come through. One half claimed it was the north gate, while the other half insisted it was the south gate.

Meanwhile the king went to see how the six ministers were doing. But there were only two of them left. Kalaf and Amet had argued and had both resigned. Halia and Harabad had fought and beaten each other so badly that they were both confined to their beds. Only Yusaf and Ymar were still trying to keep ruling together.

"I thank you for your hard work and commitment," said the king. Then he quickly appointed six more ministers: Yadi, Bidin and Paharani from the First Party, and Siwat, Husan and Burudin from the Last Party. The six men had only just returned from their tours of inspection. Now the king had two ministers too many, but he had realized that a couple of spares might come in handy.

"You must all gather in the council chamber," he said. "And the six new ministers can report back to you about their travels. They must bring their reports to me tomorrow."

Then he bid them all farewell and retreated to his own rooms.

At that same moment, something happened in the throne room that had not happened for years, not in the palace and not anywhere else. Asmian and Dasuf met! When they saw each other, they were first stunned, then angry and finally furious.

But they did not speak a word to each other, as they had not done so for ten years. They just glared, each waiting for the other to leave.

This went on for a long time, but finally Asmian took a deep breath, moistened his lips and asked: "What are you doing here?"

"I could ask you the same question!" cried Dasuf. "What are you up to?"

Now that the first words had been spoken, more could follow.

"I belong here," said Asmian haughtily.

"You boldfaced liar!" shouted Dasuf. "This is my place."

"How dare you insult me like that?!" yelled Asmian. "Do you know who you are talking to? I am the prime minister."

"What did you say?" cried Dasuf. "I'm the prime minister!"

"I wouldn't put anything past you," began Asmian, "but this is going too far!"

"Perhaps you haven't heard yet, but you've been fired," said Dasuf, interrupting him. "I am the prime minister now, and I order you to leave at once."

"Leave?" cried Asmian. "No! You leave!"

"Get out of here! Go on!" roared Dasuf.

"Help!" cried Asmian. "Throw this man out!"

Servants came hurrying and stared in bewilderment at the two mortal enemies.

"Throw this man out," repeated Asmian. "Obey me! I'm your prime minister!"

"Throw him out!" ordered Dasuf. "Listen to me! I'm your prime minister!"

The servants began to obey, but half of them helped Asmian and the other half helped Dasuf, as they did not all belong to the same party. A fierce fight ensued, in which marble columns were damaged and beautiful furniture was smashed to pieces.

Suddenly, though, there came an angry voice: "What is the meaning of this? Have you started a fight in my palace? Already?" In the doorway stood the king in person and, behind him, with pale faces, the other eight ministers.

"Asmian and Dasuf," said His Majesty furiously, "shame on both of you! Leave my palace now, and do not dare to return until your anger dies down."

"Sire, I—" began Dasuf.

"Your Majesty, tell me—" began Asmian.

But the king interrupted both of them. "I refuse to listen to either of you," he said. "Leave! If you have calmed down by tomorrow morning, perhaps I will hear your words then. But not now."

Cowed, the two prime ministers obeyed. They left the palace, angry and incredulous, and went to their homes to recover from their shock and to find some comfort with their friends and families.

When they had left, the king looked around the throne room.

"Clear up this mess," he ordered his servants. "And do not dare to disturb me again. I have important work to do." With those words, he turned around and went back to his own rooms.

"What was going on?" Jiacomo asked Laurenzo.

"A fight between Asmian and Dasuf," his brother replied.

Jiacomo laughed. "We might have expected it," he said. "They both think they're the prime minister. And they're right. Asmian is yours, and Dasuf is mine. What did you say to them?"

"I sent them both home."

"The poor men! So they still don't know which one of them is in favour with the king?"

"Let them calm down first," said Laurenzo. "At least some good has come of this."

"What's that?" asked Jiacomo.

"They just spoke to each other. For the first time in ten years!"

"Excellent!" said Jiacomo. "And maybe they'll murder each other tomorrow."

"I won't let it get that far."

"Yes, I'd like Dasuf to have a long life."

"So you think he's a good man?"

"He's good and bad," replied Jiacomo. "He's a bit hot-headed and he has a massive grudge against the First Party, but other than that I like him, apart from the small matter of him wanting me to murder you, of course. And what do you think of Asmian?"

"He has plenty of good qualities too," said Laurenzo.

"So we're both satisfied with our prime ministers," said Jiacomo. "And we both had enjoyable trips."

"Yes, most enjoyable," said Laurenzo. "But I only spoke to members of the First Party."

"And I only spoke to members of the Last Party."

"The people I met were all very nice," said Laurenzo. "Friendly and helpful."

"Just like the people I met. They were only unpleasant when they spoke about the First Party. Anyone who belongs to the First Party is old-fashioned, stupid and cruel."

"I heard that the people from the Last Party are stupid and cruel too. And they are also mean, dishonest and completely insane. They're insane because they build their towers with domes that look like onions."

"The members of the First Party are crazy because they consider pointed towers the only correct style of construction."

"The Last Party is mad because its members love swimming."

"The First Party is mad because its members love mulberry wine."

"The Last Party is malicious. The First Party is noble, good and wise. In short, it is number one in every respect."

"The First Party is useless and worthless. The Last Party is honest, plucky and full of new ideas. In short, it's the best." The brothers looked at each other and laughed.

Laurenzo said: "The First Party says that fish is poison."

Jiacomo said: "The Last Party thinks that fish is healthy. They love ships and sailing."

"The First Party doesn't," said Laurenzo. "But they grow the most delicious oranges."

"So they both have their pluses and minuses," said Jiacomo.

"Yes," said Laurenzo. "Now why don't we each tell the other what we saw on our travels through Tirania?"

The brothers spent a long time swapping stories. When they had finished, they started to make their plans for governing the country. It was late in the night when they finally gave each other a satisfied nod.

"Then that's settled, sire!"

"Absolutely, Your Majesty!"

The next day, Asmian and Dasuf were summoned separately to see the king. They both received a severe dressing-down for disturbing the peace – and in the palace of all places too!

"I don't know if I can allow you to remain prime minister," said Sutan the four hundred and sixty-seventh to Asmian. "I have heard that Dasuf is also a capable man."

"But he quarrelled with me, sire!" cried Asmian. "And besides, it was all his fault."

"So I shall not appoint him either," said the king. "I am going to do something else instead. I am going to give you both a trial, and the man who pleases me more, the one who is more peaceful, kinder and wiser, I shall make prime minister!"

And then Sutan the four hundred and sixty-seventh spoke to Dasuf. "I am going to give you both a trial," he said. "And the man I like better, the one who is more peaceful, kinder and wiser, I shall appoint prime minister!"

And so the two mortal enemies were forced to work together. They both tried their hardest, each hoping for the post of prime minister. It was not easy though, and only the fear of the other's success stopped them both from resigning.

Tirania had had many kings. Most had ruled for only a short time and their policies had been rejected by half of the population. But no one knew quite what to make of Sutan the four hundred and sixty-seventh. People told the strangest stories about him. It was understandable that he had travelled throughout the land. He was a stranger, after all, and had to get to know his kingdom. But how could it be that both parties claimed he had been their guest and that he shared their opinions? None of the ministers knew what was going on either. Why were there so many of them, more than seven? And who was in charge now, the First Party or the Last Party? And could it be true that Asmian and Dasuf had attended a meeting together? That was unprecedented, wasn't it?

Yadi, Bidin and Paharani had ventured out onto the sea without falling overboard.

Husan, Siwat and Burudin had eaten apples in a number of orchards and had not been poisoned.

The king went for rides throughout the city and gave fine speeches in which he urged his people to get along with one another. He did not just leave it at speeches though. New laws were issued, each more astonishing than the previous one.

The market would be open to members of both parties from now on. This had naturally resulted in a huge fight, and the king had turned up in person, along with his soldiers, to put an end to it. He had the worst troublemakers arrested and locked up in cells, in pairs. He always had two people from different parties imprisoned together and declared that they should not be released until they were friends.

Then he announced that all the schools would be closed immediately and replaced by one single school that every child in Tirania must attend. For the time being, lessons would take place at the palace, as no other building was large enough. The children thought this was wonderful and came home excited and full of stories every day. The king himself often popped in to see them, testing them on what they had learnt, telling them all about Babina and even playing his lute and singing songs for them. They also made new friends, children from the other party, who they had never been allowed to play with before. Their parents did not know what to think, but they did not dare to disobey the king. However, they would have liked to know which party he belonged to. Could he truly be above both parties?

And what about the ministers? They worked together, as well as they could. There was still no prime minister, as the king could not decide which one was better, Dasuf or Asmian. The two men were furious, but they were both still doing their best, hoping to be appointed by the king. They had made sufficient progress that they attended ministerial meetings together, although they sat as far apart as possible and each refused to acknowledge the other's presence when entering and leaving the chamber.

Such a situation could not continue though, and one day the ministers, Asmian and Dasuf, met in the council chamber to discuss how they could bring it to an end.

"I finally want to know where we stand," began Dasuf. "Who is in charge here, the First Party or the Last Party?"

"Both parties," said Asmian calmly. "And the king, of course."

"And do you like that?" asked Dasuf.

"No," said Asmian. "I'd rather not see your face every day. My ancestors would be spinning in their graves if they knew I was sitting at the same table as you."

Dasuf turned red, but his cousin Ymar said in a soothing tone: "Please don't argue, gentlemen."

"What should we do?" asked Dasuf. "I don't know what the king actually wants."

"Yes, you do," said Asmian. "He wants to rule impartially. That's why we chose him, isn't it?"

"Impartial?" cried Bidin, a member of the First Party. "That's not true! The king is sly and cunning, and he's playing us off against each other. When he speaks to Dasuf, he says: 'The last shall be first!' and when he sees Asmian he calls him 'Number one'. And he's laughing at all of us behind our backs."

"There's only one thing we can do," said Husan from the Last Party. "We have to work together."

"Work together?" cried Bidin angrily. "Aren't we already doing that?"

"Not in the right way," said Husan, and he continued in a whisper: "We have to work together to dethrone him! He has the same number of ministers, servants and soldiers from both parties. That's how he keeps himself safe, because he knows that if one half conspires against him, the other half will help him. Alone we are powerless, but together we can beat him."

The ministers sat silently thinking. The curtains at the windows moved gently to and fro.

"You have a point," said Bidin finally.

"It's a fine plan," said Siwat from the Last Party.

"It's an insane plan!" cried his friend Ymar.

"Yes, it's insane," agreed Asmian. "Who's going to be the new king? One of us? That will just mean more fighting!"

"Asmian is right," said Dasuf. "This plan is foolish." The others were silent.

"We can't conspire," Asmian said. "The king has been too clever for all of us. We all thought we could win him over for our own party and he let us believe that. But meanwhile he's brought us together and forced us to work as a team. He has put children from both parties in a single school, and I think in a year or two our people will be one."

"Never!" cried Bidin.

"Oh?" said Ymar. "But your party isn't that bad."

"Neither is yours," said Asmian. "I've realized, for instance, that you know more about shipping than we do and that you were right to see it as important."

"That's very noble of you," said Dasuf. "Then I am prepared to admit that in many respects you are not as awful as I thought."

"I can't hate the Last Party any longer," said Yadi with a sigh. "You see, I'm getting married to Burudin's daughter, and a man should always be good friends with his father-in-law."

"It's true," said Burudin. "I shall not forbid my daughter to marry Yadi, even though he does not belong to my party. And he has the king to thank for that!"

"I've never heard anything like it!" muttered Bidin. "Something like this would never have happened in the old days."

"But there's still one thing we don't know," said Dasuf. "Who's going to be prime minister?"

"Asmian," said Yadi.

"No, Dasuf," said Ymar.

"An hour ago, I saw the king," said Yadi. "He spoke to me and said a lot of good things about Asmian."

"That's not true!" cried Ymar. "I spoke to the king an hour ago, and he praised Dasuf with many fine words."

"That's a lie!" said Yadi.

"How dare you say that? You're the liar!"

Ymar and Yadi stood up and glared furiously at each other.

Then a cheery voice called out: "Don't argue, ministers! Yadi is telling the truth!" And the king appeared from behind a curtain! "I may not have been invited to this meeting," he said, "but I wanted to know what you had to discuss."

The ministers looked at him in horror. Then they bowed deeply, except for Ymar, who said, with a red face: "Sire, I didn't lie. You know that!"

"How dare you?!" hissed Yadi.

But then a voice spoke from another corner of the room: "Of course Ymar was not lying. I spoke with him an hour ago."

And the king appeared from behind a curtain – again!

The ministers were flabbergasted, their eyes bulging as they looked from one king to the other. Were they mistaken? King Sutan the four hundred and sixty-seventh was in the room – twice. In other words, there were two kings, both exactly the same, with the same face, the same clothes, the same red turban!

"How can you... have duplicated yourself?!" cried Asmian finally.

Dasuf was the only one with a suspicion, but he said nothing.

The kings walked towards each other and, standing side by side, they looked at their ministers.

"I am Sutan the four hundred and sixty-seventh," said one. "And I belong to the First Party."

"I am Sutan the four hundred and sixty-seventh," said the other. "And I belong to the Last Party."

"We are brothers," said one.

"Two different people," said the other.

"We don't think the same about everything."

"But we still work together."

"And we agree about the important things."

"Impartially."

"I studied the First Party."

"And I studied the Last Party."

"Then we told each other what we had learnt..."

"... and we realized that the two parties are not all that different."

"They're actually identical in one respect."

"In foolishness!"

The kings put their arms around each other's shoulders and smiled at their ministers.

"Yes," said one. "In foolishness."

"An insignificant little country," said the other, "such a tiny little kingdom, and yet there are still two parties that do whatever they can to make life difficult for each other!"

"There are Asmian and Dasuf, for instance, who hate each other simply because their families have hated each other for two hundred years!"

The ministers were still lost for words. Then Dasuf mumbled: "Deceiver!"

"Which one of us are you talking to, Dasuf?" asked the kings.

Dasuf did not reply.

"Whatever is going on?" cried Asmian.

"We shall make it clear to you," said one of the kings. "You found a poor castaway and made him king, in the hope that he would appoint you and your friends as ministers. The Last Party was furious, but luckily Dasuf found another castaway, who was prepared to take the new king's place and who would then, of course, favour Dasuf's party. Dasuf's king was able to replace yours unnoticed because he resembled him like a twin brother. The two shipwrecked men were indeed twins, and they were delighted to see each other again because each had thought the other one dead."

"So you're the deceiver!" said Asmian to Dasuf.

"Quiet, Asmian," the other king ordered. "You would have

done the same if you had been in Dasuf's position. Besides, Tirania now has what it needed. A land with two parties should also have two kings, one for each party!"

For a few moments everything was silent. Then Dasuf started chuckling. "This is so funny!" he cried. "It's actually quite hilarious!" The longer he laughed the louder it became, until finally he was roaring and clutching his belly.

Some of the ministers couldn't help joining in, and before long they were all laughing.

"Well," said one of the Sutans with a contented smile. "Those who have laughed together can no longer be enemies!"

Asmian stepped forward and asked: "Forgive me, Your Majesties, but which of you is the one I brought to Baharan who was solemnly crowned as king in this room?"

The smile disappeared from Dasuf's face. "Why do you want to know that?" he asked angrily.

"The one I appointed is the lawful king," replied Asmian. "The other is only a fake ruler."

"What does that matter?" said Dasuf. "They are both impartial."

"Exactly," said the kings. "And we will not tell you which one of us was really crowned."

Asmian sighed. "Two kings!" he said. "But that's impossible! It's unheard of – and it's against all the rules."

"We shall take it in turns to rule for a day," said one of the kings. "And we shall each appoint a prime minister. I choose Dasuf."

"And I choose Asmian," said the other. "So the two of you can take it in turns to be prime minister for the day."

"Yes, yes!" cried all of the ministers. "That's a good plan!"

"And which of us is ruling today?" asked one of the kings.

"You can do it," his brother replied.

"Fine," he replied. "Then you are now prime minister, Asmian. Do your best, even on the days when you're not prime minister. And all of you, Yusaf and Yadi, Husan and Siwat, Bidin and Burudin, Ymar and Paharani, and you, Dasuf, you must all work together to make Tirania a happy land!"

"We promise to do so," the ministers said as one.

"Then that's settled," said the king. "Now we need to announce it to the people."

The ministers raised their hands and cried out loud three times: "Hurrah!"

The king leant over to his brother and whispered: "Jiacomo, you can give the speech later. You're better at it than me."

That same day, the two kings appeared on the flat roof of their palace and addressed the crowd below. They explained exactly how they had come to be on the throne and how they had carried out their work so far. The people of Tirania were stunned at first but they came to see the funny side of the situation, and they laughed just as loud as the ministers had. And once you have laughed together, it is hard to remain angry with one another.

That evening, there was a big celebration. All of the prisoners were released, and the kings rode together through the city, surrounded by subjects from both parties. And each party said about the other: "You know, they're not as bad as I thought!"

And that was how King Sutan the four hundred and sixty-seventh restored the peace in Tirania. Of course the strife and discord were not yet over, but their mutual understanding improved by the day.

And when three months had passed, one king said to the other: "I think we can leave with easy minds now. Are you longing to get back to Babina too?"

"Just as you are, Laurenzo! And Dasuf has told me that a ship has arrived in the harbour. We can sail on that."

"Let's do so. This red turban is getting too heavy for me. I'm itching to get back to work as a goldsmith."

"Yes, I want to get back to being an ordinary person again and to speak my own language every day."

"Let's say farewell to Tirania then."

When the ministers heard that the brothers wanted to leave, they were very upset at first.

"You don't need us any longer," said Laurenzo. "You are wise enough now to choose a king from your own people without fighting about it."

"But who should be the king?"

"You must decide that for yourselves," said Jiacomo.

The ministers deliberated for a long time. Finally they reached an agreement. Asmian should become the king, as he was the most sensible of all of them. Even Dasuf agreed, as long as he could be the prime minister.

The day came for the brothers to say farewell to Tirania and in particular to its new king, Sutan the four hundred and sixty-eighth, and to Dasuf, his prime minister.

"I hope it all goes well for you," said Laurenzo.

"If it doesn't, then send a message to Bainu," added Jiacomo. "And we'll come back."

"I think we can govern by ourselves from now on," said the new king. "But we hope to welcome you again as our honoured guests."

"Both at the same time," said Dasuf, "and not as castaways."

Many people had gathered on the quay to wish their abdicated kings a safe journey. Some waved their hands, while others waved flags and threw confetti.

The brothers waved back, until they could no longer see them and the island of Tirania had disappeared from sight.

After a long journey, they arrived back safely in Bainu. Their friends welcomed them with joy and listened in amazement to the tale of their adventures.

But there were also those who did not believe them. "Who would return to Bainu if they could be king in another land?" said some, and others said: "Pfff, that country doesn't even exist! The twins just invented the entire story."

But in the chronicles of Tirania the rule of Sutan the four hundred and sixty-seventh was recorded with many glowing words, and anyone who does not believe this will have to go there and read those words for themselves.

Even though the twin brothers could have remained as kings in Tirania, instead they chose a simple life in Bainu, the city of their birth. Laurenzo devoted himself once more to the goldsmith's art, and his work was just as good as that of Philippo, his former master. The elderly goldsmith had retired and was enjoying a peaceful old age. When he died, the brothers deeply mourned his passing, as they had loved him like a father.

Laurenzo went on working, but Jiacomo had less and less to do, as his brother became so famous that people approached him directly to beg him to work for them. So Jiacomo did not need to travel to sell Laurenzo's work. When he travelled, it was for his own pleasure, but he no longer went outside of the land of Babina.

The Precious Pearl

"Give me the pearl that was entrusted to you, and I shall make you rich. If you do not, I shall take it by force."

'Palàsha', a Hindu parable

1   LAURENZO'S TASK

Laurenzo, the young goldsmith, became increasingly well known, not only in his hometown of Bainu, but also beyond. And so one day, the Duke of Forpa invited him to come and work for him for a while. Laurenzo was very pleased about this, as the duke was known as a great lover of all the arts who would only buy work that was excellent.

His twin brother was just as glad. "You're becoming famous, Laurenzo," he said. "Fancy being allowed to make something for the duke! And you'll like Forpa. It's a beautiful city. I might come and visit you there."

Laurenzo closed his workshop and packed what he needed. He said goodbye to his brother, his friends and acquaintances and to his dog, who was getting too old to go on long journeys. Then he set off in good spirits. He intended to stay in Forpa for around three months.

Forpa was in the north, in the mountains. The duke who ruled there was a powerful man; in fact, there was only one man in Babina who was more powerful, and that was the king. The duke viewed Forpa as his own little kingdom and he had done a great deal to beautify the city, such as having churches and palaces built and new parks created and planted with trees.

When Laurenzo rode into Forpa, he could not believe his eyes. The streets throughout the city were all paved, and there was not one house that did not look beautiful and well cared for. There were elegant colonnades and marble staircases up the hillsides, magnificent buildings and gardens full of flowers and greenery. The duke's palace was in the highest part of the city, and it was surrounded by a large green park, the palace grounds. There were various smaller buildings in the park: a small chapel, houses for the courtiers, and the duke's own prison.

Laurenzo stopped at the gate and dismounted from his horse. Three heavily armed guards approached him and asked what he wanted. When he had given them his name, one of them took his horse by the reins while the second took care of his bags and belongings. The third bowed respectfully and invited Laurenzo to follow him into the palace, where he was received by a solemn man, who turned out to be one of the duke's counsellors.

"Welcome to Forpa, Master Laurenzo," he said. "Did you have a good journey?"

Laurenzo replied that he had, and the counsellor told him that the duke would welcome him soon. "You will have your own house and workshop for the length of your stay," he continued, "close to the palace. The duke likes to have all his servants nearby. I shall have someone show you the way. Your bags have already been taken there."

Not long after his arrival, Laurenzo was fetched from his temporary accommodation to pay his respects to the duke. The duke was a stately man with a stern and somewhat sombre face; he was dressed in expensive clothes and looked very regal indeed. Laurenzo greeted him courteously and said that he was grateful for the opportunity to make something for the duke.

"There's no need for you to be grateful," replied the duke. "I have seen your work – at the home of the Lord of Talamura and elsewhere – and I thought that it was good. I expect you to produce something beautiful. If you do not, then you may leave."

"I shall do my best," said Laurenzo.

"I want a silver lamp for my chapel," said the duke, "and a new hilt for my sword. You must also make a large goblet, a neck chain and something else, which you can decide for yourself. You may have the most precious materials, as long as you use them to create something beautiful. Just take a look around this room. There is little here, but everything is beautiful: the furniture, the carpets and tapestries and the paintings on the walls."

Laurenzo looked and had to agree with his client's words.

"Beauty is the only worthwhile thing in this world," said the duke. "Sadly it is not to be found in humankind. I mean beauty in both senses, inside and out. I have met so many people who seemed both noble and trustworthy, but who turned out to be false and dishonest! That is why I collect works of art. They give me joy and do not disappoint me. But come," he said then, "do not let me hold you up. You may begin at once. You have a workshop with everything you need, and if you would like anything else, you can ask my treasurer. Make something, one of the items I asked for or something you would like to make yourself. In a few days' time, I shall come and see if I like your work. If it pleases me, I shall reward you amply."

Laurenzo did indeed find enough materials and tools in his workshop, and he immediately began to think about what he would make first. He did not know if he liked his customer, but this was certainly a man who knew a thing or two about art. Not the easiest of men, but a good person to work for.

An hour later, he was working away and forgot everything around him in his joy at being able to make something beautiful.

Some time went by. Laurenzo worked and the duke was satisfied with what he made. The young goldsmith wanted for nothing – he had not only materials and tools, but also pleasant accommodation and a number of servants at his disposal. Within a couple of weeks, courtiers were also coming from the palace and asking him to make items for them, and so he had little opportunity for leisure. However, he managed to take the occasional hour off now and then to wander around the city. Sometimes the duke also sent for him so that he could talk to him about art. Laurenzo still was not sure if he liked the duke or not; he was often annoyed by the man's scornful attitude towards everyone. He did not enjoy going to the palace, even though it was so beautiful. That might also have been to do with the courtiers, who looked very elegant indeed, but seemed to peer down their noses at an ordinary goldsmith.

A month went by. One evening Laurenzo was just about to get into bed when someone banged on the front door. He put on his dressing gown, picked up a candle and went to see who it was.

On the doorstep stood a man who was wrapped from head to toe in a dark cloak.

"Are you Laurenzo, the goldsmith?" the man asked.

"Yes, sir," replied Laurenzo. "How can I help you?"

"May I come in?" asked the man. "I want to speak to you in private. It is about a matter of great importance."

"My servants are already asleep," said Laurenzo. "So I am alone. Come with me to my workshop."

When they reached the workshop, the man removed his cloak and said: "You do not know me, as I arrived in Forpa just this afternoon. I am Marko, the explorer."

Laurenzo looked at his late visitor in awe. He did not know him, but he had certainly heard a lot about him. Marko, who had visited strange lands in the service of the king and had performed so many daring deeds!

"I have come at a strange hour," said Marko, "but I did not want anyone to know about my visit to you." He carefully took out a round object wrapped in silk and presented it to Laurenzo. "I have a task for you. There are two reasons why I chose you. The first is that you are a good goldsmith. The pieces you have made for the duke are truly magnificent. But the second reason is perhaps even more important: I have heard in Bainu that you are a man who can be trusted. Now open this parcel."

Laurenzo did so. Carefully, he unwrapped many layers and then he cried out in surprise. In his hand he held a pearl, as large as a coconut and gleaming like the full moon.

"Have you ever seen such a thing?" asked Marko the explorer.

"Never," whispered Laurenzo. "It's magnificent."

"There is not another one like it," said Marko. "It is my most precious possession, not only for its value, which is inestimable, but also for the sweet memories that are attached to it. It is from the distant East, and how it came into my possession is my secret. I would like you to make a silver stand for this pearl. Soon I shall cease my travels and retreat to my home to enjoy my old age in peace. I have had a special alcove made in my house, where I intend to place my pearl, so that I can always enjoy its beauty, both by daylight and moonshine. Do you think you could make such a stand? I shall pay you well – that goes without saying."

"I would be happy to make a stand for you," replied Laurenzo. "It needs to be beautiful, but very simple, serving only to enhance the beauty of the pearl."

"You understand what matters," said Marko. "Please start work at once. I shall leave the pearl here, and you must keep it safe for me. I need to set off on my travels again tomorrow, but I will be back in a month to collect it from you. I would ask you this, however: tell no one about the task I have given you, and keep it a secret that the pearl is in your home! There are many people who would like to have it. The duke, for instance, has offered me a great deal of money for the pearl. Now that I have refused to sell it to him, I fear that he will attempt to gain possession of it in some other way. So hide the pearl well and keep your silence."

"This is an honourable task," said Laurenzo, "but taking care of such a precious object is a great responsibility. Let me just measure now how large the stand needs to be. Then you can take the pearl with you."

"That will be difficult," replied Marko. "And besides, the stand will turn out better if you also have the pearl to work with. If you accept my task, you must also keep and guard this priceless object. But if you would prefer not to, then you must say so honestly."

"If you dare to entrust me with it," said Laurenzo, "I will accept the task."

"I will entrust you with it," said Marko. "And that means a great deal, as this pearl is my most precious possession." He carefully wrapped the silk around it again and placed it in Laurenzo's hands. "I shall bid you farewell for now," he said. "And I shall return for it in a month's time. I hope it goes smoothly."

"I wish you a successful journey," said Laurenzo.

When Marko had left, Laurenzo put the pearl in a safe place and went to bed. It took him a long time to get to sleep though, as he had already started to think about how he might make the stand.

The next day, he was working on a gold neck chain for the duke, but when evening came, he locked the door of his workshop. He took out the pearl, looked at it for a while and started work on the stand.

Then, just like the previous evening, there came a knock at the front door. Laurenzo quickly put everything away and went to answer the door.

A tall man, wrapped in a dark cloak, stood on the doorstep. Laurenzo thought for a moment that Marko had returned, but when the man began to speak, he recognized the voice of the duke.

"Good evening, Master Laurenzo," he said. "May I come in? I wish to look at your work and to speak with you." Laurenzo let his aristocratic visitor lead the way to the workshop. The duke took off his cloak and looked at the objects that Laurenzo had made.

"This is all very beautiful," he said. "But haven't you made anything else?"

271

"No, my noble lord," replied Laurenzo.

The duke looked around the workshop and said: "But you just received a commission for a new piece of work!"

"Oh, you mean the signet ring for your senior counsellor," said Laurenzo. "Here it is."

"No," said the duke. "I mean something else – and you know what it is!"

Laurenzo replied that he had no idea what the duke meant.

"You can stop pretending!" said the duke. "I know who came to see you last night! I am always well informed about what is happening in my city. Why else would I have spies?"

Laurenzo said nothing, but the duke gave him a cold smile and continued: "You have the pearl here that Marko the explorer brought to you!"

Laurenzo did not reply.

"Can you deny it?" asked the duke.

"No, my lord," said the goldsmith finally. "As you already know, I can no longer deny it."

"That pearl is the reason for my visit," said the duke. "And I shall come straight to the point. I want it."

"It is not me you should be asking, my noble lord," said Laurenzo, "but Marko the explorer."

"I have already asked him so many times," said the duke, "but still I do not have it. I am telling you that I must have that pearl. I wish to buy it."

"Then you should ask Marko again," replied Laurenzo. "He is the owner of the pearl."

"I want to buy it from you," said the duke. "And I can offer you lots of money. Lots and lots of money indeed."

"But how can I sell it?" cried Laurenzo. "It does not belong to me!"

"Give it to me at once," said the duke. "And I shall pay you a thousand gold pieces."

"How can you say that?" cried Laurenzo. "I can't sell something that isn't mine! Wait until Marko returns and then make your offer to him."

"You know very well that he does not want to give up the pearl," said the duke. "But I understand why you are refusing. You are afraid of Marko's anger when he returns and finds that you no longer have the pearl. But rest assured – you can tell him the pearl has been stolen, and he will understand that there was nothing you could do. If you like, I shall order my servants to testify that someone broke into your house, so that Marko will not suspect you of lying. So you have nothing to fear. Sell me the pearl."

"No, my noble lord," replied Laurenzo as politely as he could. "I cannot even contemplate selling something that does not belong to me! The pearl's owner entrusted it to me, and I shall keep it safe until he returns."

Outwardly calm, but fearful inside, he waited for the duke's reply.

"Fine," said the duke, to his surprise. "If that is how you feel, then you should not sell it. But take some time to consider my offer – and let me know if you change your mind."

With those words, the duke left and Laurenzo was alone in his workshop.

How dare he make such a suggestion? thought the goldsmith. *Marko was right to warn me about him. I don't feel comfortable now that he knows the pearl is here, even though he accepted my refusal. Just to be on the safe side, I shall hide the pearl.*

He walked all around the house, looking for a good hiding place, but he could not find one that he liked. "Maybe it would be best to bury it in the garden," he said to himself. "But first I shall look to see if there are any spies around."

When he put his head outside the door, he discovered an armed soldier on the step. "What are you doing here?" he asked.

"Duke's orders," replied the man. "Twelve of us have been ordered to guard your house. You're not allowed to leave without his permission."

Laurenzo went back inside. *Ha! I should have known!* he thought. *The duke isn't planning to take no for an answer.*

He took the pearl with him to his bedroom and hid it under the sheets at the foot of the bed. He placed a big stick within arm's reach and then tried to get to sleep. But that was not easy.

The next morning, the soldiers were still positioned around Laurenzo's house. The young goldsmith was a prisoner. Nothing of note happened during the daytime, but that evening the duke came to visit for the second time.

"Master Laurenzo," he said, "I have come to ask if you have changed your mind yet. I must have that pearl, and I will offer you five thousand gold pieces for it."

"I have already told you that I am just looking after the pearl," replied Laurenzo. "So I can never sell it."

"You are a fool!" said the duke. "You could become rich! Five thousand gold pieces!"

"Forgive me," said Laurenzo, "but I would never have expected such a proposal from you, a nobleman and the Duke of Forpa!"

"Someone like me is precisely the kind of person from whom you should expect such an offer," replied the duke. "As I have both the wealth and the power."

Neither man spoke for a moment.

"My noble lord," said Laurenzo then, "why have you placed soldiers around my house?"

"I don't want you to run off with the pearl," replied the duke. "Will you sell it to me? Yes or no?"

"No," said Laurenzo.

"So be it," said the duke, and he left.

That night and the next day, nothing happened, but Laurenzo's house was still guarded and the young man was not surprised when the duke came again that evening.

"This is the third time now, Master Laurenzo," he said, "and my patience is wearing thin. You must understand that I will stop at nothing to become the owner of that pearl. I am about to make my final offer."

"Do not say another word, sir!" said Laurenzo. "I cannot sell it, and you know that!"

"I will offer you ten thousand gold pieces," said the duke and when Laurenzo did not reply, he added: "I will also give you important commissions and recommend you to all my influential friends. I will make you famous! Give me the pearl."

"No," said Laurenzo.

"How dare you refuse?" cried the duke. "Do you not realize I can take the pearl by force? You are in my power and cannot escape."

"I am well aware of that," said Laurenzo. "I am no match for you, not like the mighty Marko the explorer. But I refuse to sell something that does not belong to me."

"I will give you one more day to change your mind," said the duke. "You know my offer. Tomorrow evening I will return. If you still refuse to sell me the pearl, I will simply take it. Farewell."

When he had left, Laurenzo decided to hide the pearl somewhere else. "But I must be careful," he said to himself, "because my servants are probably spying for the duke and as much to be feared as the soldiers around the house." He pulled up a tile in his bedroom floor, dug a hole in the ground beneath, put in the pearl and laid the tile back in place. *I am afraid it is not hidden well*, he thought with a sigh. *If the duke resorts to violence, he'll have the whole house searched and break everything open. Then he'll be sure to find the pearl.*

He spent a sleepless night.

The next morning he went to his workshop, but he got little work done. He could not stop thinking about the pearl. How could he make sure the duke did not get his hands on it? *I am powerless*, he thought. *Marko will not be able to blame me if the pearl is taken from me by force. No, but that's not true! He asked me beforehand if I dared to take on this responsibility. Now that I have said yes, I have to do whatever I can not to betray his trust in me. But how can I do that? There is only one option*, he realized finally. *I have to try to put him off. And that is only possible if I come up with a way to trick him.*

"Good evening, Master Laurenzo," said the duke when he came that evening. "What is your decision? Will you sell me the pearl?"

"Well, you see," began Laurenzo, "it's like this, my noble lord—"

"Don't try to talk your way out of it," said the duke, interrupting him. "Will you sell me the pearl? Yes or no?"

"I'd rather not," said Laurenzo. "I think—"

"Silence!" said the duke. "I've given you enough chances. Now I'm going to take the pearl and give you nothing in return."

"Oh, but listen to me, noble duke!" cried Laurenzo. "You have misunderstood me. Or rather, I have not told you the truth. The truth is that I also admire the pearl. I think it is the most beautiful thing I have ever seen, and I cannot part with it. That is why I do not wish to sell it. Yes, from the very beginning I have dreaded the day when I would have to return it to Marko the explorer. You are more powerful than I and you can take it from me, but I beg of you, please let me keep it for just a little longer, so that I can enjoy its beauty and imagine that it belongs to me! You can have it for the rest of your entire life."

The duke gave him a searching look. "Are you telling the truth now?" he asked.

"Yes, my noble lord," replied Laurenzo.

"I can understand your feelings," said the duke. "This pearl has no equal in the whole world. That is why I want it." He fell silent for a moment and looked thoughtful. "Fine," he said then, "you may keep it for one more day. But I will not give you that day for nothing. It will cost you one hundred gold pieces!"

"I shall give them to you," said Laurenzo.

"And do not imagine you will receive any payment for the pearl tomorrow! It is too late to sell it to me. Tomorrow I will take it – and now you will pay me one hundred gold pieces."

"Fine," said Laurenzo, and he paid.

"Farewell," said the duke, when he had taken the money. "Enjoy the pearl for the night and the day you may still have it!"

He left and Laurenzo thought to himself: *What a vicious, greedy and dishonest man the duke is! Now I have one day but I shall try to get more time, even if it costs me all of my money. I promised Marko that I would keep the pearl safe, and I hope I will be able to do so. Oh, if only he would come back!*

The next evening, the duke came to demand the pearl again, and once again Laurenzo was able to buy another day's delay for one hundred gold pieces. The same happened the following evening.

Laurenzo was still locked up inside his house, but he was well looked after. He was even allowed visits from the members of the court, who came to order various pieces from him. He did not dare to confide in any of them, however, fearing that they might betray him to the duke. During the daytime, he worked, although his heart was burdened with worry.

On the fourth evening, the duke was no longer satisfied with one hundred gold pieces; he wanted twice the amount. Laurenzo paid, but he knew that he would soon run out of money if this continued. So he worked twice as hard on the orders for the courtiers, as that would allow him to make some more money.

This went on for some time, until ten days had passed since the duke's first visit. Then Laurenzo ran out of money.

"I have nothing left," he said to the duke. "But I have another suggestion. I will work for you and make whatever you want, and you do not need to pay me anything for my work."

"Fine," said the duke. "Make a ring for me, and you can have another day with the pearl."

For three days, Laurenzo worked and worked, barely giving himself the time to eat or to drink, and he made a ring, a neck chain and a silver dagger for the duke.

"These things are very beautiful," said the duke, "but they are nothing in comparison to the pearl. I do not want to wait any longer. Give it to me this instant."

"Noble duke," said Laurenzo, "supply me with materials, as I have run out, and I will make a masterpiece for you. Just leave the pearl with me for one more day."

"No," said the duke.

"I have money in Bainu, where I was born," said Laurenzo. "Let me send a message."

"That will take too long," said the duke. "Give me the pearl. You've had enough time to look at it now."

"You know that I have to make a stand for it," said Laurenzo. "Let me finish that first. Then you will have the most beautiful of objects, and it will be complete."

"Fine," said the duke, "finish the stand. But I will allow you no more delays after that."

When he had left, Laurenzo sighed a deep sigh. How would he be able to protect the pearl until Marko returned? Only half of the time had passed. But he did not want to lose heart. *I shall look after what has been placed in my care,* he thought fiercely. *Besides, I do not want the duke to have the pearl – not him of all people! Oh, if only Jiacomo were here, someone I can trust. I feel so alone, surrounded by enemies.*

He began to work on the stand, as slowly as he dared.

"Is the stand ready?" asked the duke, when he came back the next evening.

"Not yet, my noble lord," replied Laurenzo.

"Show me how far you have got," ordered the duke.

Laurenzo did as he was told.

"Don't think you can fool me!" said the duke angrily. "You can work much faster than this! I will allow no more delays. I will have the pearl and the stand the day after tomorrow – and if the stand is not finished, I will just take the pearl!"

Laurenzo did not reply.

"Do you understand?" asked the duke.

"Yes, my lord," said Laurenzo. "And yet I would ask you to please grant me a little longer with the pearl. I may have no money left, but I have plenty of strength to work. I will make the most beautiful things for you."

"I don't need them," snapped the duke. "All I want is the pearl. The precious pearl that has no equal. Finish the stand. The day after tomorrow I will come here for the last time."

Laurenzo looked at him and saw that he meant it. He bowed his head and fell silent.

"Just look at yourself!" said the duke. "You've wasted your money and worked your fingers to the bone, and all for something that does not even belong to you. Why? You will still have to hand over the pearl."

Laurenzo raised his head.

The duke gave him a penetrating gaze and said: "You didn't want to keep the pearl for yourself! You were cunningly trying to delay matters until Marko returns. Is that not so?"

"It's true," said Laurenzo. "I beg you, my lord, please do not commit an injustice!"

"Silence!" cried the duke. "You are crafty, but I refuse to be deceived any longer! Where is the pearl?"

"I won't tell you," replied Laurenzo.

"You will give it to me the day after tomorrow," said the duke, "*with* the stand. I have set my mind on owning it, and I will get it, by hook or by crook. I shall double the guard around your house. You will not escape from me, you impudent goldsmith!"

Now it's all over, thought Laurenzo, when the duke had left in a state of great agitation. *There's no suitable hiding place in the house, and there's no one I can turn to for help. But I will not complete the stand. I will do that only for Marko the explorer.*

So there he sat with the pearl, imprisoned in the beautiful house near the duke's palace in Forpa. And he felt very lonely indeed.

2   JIACOMO TO THE RESCUE

Meanwhile his twin brother, Jiacomo, was thinking to himself: *I'm getting a little bored with Bainu. Why don't I go to Forpa and pay Laurenzo a visit?*

And so, one fine morning, he rode into Forpa. He had been there on his travels before, but he still admired all the beautiful things that there were to see. He had not ridden far into the city when an aristocratic gentleman stopped him and said: "Hey, Master Laurenzo, fancy seeing you out on the street! Have they released you from house arrest?"

"What do you mean?" asked Jiacomo. Although he realized that he had been mistaken for his brother, the question was still very puzzling.

"Well, the duke has forbidden you to leave your house, has he not?" said the gentleman. "I saw the guards outside the house this morning."

"Oh," said Jiacomo casually, "that matter's been settled. Good day to you, sir!"

"Ah, so what exactly was the problem between you and the duke?" the man asked curiously.

"I'll tell you another time," replied Jiacomo. He politely doffed his hat and rode on, wondering what on earth was happening. Respected goldsmiths did not get locked up in their houses, did they?

The closer he came to the palace, the more serious his expression became. He felt a sense of impending doom. *Come on*, he thought finally, *don't start worrying before you know what's happening. There could be a very simple explanation for Laurenzo's house arrest.* But no matter how hard he thought, he could not come up with one.

Laurenzo had written him a letter during the first couple of weeks of his stay and had said that he was living near the palace. So Jiacomo rode into the park, wondering in which of the buildings his brother might be staying. Seeing lots of soldiers standing in front of one of the houses, he dismounted from his horse and headed straight there.

When the soldiers saw him, their jaws dropped. Their commander came towards him and cried: "However did you get here, Master Laurenzo? You know you're not allowed to leave your house."

"Why not?" asked Jiacomo.

"Duke's orders. So how did you manage to get out without anyone noticing?"

"I'm not going to tell you," replied Jiacomo. "You should have paid more attention. But don't worry," he added, "I'm going back inside now."

He threw the reins of his horse into the hands of one of the soldiers, walked up to the house and knocked on the door. Anxiously, he waited for it to open, hoping the guards wouldn't ask themselves why he didn't simply unlock it and wondering how they would react when Laurenzo came to answer the door. But it was not Laurenzo who came; a stranger, probably a servant, appeared and stared at him in surprise.

"Master Laurenzo!" he cried. "I thought you couldn't go outside!"

"Well, you see that I can," said Jiacomo. "May I come in?"

"Of course!" said the servant. "And please be quick about it. It's just as well the duke didn't see you. I thought you were in your workshop."

Jiacomo headed inside, waited for the servant to leave and then went in search of his brother's workshop. *No matter what's going on*, he thought, *it can't hurt to let people think that Laurenzo can be in two places at once. No one here seems to know he has a twin brother.*

Outside, the commander was hauling his soldiers over the coals. "You are hopeless!" he cried. "One of you must have let him slip through! If it happens again, I will report it to the duke, and you know how strict he is!"

Jiacomo tried a door and found it was bolted from the inside. Knocking, he said quietly: "Let me in!"

It was exactly as he had hoped: the door opened and his brother was standing before him. When Laurenzo saw

Jiacomo, he looked surprised at first, then delighted – and finally worried.

"Quick," whispered Jiacomo. "They mustn't know I'm here."

Laurenzo let him in, carefully closed the door and said: "So what *are* you doing here?"

"I just came to visit you," replied Jiacomo. "Why have they imprisoned you?"

"I'm so glad you've come," said Laurenzo.

"So am I," replied Jiacomo. He gave his brother a worried look and asked: "So what's wrong? Talk quietly. No one must know I'm here. They think that I'm you, you see! The guards outside were so surprised that they almost fell over. They had no idea how Master Laurenzo could have left the house without being noticed. But now tell me what's happened. Why have you been locked up?"

Laurenzo told his brother everything that had happened – all about the pearl and the duke's demands.

"The villain!" whispered Jiacomo furiously. "He's abusing his power."

"And you understand why I don't want to give him the pearl?" asked Laurenzo. "Yes, of course you do. Marko the explorer entrusted me with that pearl, and I want to be able to return his property to him."

"Indeed. That goes without saying," said Jiacomo. "Come on, let's think about how we can smuggle the pearl away from here and get ourselves to safety."

"The first part is possible now that you're here," said Laurenzo. "But the second part will be trickier – at least for me."

"That means for both of us," said Jiacomo. "I won't abandon you. The duke is coming tomorrow evening, isn't he?"

"Yes."

"Have you finished the stand yet?"

"Almost. I could easily do it in a couple of hours."

The brothers began a whispered discussion. They did not agree on some points, but eventually they had a plan.

"I'm still not keen on it," said Jiacomo. "It's too risky for you."

"There's no other way," said Laurenzo. "This task is *my* responsibility."

As the sun set, the front door of Laurenzo's house opened, and the young goldsmith came out, carrying a round bundle in his hands.

The soldiers' commander walked over to him and said: "I'm sorry, Master Laurenzo, but you know you mustn't leave without the duke's permission."

"Yes, I know that," replied Laurenzo. "But it's the duke I want to speak to. I have here something that he would like to own, and I shall finally give it to him. Then at least I'll be free to come and go as I please."

"Oh," said the commander, "so that's it! I know the duke wants something from you, although I don't know what it is. But shouldn't you wait for him to come here himself?"

"No," replied Laurenzo. "I've already waited too long. The duke will be grateful if you and your men take me to him."

"Fine," said the commander and he ordered most of the soldiers to take Laurenzo to the palace. Two of them had to stay behind to guard the house.

Soon after that, the duke was surprised by a message that the goldsmith wished to speak to him. "Aha, finally!" he said. "Bring him to me."

Laurenzo was brought in, surrounded by soldiers.

"So at last you've seen sense," mocked the duke. He sent the soldiers away and then asked: "Have you come to bring me the pearl?"

"Noble duke," said Laurenzo. "I shall give you the pearl, but I am doing so reluctantly and only because I have been forced to do so. I am ashamed because I was not able to do what Marko asked me to do, but you are more powerful than I am, and so I shall have to yield to you. I would only ask you this: grant me permission to leave this city at once and to return to Bainu, where I can work in peace as a simple goldsmith, far away from dukes and precious pearls."

"Permission granted," said the duke. "I too would like you to leave my city and never return. Now give me the pearl."

Laurenzo appeared to hesitate. "I really would rather not," he said.

"Give me the pearl!" the duke repeated furiously.

Laurenzo handed over the bundle he was carrying.

"Thank you," said the duke icily.

Laurenzo bowed and made to leave.

"Wait a moment," said the duke, carefully starting to open the parcel.

"Must I suffer my defeat even longer?" said Laurenzo. "Please, my noble lord, let me go." And he headed for the door.

"Wait!" said the duke and he called for his servants. "Take him from this room," he ordered them, "but do not release him."

All alone, the duke continued unwrapping the bundle. At first he thought he really had the pearl in his hands, but when he looked closer, his face froze. It was not the pearl, but a coconut painted white and pink!

He hurried out of the room and Laurenzo, who saw him coming, tore himself away from the servants and ran off.

"Grab him!" shouted the duke. "Don't let him escape! He has deceived me!"

The palace was big and there were lots of servants walking around. So it was not long before Laurenzo was captured and brought before the duke.

"Take him to the prison," said the duke, "and lock him up. And send soldiers immediately to guard his house. No one must go in or out. Quick!"

Then he called a few of his most trusted servants and went with them to the goldsmith's house to fetch the pearl.

But the pearl was nowhere to be found.

When Laurenzo had gone to the duke with the guards, Jiacomo had escaped from the house with the pearl. This had not been too much of a challenge, as the two men who had stayed behind could not guard all four sides of the house.

Carrying the carefully packaged pearl, he calmly walked out into the palace grounds and into the city. He went into several shops and then entered an inn in a quiet street. A little later, when he left the inn through a back door, no one would have recognized him, as he had disguised himself with ragged clothes and a red fake beard. Dressed in this disguise, he walked back to the palace grounds, still carrying the pearl.

At Laurenzo's house, everything was in turmoil. There were soldiers surrounding the building, and servants bustling around and looking worried. Jiacomo wandered up to one of the soldiers and said: "What a commotion! What's going on?"

"Clear off!" said the soldier. "You have no business here."

"I'm already leaving," said Jiacomo. "I'm already leaving, my good man!" But he stayed where he was and continued: "That clever goldsmith lives here, doesn't he?"

"That clever goldsmith is in prison," said the soldier.

Jiacomo managed to conceal his reaction. "No! Really?" he cried. "He's in prison? Then he must have done something very bad."

"I'm sure he did," said the soldier. "And now clear off, you tramp! No one is allowed to come anywhere near this house."

"I'm already leaving!" repeated Jiacomo. "Do you have anything to spare for me, brave soldier? I'm a poor man and I could use a coin or two."

"Away with you!" yelled the soldier.

Jiacomo did as he was told and walked on through the palace grounds. Close to the prison, he stopped. *This is exactly what I was afraid of*, he thought with a sigh. *I knew the duke wouldn't let Laurenzo go before he'd opened the parcel. But sighing isn't going to do us any good. I'd better think about how to get him out of there.*

He sat down close to the palace gate, in a spot with a good view of the prison. Then he took out a wooden bowl, put it on the ground in front of him and asked everyone who passed by for a little change. And while he waited, he took a look around and pondered the problem.

The duke called for the commander and asked if he had guarded Laurenzo's house well.

"Absolutely, my noble duke," he replied. "No one has gone in or out." He did not mention that Laurenzo (or so he thought) had gone out for a while and then returned, as he was very afraid of his master.

The other soldiers said the same: they swore that they had not seen Laurenzo leave the house.

The duke went to the prison and entered Laurenzo's cell.

"Where is the pearl?" he asked.

"Go and look for it yourself," said Laurenzo.

"How dare you defy me?" cried the duke. "I have had your house searched. My men knocked on all of the walls and took up the floors and searched every nook and cranny, but the pearl isn't there. Where have you hidden it?"

"I swear that I have not smuggled it out," said Laurenzo. "But that's all I'm telling you."

"And as a result you're in prison," said the duke. "It really is about time you gave me that pearl."

"Duke," said Laurenzo, "I have given you all of my money and worked for you so that I could keep the pearl. Do you think a prison sentence will change my mind?"

The duke looked at him and replied: "If you wish to remain stubborn, I shall have to resort to other measures. You shall have nothing to eat until you have told me where the pearl is! Hunger will surely change your mind."

With those words, he left Laurenzo's cell, ordering the guards to keep a very close eye on the prisoner and not to feed him under any circumstances, and then he retreated to his palace.

It was completely dark now and the palace grounds were very quiet. There were only soldiers out and about, by the palace and around Laurenzo's house. Jiacomo stood up from his spot, thinking: *Good, now I can get started. But first I'll hide the pearl in the place that Laurenzo and I agreed.*

When he had done that, he left the area. Before long he returned, but now he had exchanged his begging bowl for a lute. Playing and singing, he went from house to house. Some of the courtiers chased him away; some of them threw him a coin or two. Finally he stood singing and playing in front of the prison. It happened exactly as he had hoped: one of the jailers came out and asked him to step inside. "My friends and I have to guard a prisoner," he said, "and it's a dull old job. If you play for us, we won't fall asleep."

And so Jiacomo ended up inside the prison, playing their favourite songs for all the jailers in turn. With his playing and his singing and his happy conversation, he soon made friends with them. So it required little effort for him to learn that there was only one prisoner at that moment – Laurenzo – and that he had to be guarded very closely. He also found out where Laurenzo's cell was and that it had only one door, which opened into the main room, where the jailers kept watch night and day.

It was late when Jiacomo left, but he promised to return soon.

The next morning, he kept his promise, and he heard something that really shocked him. Laurenzo was not being fed. He found it hard not to show his alarm, but the thought that he had to save his brother helped him to keep a calm expression.

I need to hurry! he said to himself. *Laurenzo must be released before he's starving – and sick!*

When evening fell, he went back to the prison for the third time. The jailers, who were sitting in the main room and playing cards, were delighted to see him. Jiacomo played his lute and sang:

> "Sing and play! Play and sing!
> Dance around, dance in a ring!
> The moon shines brightly in the dark.
> The oak trees whisper in the park!
> Flash your knife,
> and guard your life!
> Fill your cups, my friends, with wine!
> Wine so red, wine so fine!
> Wine, glow, wine, flow, fill your cup!
> Fill your cup and drink it up.
> Pick it up and drink it down,
> and let your singing fill the town.
> Wine to drink the whole night through!
> Wine for me! Wine for you!"

He took out a bottle of wine, held it up and said: "We're in luck. Who wants some?"

"Me! Me!" cried all of the jailers, forgetting that they were not allowed to drink on duty.

Cups were fetched, and Jiacomo filled them. The jailers drank and when the cups were empty, Jiacomo took out a second bottle and poured again. He picked up his lute and played, but he did not drink, although he pretended to. And when the jailers were very merry, he sidled up to their boss and stole the keys from his keyring.

Suddenly, though, there was a loud sound of footsteps and some of the duke's soldiers came into the room. They looked most surprised when they saw the happy scene. Startled, the jailers put down their cups and tried to look as alert and vigilant as possible. Jiacomo stopped playing and put on an innocent face.

"We were sent by the duke," said one of the soldiers in an ice-cold voice. "Our noble lord wishes to know how his prisoner is faring."

"Fine, fine," replied the head jailer, quickly standing up. "Well, as fine as a man can be faring when he's not allowed to eat."

"Let us into his cell," ordered the soldier. "We need to ask him something."

"Certainly," said the jailer, reaching for his keyring and realizing his keys were gone. Horrified, he looked at the musician. But he'd gone too!

"I indicated that your visitor should leave," said the soldier who was standing by the outside door. "You know no unauthorized persons are allowed in the jail!"

The head jailer said nothing. He did not dare to tell him that his keys had disappeared, as he was afraid he would be punished for his negligence. So he whipped out his spare key and opened the door of Laurenzo's cell.

Laurenzo was lying on his bunk, but he got up when the soldiers came in.

"The duke sent us," they said. "Have you changed your mind yet?"

"No," replied Laurenzo.

The soldiers turned and left the cell and the prison. The guard locked the door again and warned his mates to keep a very close watch. He was very worried about the loss of his keys, but he reassured himself: *We're all out here in front of the door and there's no way he can escape, because he'd have to come past us.*

Laurenzo had gone to lie on his bunk again. His stomach was rumbling and he was in a sombre mood. The only thing he was glad about was that the pearl should be safe by now. Sighing, he looked out through the bars in the small window; he could see a bit of sky and the full moon, which was as round and gleaming as the pearl.

A while after the soldiers had left, he heard footsteps outside. Then a small package came flying in through the window. Laurenzo leapt to his feet and picked it up. There were three keys and a note inside – it was from Jiacomo! He went over to the window and tried to read the note by the light of the moon. It was difficult to decipher, but he managed.

This is what it said:

> One of these keys fits the door of your cell. Soon – either tonight or early tomorrow morning – you'll hear me whistling outside. Then there'll be some noise: shouting and people going to and fro. Unlock your door and peek out into the room. The jailers will probably have disappeared. Then head quickly out of the prison and go around to the back, where you'll find a long cloak under a tree. Wrap yourself up in it, leave the palace grounds and go to the inn

opposite the entrance to the park. Wait for me. I'll be there soon.

Don't hesitate. Do exactly as I have written. Good luck!

Jiacomo

Dear Jiacomo, thought Laurenzo. *I hope he's not in any danger himself. Has he bribed the guards?*

Very early the next morning – the sun had not yet risen – Jiacomo walked back into the palace grounds. This time he was not in disguise. As he came close to the prison, he began to whistle, a cheerful tune from his childhood, but when he reached the gate, he shouted loudly: "Hey, hey, come out here!"

The jailers heard it and one of them went outside to tell him to be quiet. And there he saw Jiacomo, with his hands on his hips and a smile on his face.

"Good morning!" called Jiacomo cheerfully. He took a step forward, so that the light of the lantern above the gate could shine onto his face. "Good morning! I bet you didn't see this coming, did you? I've escaped!"

The jailer, who was sure it was Laurenzo standing before him, was so surprised that he was rooted to the spot. He let out a cry, which made the jailers inside leap to their feet.

Jiacomo took a few steps back, laughed out loud and shouted: "You lot let me escape! I'm free!"

The guard called his fellow jailers: "Help! Quick! The goldsmith has escaped! Catch him! Catch him!"

Jiacomo turned and ran away as quickly as he could. The

jailers raced after him, without stopping to think about how exactly Laurenzo might have escaped. Jiacomo sprinted straight through the park, swerving around trees and jumping over flowerbeds. He had soon opened up a big lead.

"Stop him! Catch him!" yelled the jailers. The soldiers who were standing guard by the palace and around Laurenzo's house joined in the hunt. Their shouting made the lights go on in various houses, and sleepy people peered out of the windows, even from the palace.

Jiacomo would surely have escaped if one of the jailers had not come up with the idea of stopping, picking up a stone and throwing it at him. To Jiacomo's misfortune, the throw was a good one. It hit his head. He felt dizzy – and he fell. He was soon back on his feet, but by then his pursuers had caught up with him – and he was captured!

"Ha! Now we've got you again!" panted one of the jailers. "And this time we won't let you go!" They led Jiacomo away, but at the palace they ran into the duke, who had woken up because of all the noise. When he heard what had happened, he became very angry and he yelled at the jailers until they were all trembling.

"I shall guard him myself," he said finally. "Bring him into the palace. He won't escape from there!"

Laurenzo had done as Jiacomo told him and had calmly walked out of the prison, with no idea that the jailers were now after his brother. He found the cloak, wrapped himself in it and easily made it to the inn opposite the park entrance. Filling his empty stomach with bread and cheese, he waited for Jiacomo.

But when the morning went by and his brother did not come, he became worried. He wrapped the cloak around himself again, pulled the hood over his head, and then it was his turn to go to the palace grounds to find out what had happened. Various people told him that Master Laurenzo had escaped but had immediately been captured again and locked up inside the palace. When he heard that, he felt defeated. How could he ever free his brother from the palace? There was only one way he could think of...

And so it happened that an astonished servant came to tell the duke that Laurenzo the goldsmith wanted to speak to him. "Not the Laurenzo who's locked up, but another one," he added. "He's at the gate."

"What nonsense is this?" cried the duke. "There is only one Master Laurenzo."

"I thought the same, my lord," said the servant. "But the one at the gate says he is the goldsmith and, on my word of honour, he certainly looks like the goldsmith."

"A strange story," said the duke. "Fine, let him in."

When the young man was standing before him, he could not help but look surprised. How could this be Laurenzo? The goldsmith was imprisoned in one of the dungeons beneath the palace, wasn't he?

"Make no mistake," said the young man. "I am Laurenzo the goldsmith. The one who is in prison is Jiacomo, my twin brother. He does not know a thing about this business and has nothing to do with it. So you must set him free and keep me here."

"Twin brother!" cried the duke. "Now I understand how you escaped! Are you really Laurenzo?"

"I am the man you robbed of money and freedom for the sake of a pearl you wanted to own."

"Why did you come here?" asked the duke. "You were safe!"

"I can't let my brother pay for something that concerns only me, can I? Set him free, Duke, and imprison me."

"Do you have the pearl with you?" asked the duke.

"No, my lord," said Laurenzo.

"So where is it?"

"I will not tell you," replied Laurenzo.

"Does your brother know where the pearl is?"

"No, my lord," said Laurenzo.

"I don't believe a word of it!" cried the duke. "He must have helped you to smuggle the pearl away. I don't know how, but I'm sure the resemblance between the two of you played some part in it."

"My brother helped me to escape," said Laurenzo, "but he knows nothing about the pearl. I have not yet had the chance to tell him about it."

The duke narrowed his eyes and studied Laurenzo. "I shall ask him myself," he said after pausing for a moment. "If he truly does not know, of course I will set him free. But you may not leave until you tell me where the pearl is."

Laurenzo did not reply. *I hope Jiacomo pretends not to know anything about the pearl,* he thought. *He'll surely be bright enough to realize he should do that!*

The duke called his servants and ordered them to imprison the goldsmith.

When Laurenzo had been taken away, the duke paced up and down for some time, with a frown on his face and deep in thought.

Then he sent for one of his counsellors and gave him some instructions. A couple of hours later, he headed to the dungeon where Laurenzo was imprisoned.

Laurenzo's dungeon was closely guarded and he was also in chains. But he looked at the duke proudly and without fear.

"Don't ask me anything," he said. "I won't answer you anyway."

"Look out of the window," ordered the duke. "If you stand on tiptoe, you can see the courtyard. Look – and tell me what you see."

Laurenzo looked – and turned pale.

"A gallows," he said.

"Exactly," replied the duke. "And if you do not tell me where you have hidden the pearl, you will be hanged there before sunset. So speak now, or it will cost you your life."

Laurenzo said nothing.

"You still refuse to answer?" cried the duke. "Is that pearl worth your life?"

Laurenzo bowed his head. After some time, he looked up at the duke and said in a serious voice: "I promised to keep and to protect that pearl. Of my own free will, I accepted the responsibility. If I give in to you now,

I will have lost more than that pearl. This time it was a pearl that was entrusted to me, but another time it might be something even more precious. But whatever it might be, I shall take care of it. If I give you what you want, you will have beaten me through your evil actions! If I do as you ask, I will not only be giving you the pearl, but I will also be handing the victory to the forces of evil!" He sighed and said: "Why am I still talking? You don't understand anyway, and that doesn't matter. Kill me, if you wish, but I will remain silent."

"Fine," barked the duke and he left. He went to Jiacomo's cell and said: "Where is the pearl?"

Jiacomo just looked at him haughtily and did not reply.

"Where is the pearl?" repeated the duke.

Jiacomo remained silent.

"You know where it is," said the duke, "even though you are not Laurenzo the goldsmith, as you led me to believe, but his twin brother." Jiacomo looked at him in horror. "Ha, you weren't expecting that, eh? Yes, I know that you are not Laurenzo. How else could he have escaped? And I also know that you know where the pearl is."

"The pearl?" said Jiacomo with a look of surprise. "I don't know anything about any pearls."

"That is a lie," said the duke.

"I truly don't," Jiacomo insisted. "I don't understand what you want from me. Why have you imprisoned me here? I have done nothing to you."

"Tell me where the pearl is, and I will free you," said the duke.

"I really don't know!" cried Jiacomo.

"You're just as pig-headed as your brother," said the duke. "Look out of the window, and you will see a gallows. If you remain silent, you will die. What do you say now?"

"That would be a wicked deed!" cried Jiacomo.

"Where is the pearl?"

"I don't know," replied Jiacomo. "It's none of my business."

"Indeed," said the duke, "it is not your business. Your brother must decide for himself what to do, as he was given the pearl to look after. But you don't need to go to the gallows for a matter that concerns only your brother, do you?"

"Indeed. That goes without saying," said Jiacomo. "So you have to let me go."

"Tell me where the pearl is," ordered the duke, "or I will have you hanged before the sun sets."

Jiacomo let out a sigh. "I don't want to be hanged," he said. "But I will not tell you."

"You fool!" cried the duke. "Why not?"

"My brother has done everything in his power to keep that pearl out of your hands," replied Jiacomo. "And now you want me to make all of his efforts in vain? Besides, I do not wish you to have the pearl, and I am glad that, even with all your power, you will not get what you want. I would rather die than tell you."

The duke said nothing, turned around and left.

Outside the dungeon, one of his counsellors came up to him. "The gallows is ready, my noble lord," he said. "When will justice be done?"

"Before sunset," replied the duke.

"Everything is prepared," said the counsellor. "I have also sent for the executioner. You are a strict yet just ruler."

"So you agree that the two prisoners should be hanged?"

"Of course, most exalted duke."

"Do you know what they have done?"

"No, my noble duke."

"Then how do you know that I am just?"

"I would never dare to doubt it!" cried the counsellor. "I know the two prisoners have refused to give you valuable information – and for that reason alone they deserve severe punishment."

"As you say," said the duke. "Summon all of my counsellors and my judges, my high functionaries and generals and everyone of any significance and have them gather in the large council chamber."

"Your will shall be done," said the counsellor, hurrying away.

The duke stood there for a moment, deep in thought, and then returned to Laurenzo's dungeon.

"I have come to attempt to persuade you for the very last time," he said. "Where is the pearl?"

He looked intently at Laurenzo, but Laurenzo did not respond.

"I have been to see your brother," said the duke. "But he is just as stubborn as you."

"My brother!" cried Laurenzo. "You were going to set him free!"

"I would have done so – if he did not know where the pearl is."

"He doesn't know," said Laurenzo.

"He does know, but he won't tell me," said the duke, before continuing: "Now listen carefully. I will set both of you free if you tell me where the pearl is. If you do not tell me, I will set you free, but I will hang your brother!"

Laurenzo stared at him. "No..." he whispered. "You could not be that cruel!"

"Speak," said the duke. "It is the pearl or your brother's life."

"You have won," said Laurenzo. "I cannot remain silent at Jiacomo's expense. I shall tell you. The pearl is hidden—"

"Not yet," the duke said, interrupting him. "I want you to tell me later, in the presence of witnesses." And he quickly left the dungeon.

He went straight to Jiacomo's dungeon. "I have just been to see your brother," he said. "He is silent, like you."

"Is Laurenzo here?" cried Jiacomo.

"He came to me himself to give his freedom in exchange for yours."

"I might have expected that," said Jiacomo in dismay.

"So now will you tell me what I want to know?"

"No," said Jiacomo.

"If you tell me where the pearl is, I will set you and your brother free. If you do not tell me, I will set you free, but your brother will die!"

Jiacomo turned deathly pale. "You viper," he said.

"What is your answer?" asked the duke.

"Of course I will tell you," said Jiacomo. "I have no choice."

"Fine," said the duke. "Later you will show me the way to the pearl, in the presence of witnesses."

And he left the dungeon.

Soon after that, all the important people of Forpa gathered in the council chamber. The duke was the last to enter. He sat down on his throne and ordered two servants to bring the two brothers before him – but in such a way that they would not see each other until they arrived in the chamber.

Laurenzo and Jiacomo entered through two opposite doors and, when they saw each other, the colour drained from their faces.

"Step forward," ordered the duke.

The brothers went closer; they stood side by side in front of the duke. And everyone in the room gazed curiously at them.

The duke looked at the brothers and then at the crowd and said: "I have brought you all here to listen to what these young men and I have to say to one another. I need to tell you that I am looking for a pearl, a precious pearl. I have searched for a long time, and now I have found it."

Jiacomo leant over to Laurenzo and whispered something in his ear. Laurenzo whispered back.

"Laurenzo and Jiacomo," said the duke, "now tell me where I can find the pearl."

"I'll tell him," began Laurenzo.

"No, I'll tell him," said Jiacomo.

"So are you telling him for my sake?" Laurenzo asked his brother.

"And are you telling him because of me?" was Jiacomo's question in return.

"Well, in that case, you should stay silent," they both said at once.

"Silence!" cried the duke. "You do not need to tell me anything. I have already found the pearl!"

He rose from his seat and said in a loud voice: "I have found the pearl, the pearl whose existence I doubted at first! And not just one of them, but two." He approached the brothers, laid his hands on their shoulders and spoke: "The first pearl I found was you, Laurenzo! And the second pearl is you, Jiacomo! I tried everything, Laurenzo, to take away the pearl with which you were entrusted, but you protected it and could not be bribed with gold or intimidated by threats. And you, Jiacomo, stood by your brother and helped him, no matter how difficult it became. Two brothers, true to a promise, true to themselves, true to each other – two pearls the like of which is hard to find!"

A murmur went around the room. Laurenzo and Jiacomo looked in bewilderment at the duke and then at each other. They could not believe their ears!

"You are free," said the duke. "And more than that, I consider it an honour to have met the two of you. You, Master Laurenzo, will get back all the money I have taken from you. And I ask you both forgiveness for the fear and hardship and sadness I have caused you."

Then he ordered everyone to leave the council chamber, saying that he would explain it all to them later. "Leave us," he said, "and send in the guest who has been waiting half an hour to be received: Marko the explorer."

Then he pulled up two chairs for the brothers and poured them each a cup of wine. "Drink," he said, "and you will soon feel better."

Then Marko the explorer entered the room. He froze in astonishment when he saw the two brothers.

"Welcome," said the duke. "You have come to collect your pearl. Ask these brothers where it is, and you will have it returned, just as beautiful as when you left it – or no, more beautiful, as now it has a story attached."

And he told the explorer what had happened.

"You know, Marko," he said, "that I wanted to own your pearl. So I went to Laurenzo and offered him a lot of money for it. He refused, however, to sell something that did not belong to him – three times in a row, even though the last time I offered him far more than I offered you! At first I was surprised, then angry, and then I felt respect for his incorruptible honesty. *But*, I thought, *if I really want it, I can get the pearl. Even if he is not interested in money, he will surely give in to threats.* So I tried it that way too. I demanded all of his money and his labour, but he stood firm. Every night I went to him and said: 'Give me the pearl.' I could of course have taken it by force, but by then it was not so much that I wanted the pearl and more that I was curious to see how long Laurenzo would persist in his refusal. I decided to test him to the limit. If he did not give in, I would not only forget about the pearl (as I had already decided to do, as his response had filled me with shame), but I would return everything I had taken from him, and more besides. Then along came Jiacomo, who helped his brother and saw his task as his own. I was amazed and wanted to know the extent of their loyalty. I tested them both to the limit, but they remained strong and, above all, loyal to each other. Then I knew that I had found more than I had been looking for at first, more than a pearl of great value."

The duke looked at the brothers. "Forgive me," he said. "Perhaps I went too far. But I shall try to make up for what I have done to you."

"Yes, you certainly did go too far," said Marko the explorer. "But perhaps the brothers will not be angry, because they have proved that they could pass your test, and because they have perhaps changed you for the better by doing so." Turning to the brothers, he said: "I thank you for the way you protected the pearl that I entrusted to Laurenzo. I could never have imagined that it would cause you so many difficulties."

"We shall return it to you at once," said Jiacomo. "We'll be happy when it's back with you – and we're rid of the burden!"

Marko smiled. "I can understand that," he said. "Are you Laurenzo, or his brother?"

"I am his brother," replied Jiacomo. "Laurenzo can tell you where the pearl is. This task is his responsibility, after all."

"It is hidden on a ledge above one of the palace windows," said Laurenzo. "To the left of the gate, the fifth window."

"Above a window of my palace!" cried the duke. "Under my very nose!"

"The closer, the better," said Jiacomo. "It's the last place you would look."

"Excellent thinking," said Marko the explorer. "I shall go and fetch it soon. I'm sure the stand is not yet complete, is it, Master Laurenzo?"

"Yes, it is. I finished it on the day Jiacomo came to me."

"Now I must thank you and your brother once again," said Marko, "as money alone is not enough." He shook the two young men by the hands. "Please excuse me for a moment," he said then. "And I shall fetch the pearl from its hiding place."

"I have a request for the two of you," said the duke to the brothers, when Marko had left. "Don't return to Bainu, but stay here, at my court. I shall make you both my counsellors. I don't think I could find any better men!"

The brothers looked at each other. They did not have to think about it for long.

"Thank you, my lord," said Laurenzo, "but I would rather remain a goldsmith and carry out my work in my hometown."

"I would also prefer to continue my normal life," said Jiacomo. "We would not feel at home at court."

"I understand," said the duke. "But remember this: I hold you in the greatest respect and if you ever have need of me, you can always count on me. Do not leave right now though. Stay for a while as my honoured guests, so that you will have

308

pleasant memories of Forpa. I hope you don't bear me a grudge, and that you will prove this by accepting my invitation."

The brothers looked at each other again.

"Fine, we shall stay for a while," said Jiacomo. "But please don't honour us too much! And please don't compare us to pearls again, as we've both had more than enough of pearls!"

Then Marko came back with his pearl, which shone like the full moon. And even though Jiacomo had said that he and Laurenzo wanted nothing more to do with pearls, they still gazed at it in wonder.

And Marko said: "I'm not planning to keep it just for myself any longer. I'll make sure it's in a place where everyone can enjoy its beauty. I shall present it as a gift to our land, to Babina, and I hope that it will no longer arouse anyone's greed, but that people will look at it in the same way as they look at the moon, without longing to own it for themselves."

Laurenzo the goldsmith was now truly a master of his trade, and his fame reached far beyond the borders of Bainu. He received so many commissions that he barely had time for anything other than work, unlike his brother, Jiacomo, who roamed around and took life easy.

But one day Laurenzo decided that he had had enough of all that hard work...

The Knight of the Red Rose

> *From the east to western Ind,*
> *No jewel is like Rosalind.*

SHAKESPEARE: As You Like It

It was summer in Bainu, glorious summer. Laurenzo, the young goldsmith, was busy in his workshop, but in the middle of the morning he put down his tools, wiped his forehead and said to his apprentices: "Tidy everything away and go outside. Go for a walk in the fresh air or rest in the shade of a tree. No one should stay inside on a day like this."

When the happy apprentices had left, Laurenzo changed his clothes, saddled two horses and rode away on one, leading the other by the reins. He rode through the streets of Bainu, until he came to Antonio's Tavern. His brother, Jiacomo, was sitting there under the awning, playing chess with the innkeeper.

"Good morning," said Laurenzo. "Would you like to come with me, Jiacomo? I'm off for a ride through the woods and fields outside the city."

Jiacomo widened his eyes and asked: "Whatever could be wrong? Master Laurenzo is abandoning his work! Shouldn't he be making jewellery for the wives of the rich gentlemen of the town or a chandelier for the cathedral?"

"The gleam of the gold made me long for the gleam of sunshine," replied Laurenzo. "I'd rather have the colour of the sky than the colour of sapphires, and the green of plants and trees rather than the green of emeralds. Which is why I'd like to get out of the city."

"Where to?" asked Jiacomo, moving one of the pieces on the chessboard.

"I don't know," said Laurenzo.

"And it doesn't matter," said Jiacomo. "Of course I'll come with you. Over the hills and far away!"

The innkeeper objected. "Finish this game first," he said.

"It's over," said Jiacomo. "Checkmate in four moves." He stood up and climbed onto the horse that Laurenzo was leading. "See you later, Antonio!" he called cheerfully. "We're off into the countryside, far from dusty chess pieces and cold jewels."

The brothers rode away, leaving the innkeeper looking in surprise at the chessboard. "Checkmate in four moves," he muttered after a while. "I do believe he's right!"

Meanwhile, the brothers were riding out of the city gate. Jiacomo sang:

> *"Over the hills and far away,*
> *over the hills and far away,*
> *who'll ride with us on this fine day?"*

They rode for quite some time, through fields and meadows. The sun climbed higher, and the day became very warm. As they came to a fork in the road, Laurenzo said: "Let's take the one on the right. There's a small inn at the end of it, where we can rest in the shade and enjoy a cup of cool wine."

"I like the sound of that," said Jiacomo. "But you're mistaken. The inn you're talking about is at the end of the road on the left, not the right. The road you want to follow leads to the estate of some nobleman or other."

"No, that's not right," said Laurenzo. "You're the one who's mistaken. The inn's this way."

They talked about it for a while, but could not agree. Finally Jiacomo said: "Fine, you take the one on the right, and I'll take the one on the left. Whichever of us turns out to be correct and arrives at the inn should wait there for the other one, who will treat him to a cup of wine."

Laurenzo thought this was a good solution and so the brothers said that they would see each other later, and each went the way he thought was right.

Jiacomo had to ride for a long way, but he came to the inn. *I knew I was right*, he thought. *I know this area better than Laurenzo does.* He made himself comfortable inside the cool inn, ordered a cup of wine and waited for his brother to arrive.

Laurenzo had taken the wrong path, but it led him to an adventure.

After riding for a while, he came to a beautiful wood, almost like a park, filled not only with trees but also all kinds of flowers that were blooming brightly. He soon realized that he had in fact been mistaken and that the inn was not along this road. But he went on riding for a while, as the woods were so beautiful and cool. When he came to a rosebush with velvety dark red roses, he picked one and tucked it into his buttonhole. Then, spotting a bend in the

313

road ahead, he decided to turn around when he reached that point. Jiacomo must have found the inn already and would be waiting for him.

When he reached the bend, he stopped his horse. But instead of turning around, he stared in surprise. Right in front of him, under the tall trees, he saw a charming scene. A large group of people were sitting on the soft green grass, and between them a snow-white sheet was spread out, with bowls of bread, fruit and other food on it, and cups of sparkling wine. Most of the people were young; there were men with smiling rosy faces and women who looked like flowers. Laurenzo watched them for a few moments and then started to ride back. But at that instant one of the young men caught sight of him. Giving a cry, he leapt to his feet.

"There he is!" he cried. "It's the Knight of the Red Rose!"

The people on the grass all turned to look at Laurenzo. Some of them jumped up and came running towards him, surrounding his horse.

"Welcome!" they cried. "Welcome, Knight of the Red Rose! You're finally here. We've been waiting so long!"

Laurenzo looked at them in surprise, as he did not know any of these people.

"Come along, sir knight," said one of the young people, "get down from your horse. Your bride awaits!"

Laurenzo was more or less forced to climb off his horse and with much laughter he was led to the spot beneath the trees, where the rest of the company greeted him eagerly.

They must be playing a prank on me! thought the young goldsmith. But they all looked so happy that he could not be angry with them. Instead, he took off his hat and gave them a deep bow.

"Long live the Knight of the Red Rose!" cried one of the young people, and this wish was repeated, along with cheers.

"Long live Lady Rosalinda!" cried another, and this wish too was greeted with cheers.

Then everyone stepped aside and made way for three people who came towards Laurenzo. The first was a portly older man, the second a stately lady, and the third a young woman. The man stood before Laurenzo and said solemnly: "My wife and I greet you, sir knight, our future son-in-law. And meet our daughter, about whom you have heard so much, and whom you are now seeing for the first time in years: Rosalinda!"

Laurenzo looked at the young lady and was struck dumb. Never before had he met anyone who made such an astounding first impression on him. She was as lovely as a newly blossoming rose.

Then the gentleman shook him by the hand, as did his stately wife, but the young woman stood motionless, with her eyes lowered.

"A toast!" cried someone. "A toast to the young couple, to the knight and his bride!"

Before he knew it, Laurenzo was sitting on the ground with the group, Rosalinda on one side and her mother on the other. The young woman's father was the only person standing, with a cup in his hand.

Laurenzo had still not spoken a word; he was utterly confused. He wondered if these happy people were really playing a prank on him... or if they thought he was someone else. The true reason for his silence, though, was Rosalinda, the young lady they called his bride. He was seeing her for the first time in his life, but he already knew that he wished she were his bride for real. He kept looking at her and heard nothing of the speech that her father gave. However, he noticed that, unlike the rest of the company, she did not seem happy. When the speech was over, he downed the cup he had been given and tried to pull himself together. Standing up, he looked around in embarrassment, suddenly ashamed because he had not said at once that he was not the man these people had taken him for.

At that moment, a tall young man came walking along the road, leading a horse by the reins. He stopped to watch them. Noticing him, Rosalinda's father turned and asked Laurenzo: "Who is that gentleman? Do you know him, Sir Reinout?"

Laurenzo looked and shook his head. But before he could say anything, the stranger waved at him and called out: "Greetings, Sir Reinout! Won't you invite me to your party?"

Laurenzo was even more confused now, as he truly did not know this young man. *This is becoming more peculiar by the moment*, he thought. *Apart from Jiacomo, there's surely no one else who looks just like me, is there?*

The stranger left his horse, came closer and repeated his question: "How about inviting me to your engagement party?"

Rosalinda's father asked the stranger who he was.

"An old friend of this knight's," replied the young man, "of the Knight of the Red Rose."

"Any friend of Sir Reinout's is welcome here," said Rosalinda's father and, turning to Laurenzo, he said: "Why don't you introduce your friend?"

"Jiacomo is my name," said the young man, giving Laurenzo a wink.

Now Laurenzo had another reason to look surprised, although of course it could just have been a coincidence that the stranger shared his brother's name. "I don't know you..." he began hesitantly, but he was interrupted with the words: "But you must remember me, my dear Reinout! From that pleasant evening at the inn in Puna, three months ago. You spoke about many things, including Rosalinda, your peerless bride!"

The young man wiggled his eyebrows and gave Laurenzo a meaningful look, as if trying to tell him something. And so the goldsmith fell silent.

"Do you know each other, or not?" asked Rosalinda's father.

"Yes, now I remember," said Laurenzo weakly. He wasn't sure what to do – should he continue to play the game or put an end to it?

The new guest bowed to Rosalinda and her mother and then sat down. Rosalinda's father also sat, with a little difficulty. Laurenzo realized that he was now the only one standing and that everyone was looking at him expectantly – except for Rosalinda, who was staring down at the cup in front of her.

"Noble company," began Laurenzo a little shakily, "I thank you for your warm welcome, but I must say that I don't quite understand why—"

The young man who was called Jiacomo clapped his hands. "An excellent point!" he exclaimed. "Sir Reinout does not understand why we are not playing hide and seek. That's the

318

done thing at engagement parties. Let the girls hide – and the men must seek!" Leaping to his feet, he cried: "Yes, that's the thing to do! Come on, let's begin right now!"

All of the young people stood up, calling out: "Yes, hide and seek! Let's play hide and seek!" The girls took one another by the hands and ran away to hide.

"Now we must each try to find the one we like best," said the young man who was called Jiacomo. "We'll count to ten and then go after the girls."

Rosalinda's father laughed out loud. "Bring them back soon," he said. "You still need to finish my feast. That's young people for you – they would rather play than eat!" Rosalinda's mother said nothing, but watched the girls as they disappeared into the trees.

"Come on!" cried the young man called Jiacomo. "The count to ten is over. Let's go and seek!"

Laughing, the young men rushed into the woods. Jiacomo took Laurenzo by the arm and pulled him along. Soon it was just the two of them; the others had scattered in every direction. Then Laurenzo stopped.

"Go on," the other young man said. "Aren't you going to look for Rosalinda, your lovely bride?"

"I have something to tell you," said Laurenzo. "Half an hour ago I had never met any of these people and now I'm supposed to be going in search of my bride! I'll be honest with you – Lady Rosalinda is not my bride."

"Of course she's not. I know that," replied the young man calmly.

"You know?" cried Laurenzo. "Then why did you call me Reinout, the Knight of the Red Rose? Who is that knight and why does everyone think I'm him? Who are all these people? And what is Rosalinda's father's name?"

"That's a lot of questions all at once," said the young man, laughing. "I know you aren't Sir Reinout, because I've met you before. Stop pretending you don't remember! It was in Puna, as I said. You are my namesake, Jiacomo!"

"Then you're mistaken," said Laurenzo. "Although that's understandable. Jiacomo's my twin brother."

"Your twin brother?" said the young man. "Ah, then you must be the goldsmith."

"Yes, my name's Laurenzo."

"Laurenzo the goldsmith. You're famous, aren't you? I heard that you've worked for the Duke of Forpa."

"That's right," said Laurenzo. "But now you must answer my questions, Jiacomo!"

"Fine," said the young man. "If you will first tell me how you ended up among this group of people." So Laurenzo told him.

"Ah, now I understand," said the young man. "Well, you're on the estate of Rosalinda's father, Cristiano di Dididi, also known as the Lord of the Feasts. And you've been mistaken for Sir Reinout, the son of the Count of Rosanjia, the prime minister. The count and Lord di Dididi are old friends and they agreed years ago that the daughter of one would marry the son of the other. Naturally, though, they didn't ask their children's opinions on the matter. Sir Reinout has spent a lot of time travelling, so he and his future bride have met only once, when they were children and could barely talk. One day, though, the time came to celebrate the engagement, and Lord di Dididi obviously decided to hold a feast to mark the occasion. A party in his park, as you've seen. Sir Reinout would finally meet his bride, and it was agreed that he would wear a red rose on his chest so that he might be recognized. As you may know, the counts of Rosanjia have a red rose in their coat of arms, and a rose is also fitting for the name of Lady Rosalinda. So when you came riding along with a red rose on your chest, everyone thought you were the knight!"

"If only I were!" sighed Laurenzo, running his fingers over the rose. "Now all I can do is offer my apologies and quickly leave."

"You're not telling me you've fallen for Lady Rosalinda, are you?"

"What business is that of yours?" said Laurenzo. "But then why shouldn't I tell you? I fell in love with her the moment I saw her."

"But if that's true, then you can't leave!" cried the young man who was called Jiacomo.

"What else can I do?" said Laurenzo with a sigh.

"All's fair in love and war," said Jiacomo quietly. "Let everyone continue to believe that you are Sir Reinout and take your chance to win the lady's heart."

"Absolutely not!" replied Laurenzo, a little angrily. "I shall tell them who I am. I have no need to be ashamed of my name. Besides, the real Reinout will soon come along, wearing a red rose, just like me."

Jiacomo looked all around and then whispered: "Shall I tell you something? I know Sir Reinout, and I know a thing or two about him as well. He's not interested in the marriage that his father has arranged for him. He might not even turn up!"

"Then he is a fool," said Laurenzo. "How can he be against the marriage if he doesn't even know Rosalinda?"

"I'm not certain," said Jiacomo, "but I've heard that he loves another lady, just as you love Rosalinda. So I would advise you to stay here and play your part."

"I want to stay," said Laurenzo, "but under my own name."

"That would be very foolish of you," said Jiacomo. "Even if you were the king himself, Lord di Dididi would be furious with you if you told him now. He is a man who does not like to be crossed, and he is determined that his daughter will marry Sir Reinout of the Red Rose. She will have to marry him, whether she wants to or not, even if he should turn out to be a villain or a beggar."

Laurenzo frowned and sighed again. Then he shook his head. "You're right when you say that I should stay here," he said. "But you're not right to suggest that I should deceive my host."

"If you want to be stubborn, then have it your own way," replied Jiacomo. "But before you come to a decision, you had better go and seek Rosalinda. I can hear laughter and shouting among the trees. I'm sure a lot of the young ladies have already been found. I'm going to look for one too – and if you don't hurry, I might just find your Rosalinda!" And before Laurenzo could reply, he was gone.

Deep in thought, the young goldsmith began walking through the woods. He heard sounds all around: the cracking of twigs under tiptoeing feet and whispers and quiet laughter. Then he stopped and thought to himself: *My brother's namesake is right. Why should I not try to find Rosalinda first?*

He had previously proved himself to be a good tracker, and he also received a little help. From behind a tree came a giggling girl's voice, which said: "Sir Reinout, walk straight on and you will find your bride for sure!"

He did as he was told and found himself in a dense part of the woods, where he had to make a path for himself through branches and undergrowth. There he heard another voice, whispering through the bushes: "Now go left and you will find your bride, your Rosalinda!"

Laurenzo turned left and followed a trail of flattened grass. After a while, he saw some movement in the trees. He quietly crept over there – and yes, it was Rosalinda!

"Found you!" he said, walking up to her.

The young lady backed away.

"You're not scared of me, are you?" asked Laurenzo.

"Certainly not," replied Rosalinda coldly. "I'm just surprised that you were able to find me. My friends must have revealed my hiding place to you."

"They helped me," Laurenzo admitted. "But I would still have found you, even though it might have taken a little longer."

"Then let us return to Father and Mother," said Rosalinda, turning around.

"Oh, but wait!" cried Laurenzo. "I'm so happy to speak to you alone for a moment!"

"Why would you wish to speak to me alone?" said Rosalinda. "We have nothing to say to each other."

"But I have plenty to say," replied Laurenzo.

"There'll be enough time for that later," said Rosalinda. "After all, we have to get married!"

"We have to?" asked Laurenzo.

"Yes, as our parents agreed, Sir Reinout."

"Rosalinda," said Laurenzo, "Lady Rosalinda, I noticed that you were the only one who did not look happy at the party in your honour. Why was that?"

The young lady stared at him with a serious expression. "Why should I be happy?" she replied. "Because I have to celebrate my engagement to a man I did not choose for myself?"

"Do you... Do you love someone else?" asked Laurenzo.

"N-no," said Rosalinda. "And that's just as well, as I will have to marry you anyway, Sir Reinout."

"Dear Rosalinda," said Laurenzo, "you don't have to marry me. I am not Sir Reinout, even though I am wearing a red rose."

Rosalinda stared at him in surprise. "What are you saying?" she cried. "You're not Sir Reinout?"

"No, Lady Rosalinda," he replied, "my name is Laurenzo." And he told her how he had come to be mistaken for the knight. "So do not be sad," he concluded, "as you do not have to marry me."

For the first time, Rosalinda smiled at him. Laurenzo smiled back at her and sighed.

"Why are you sighing?" asked Rosalinda.

"Because I'm not really the Knight of the Red Rose," replied Laurenzo. "Now I have to go away and I shall never see you again."

"Oh no, you mustn't go!" cried Rosalinda. "We've only just met." Then she sighed too and said: "Oh, Laurenzo, I wish you really were the Knight of the Red Rose."

"Why?" asked Laurenzo in surprise.

After all, a minute ago Rosalinda had made it clear that she did not want to marry that knight.

The lady blushed and did not reply.

Laurenzo's eyes began to gleam and then he told her how much he loved her, even though he had known her for only a short time. "Oh, Rosalinda," he said, "if I love you this much now, then in a week's time my love will know no bounds!"

Rosalinda heard his words and replied: "Laurenzo, I believe that I love you just as much. At first I didn't want to let it show, as I had made up my mind not to love the man my father had chosen for me without even asking for my opinion. But now I wish you really were Sir Reinout, so that I would have to marry you, whether I wanted to or not!"

Then they took each other by the hand and walked through the woods, feeling happy and worried at the same time.

After a while, Laurenzo said: "Rosalinda, I shall go to your father and tell him who I am and ask him to receive me as his guest."

"Oh no, Laurenzo!" cried Rosalinda, stopping him in his tracks. "You do not know my father. He has many good qualities, but he is very quick-tempered and I do not know anyone who is as stubborn as him. He chose Sir Reinout for me and he will never admit that he made a bad decision. If you tell him now who you are, he will become furious and chase you away. No, we need to think about this carefully."

"What do you want me to do?" asked Laurenzo.

"If Sir Reinout has still not arrived, you must continue to play the role."

"Absolutely not," said Laurenzo. "I want to be who I am! I am Laurenzo the goldsmith, and I can hold my own against any nobleman, even if he has ten red roses in his coat of arms! I will always keep the rose I am wearing now, a rose I picked by chance – because I have it to thank for meeting you."

"Wear it, Laurenzo," said Rosalinda, "and remain the Knight of the Red Rose, just for a while!"

"Don't you want to marry a goldsmith?" asked Laurenzo.

"I want to marry you, no matter what you are," said Rosalinda. "But do not do anything hasty. You must make my father so fond of you that he wants only you as his son-in-law, even after you confess that you are Laurenzo the goldsmith. I shall whisper our secret to my mother, and then she will likely help us to put Father in a favourable mood."

By then, they were nearing the place where the white sheet lay on the ground and most of the company was already waiting for them.

"I don't see any new guests, so Sir Reinout has not arrived," whispered Rosalinda. "Will you do it, Laurenzo?"

"I shall play my role," the young man promised, "because you have asked me to."

Laurenzo sat on the grass with the happy group and played the part of Sir Reinout of the Red Rose as well as he could. And yet he did not feel entirely at ease. What if the real knight turned up? But when he looked at Rosalinda, he forgot his worries.

"Right," said Lord di Dididi, when all of the plates and dishes were empty. "What do you want to do now? I suggest sitting here for a while and making some music. And then we men can go and shoot a few arrows. I've heard, Reinout, that you are a master archer and I'm keen to measure my skills against yours."

Laurenzo was startled. He had never even held a bow or arrow before, so now his deception would be sure to come out. "Ah," he said, "but I haven't done it for so long."

"Oh, but Father, I promised to show him the flower garden," said Rosalinda, who clearly understood Laurenzo's dilemma.

"He can do both, can't he?" said Lord di Dididi. "Reinout, you can show me your skills later!"

"They're expecting a lot from you, my friend," said the young man who was called Jiacomo. "Let's hope they're not disappointed!" He gave Laurenzo another wink. "Don't look so worried," he added. "You'll put on a fine show, as sure as my name is Jiacomo."

Laurenzo was startled again, but this time for a completely different reason. Jiacomo! He had not thought about his brother at all, but he had been waiting for him all this time at the inn. He leant over to Rosalinda and whispered: "Allow me to leave for a moment. I'll be back soon."

"Where do you need to go?" asked Lady di Dididi, who had heard his words.

"To see... To see a servant of mine," replied Laurenzo. "He's waiting for me at a nearby inn."

"Ah, the Three Lemons," said Lord di Dididi. "I shall send one of my men."

"I'm afraid that won't work, my lord," replied Laurenzo. "I need to speak to him in person. But I shall ride quickly."

"Then go at once," said Lord di Dididi, and he accompanied Laurenzo to his horse and showed him a shorter way to the inn, straight through the woods. The young man thanked him, said "I'll be back soon," and galloped away to tell Jiacomo why he had been away for so long.

Jiacomo had indeed been wondering where his brother was, but he was not too concerned. *Laurenzo can take care of himself,* he thought as he ordered another cup of wine. Then he leant back in his chair, rested his legs on another chair and dozed off.

A little later, he woke up and realized that Laurenzo was still not there. At that point, he did become slightly worried. He paid for the wine (which should have been Laurenzo's treat), left the inn and rode back down the road until he reached the fork in the road. He went along the road his brother had taken and followed his trail through the beautiful woods, eventually coming to the place where Laurenzo had seen Lord di Dididi and his family and guests, but there was no one there, as everyone had left by then. A little further on, there was a large house with a lawn in front of it, and on that lawn lots of men were shooting arrows at targets. Young ladies in beautiful dresses stood watching and cheering when there was a good shot.

Jiacomo stopped his horse and thought to himself: *I'll go and ask those people if they've seen Laurenzo.* He hopped off his horse and walked over to the archers.

One of them, a portly older man, saw him coming. "Hello!" he cried. "You're back! Come on over here and show us what you can do!"

So Laurenzo's been here, Jiacomo thought, and he politely said: "I'd like to ask you, sir, if you—"

The portly man pushed a bow into his hands and repeated: "Go on, show us what you can do!"

"Hit the bull's-eye three times, Sir Reinout!" cried one of the young men. "Lord di Dididi has already hit it twice!"

Jiacomo looked at him in surprise. He was used to being mistaken for his brother but this time he wasn't being called "Laurenzo", but "Sir Reinout".

"Come along, young man," said Lord di Dididi, "show me that you deserve your reputation as a good archer!"

What on earth is going on? thought Jiacomo. *Laurenzo has no idea how to use a bow and arrow, and since when has his name been Sir Reinout?* As he was thinking this, he nocked an arrow and drew his bow. Squeezing one eye shut, he aimed, and fired.

"Bull's-eye!" yelled one of the young people.

Jiacomo could use a bow and arrow, of course, as Jannos, the master thief, had taught him the skill of archery. Everyone cheered for him and then he had to shoot again. Another arrow zoomed off and hit the bull's-eye. Three times in a row he hit the target, and so he was the winner of the game.

"You shoot even better than I imagined, Reinout!" Lord di Dididi praised him.

Jiacomo bowed and opened his mouth to explain that he was not Sir Reinout, but then he heard a sweet voice behind him, which said: "You're back so soon, Reinout. But you've lost your rose!" He looked round and saw a beautiful young woman smiling at him. It was Rosalinda, but of course he had no way of knowing that.

"He can always find a new rose," said Lord di Dididi. "But you must give your future husband something else, Rosalinda! A kiss for the victor!"

The young lady blushed and laughed. Jiacomo stared at her, open-mouthed.

"Well, you youngsters? Get on with it!" cried Lord di Dididi.

Rosalinda put her arms around Jiacomo's neck and kissed him. Then she looked at him, frowned and let go. The others

clapped their hands, but Rosalinda turned around and walked towards the house.

"Yes, you did return quickly," said Lord di Dididi, slapping Jiacomo on the shoulder. "You must have ridden very fast. And then hitting the bull's-eye three times too! My goodness me! Did you speak to your servant?"

"My servant?" asked Jiacomo.

"Yes, your servant. At the inn."

"Which inn?"

"The Three Lemons, of course!" cried Lord di Dididi. "That was where you were going, wasn't it?"

"Oh, so I rode to the inn," said Jiacomo. "How long ago was that, sir?"

"You probably know that best," replied Lord di Dididi, giving him a rather puzzled look.

"Good heavens!" cried Jiacomo. "I must return at once! I've forgotten something. Forgive me, sir, I have to go!"

He turned around, ran to his horse, jumped onto it and rode away. Lord di Dididi stared after him in surprise.

"That young man is acting a little strangely," he said to his guests. "But then it is a special day for him. And he's very good with a bow and arrow!"

When Laurenzo came to the inn, his brother was no longer there. So he rode back, this time along the route that Jiacomo had taken, in the hope that he might be able to catch up with him.

At the fork in the road, the two brothers met.

"Ah, there you are!" cried Jiacomo. "What have you been up to all this time? When I went to ask the people on that estate if they'd seen you, they first greeted me as Sir Reinout, then they put a bow in my hand and told me I had to hit the bull's-eye. And finally a beautiful young woman came along, threw her arms around my neck and gave me a kiss!"

Laurenzo's face clouded over when he heard those last words. "What did you say?" he cried furiously. "How dare you take advantage of our resemblance? You made Rosalinda believe that you were me! Mind your own business and keep your nose out of mine." Then he rode past Jiacomo and galloped away.

Jiacomo stared after him. "This is too much for me," he muttered. "He can stew in his own juice. I'm going home!" And he rode slowly back to Bainu.

Laurenzo rode on without looking back, almost until he reached the Di Dididi estate. He was still angry with Jiacomo for allowing Rosalinda to kiss him without explaining that he was not who she thought.

It was already late in the afternoon when he climbed off his horse at the estate. A servant came to meet him and said: "Everyone is waiting for you inside the house. I shall take your horse to the stable."

Lord di Dididi had laid on another feast in the most beautiful room of his house. Laurenzo was given the seat of honour. The food was delicious and the company was merry, but the young man could not really enjoy either. He still felt uncomfortable pretending to be Sir Reinout, and he was beginning to regret the harsh words he had spoken to Jiacomo.

"You're a very good archer," the other Jiacomo said to him. "I didn't think you would win."

Laurenzo sighed. Jiacomo had done that for him! No, he was not having a good time at all and, to make matters worse, Rosalinda did not seem as happy and friendly as before.

After the meal, there would be dancing.

"The musicians have already arrived," said Lord di Dididi. "You'll be staying, won't you, Reinout? You can sleep here."

"I don't know if that will be possible," replied Laurenzo hesitantly.

"Your father's obviously expecting you at home," said Lord di Dididi. "It's a shame he was too busy to come. When the king can spare him, I shall have another feast and he will be the guest of honour."

Laurenzo bowed. *What have I got myself into?* he thought gloomily. *He's going to be so furious when he discovers my deception!*

When he was dancing with Rosalinda, he felt happier though. The young lady, however, was quiet and serious.

"What's wrong, Rosalinda?" whispered Laurenzo.

"Do you love me?" she asked.

"You know I do, Rosalinda!"

"When Father told me to kiss you this afternoon, you looked at me so strangely – as if you didn't know me at all!"

Laurenzo stopped. "Rosalinda," he said, "come with me to a place where no one can overhear us and I shall tell you why."

They went into the garden, where Laurenzo told Rosalinda that it had been his twin brother who was there that afternoon, and he added: "I'm ashamed of myself, because I treated him most unkindly. So I think I should go home now and explain everything to him. Would you mind, Rosalinda?"

"Of course not," she said. "But you must promise me that you will come and visit me again tomorrow."

"I shall come. As Sir Reinout or as Laurenzo?"

"As the Knight of the Red Rose," replied Rosalinda. "And I shall gradually prepare Father."

"I don't like this at all," said Laurenzo. "At some point it will all have to come out. And I would like to have a word with this Sir Reinout!"

Soon after that, he said farewell to the Di Dididi family and rode back through the dark woods and the lonely fields to Bainu.

It was long after midnight when Laurenzo got home. Jiacomo was already in bed, but he was still awake. So Laurenzo was able to tell him the whole story and to apologize.

"Oh, stop it!" said Jiacomo with a yawn. "I can understand why you were angry. That Rosalinda's a nice girl. She'd make a good wife for you." Smiling at his brother, he added: "There's no need for you to be jealous, because I'm not planning to fall in love with her. But I can't help it if she mistakes me for you."

Laurenzo gave a deep sigh. "I have so many obstacles to overcome," he said. "Her father still thinks I'm Sir Reinout. What should I do about that? And I'd also like to know why the real Reinout didn't turn up."

Jiacomo yawned again. "It's too late to be thinking about that now," he said. "Go to bed and have a good night's sleep. Tomorrow will bring a fresh start and a clear mind."

"That may be good advice," said Laurenzo. "I really am tired. Oh, and there was something else I wanted to ask you. What do you know about this Jiacomo, the man who met you in Puna?"

"I met a number of people in Puna," replied Jiacomo sleepily. "But someone with the same name as me? I don't remember..." Then he opened his eyes wide and continued: "An inn in Puna, you say? Ah yes, then I may well have met him."

"He's tall and thin," said Laurenzo, "with curly brown hair."

"Yes," mumbled Jiacomo. "I know him... Jiacomo!" He turned over and said: "Talk tomorrow. Sleep now."

Laurenzo went to bed too, and for the rest of the night he dreamt about Rosalinda. But he also dreamt about a masked knight with a red rose on his chest, who wanted to steal his bride away.

The next morning, Laurenzo said to Jiacomo: "I'm going back to see the Di Dididi family soon. But I'll tell them honestly who I am."

"Good," said Jiacomo. "You're no less worthy than that Sir Reinout, even if he does have a coat of arms with a red rose. You're the best goldsmith in Babina – and you were also a king for a while. There aren't many people who can say that!"

"I just wonder where the real Sir Reinout is," muttered Laurenzo.

"Don't you worry about that," said Jiacomo with a smile.

After breakfast, Laurenzo dressed in his smart clothes and picked out a few of the finest pieces of jewellery he had made. He told his apprentices what to do while he was away, said goodbye to his brother and rode to the Di Dididi estate.

When he got there, he asked to speak to the gentleman of the house. Lord di Dididi received him very warmly. "Welcome, Sir Reinout," he said. "I'll let my wife and daughter know that you're here."

"My noble lord," said Laurenzo, "I have something to confess. Let me tell you first that I love your daughter above all else and that I want nothing more than to make her happy."

"Nicely said, my dear Reinout," said Lord di Dididi.

"My lord," said Laurenzo, "my name is not Reinout! I am not the Knight of the Red Rose! My name is Laurenzo and I am a goldsmith from Bainu."

"What are you saying?" cried Lord di Dididi.

"I am not the man you thought I was. You took me for someone else," replied Laurenzo, and he began to explain how it had come about.

But Lord di Dididi did not even let him finish speaking. Turning red with fury, he roared: "So you are an impostor! Then how dare you show your face here again?"

"My lord," said Laurenzo, "I love your daughter. I may not be a knight, but I have no need to be ashamed of my name. I beg your understanding for my deception. Please bear in mind that—"

"Silence!" cried Lord di Dididi. "Out of my sight, you villain of a smith or whatever you are! Leave my house or I shall have you thrown out!"

Laurenzo was forced to leave. He slowly rode back to Bainu in a melancholy mood.

As he approached the city, two men on horseback came galloping up alongside him. They were servants of Lord di Dididi. "My noble lord!" they called out. "Our master sends his apologies and asks if you would return."

"I am not sure I want to," said Laurenzo haughtily.

"Lady Rosalinda would also like to speak to you," said the servants.

"That's a different matter," replied Laurenzo. He turned his horse around and rode back.

When he came to the house a second time, Lord di Dididi was already waiting for him.

"I'm glad you have returned, my boy," he said a little sheepishly. "You must forgive me for my outburst."

"You must forgive me for my deception," said Laurenzo, also a little sheepishly. "You see, I fell in love with your daughter the moment I saw her—"

"And you also realized that she would not love a man who had been chosen by her father," said Lord di Dididi, finishing his sentence for him. "You're a clever man, Knight of the Red Rose! But you still shouldn't have tried to fool me." He slapped Laurenzo on the shoulder and said: "Come with me. My wife and daughter are waiting for you."

Laurenzo followed his host, rather surprised by his sudden change in behaviour.

Lady di Dididi greeted him kindly and her daughter threw her arms around him. Then they all sat down together and Lord di Dididi had four nice big cups of wine poured for them.

"So tell me," he said to Laurenzo, "where did you leave your red rose?"

"I put it in a vase," replied Laurenzo. "And I will keep it for ever."

Lord di Dididi smiled and said to his daughter: "Well, Rosalinda, are you happy with the husband I have chosen for you?"

Rosalinda did not reply, but stood up and said to Laurenzo: "Will you come with me? I'd like to show you the flower garden."

"Wait a moment, Rosalinda," said Laurenzo. "I have brought a gift for you. Maybe your parents would not mind if I gave it to you now." He took out a parcel and presented it to her.

Thanking him, Rosalinda unwrapped it. The parcel contained some exquisite pieces of jewellery: a necklace, a pair of earrings and a beautifully crafted golden ring. "Oh, they're lovely," whispered the young lady.

"A magnificent gift," said her father. "You have excellent taste. Where did you buy these things so quickly, son-in-law?"

"I made them myself," replied Laurenzo.

"Yourself? You're able to make something like that yourself?" Lord di Dididi cried in surprise.

"Yes, of course," said Laurenzo. "I am a goldsmith, after all." Rosalinda cast an anxious glance at her mother.

"A goldsmith?" said Lord di Dididi. "I don't understand, Reinout! I thought you were a military man."

"He is!" cried Rosalinda. "He's just joking."

Her father frowned. "Now who's telling the truth?" he barked. He looked at Laurenzo and asked: "What is your name and who are you?"

"My name is Laurenzo, son of Ferdinand," replied the young man. "And by trade I am a goldsmith."

"How can that be?" cried Lord di Dididi. "My wife and daughter swore to me that you were Reinout, the Knight of the Red Rose. They told me you'd pretended to be this Laurenzo because you knew Rosalinda wanted nothing to do with the man I'd chosen for her."

"No, my lord," said Laurenzo. "It's like this—"

"Don't listen to him, Father," cried Rosalinda. "He is the Knight of the Red Rose, the man I want to marry!"

"But this young man says he is someone else!"

"Now don't be angry," his wife said in a soothing tone. "You like this young man. You said so yourself. And he is Rosalinda's Knight of the Red Rose. Who else could he be?"

Laurenzo looked at one and then the other. He realized what must have happened. Rosalinda and her mother had managed to persuade Lord di Dididi that he really was Sir Reinout. That was why he had been asked to return. He did not know what to say. He would have preferred to be Laurenzo the goldsmith, but he did not really dare to contradict Rosalinda and her mother.

Lord di Dididi stood right in front of him and roared: "Are you Laurenzo the goldsmith, or Reinout of the Red Rose? If you're one, I'll beat you to a pulp, and if you're the other, you may marry my daughter!"

"I won't let myself be beaten to a pulp," shouted Laurenzo. "And I'm going to marry your daughter, no matter what my name is!"

"So you *are* Sir Reinout!"

Lady di Dididi laid her hand on her husband's arm and said: "Is this any way to treat a guest, whoever he is and whatever he does? He would be right to leave in anger."

Lord di Dididi swallowed, coughed and replied grumpily: "My guests will never have any cause for complaint. The guests I have invited here myself, that is. And by all the red roses in the world, I surely have the right to know which young man my daughter wants to marry, don't I?"

"Yes, you have the right," said Laurenzo, who had had enough of all the confusion by now and thought it was finally time to clarify matters.

Lord di Dididi looked at him sharply and raised his hand. "Wait a moment, young man," he said, suddenly much calmer. "My wife and daughter say one thing and you say another. Experience has taught me not to argue with Lady di Dididi! I shall make it easy for you by forbidding you to tell me who you are. I don't want to know, do you hear me? I shall call you the Knight of the Red Rose, and I don't care if your name is Reinout or Laurenzo, or Marko or Antonio. Tell me nothing. I shall find out myself what I want to know. You are my guest. Now sit down and finish your wine!"

Laurenzo obeyed without saying a word. That seemed to

be the best course of action. He did not have another opportunity to speak to his host, as more guests arrived then, most of whom he had already met the previous day. They greeted him as the Knight of the Red Rose, and Rosalinda whispered to him that that was exactly what he was. "You're *my* Knight of the Red Rose" – that was how she put it.

The hospitable Lord di Dididi welcomed everyone cheerfully, and then briefly stepped out to talk to one of his servants. Soon after, he returned and announced that lunch was ready. Laurenzo joined them, but he ate little and he said even less. After the meal, which lasted a long time, Lord di Dididi took his guests to a large room with all kinds of musical instruments.

"Everyone must pick up an instrument!" cried Lord di Dididi. "Strum the lutes, blow the flutes, play on the trumpets. And if you can't play, then you must sing!"

There was music and singing, and Laurenzo sang a duet with Rosalinda.

A while later, a servant came in and informed Lord di Dididi that two men from Bainu wanted to speak to him.

"Aha," said Lord di Dididi. "I've been expecting them. We must stop making music – at least for now, but maybe longer! Send them in," he ordered his servant.

The two men soon entered the room. One of them was old, and the other was young. They were both dressed in grey coats upon which a red rose was embroidered.

"Ah, look, two servants of the House of Rosanjia," said Lord di Dididi, with a sideways glance at Laurenzo. "They have ridden here at my request. I thank you for coming so quickly," he said to the two men. "Soon you may rest for as long as you want. But first I would like to ask you a question. Do you know Sir Reinout, your master's son?"

"Yes, my lord," replied the younger of the two servants.

"Very well indeed, my lord," said the older man. "I've known him since he was a child."

Lord di Dididi pointed at Laurenzo, who was standing beside Rosalinda. "Then I'm sure you can tell me," he said, "if this young man is Reinout, the Knight of the Red Rose."

The two servants looked at Laurenzo. Then they approached him and gave him a deep bow.

"Greetings, Sir Reinout," said one.

"Do you have need of us?" asked the other.

Laurenzo stared at them, his eyes wide. This really was becoming stranger and stranger! But Lord di Dididi said with satisfaction: "So this young man is Sir Reinout, the son of the Count of Rosanjia."

"Yes, my lord," said the servants. "This is Sir Reinout!"

"Thank you," said Lord di Dididi. Turning to Laurenzo, he said apologetically: "Forgive me, Reinout, but I had to be certain."

"So you really are Sir Reinout, Laurenzo?" cried Rosalinda. "Why did you lie to me? Why didn't you tell me?"

The other guests listened and looked with open mouths.

"Calm down, Rosalinda," said Lord di Dididi. "This young man has remained the same person, even though he does not appear to be who you thought he was. Everything is now as it should be."

But Laurenzo cried out: "It most certainly is not! I've had enough of this comedy of errors! Tell me," he asked the servants, "do you really think I am Sir Reinout of Rosanjia?"

341

"Y-yes, my lord," stammered the servants.

"Lies!" cried Laurenzo. "I do not know you, and you do not know me. Is everyone conspiring to turn me into someone I am not? I am Laurenzo the goldsmith, and yesterday I simply had the fortune – or perhaps the misfortune – to pick a red rose and to wear it on my chest!"

These words caused some consternation, but Laurenzo paid no attention. He stared at the servants and seemed to be thinking about something. Then his face lit up. "Oh, I am such a fool," he said. "Now I understand everything. Where's your master?" he asked the servants. "I mean the real Sir Reinout."

"I d-d-don't understand..." one of them stuttered.

"You understand perfectly! Come on, you two are riding back to Bainu with me, and we shall pay your master a visit. Sir Reinout of the Red Rose, who did not respond to his father-in-law's invitation and who did not wish to pay his respects to his bride!"

"But we've just come from Bainu," the servants protested. "Our horses are tired."

"Then we shall borrow some horses from my host." Laurenzo turned to Lord di Dididi. "I'm sure you won't mind, will you?" he said.

"Yes... no... what do you want?" the man cried. "I have no idea what's going on. None whatsoever!"

"But I do," said Laurenzo. "I promise to return before this evening – *with* Sir Reinout. Then you can decide for yourself which man you choose as your son-in-law."

He bowed to the lord and lady and nodded at the guests. But to Rosalinda he gave a kiss, and he said: "Red rose or no red rose, I love you, Rosalinda!"

Then he and the servants left the room, and soon the three of them were galloping back to Bainu.

Stunned, the guests put down their instruments, and Lord di Dididi dropped into a chair. "I know one thing for sure," he wailed. "I'm sick of the sight of roses!"

Laurenzo rode to Bainu with the two servants from the House of Rosanjia, without giving himself or them a moment's rest.

"Take me to Sir Reinout at once," he ordered, when they reached the city.

The servants looked at him with unhappy faces and came up with all kinds of excuses.

"Silence," Laurenzo said impatiently. "I shall find him myself."

Then he suddenly stopped his horse and cried: "And just look! I've found him already!"

They were just riding past Antonio's Tavern, and there was Laurenzo's brother, Jiacomo, sitting under the awning and talking and drinking with the other young man who was called Jiacomo.

Laurenzo dismounted and walked over to them. "Good afternoon, brother," he said. "Good afternoon, Sir Reinout!" He called the servants over and asked them: "Is this not your master, Sir Reinout of the Red Rose, the son of the Count of Rosanjia?" The servants were reluctant to answer.

The young man who had called himself Jiacomo stood up and said: "Answer him, my good men."

"But what should we say?" asked the servants. "We did as you told us, but he didn't believe us and he said we were lying!"

"Of course he didn't believe you," said the young man, laughing. "But you did your best and you may go, with my thanks." He bowed to Laurenzo and said: "So you have guessed who I am. Sir Reinout at your service. Sit and have a beer with us."

"No," said Laurenzo. "First you can come with me to Lord di Dididi to tell him who you are and who I am, and to explain your behaviour." He looked at his brother and continued: "You must have known, Jiacomo, who your so-called namesake was. So why didn't you tell me?"

Jiacomo laughed. "I thought you should find out for yourself," he replied. "And you have now, haven't you? You could have worked it out right away, if your mind hadn't been on other things. I never met a namesake in Puna, but I did meet a certain Sir Reinout. This morning he came to the workshop and asked for you. As you were not there, I invited him to come for a drink with me."

"But you still have a lot to explain to me, Sir Reinout," said Laurenzo. "I know why you don't want to marry Rosalinda – luckily for me – but I don't understand why you had to stage this comedy of errors, even to the extent of ordering your servants to address me as their master. You have to come with me to Lord di Dididi's house at once, as I've promised to return there before this evening."

"Oh!" cried Sir Reinout. "Do I really have to stand in front of that stern father and allow him to unleash a storm upon my poor head? And I don't even dare to imagine what my own father's going to say when he hears about this."

"It's all your fault," said Laurenzo without any sympathy.

"Don't you have me to thank for your young lady's love?" exclaimed Sir Reinout.

"I have a red rose to thank for that," replied Laurenzo. "But I'm glad you love another lady. I couldn't bear it if you were to marry my Rosalinda."

"So then you should be grateful to me," said Sir Reinout. "Listen, Laurenzo, and I will explain everything to you. And please don't be angry with me. It had been agreed and arranged that I would marry Rosalinda, but on my travels I met a young lady whom I came to love above all others. Cecilia is her name, and even if Rosalinda were ten times as beautiful and intelligent, I could not love her more; my heart belongs to Cecilia. My father, however, didn't want to hear about my love. He had, on my behalf, given my word

345

to Rosalinda, and he said it was my duty as a knight to remain true to her, even though I did not know her. So I reluctantly set off for Lord di Dididi's house. That was only yesterday morning, even though it seems like longer ago. When I saw the group in the distance, sitting on the grass, my heart sank into my boots, and I tore the red rose from my chest. I hated it, as it reminded me that I would have to abandon Cecilia. I wanted to turn around and to ride away, but curiosity drove me onwards, just to see what she looked like, the young lady my father insisted I should marry.

"You'll understand my surprise when I saw that another man was already sitting beside her, a young man with a red rose on his chest, who was being addressed as her betrothed. I knew the young man, or I thought I knew him, as a certain Jiacomo. I wanted to find out how he had ended up there in my place, and so I went up to the merrymakers and introduced myself as his friend. He was called Jiacomo – or so I thought at the time, but later I heard that you were his brother, Laurenzo – and he was calling himself Sir Reinout. So I, the real Reinout, called myself by his name: Jiacomo."

Sir Reinout fell silent for a moment, and then nodded at Laurenzo and went on: "You know what happened next. I saw that you had fallen in love with Rosalinda. She's a charming girl, and if I had not met Cecilia, I would have had no objections to marrying her. Then I suddenly saw a solution for my problems. *If Laurenzo marries Rosalinda, I can marry Cecilia*, I thought. But it wouldn't be that easy, as I had heard a great deal about Lord di Dididi's stubborn nature. So it seemed better to me that you, Laurenzo, should continue to present yourself as the Knight of the Red Rose for the time being – just until Lord di Dididi liked you so much for your own sake that he would accept you as his son-in-law—"

"Or until he noticed that you, Reinout, had not kept your promise, and would be so angry with you that he would not want you as his son-in-law in any case!" said Jiacomo, interrupting him.

"That was another possibility," said the young knight calmly. "Today, when a messenger from Lord di Dididi came to our house to ask if I was at home, and if I was not, then to request that a couple of servants should come to his house, I realized that he'd become suspicious. So I ordered two of my men to play along with the game. Sadly, Laurenzo, you did not wish to keep it going."

"The game's over," said Laurenzo.

"But how did you know I was Sir Reinout?" asked the young nobleman.

"When the servants came and, as you said, played along with the game, I realized that only Sir Reinout could have ordered them to do so. You were the only one, except for Rosalinda and my brother, who knew who I really was. Besides, you called yourself Jiacomo, the name of my brother, for whom you took me at first. And that was it. So now we must go to Lord di Dididi. I shall ask him for the hand of his daughter, and then you can marry your Cecilia!"

"Can I come too?" asked Jiacomo. "I'd like to renew my acquaintance with my future sister-in-law and her parents."

Before the afternoon had come to an end, the three young men arrived at Lord di Dididi's house. A coach with two horses

347

stood in front of the house, and the sight of it alarmed Sir Reinout somewhat.

"That's my father's coach!" he exclaimed. "Why should he have come here? I thought he was too busy with government affairs to leave the capital."

They climbed down from their horses and a servant came outside to welcome them.

Jiacomo, however, did not want to go into the house.

"That would only cause more confusion," he said, laughing. "I'll stay and wait in the garden until you've explained everything."

Laurenzo and Sir Reinout went inside, where they met not only the Di Dididi family, but also a tall gentleman with a forked beard.

"My father," whispered Reinout to Laurenzo.

"Here he is at last!" cried Lord di Dididi. "But not alone this time." And he asked the Count of Rosanjia: "Do you recognize your son, my dear friend?"

"I'm afraid I do not," replied the count. "My son is a knight and he wears a red rose in his coat of arms. But a knight always keeps his promises, and I'm afraid that my son has not done so. And so I can no longer see him as a knight – or as my son!"

"Forgive me, Father," said Sir Reinout, "but the promise you speak of was given by you, not by me! Must I keep promises I have not made myself?" He bowed to the Lord and Lady di Dididi, and he bowed even more deeply to Rosalinda. "I am Reinout of Rosanjia," he said. "The Knight of the Red Rose."

"Well, well, well!" cried Lord di Dididi. "The Knight of the Red Rose! That is a name I can no longer stand to hear! Why did you lie to us and deceive us? Why did you and your friend play a game for my daughter's hand? I know one thing for sure: you will not have my daughter!"

"My noble lord," said Sir Reinout, "and my beautiful young lady, I beg you both to forgive me. But please do not be angry with Master Laurenzo for chancing to pick a red rose and falling in love. Let him explain it all to you."

Then Laurenzo, with Sir Reinout helping out now and then, told them almost everything that needed to be told.

Then Lady di Dididi spoke up. "You see? That's what happens!" she said to her husband and to the count. "That's what happens when you don't allow your children to make their own choices. Just be glad that everything has turned out so well and that Reinout can marry Cecilia and that our daughter can marry Laurenzo. And don't be angry any longer, but laugh instead at this comedy of errors!"

Lord di Dididi followed her advice. "Laurenzo," he said brightly, "I accept you as my son-in-law and I hope that you and Rosalinda will be very happy together!"

"And I forgive you," said the count to his son. "Allow me to become acquainted with Lady Cecilia soon, and I shall be glad to accept her as my daughter-in-law."

They all smiled happily at one another.

"It may just take me a little time to become accustomed to your name," said Lord di Dididi to Laurenzo. "Goldsmith is a fine trade. And you can use a bow and arrow as well as the best of knights!"

"Ah!" cried Laurenzo. "I have another misunderstanding to clear up! I can no more use a bow and arrow than Sir Reinout can make jewellery. I have never even held a bow in my hands before!"

Now Jiacomo was fetched, and there was even more reason for surprise.

"This is becoming more and more like a comedy of errors," said Lord di Dididi. "Laurenzo was playing the Knight of the Red Rose and Sir Reinout called himself Jiacomo. And the real Jiacomo was Laurenzo's twin brother." He was slapping his knees and laughing away. But then he exclaimed: "Rosalinda, how are you ever going to manage? Will you be able to recognize your own husband?"

He told Laurenzo and Jiacomo to stand side by side and asked: "Rosalinda, now tell me, without hesitation: which of the two is Laurenzo?"

Rosalinda looked at each of the brothers and smiled mischievously. "May I kiss both of you?" she asked. "Then I will know which one is Laurenzo."

"I have no objections," said one of the brothers cheerfully.

"As you wish," grunted the other.

Rosalinda took the second one by the hands and said: "Dear Laurenzo, you're not jealous of your brother, are you? I love you, but I will kiss Jiacomo as my brother, because that is what he will soon be."

"Laurenzo," said Jiacomo, "I wish you good luck with a wife like that!"

Then Laurenzo laughed too, and Rosalinda kissed first him and then his brother. The others came crowding around the couple, wishing them all the best.

"And now," said Lord di Dididi, "we shall celebrate with another engagement party. Sir Reinout, go and fetch your bride too, and then the party will be complete!"

It happened as the Lord of Feasts had said. There was dancing and singing, laughter and music. But late in the evening, Jiacomo, walking all alone in the garden, looked up at the moon and sang:

> *"Other men have found a bride.*
> *Sing ha! Sing ha! Sing trala la la!*
> *And I have laughed, and I've not cried.*
> *Sing ha! Sing ha! Sing trala la la!*
> *But I am one man all alone.*
> *Oh, hear my deep and sorry sigh.*
> *And the moon hangs sad upon a silver thread*
> *so lonely in the dark, dark sky!*
> *Sing ha! Sing ha! Sing trala la la!"*

When Laurenzo, the goldsmith, was married to the sweet Rosalinda, many people said to his twin brother, Jiacomo: "Should you not start working too, like your brother, and settle down and look for a wife?"

But Jiacomo replied: "On my journeys and adventures, I earn enough money to live on. I know of no work for which I am well suited. The only skill I have is something I would rather not speak about. And, as far as a wife is concerned, I like many girls, but I am not in love with any of them."

Then people laughed and said: "Well, you can't be identical in every way!"

And Jiacomo laughed too. "One of us must continue to look for adventures," he said. "Although I sometimes fear that I will never experience as much on my own as with Laurenzo."

He was delighted that his brother had found a lovely wife, but he did notice that their life had changed. Laurenzo preferred to stay at home now, and he had lots of work to do too.

And yet, one day, Jiacomo did find work that he was well suited for, even though it was something very different from that of his brother.

The Ring with the Blue Stone

"I am a master thief. For me, locks and bolts do not exist, and whatever I desire becomes my property."

GRIMM: 'The Master Thief'

1 THE FIRST TASK

One evening, Jiacomo was bored. He was alone at home, as his brother, Laurenzo, had gone with his wife to visit his parents-in-law.

I know, thought Jiacomo, *I'll go to the inn. I'm sure to find some good company there.* He picked up his lute and walked to his friend Antonio's tavern.

Antonio welcomed him warmly and said: "Sit down, Jiacomo, and play for us."

The inn was rather full, and Jiacomo knew most of the customers. He ordered a cup of wine, tuned his lute and played. Before long, lots of people were singing along, and it was an enjoyable evening.

Now, in the inn that evening, there was an unpleasant man called Ludovico. He had been jealous of Jiacomo for some time, because he was so cheerful and everyone liked him.

353

And when Jiacomo stopped playing to finish his drink, this Ludovico spoke to him.

"I have no idea," he said, "what you're so happy about! After all, you don't have much to be proud of, do you?"

"What do you mean?" asked Jiacomo, surprised.

"Well, just take a look at your twin brother. You're identical in appearance, but he's so different from you. He's a famous goldsmith and moves in high circles. And what can you do? Nothing! He's married a beautiful woman, but you couldn't even support a wife."

"Then it's just as well I'm not thinking of marrying," said Jiacomo. "I'm free and I'm happy."

"Aren't you jealous of your brother?" Ludovico persisted.

"Why should I be jealous?" cried Jiacomo.

"He's famous throughout Babina. You're not. You're just the brother of Laurenzo, the great goldsmith."

Jiacomo laughed. "Yes, he's famous," he said. "That's true and I'm proud of him. But I could have been just as famous as him... if I had wanted to be."

"Pah," scoffed Ludovico. "You're just saying that!"

"No, really!" cried Jiacomo. "Laurenzo is a master goldsmith, but I could have been a master thief. Yes, a thief! Someone who knows about these things said I have a great talent for it." He looked at the other customers around him, the familiar faces and the unfamiliar ones. "I could, if I wanted to, steal all the money from your purses," he continued. "I could take the valuables from your homes, the silver from the drawers, the jewels from the cabinets. I could steal anything I wanted, without getting caught. There is no bolt I cannot slide, no lock I cannot open!"

"So why don't you do it?" asked Ludovico.

"Because I'm too honest," replied Jiacomo. "And for that reason I have missed out on a glorious – or notorious – career!"

"You're just boasting!" cried Ludovico.

But Jiacomo would not allow himself to become angry. He took out his lute again and sang:

> *"Oh, I can steal just anything:*
> *gold cup, candelabra, ring.*
> *No bolt or bar can hold me back.*
> *There is no safe I cannot crack.*
> *No fence, no gate and no brick wall*
> *will keep me from my glittering haul.*
> *No soldier and no guard with knife*
> *is any threat to my dear life!*
> *And if it did not bring me grief,*
> *then I would be a master thief."*

Then he paid for his drinks, stood up and said that he was going home.

When he had left the inn and was walking home through the dark streets, someone suddenly tapped him on the shoulder and said: "Good evening." Jiacomo turned around and saw a young man he recognized as one of the guests from the inn. "Oh, good evening," he replied.

"There's something I'd like to ask you," said the man, walking along beside him. "Is what you said just now at the inn true? Are you really a master thief?"

"I *could* have been a master thief," replied Jiacomo.

"Can you prove that? Or were you just bragging?"

"Well, there might have been a little exaggeration involved," said Jiacomo with a smile. "But why do you want to know, if I might ask?"

The young man looked around and said quietly: "I can give you the opportunity to prove that you can steal."

"I've already proved that," said Jiacomo. "And I'm not doing it again."

"I'll pay you well," whispered the young man.

Jiacomo stopped. "Listen," he said, "I've been in prison twice – once for something bad that I *didn't* do, and once for something good that I *did* do. But I don't want to end up in jail for something bad that I did do."

"Oh, but you said yourself that you wouldn't get caught!" said the young man. "Besides, I don't want to ask you to do anything bad. You just need to steal back something that belongs to me!"

"Ah," said Jiacomo, "so you want to put me to the test?"

"No, that's not it either," replied the young man. "I want you to steal something that belongs to me, but that I no longer have in my possession, something that was stolen from me."

"If someone has stolen something from you, then they're a thief, and thieves should be reported to the sheriff. That seems to me like the best way to get your property back."

"But I can't do that!" the man replied. "I shall explain everything to you. But we need to go to a place where I can speak without being overheard."

"Then come to my house," suggested Jiacomo. "My brother and his wife are not there right now, so we can take our time to talk."

Soon they were in Laurenzo's workshop. Jiacomo lit the lamps and took a good look at his new acquaintance. He appeared to be a respectable young man, dressed in fine linen and beautiful velvet.

The man saw the way Jiacomo was looking at him and said: "First let me introduce myself. You might know my name: Dia Porta. Fernando Dia Porta."

Jiacomo had indeed heard that name before. It was the name of an old and illustrious family that had played an important role in the history of Babina. He bowed and said: "And, as you probably know, my name is Jiacomo. Please, sit down and tell me what is on your mind. Would you like a drink?"

Fernando Dia Porta sat down, but refused a drink. Then he said: "I shall tell you everything that needs to be told, and I shall start at the beginning. When you've heard the whole story, perhaps you will be willing to help me. Have you ever heard of Konrad and Katrina?"

"Of course!" said Jiacomo. "The most devoted couple ever to have lived in Babina!"

"They died two centuries ago," said Fernando, "and still their praises are sung by minstrels, and poets write verses about them. You know that after many difficulties they married each other: Konrad Dia Porta and Katrina, his bride. I am their descendant, as I am a Dia Porta from Sfaza. Now what you need to know is that Konrad gave Katrina a ring as a gift, a ring of white gold with a sapphire in it. When they died, their son inherited that ring. The ring has been in our family ever since. When the oldest son of a Dia Porta wanted to marry, his mother gave him the ring to give to his chosen one. It was said that the ring would win him his bride's love.

In any case, the ring has ensured that
every Dia Porta has had a happy marriage, for two centuries now."

"I have heard this story before,"
said Jiacomo. "My brother told it
to me; he knows a lot about such
things. But I can't say that I believe
it. How can an ordinary ring make
someone fall in love?"

"The ring that Konrad gave
to Katrina is no ordinary ring!"
cried Fernando. "It clearly has a
strange and wonderful power. But
listen, my story is not yet over. I
was the only son, and when my
parents died, I inherited not only lots of money, but also
the ring, the ring I would one day give to my chosen one.
I inherited so much money that I thought it would never
run out. But I shall be honest with you and admit that I was
wrong. Within two years, I squandered everything, leaving
me with nothing but my estate, a pile of debts – and the
ring. The people I owed money to made life very difficult
for me, before finally threatening to have me thrown into
jail if I did not pay up immediately. I was desperate and
bitterly regretted my extravagance, but that did not help
me. Where was I supposed to get the money from? Well,
I had a friend – at least I thought he was a friend – and
he was very rich. I went to him and asked for his help. He
was willing to lend me some money, and as a guarantee of
repayment he asked for the ring. He promised, though, to

give it back as soon as I had paid my debt. I agreed to his condition, paid back the money I owed and resolved to live frugally and to work hard, so that I could reclaim the ring as soon as possible. Six months later, I had a stroke of luck. I inherited some money from a distant relative, which made me as wealthy as I had been before. So I went straight to my friend to give him his money with interest and to ask for the ring back. But what do you think he did? He would not take the money and said that he had bought the ring from me! He refused to give it to me! He still has it now, but I can't accuse him of theft. We didn't put our agreement in writing because I trusted him, and so I can't prove to any judge that I never sold the ring, but only left it with him as a guarantee."

"That's a tricky situation," said Jiacomo.

"He's such a viper! And now I have fallen for a lovely lady, Mariana, the daughter of the Lord of Arca, the Lord Chief Justice. But how can I ask for her hand without giving her the ring? The worst of it is that I have heard my former friend also has his eye on her. I am sure he is planning to give her the ring, the white ring with the blue stone, the ring that belongs to me!"

Fernando sighed, looked at Jiacomo and continued: "So now I have told you everything honestly. I know of only one way to get the ring back... and that is to steal it, although it can't really be called stealing, as the ring belongs to me. And that is the task I would like to entrust to you."

"Why don't you do it yourself?" asked Jiacomo.

"I wouldn't know how to," said Fernando Dia Porta. "I've never stolen anything in my entire life. Besides, my treacherous friend is on his guard against me. He doesn't know you, so it will be easy for you to take the ring from him, even if you were not a master thief."

When Jiacomo did not reply, he went on: "Please help me! Give me back what belongs to me, the ring that is priceless to me. You can name your reward."

"If you have told the truth, my lord Dia Porta," said Jiacomo, "then I would be doing a good deed."

"Do you doubt my word?" asked Fernando, a little angrily.

"I will accept the task," said Jiacomo. "I shall get your ring back for you."

"Thank you," said Fernando. "You have made me very happy. How much money do you require?"

"I won't ask for much," replied Jiacomo. "Two hundred ducats."

"Let's make it three hundred," said Fernando.

"Fine," said Jiacomo, "I accept." He stood up and fetched paper, pen and ink. "I'm going to put this in writing," he said, "as I've learnt from your story that it's wise to do so."

"Please do," said Fernando. "But I would ask you one thing: talk to no one about this task, not now and not later."

Jiacomo promised not to. "And there are some things I need to know as well," he continued. "Firstly, the name of your friend and the place where he lives."

"Don't call him my friend!" said Fernando. "But his name is Pidras Pidri. He is a merchant by trade and he lives on the market square." He also gave Jiacomo his own address and added: "And I can tell you that Pidras Pidri has recently paid a lot of visits to the home of the Lord of Arca, whose daughter we both admire. Tomorrow evening, the lord is giving a big party – a masked ball – to which I have received an invitation. I think that Pidras Pidri will also be there, to poison my pleasure."

"Will he be wearing the ring?" asked Jiacomo.

"I wouldn't be surprised!"

"A masked ball," said Jiacomo, "is a fine thing, as the merrymakers will make themselves unrecognizable." He gave a quiet whistle, dipped the pen in the ink and wrote down some words, which he read out to Fernando:

"*I, Fernando Dia Porta, hereby instruct Jiacomo, son of Ferdinand, to steal a ring for me from Pidras Pidri, which belongs to me by right. For carrying out this assignment, I shall pay Jiacomo three hundred ducats.*

"Will you sign this?" asked Jiacomo.

Fernando signed.

Jiacomo promised to bring him the ring within two weeks. Then Fernando said goodbye and left.

Jiacomo folded up the paper and put it in his pocket. "Excellent," he said out loud. "Finally another adventure! I shall steal that ring – and my only objection is that the task is not difficult enough for Jiacomo the master thief."

The next morning, Jiacomo got up early and after breakfast he went into town. He lingered outside an elegant house on the market square and rushed to help when one of the servants came along with a heavy basket full of groceries. Then they had a nice chat by the back door. He did the same at the house of the Lord of Arca, the Lord Chief Justice, where servants were coming and going, busy with the preparations for the party. After that, he paid a visit to two tailors: old

Baptiste, where he and Laurenzo bought their clothes, and the sophisticated Ramon, who made clothes for the upper classes. Then he headed home for lunch.

"Laurenzo," he said to his brother, "I've ordered some clothes, but I don't have enough money to pay for everything. Could you lend me some? You'll get it back in two weeks."

"What do you need new clothes for?" asked Laurenzo, sounding rather surprised.

"I'm going to a party tonight," replied Jiacomo. "So I need to look presentable, don't I?"

"Of course you can borrow some money," said Laurenzo. "What kind of party is it?"

"A masked ball."

"Lovely," said Rosalinda, Laurenzo's wife. "And will there be any nice girls at the ball?"

Jiacomo had not even thought about that. "Maybe," he said. But that was all he would say, and his brother and sister-in-law thought he was acting very mysteriously indeed.

"Maybe he's in love," said Rosalinda, when Jiacomo had left.

The Lord Chief Justice, the Lord of Arca, was giving the party that night to celebrate the birthday of his only daughter, Mariana. The large halls and rooms looked magnificent. They were decorated with flowers, and hundreds of candles were shining in crystal chandeliers. The most beautiful sight, though, was the guests in their luxurious clothes – the men with their wide sleeves, and the women in their dresses with trains. Everyone wore a mask – white, black, green, red, some decorated with beads or precious stones – and the women had jewels around their necks and in their hair.

At the entrance to the largest room, the Lord Chief Justice himself stood welcoming his guests. He was the only one who was carrying his mask in his hand instead of wearing it on his face, but he was the host, so everyone had to be able to tell who he was. He looked very distinguished, dressed simply in a long black cloak trimmed with fur and with a black velvet cap on his grey locks of hair. He was a serious man, who was not fond of extravagant finery.

Beside him stood a blonde woman. Her dress and her mask were silvery white. The Lord of Arca warmly welcomed his guests, although there were many he did not know because of their disguises. Fernando Dia Porta was there, and Pidras Pidri too, but luckily they did not recognize each other.

The musicians started to play, and the first dance began. Fernando and Pidras both thought they knew which masked woman was Lady Mariana and they headed straight for her. Pidras reached her first, but as he was about to bow and ask her for a dance, someone tugged on his jacket.

Angrily, he turned around. It was one of the judge's servants. "Forgive me," the man whispered, "but aren't you Pidras Pidri? My master would like to speak to you for a moment."

Pidras Pidri made his apologies to the young lady and followed the servant to a small side room, where he found the Lord of Arca – who had put on his mask in the meantime – waiting for him.

"You wanted to speak to me, my noble lord?" asked Pidras Pidri.

The judge ordered his servant to leave, closed the door and then said quietly: "Ah, Pidri, is it true that you wear a precious ring on your finger?"

Pidras Pidri looked at his gloved hands and replied that it was indeed true.

"It would take a long time if I were to tell you the whole story," said the Lord of Arca, "but I have heard that there are people who would like to steal your ring, and I fear that you are not safe from them even here in my house."

Pidras Pidri was a little startled. "I was afraid something like this might happen!" he said. "But no one will steal my ring. It is my property and I always guard it well."

"And yet I am concerned," said the Lord of Arca. "I should find it most regrettable if you were to be robbed in my house. I don't need to tell you that I've taken every precaution. Nevertheless, to be on the safe side, I would ask you to put the ring in my safe. At the end of the evening, you can take it back out, and until then you will be free to celebrate my daughter's birthday without any nagging worries."

"That's very kind of you," said Pidras Pidri.

"It's my duty as your host," said the Lord Chief Justice. "But I would add that I have a particular interest in ensuring you do not encounter any unpleasantness. You are, after all, a good friend of mine – and even more so of my daughter! And perhaps you will become more than a friend one day – who knows?"

Pidras Pidri smiled, both delighted and flattered. "I thank you," he said, "and I accept your generous offer. You see, this ring is very dear to me!"

"And you are dear to me," said the Lord of Arca. "So give me your ring, and I will put it in my safe at once."

Pidras Pidri gave him the ring, and the Lord Chief Justice opened an iron safe in the corner of the room, placed the ring inside and closed it again.

"Would you like to keep the key?" he asked. "Or shall I?"

"Please keep it for me, my noble lord," said Pidras Pidri. "And let me thank you once again."

"Now return to the dance," said the Lord Chief Justice. "My daughter is in the ballroom." He walked his guest to the door and wished him an enjoyable evening.

No sooner had Pidras disappeared than the Lord of Arca changed completely. He hurried to the safe, opened it, took out the ring and slid it onto his little finger. Then he took off his long black cloak, removed his cap and mask and his grey locks of hair. He was no longer the Lord of Arca, but Jiacomo, the master thief! The young man put the clothes and the wig in the safe, closed it again and left the key in the lock. *Good*, he thought with satisfaction, *that was easy!*

The only danger was that the judge himself might have come in, but luckily he didn't. And as for Pidras Pidri, he really is a very stupid man!

He walked to the mirror and looked at himself in the new clothes that he had put on beneath the black cloak. "You look most presentable," he said to his reflection. "I think you can stay at the party for a while." He took out a second mask and put it on, pulled on a pair of gloves and cheerfully headed for the ballroom.

And there, in the ballroom, is where he saw her.

The musicians were playing and the merrymakers were dancing. Elegantly, they spun around one another, performing the most complicated steps with the greatest of ease. Jiacomo stood watching for a while. Everyone's clothes were colourful, but there was one young lady who was dressed entirely in silvery white, and he could not keep his eyes off her. She was the most elegant of all and her hair was the colour of pale gold.

Oh, he thought, *I wish she would take off her mask, so that I could see her face.*

She danced with Fernando Dia Porta and then with Pidras Pidri, and he envied them both. Then the music stopped for a moment and, fluttering her fan, she walked in his direction. Pidras Pidri and Fernando both followed her and bowed to her as soon as the music began again. But Jiacomo beat them to it! He had already taken the young lady by the hand and soon they were dancing together – and it was wonderful!

Jiacomo looked into her eyes, which sparkled darkly behind her mask, and he thought: *I can see so little of her face, and yet she has made more of an impression on me than anyone ever before.* He talked to her and found that he had never heard such a sweet voice. He asked what her name was, but she would not say, as all names must remain unknown at a masked ball.

Then – too soon! – the dance was over.

Jiacomo had only wanted to stay at the party for a short while, but now he had changed his mind. He stayed there, and no one suspected that he had not been invited and that he had just stolen a precious ring from one of the guests. He danced one more time with the young stranger and then he asked her into the garden, which was illuminated by lanterns in the trees and the moon in the sky.

"Would you grant me a request, my lady?" he asked. "And then I shall tell you a secret."

"Do you think I'm curious about your secrets?" she asked.

"Maybe," replied Jiacomo, "if I tell you that the secret could be dangerous for me."

The lady laughed.

"Please," Jiacomo continued, "would you take off your mask? Just for a moment?"

"Why?"

"I would so like to see your face," he replied. "I want to know if you look as you do in my dreams."

"Your dreams?" she said. "No, don't ask me to do that. You could be disappointed."

"That's impossible," said Jiacomo. "You might look different, but you could not disappoint me."

"Well, here goes then," said the young lady, laughing as she took off her mask. "Do I look different?" she asked a little shyly, when Jiacomo said nothing.

"I don't remember," he said. "Now that I've seen you, all of my earlier notions have disappeared."

"If you keep staring, you'll go blind," said the lady after a while, smiling as she put her mask back on. "Now, tell me, what is the secret that you had for me in return?"

"I thought you weren't curious," said Jiacomo, "but fine, here it is. I am an uninvited guest – that is my secret. Now you can tell the host and have me thrown out if you like. I put my fate in your hands!"

"Oh!" said the lady. "So why did you come here? Who are you? Let me see your face too!"

Jiacomo, in turn, took off his mask and said: "I no longer remember why I came here! All I know is that I am in love."

The lady did not reply at first. Then she said: "I have never met you before."

"And I have never met you," said Jiacomo.

"Who are you?" she asked.

"You told me yourself that all names at a masked ball must remain secret. But I shall tell you mine... if you tell me yours."

"Wait until midnight," said the lady. "Then everyone has to take off their masks and reveal their identities."

"I'm afraid I cannot stay that long," said Jiacomo with a sigh, as he put his mask back on. "So will you dance with me one more time, my sweet lady?"

They returned to the ballroom and danced together again. Then the young lady danced with a few other young people while Jiacomo stood in a quiet corner, watching her. When one of the servants walked past, he stopped him and said quietly: "Have pity on a troubled heart. Who is the young lady in white with the golden hair?"

The servant gave Jiacomo a sympathetic look and replied: "Don't you know? She is Mariana, the daughter of my master, the Lord Chief Justice."

Lady Mariana! thought Jiacomo. *Mariana! Oh, why did I stay at this party? Lady Mariana, the daughter of the Lord of Arca, for whose hand in marriage noblemen and wealthy merchants are competing. Whatever was I thinking to fall in love with her? I'm going home. I must be away before twelve.*

He went back to the small side room, took the bundle of clothes from the safe and disappeared in the same way he had come: through the garden and over the wall.

"How was the party?" asked Laurenzo the next morning.

"Oh, fine," replied Jiacomo. "Very nice."

"You look a bit pale," said Rosalinda. "It must have been a late night."

Jiacomo sighed. "I didn't sleep well," he said.

"That's not like you," said Laurenzo. "Where was this party? And who was the host?"

"The Lord of Arca."

"The Lord Chief Justice? He invited you, did he?" asked Laurenzo with surprise.

"No," said Jiacomo. "I just went. There's no way such a proud and distinguished gentleman would invite me to his party."

"He's very pleasant," said Laurenzo. "Not at all proud."

"So you know him?" cried Jiacomo. Now it was his turn to be surprised.

"He's bought various things from me. In fact, I'm working on a silver belt for his daughter right now."

"No! Really?" cried Jiacomo. "Whoever would have thought it? Do you know his daughter?"

Laurenzo shook his head. "No," he said, "I've never met her." He looked enquiringly at his brother, but did not ask any questions.

A little later, Jiacomo followed him to his workshop.

"Laurenzo," he said, "when will Mariana's belt be ready? I mean, the belt for the Lady of Arca."

Laurenzo smiled. "In a couple of hours, if I start work on it now," he replied.

"And when it's ready, are you going to deliver it yourself?"

"I usually do with such a valuable piece."

"Oh, Laurenzo, may I take the belt in your place?"

Laurenzo looked at his brother and smiled again. "Come on!" he said. "Out with it."

371

"I'm in love," said Jiacomo. "In love with Mariana! But she's a noble young lady, and her father will never invite me into his home. I must see her again! Let me take the belt in your place. No one will notice."

"And do you intend to make Mariana think that you are me?"

"No, Mariana will know that I am Jiacomo. Laurenzo, you have to say yes!"

"I can't refuse you," said Laurenzo. "Just do it – and don't disgrace me!"

"Thank you," said the delighted Jiacomo. "And Laurenzo, will you finish the belt quickly? Start it right away. Will you do it before you do anything else?"

"I shall hurry," promised Laurenzo.

That afternoon, the Lord of Arca received a visit from Master Laurenzo, the goldsmith. At least he thought it was the goldsmith. He had met him only a few times, but even if he had known him well, he would not have noticed that anything was amiss. They said in Bainu that there was only one person who could tell the twin brothers apart, and that was Laurenzo's wife, Rosalinda.

The Lord Chief Justice greeted the supposed goldsmith very warmly. "I am sorry that I had to keep you waiting for a moment," he said. "But the sheriff was with me. Something unpleasant occurred last night. A precious piece of jewellery was stolen from one of my guests."

"Oh dear," said Jiacomo, "that's bad news."

"And in a particularly cunning way too," said the Lord Chief Justice. "But I won't bore you with that. You've come to bring the belt, haven't you?"

Jiacomo nodded, opened the box he was carrying and showed him the silver belt. The Lord of Arca was full of admiration for the piece.

"Magnificent!" he said. "I shall give my daughter this belt when she marries."

"Is your daughter going to marry?" asked Jiacomo, his heart pounding away.

"Well, it will happen one day," said the Lord Chief Justice. "I don't want to rush her, but I don't think it will be much longer now. She has plenty of suitors to choose from."

"My noble lord," said Jiacomo, "I am glad you like this belt. However, I'm not certain it will fit your daughter. It might need a link adding or removing. But I imagine you don't want the young lady to find out about the gift, eh?"

"Oh, she already knows about it," said the Lord of Arca. "I shall send someone to fetch her. Then you can see if the belt fits."

That was the answer Jiacomo had been hoping for. Now he would see Mariana again!

Soon she entered the room. She looked a little startled to see him, but she said nothing.

"Mariana," said her father, "this is Master Laurenzo, the goldsmith. He would like to know if the silver chain belt he has made for you fits properly."

Jiacomo bowed deeply to Mariana. She blushed and smiled at him.

"Greetings, Master Laurenzo," she said, "you have a name of great renown." She put on the belt, and it was a perfect fit.

"Don't thank me yet," said the Lord of Arca. "You will not receive it from me until you marry."

Mariana took off the belt. "Then I must marry soon," she said with a smile. "Even if it is only to own this beautiful belt."

"Do you know what would be even more beautiful?" said Jiacomo. "If you had a bracelet to match in the same style. And maybe a necklace and a pair of earrings."

Mariana smiled and looked at her father.

"Hmm," he said. "That would indeed be most fine."

A servant came in and told his master that the sheriff wanted to ask him something else. "Excuse me for a moment," said the Lord Chief Justice and he left the room.

Jiacomo looked at Mariana. "So we meet again, my lady," he said. "And now I know your name too."

"And I yours," she said. "Why did you leave yesterday evening? I didn't see you at midnight."

"I was afraid that it would come out that I was an uninvited guest," replied Jiacomo. "I feared your father would be angry."

"Father was very angry, but that was later and for another reason. I'm glad that you are Laurenzo the goldsmith!"

"Why, Lady Mariana?"

"I was afraid for a moment that you had something to do with the theft. Did you know that something was stolen yesterday evening?"

"Your father told me," said Jiacomo. "So you suspect me?"

"No, I didn't really believe you had done it, but I had to admit to myself that it was possible. Please forgive me, Master Laurenzo! Now I can only laugh at my fear. A goldsmith would never steal a ring. He can make rings himself, as many as he wants!"

"Don't say that," said Jiacomo, smiling. "A goldsmith might

in fact be very interested in obtaining a ring, if it were old and special. But I can assure you that Master Laurenzo would never steal anything! And I would never take the property of another man."

"I believe you," said Mariana. "And I promise that you will receive an invitation next time we have a party."

"I thank you, my sweet lady," said Jiacomo. He wanted to say something else but he held his tongue because the Lord of Arca returned.

"Master Laurenzo," he said, "you must make a matching bracelet too, and maybe something else. I shall have a think about it."

Jiacomo bowed. "It would be my great pleasure to make more jewellery for your daughter," he said.

But it was, of course, Laurenzo who had to make it! Jiacomo went to his workshop and said: "Do it quickly, Laurenzo! So that I can take the bracelet to her. And then maybe a necklace and a ring..."

"Stop it!" cried Laurenzo. "Don't you think I have enough work to do?"

"But this is a large and important commission," said Jiacomo. "The Lord of Arca is a powerful man."

"And his daughter is charming and beautiful," added Laurenzo. "Did you speak to her?"

"Yes," said Jiacomo. His face clouded over a little. It had not gone entirely as he had hoped. Mariana still did not know that he was Jiacomo, instead of Laurenzo the goldsmith. He had to tell her. But what would she think? Would she suspect him of the theft again?

"Oh yes," he said out loud. "I need to take the ring to Fernando too."

"What are you talking about?" asked Laurenzo.

"Oh," said Jiacomo, "I've been given a job to do as well. But I promised not to talk about it, so I can't tell you anything."

That evening he went to his room, took out the ring and looked at it. Although he didn't believe in the power of the ring, he still didn't like the thought of Fernando giving it to Mariana.

He put the ring away, picked up his lute and went outside. Then he wandered around the town until he somehow found himself outside the grand house where Mariana lived. In the blink of an eye, he had climbed up onto the wall that surrounded the garden. He looked at the illuminated windows. One of the windows opened and, to his joy, he saw Mariana leaning out. Strumming his lute, he sang:

> "If I were a thief, I would steal for you, Mariana!
> If I were a star, I would sparkle for you, Mariana!
> If I were the sun, I would shine for you, Mariana!
> If I were a poet, I would rhyme for you, Mariana!"

"Who's there?" called Mariana.

"You can have three guesses, Mariana," said Jiacomo. "Am I Fernando Dia Porta?"

"Fernando? No!"

"Am I Pidras Pidri?"

"Oh no," said Mariana.

Jiacomo jumped down from the wall, walked through the garden and stopped under her window.

"So who are you going to marry, Mariana, Fernando Dia Porta or Pidras Pidri?"

Mariana laughed. "What an impertinent question," she said. "Why would I marry either of them? Neither has asked me."

"But if they were to ask you, Mariana, which one would you say yes to?"

"I've never thought about it," replied Mariana. "And now I shall guess for the third time. You are Laurenzo."

"Wrong three times!" said Jiacomo. "I'm not Laurenzo!"

"But I can see you," said Mariana. "I can see you very clearly. You are Laurenzo!"

Then a voice called from inside: "Lady Mariana!"

"I have to go," said Mariana. "Farewell, Laurenzo!"

A white flower fell at Jiacomo's feet, but the young lady herself had disappeared. Jiacomo picked up the flower and went home, more in love than ever. But he still had not told her who he was.

For the next two days, Laurenzo felt rather besieged. His brother kept hanging around the workshop and encouraging him to get on with the bracelet for Mariana as quickly as possible.

And when Jiacomo was not in the workshop, he was swooning about and trying to compose love poems.

When the bracelet was finally ready, Jiacomo cheerfully set off with it to the house of the Lord Chief Justice. He saw Mariana again, but her father stayed with them the entire time, so he had no opportunity to tell her what was on his mind. He did not dare to tell the Lord Chief Justice himself who he actually was, although he realized he would have to do so at some point. Fortunately, he – or rather, Laurenzo – had received a third order: a pair of earrings for Mariana.

That same evening, he was sitting up on the wall again with his lute and waiting to see if Mariana would appear.

Mariana was in her chamber, but she was not alone. A friend was visiting her. At a certain point, the two young ladies heard soft music. Jiacomo had become impatient and he was strumming his lute.

"Listen!" said the friend. "What's that?"

Mariana just blushed and said nothing.

"An admirer," said the friend. "Who is it, Fernando Dia Porta or Pidras Pidri?"

"No! Neither of them!" replied Mariana.

"So who is it then?" asked the friend, and she kept on asking until Mariana said: "It's Laurenzo the goldsmith."

Her friend gasped and cried out: "Laurenzo the goldsmith? Oh, that's not right! He recently married Rosalinda, the daughter of Lord di Dididi!"

Jiacomo saw Mariana appear at the window and, delighted, he headed over there. But when he looked up, something happened that he was not expecting. The lady emptied a jug of water over his head and then slammed the window shut. Deeply dismayed, Jiacomo went home.

When Laurenzo had finished the earrings, Jiacomo delivered them. The Lord Chief Justice praised them highly and ordered a necklace, but Jiacomo did not get to see his daughter.

2 THE SECOND TASK

"This ring I shall give to the lady I love."

TITO DRASTA: 'The Florentine Ring'

"Come out with us," said Laurenzo the next evening. "They're performing a play on the market square."

But Jiacomo gloomily shook his head and said that he was not in the mood. No matter what Laurenzo and Rosalinda said, he would not change his mind and so he stayed alone at home with his sad thoughts of Mariana. He could not spend too long dwelling on those thoughts, however, as there came a knock at the door. He opened it to find a young man standing on the doorstep. At first he did not know who it was, but when the man began to speak, he recognized him. It was Pidras Pidri!

"Good evening," the man said. "This is the house of Laurenzo the goldsmith, isn't it?"

"Yes, sir," replied Jiacomo, "but my brother is not at home."

"Ah, then you must be Jiacomo. You're the one I want to talk to. May I come in?"

"Of course," said Jiacomo. He let the visitor in, wondering why the man wanted to speak to him.

"You don't know me," said the man with a bow, "but my name is Pidras Pidri. I shall tell you why I have come to visit you. A few weeks ago, I was staying at an inn on the plain, a place called the Two Brothers. The innkeeper is apparently a good friend of yours."

"Jannos!" said Jiacomo. "How is he?"

"He sent his best wishes," said Pidras Pidri. "He told me how the inn came by its name. It's named after you and your brother, isn't it? He also told me that your brother is a skilful goldsmith and that you are... a skilful thief!"

"What—" began Jiacomo.

"Oh, I know you never steal," said Pidras Pidri, interrupting him. "But you could be a skilful thief if you wanted to. Is that better?"

"Yes, that's better," said Jiacomo.

"I am interested in your talents," Pidras Pidri continued. "I would like to make use of them."

"Oh, no," said Jiacomo with a serious face. "I don't want to steal."

"Please, let me finish. If I take something that belongs to me, that's not theft, is it?"

Jiacomo stared at his visitor with wide eyes. "No," he said slowly, "it's not."

"I am in a difficult situation," said Pidras Pidri. "May I share it with you?"

"Of course," said Jiacomo. "Please sit down. Would you like a drink?"

"Yes, please," said Pidras Pidri. And when Jiacomo had poured two cups of wine, he leant back in his chair and began: "I used to have a friend, who is my friend no longer. Fernando Dia Porta is his name. You may have heard of him – he comes from an illustrious family. Fernando, however, has dishonoured his family name. He is a spendthrift and a good-for-nothing. One day, he found himself in financial difficulties and he came to me for help. The people he owed money to meant to throw him into jail if he didn't immediately pay back all the money he owed. He had just one item left of his former riches, an old ring, which he offered to sell to me. I bought that ring to help him out – and I paid far more than its value too. Some time later, Fernando regained his former wealth and regretted that he had sold his ring. He came to me again, and said he wanted it back. But I had found a purpose for the ring in the meantime and so I refused to sell it back to him. Which was my right, was it not?"

"Certainly," said Jiacomo. "That was your right."

"But Fernando had a different opinion about it. He became furious and even had the nerve to say I had stolen the ring from him! We argued and have not spoken since then."

Pidras Pidri emptied his cup and said: "You might not understand why I'm telling you all of this, but it will soon become clear."

I think it's already clear, thought Jiacomo, but he said nothing.

"I knew Fernando would not take no for an answer," continued Pidras Pidri. "He would do whatever it took to get back the ring that he had forfeited through his own fault. And indeed, now he's succeeded! Not long ago, the ring was stolen from me in a most cunning manner. I have no proof, but I am convinced that Fernando has the ring once again!"

"But," said Jiacomo, "is this not a matter for the sheriff? Make a complaint against Fernando and get your property back that way."

Pidras Pidri sighed. "That's the problem," he said. "I have no proof and I can't just accuse a nobleman like Fernando Dia Porta. I can't even prove that I bought the ring from him in the first place, as I was foolish enough not to have it put in writing. I trusted Fernando. I thought he was my friend!"

"Yes, that does indeed make it tricky," said Jiacomo. He was having difficulty keeping a straight face. "But what do you think I can do to help?" he asked.

"Steal back the ring for me from Fernando Dia Porta," replied Pidras Pidri. "You already said it: it's not theft, as the ring is my property."

"Why don't you take it yourself?" asked Jiacomo.

"Because Fernando is on his guard against me! And I wouldn't know where to start. Master Jiacomo, do this for me! I will, of course, pay you for your services."

"Hmm," said Jiacomo. "Why are you so attached to this ring? There are plenty of rings in the world! You could have another one made. My brother is a master at making such things."

"There's a story attached to this ring. They say it was a gift from Konrad to his beloved Katrina. And it's said that when a man gives this ring to a woman, she will fall in love with him."

"Do you believe it?" asked Jiacomo.

"No... Yes..." said Pidras Pidri. "Well, I believe some of it. That's why I would like to have my ring back. To present as a gift to a young lady!"

"I see," said Jiacomo and he was silent for a while. Then he stood up and said solemnly: "Pidras Pidri, I will accept this task! For three hundred ducats, I will steal the ring from Fernando Dia Porta and give it to you."

Pidras Pidri stood up too and said: "My thanks, Master Jiacomo!"

"But permit me to write this down," Jiacomo continued. "You have seen for yourself that such things should not be neglected."

"You are right," said Pidras. "On one condition: tell no one about this job – or you will regret it."

"Yes, it will remain a secret," said Jiacomo. He took a piece of paper and wrote: *I, Pidras Pidri, hereby instruct Jiacomo, son of Ferdinand, to steal a ring for me from Fernando Dia Porta, which belongs to me by right. For carrying out this assignment, I shall pay Jiacomo three hundred ducats.*

He asked Pidras Pidri to sign this document and then said: "Just one more thing, sir. What does this wondrous ring look like?"

"It's made of white gold," replied Pidras Pidri, "with a blue stone in it, a sapphire."

"You will have it back within two weeks," promised Jiacomo with a bow.

When Pidras Pidri had left, Jiacomo sat down and burst out laughing. "This is a fine old muddle," he said to himself. "Now I have the ring, but I don't know which one it belongs to. How can I find out who told the truth?" Then he sighed. *Should I just give the ring to Mariana myself?* he thought. *Then perhaps she'll want to see me again.*

The next morning, Jiacomo went to Laurenzo in his workshop. "Laurenzo," he asked, "will you make something for me?"

"Again?" cried Laurenzo. "I'm working on a necklace for Lady Mariana, and it's nowhere near finished."

"Oh, this is something completely different," said Jiacomo. "Take a look." And he placed an object before Laurenzo.

"It's a beautiful ring," said Laurenzo. "The setting of the stone is old-fashioned – it must have been made more than a hundred years ago."

"Would you be able to make a copy of it?" asked Jiacomo. "So that no one can tell the difference?"

Laurenzo examined the ring from all sides. "I could," he said finally. "But it will be expensive. I need to find a sapphire of the same size, and white gold isn't cheap."

"Couldn't you use silver instead of white gold?" asked Jiacomo. "And a piece of blue glass that looks like a sapphire? It can't cost more than three hundred ducats."

"How did you get this ring?" asked Laurenzo." And why do you want me to copy it? I don't really like doing this kind of work, and I don't like fake stones."

"Neither do I," said Jiacomo. "But I'd still like you to do it. And it needs to be ready soon."

"Then tell me why!" cried Laurenzo. "You never used to have secrets from me, Jiacomo!"

"No," said Jiacomo. "I have promised not to speak about it, otherwise I swear I'd tell you. It's a really strange story. Will you do it, Laurenzo? I'll pay you three hundred ducats."

"Go on then," said Laurenzo, looking at the ring again.

"And no one will be able to tell the difference?"

"An expert would obviously be able to see it."

"But an ordinary person like me?"

"They wouldn't notice," said Laurenzo with a smile. "Unless they already knew."

"Good," said Jiacomo. "Then copy this ring. And don't tell a soul about it, Laurenzo!"

"What about the necklace for Lady Mariana?"

"That can wait," replied Jiacomo.

Two days later, Laurenzo had finished the copy of the ring. Jiacomo greatly admired his skill and, after some thought, he said: "Would you make me another one?"

"Another one?" exclaimed Laurenzo. "What do you intend to do with all these rings?"

"To give them to some of my acquaintances," replied Jiacomo. "I'm sorry I can't tell you more."

"I'm only doing it because it's you," said Laurenzo. "I wouldn't take on a job like this for anyone else."

"Thank you," said Jiacomo. "Can you do it quickly, Laurenzo?" And he thought: *Until I discover the true owner of the ring – Fernando Dia Porta or Pidras Pidri – I shall keep it safe. And I will find out whose it is, or I will not have carried out my tasks properly.*

A couple of days after that, Laurenzo was sitting in his workshop, putting the finishing touches to the second copy of the ring. Then there was a knock at the door. One of the apprentices went to answer it.

It was Mariana, with an elderly lady companion.

"Good morning," Mariana said in a haughty tone. "May I speak to Master Laurenzo, the goldsmith?"

The apprentice let her in, while her companion stayed outside. Laurenzo rose to greet the noble young lady. He did not know that she was Mariana; he only knew her father, the Lord of Arca.

"Master Laurenzo," said Mariana, "at my father's request, you have made for me a belt, a bracelet and a pair of earrings."

Ah, thought Laurenzo, *she must be Mariana.*

"That's right, my lady," he said. "I'm working on the necklace now, but it's not finished yet."

"I have come here," continued Mariana, "to tell you that you do not need to complete the necklace and that you do not have to make anything else for me in future. I have no need for your work."

Laurenzo looked at her, rather surprised. *She's angry,* he thought. *Wait a moment, does she think that I'm Jiacomo, or that Jiacomo is me?* And he said: "As you wish, my lady. I must say, though, that I am sorry to hear it. Do you not like my work?"

"I find no fault in your work," replied Mariana in a chilly tone. "But I do in your behaviour, Master Laurenzo."

She was about to leave, but Laurenzo called out: "Lady Mariana, I think there's been some kind of misunderstanding!"

Mariana looked even haughtier. "I do not believe so," she said. "Good day, Master Laurenzo. And give my good wishes to your *wife!*"

Ha! thought Laurenzo. *Now I understand!* And he said: "Truly, my lady, I am not who you think I am. Come with me, and I shall introduce you to my wife and my brother, whom you know better than me."

"Your brother?" said Mariana in surprise. "Most definitely not! I have no wish to meet your family. Let me go, or I will become angry."

"But you are already angry," said Laurenzo. "I beg you, my lady, do not leave! I assure you that you already know my brother." He raised his voice. "Jiacomo!" he called. "Come here!" Then he told his apprentices to leave the workshop.

Mariana stood in the doorway, wondering whether to leave or not. Then Jiacomo came in. As soon as he saw her, he blushed. Mariana looked in surprise at one brother and then the other.

"This is my twin brother, Jiacomo," said Laurenzo. "He went in my place to deliver the jewellery that your father had ordered. But I did not think he would also take my name. I should also add that this is the first time you and I have met, my lady. If you are angry, then please be angry with Jiacomo. I'm sure he deserves it."

Jiacomo and Mariana were staring at each other, but the lady no longer appeared to be quite so angry.

"Forgive me, Mariana," Jiacomo said finally. "I kept wanting to tell you that I am not Master Laurenzo, but something always got in the way, and I didn't quite dare." Then he asked her why she was angry.

Now Mariana blushed. She lowered her eyes and did not reply.

"I'm not sure," said Laurenzo after a moment of silence. "But I think she was angry with me – although it was actually you – and with my... wife?"

"Oh!" cried Jiacomo in delight. "So you *do* love me, Mariana? You know that I love you, don't you? So, so much! Yes, yes, Mariana! I love you! Do you love me too?"

Mariana said slowly: "I don't know. I don't know, Jiacomo."

"So do you love another man, Mariana?"

"No," the lady replied. "That's not it."

"Oh, Mariana, if I were a nobleman, like Fernando Dia Porta, or a wealthy merchant, like Pidras Pidri, I would go to your father and ask for your hand in marriage. And what would you say, Mariana?"

Mariana smiled. "If I loved you," she said, "it would not matter to me if you were rich or poor, famous or unknown. But I have known you for such a short time, Jiacomo, and I was mistaken too, confusing you and your brother."

"That was my fault," said Jiacomo. "You see, I was so eager to get to know you better, and posing as my brother gained me access to your house."

Looking around, he noticed that Laurenzo had silently slipped out of the room. He saw the rings on the table; the ring of Konrad and Katrina and the copies that Laurenzo had made. He picked them up and studied them carefully. Then he put the fake rings back down and showed Mariana the real one.

"Mariana," he said, "I love you and would do anything to win your love. Here, take this ring and wear it to show that you are no longer angry with me."

"What a beautiful ring," said Mariana. "How did you get it? Is it yours? But I can't accept it. It's far too precious a gift."

"Wear it for a while," Jiacomo persisted. "For a day, a week. This ring doesn't actually belong to me. I stole it."

Mariana laughed.

"You see, now you're laughing," said Jiacomo. "You don't believe me. I stole it, I tell you, but I am no thief – on my word of honour! Listen, I am not giving you this ring as a gift, and you are not accepting it as one. We are just pretending. You are keeping it safe for me, but you must act as if you received it from me as a gift. It is very old and there is a story attached to it that I can't tell you yet. Take the ring, Mariana, and wear it as a reminder of my love!"

Mariana shook her head. "You are talking so strangely," she said, "that I don't understand a thing. But fine, I shall do as you ask." She took the ring and slid it onto her finger. "I have to leave now though," she continued. "My companion will be wondering where I've got to."

She left, but before she stepped through the doorway, she looked back and said: "Tell your brother that he should finish that necklace after all."

Later, Jiacomo walked up and down the workshop, playing his lute and singing:

> *"Konrad had a ring.*
> *A wondrous ring, a fine old thing!*
> *And what did he do with that ring?*
> *He gave it to Katrina!*

Oh, it was a wondrous ring,
a ring of white and blue,
he gave it to Katrina,
his sweetheart, oh so true.
Oh, hear now what I say
of the blue and white gold ring.
A wondrous ring,
a fine old thing,
and if you were wondering,
Konrad gave it to Katrina."

The apprentices put down their work and started clapping along. But Laurenzo said: "You still have a lot of explaining to do, Jiacomo! And if not to me, then to the Lord of Arca."

Jiacomo stopped singing and replied: "You're right, Laurenzo. Sadly some things are hard to explain." He sighed. *I must tell him that I am not Master Laurenzo,* he thought. *But I would rather not tell the Lord Chief Justice that I attended his party as an uninvited guest. Mariana knows, and I would also dare to tell her why I was there. But Fernando and Pidras won't let me. And they're both waiting impatiently for their ring! Which one of the two was telling the truth?*

Turning back to Laurenzo, he said: "Will you give me the two imitation rings? I have an errand to run. I'll pay you soon. Oh, Laurenzo, do you think I have a chance with Mariana? If only I were a famous goldsmith, like you, or if I knew another trade, apart from stealing."

"You have stopped stealing, haven't you, Jiacomo?" said Laurenzo. "You could do a great deal better if you wanted to, as you have often proved."

"Just let me do what I can for now," said Jiacomo. "Which is to put these rings in boxes and take them to the gentlemen who ordered them."

Jiacomo took one ring to Fernando Dia Porta and one to Pidras Pidri. They were both delighted and each gave him the promised three hundred ducats, which Jiacomo later paid to Laurenzo.

Fernando and Pidras suspected nothing of the trick that had been played on them. And they both made the same decision. They would go straight to the Lord of Arca, ask him for his daughter's hand in marriage and offer her the ring.

And it just so happened that they both arrived at the door of the Lord of Arca at the same time. They were not pleased to see each other there, and each glared at the other.

"I wish to speak to the Lord Chief Justice," said Pidras Pidri to the servant who opened the door, "about a most important matter."

"I also wish to speak to the Lord of Arca," said Fernando. "At once, if possible. It is about a question of the greatest importance."

"That may well be, sir," said Pidras to Fernando, "but I was here first."

"You are lying, sir," snapped Fernando. "You were not first. We arrived at the same time. And as my visit is more important, I want to go in first."

Eventually they went in together and the servant allowed them both to see the Lord Chief Justice at the same time. But when he had greeted them and asked what they wanted, the difficulties began all over again.

"I wish to ask you a most important question," said Pidras Pidri. "Might I speak to you alone?"

"I too have something important to say," said Fernando Dia Porta. "And I would ask you to listen to me first, in private, if you please."

"Really!" said Pidras. "I was here first and I am not thinking of leaving until you have heard my request."

"And I tell you I'm not going until I have presented my request to the Lord of Arca!"

They glared furiously at each other and would have said much more if the Lord Chief Justice had not intervened. "Please don't argue, gentlemen," he said calmly. "If neither of you is prepared to leave and neither will let the other speak first, then you must both speak at the same time. And I shall see if I can understand what you say."

"I wish to ask you for the hand of your daughter, Mariana," the two young men said as one. Then they glared furiously at each other again before turning hopefully to the Lord of Arca.

He stroked his chin and answered thoughtfully: "I know both of you. You are both young and healthy, and are what people refer to as a 'good match'. In addition, I have not heard anything bad about either of you. In short, I would be prepared to accept either of you as my son-in-law and I give no preference. So it seems that it would be better to ask your question of my daughter herself. I have told her that she may make her own choice, and I shall accept the man she chooses."

So Fernando and Pidras went to Mariana, still together, as neither would allow the other to go first.

The young lady welcomed them warmly and asked them what the purpose of their visit was.

"Fair maiden..." began Fernando.

"Beautiful Mariana..." began Pidras.

Then they both said at the same moment: "Will you marry me?"

Mariana looked at one, then the other, and paused before answering. The two men began to declare their love for her, but they kept interrupting each other until they finally fell silent, their faces red.

Then Mariana said: "Fernando Dia Porta and Pidras Pidri, I feel truly honoured by your proposals of marriage. I have a very high opinion of both of you, and I am therefore sorry that I cannot return your love. So I must sadly decline."

"Oh, Lady Mariana!" cried Pidras Pidri. "Does my love not kindle the same in you? I adore you. I give you my word!"

"Not as much as I adore you!" cried Fernando. "Fair maiden, I cannot force you to love me and I shall leave if you order me to, but please accept this gift from me. Whether you wish to marry me or not, take what I am giving you as proof of my sincere love!" And he gave Mariana the parcel he was holding.

"Accept my gift too, Lady Mariana," said Pidras Pidri. "Whether you love me or not, take it as proof of my love, which is beyond words." And he too gave Mariana a parcel.

"Fernando and Pidras," said the lady, "I thank you for your kindness, but I cannot accept your gifts."

"Please!" cried Pidras. "Just open it!"

"Please!" begged Fernando. "Try it on! Just for a moment! You have already turned me down. Do not make me even more miserable."

So Mariana kept the parcels and carefully began to open the first of the two. Her admirers watched anxiously.

"Oh, a ring!" cried Mariana. Her surprise was understandable, as she saw at once that the ring was the double of the one she had received from Jiacomo and which she was now wearing on a chain around her neck.

"You must put this ring on your finger," said Fernando, "and wear it as a reminder of me."

"Excuse me!" said Pidras. "That ring is a gift from me, Lady Mariana! Wear it and—"

"Don't listen to him!" Fernando interrupted. "That was my parcel and it's my ring! My gift, Lady Mariana!"

"No, it's not!" shouted Pidras. "You're mistaken! This is my ring. I know my own gift, don't I?"

"Wait a moment," said Mariana. "First let me open the other parcel."

When the second ring appeared, all three of them stared in amazement.

"They are exactly the same!" cried Mariana. She did not mention the ring she was wearing on the chain around her neck.

Her two admirers looked at the rings and then at each other and then back at the rings.

"How did you...?" said Fernando to Pidras.

"Where did you...?" said Pidras to Fernando.

They fell silent, as they were speechless.

Then Fernando spoke up. "My ring is the ring of Konrad and Katrina," he said.

"No, that's *mine*!"

"You stole my ring!"

"Liar! You stole mine!"

"Gentlemen," said Mariana, "please don't argue!"

The two young men each took a ring and looked closely at it. Then they looked at each other.

"This ring is fake!" cried Fernando.

"I have been deceived!" roared Pidras.

"Did you...?" began one.

"So you did too?" asked the other.

"Jiacomo!" whispered Fernando.

"Jiacomo!" cried Pidras.

"Yes, Jiacomo," said Fernando. "He has deceived me!"

"He has deceived us both! The villain!"

"I'm going to see him!"

"I'm coming too!"

"Yes, we'll go together!"

For a moment, the two men forgot that they were enemies. They quickly muttered their apologies to Mariana, said goodbye to her and hurried away, with the rings in their hands.

Still surprised, Mariana watched them go. Then she called a servant and said: "Quick! Run to the house of Laurenzo the goldsmith and ask his brother, Jiacomo, to come and see me at once."

Fernando Dia Porta and Pidras Pidri stormed into Laurenzo's workshop. The goldsmith had just told his apprentices that their work was over for the day and that they could tidy up. The two men naturally thought he was Jiacomo and they greeted him with the words: "You villain! How dare you try to make fools of us?"

"Who are you, gentlemen?" asked Laurenzo. "And how dare you come bursting into my workshop and address me in such a manner?"

"Oh, the cheek of the man!" cried Pidras. "Now you're acting as if you don't know us!"

The two men stood right in front of the goldsmith and held the rings under his nose.

"Tell us now," ordered Fernando Dia Porta. "Where did these rings come from?"

Laurenzo looked at the rings and replied: "I made them."

"Ah, so you confess," said Pidras Pidri, grabbing hold of him. "Then come with us to the sheriff – and receive the punishment you deserve!"

Laurenzo pulled himself free and said angrily: "I will not be insulted and dragged away without knowing the reason why!" But meanwhile he was thinking: *What on earth has Jiacomo been up to?*

The apprentices also came over to defend Laurenzo. Fernando and Pidras realized now that this was not Jiacomo, but his brother, the goldsmith. That confused them for a moment, but then Fernando cried: "You know all about it! You said yourself that you made these rings. So where is the real ring? And where is your brother?"

"Jiacomo has just left," said one of the apprentices. "I don't know where he went."

"Then you must come with us," said Fernando to Laurenzo.

"That's right," agreed Pidras. "We are officially accusing you and your brother of theft and deception. And I would advise you to confess at once."

"I have nothing to confess," said Laurenzo. He did not let them see that he was worried. Had Jiacomo done something foolish? Laurenzo decided to remain silent, even about what little he did know. His brother could explain it all when he returned.

So Fernando and Pidras received no answer to their questions, and they became more and more angry. Eventually they ran off to fetch the sheriff and to make a complaint to the Lord Chief Justice, so that the two brothers would receive the punishment they deserved.

Soon many people in Bainu knew that Laurenzo the goldsmith and his brother, Jiacomo, had been summoned before the judge. The accusers were Fernando Dia Porta and Pidras Pidri, both respectable men, and they were accusing the two brothers of theft and deception. Three judges would handle the case, and one of them was the Lord Chief Justice himself, whose daughter, Mariana, was loved by the accusers. This was going to be an interesting case!

Most people did not believe that Laurenzo was guilty. As well as a skilled goldsmith, he was known as a good man; only those who were jealous of him said that there might be some truth to it. As for Jiacomo: he too had many friends who swore that he was as honest as the day is long, but even they had to admit that Jiacomo had boasted about his ability to steal.

When the case came up, the court was full of people who were interested to see what would happen. Everyone looked curiously at the judges in their robes and the accusers in their colourful clothes. But what they looked at most was the brothers, who resembled each other so closely that no one could say for certain which was one and which was the other. To many people's astonishment, one of them was wearing a lawyer's robes. Antonio, the innkeeper, claimed that it was Jiacomo.

"Yes, that's Jiacomo," he said. "He told me himself that he would be his own lawyer. Not for Laurenzo, though, because his brother has not done anything wrong and knows nothing about the whole business. Jiacomo told me that himself. He was furious when his brother was accused. They love each other, those two, whatever else people might say about them."

The Lord Chief Justice banged his gavel on the table, as a sign that there should be silence in court. Then, in a clear voice, he declared the hearing open.

First the charges were read out. Fernando Dia Porta and Pidras Pidri accused the brothers Laurenzo and Jiacomo of having stolen a valuable ring from them and exchanging it for two counterfeit versions made by Master Laurenzo.

"Thank you," said the Lord Chief Justice. "Before we begin, I would just like you to clarify a point for me. To whom does this stolen ring belong, to Fernando Dia Porta or to Pidras Pidri, or to both of them together?"

"It's mine, my lord," said Fernando.

"It's mine, my lord," said Pidras Pidri.

"I see," said the Lord Chief Justice. "So there are two real rings and two counterfeit ones. You've shown me the fake ones; so, according to you, the real ones must be in the brothers' possession."

"That's right, my lord," said Fernando. "But there is only one real ring."

"One real ring," said the Lord Chief Justice. "And you both say it belongs to you?"

"Yes, my lord," said Pidras Pidri. "But that's not the point. We are accusing these two brothers because they stole that ring and gave each of us a fake ring instead, telling us that it was our ring."

"Your ring?"

"Yes, my lord," said Pidras and Fernando at the same moment.

The Lord Chief Justice turned to the brothers and asked: "Which of you is Laurenzo the goldsmith?"

"That's me, my lord," replied the one without the robes.

"Do you admit that you made the two fake rings?"

"Yes, my lord," said Laurenzo.

"Will you tell me why you did that?"

"I can tell you," said Jiacomo. "He did it because I asked him to."

"Is that true?" the Lord Chief Justice asked Laurenzo.

"Yes, my lord," he replied.

"Do you know why your brother asked you to do that?"

"Well..." Laurenzo began hesitantly. "He—"

"He doesn't know anything about it," said Jiacomo, interrupting his brother.

The Lord Chief Justice frowned and said: "Will you wait to speak until I ask you a question?"

"My lord," said Jiacomo, "you should be questioning me, not my brother! He doesn't know why I wanted to have the ring copied. Laurenzo, don't go thinking that you need to protect me! I'm already sorry enough that you're standing here in front of the judge because of me."

"Would you please stop straying from the subject!" said the Lord Chief Justice. "You are Jiacomo, the brother of Laurenzo. You instructed your brother to make two copies of the ring. Is that right?"

"Yes, my lord," said Jiacomo. "And I paid him to do so. But I did not tell him why or what the purpose of the rings would be."

"Is that true, Master Laurenzo?" asked the Lord Chief Justice.

"Yes, my lord," replied Laurenzo. "And I do not believe that my brother has done anything wrong. I know him."

"Your brother must prove that himself," the Lord Chief Justice said. "Jiacomo, tell me how the real ring came into your possession, whether you still have it and why you had copies made. All these facts combined do indeed sound like theft and deception but I shall not pass judgment until I have heard your story. Do you have a lawyer to defend you?"

"I shall defend myself," replied Jiacomo with a bow. "As these borrowed robes are intended to indicate. I admit, my lord, that I had that wondrous ring in my protection, and I admit that I stole it. But I deny that I am a thief! Each of the two accusers, Pidras Pidri and Fernando Dia Porta, recently gave me a task. I was not allowed to talk to anyone about it, but now that they have accused me, I consider myself released from that promise. Now I shall tell you how the ring came into my possession."

He explained how Fernando Dia Porta first came to him to ask him to steal the ring that belonged to him, and said that he had accepted this task and then carried it out.

"So," said the Lord Chief Justice, "you were the man who dared to impersonate me at my own party!"

Then Jiacomo explained how Pidras Pidri came to him later, with a similar story and asked him to steal the ring from Fernando. He told him everything that needed to be told.

"I found myself in a very difficult situation, my lord!" said Jiacomo. "I had stolen the ring with the intention of returning it to its rightful owner. But which one was the rightful owner? One of the two gentleman had lied, but I truly did not know which one! If I gave the ring to the wrong man, then

the accusation would have been justified, and I really would have committed a theft! That is why I asked my brother to make two rings for me, exactly the same as the first. I gave one to Fernando Dia Porta and one to Pidras Pidri and decided to keep the real ring until I knew whose it was!" There was laughter in the courtroom.

"I see," said the Lord Chief Justice. "And do you know that now?"

"Not yet," replied Jiacomo. "But I intend to find out."

"Braggart!" cried a voice. It was Ludovico, the unpleasant man from the inn, who was up in the public gallery.

The Lord Chief Justice called for silence in court and turned to the two accusers. "Fernando Dia Porta and Pidras Pidri," he said, "is this story true? Did you instruct Jiacomo to steal the ring for you?"

"Yes, my lord," they both replied.

"One of you has lied," said the Lord Chief Justice. "Tell me truthfully, who is the rightful owner of the ring that belonged to Konrad and Katrina?"

"Me!" the two men cried at the same moment.

The Lord Chief Justice frowned and said: "You have accused these brothers, but one of you is himself a thief. I would ask that man to stop lying and therefore perverting the course of justice."

But each of them continued to insist that the ring was his property.

"Silence!" cried the Lord Chief Justice, losing his patience. He turned back to the brothers. "Master Laurenzo," he said, "you are cleared! You are free to go in peace. But I am not yet finished with you, Jiacomo! Your actions were clever and your defence was ingenious. You were right not to give the ring to either of these gentlemen. But you should not have kept the ring yourself, as you knew it did not belong to you! As long as it is in your possession, the rightful owner could accuse you of theft. So where is the ring?"

"I do not have it with me," replied Jiacomo.

"Where is it?" asked the Lord Chief Justice.

"My noble lord judge," said Jiacomo, "might I ask you something first? Would you ask Fernando and Pidras to tell you what they intended to do with the ring? That's if you do not already know."

"What does that matter?" said the Lord Chief Justice.

"It matters a great deal!" said Jiacomo. "What did Fernando and Pidras want to do with the ring? Or do they not dare to say what they both told me – and what you too should know?"

The Lord Chief Justice thought for a moment. "Fine," he said. "Fernando Dia Porta and Pidras Pidri, answer this question: what purpose did you have for the ring?"

The two men did not hesitate to answer. "We wanted to give it to Mariana of Arca," they said as one.

"Your daughter," added Pidras.

"That is true," said Jiacomo. "And I knew that. So I did the best thing that I could have done with the ring. I acted as these men – one of whom is the rightful owner – wished. I gave it to Lady Mariana of Arca! Perhaps she would step forward to testify on my behalf."

The courtroom filled with laughter and chattering. The Lord Chief Justice completely lost his composure. "What?!" he exclaimed. "Mariana knows about this?"

And indeed, his daughter stepped forward and raised her hand. In her palm, the ring glittered, white and blue.

"This is the ring that Jiacomo gave me," she said. "And I shall repeat the words that he spoke when he did so: 'Wear it for a while, for a day, a week. This ring doesn't actually belong to me. You are keeping it safe for me.'" She put down the ring before her father and added: "Here it is. Now you can return it to whoever is the owner, Fernando or Pidras."

Some of the people in the public gallery clapped at that point. Recovering from his surprise, the Lord Chief Justice called for silence. He asked Fernando and Pidras to look at the ring, and each declared that it was his own.

"Lady Mariana has testified in your favour," he said to Jiacomo. "You stole and yet you did not steal, and I do not know of any law that would allow me to punish you!" Then he spoke to Fernando and Pidras. "You, the men who accused Jiacomo and Laurenzo," he said, "have also accused yourselves. One of you is a thief and if he does not confess, suspicion will continue to surround both of you! And then I will be unable to return the ring to either one of you. So I would advise you to answer my question honestly: to whom does the ring belong?"

"Me," they both said at once.

The Lord Chief Justice frowned again and had a whispered discussion with his fellow judges. Everyone watched anxiously, except for Fernando and Pidras, who were glaring furiously at each other once again.

Then the Lord Chief Justice said in a solemn voice: "Now hear my judgment in the case of Fernando Dia Porta and Pidras Pidri against Jiacomo and Laurenzo. The brothers are free to go, and as for the fake rings, the accusers may keep them as replacements for the ring they both claim to own. If the owner's identity should be discovered, his ring shall be returned to him. The other will then be obliged to buy the owner's fake ring for three hundred ducats. Until then, however, the real ring shall remain in the custody of the court."

One of the judges said: "Why, Lord Chief Justice, do you not leave everything as it was? Give the real ring to Lady Mariana. Then at least the owner's wish will have been satisfied."

"I can hardly suggest giving the ring to my daughter, can I?" said the Lord Chief Justice."

"And I object!" cried Pidras Pidri. "That ring is mine, on my word of honour! And I want the court to return my property to me!"

"The ring is mine!" cried Fernando. "As truly as my ancestor was called Konrad! But you may give it to Mariana as my gift."

"Silence!" cried the Lord Chief Justice, banging his gavel. "I have decided to do as my honourable colleague advised. The ring shall go to my daughter, Mariana... if she will accept it."

But Mariana shook her head and said: "No, Father, I mean Lord Chief Justice, I would rather not take it."

"Then the court shall keep the ring," decided the Lord Chief Justice. "And I hereby close the hearing."

Then he ordered everyone to leave the room, except for Jiacomo, Fernando and Pidras Pidri. Everyone obeyed his order, but Laurenzo and Mariana asked if they might stay too. The Lord Chief Justice gave them permission to do so.

When all the others were gone, he said: "Good, now the new case can begin. So who *is* the owner of the ring?"

"I know the answer now," said Jiacomo calmly.

The Lord Chief Justice looked at him thoughtfully. "So you know too?" he said. "Then speak, Jiacomo, but do not accuse anyone without a good reason."

"Fernando Dia Porta is the ring's owner," said Jiacomo.

"As I've said all along," said Fernando.

"Lies!" cried Pidras.

"Don't say that, Pidras," said Jiacomo. "I'm sorry for you, as I know the reason for your dishonesty and can well understand your feelings. But you are the one who lied."

"How do you know that?" asked the Lord Chief Justice with great interest.

"Fernando Dia Porta and Pidras Pidri both believed in the miraculous power of the ring; they were both in love with Lady Mariana. So the real owner would be happy for her to have the ring, because then she would fall in love with him. But the false owner would realize that the stolen ring, now that he had lost it, could no longer be called his property in any way. His chances would be lost if the ring were given directly to Lady Mariana! When there was talk of giving Mariana the ring, Fernando approved, but Pidras Pidri wanted to have it back. So Fernando Dia Porta was the true owner."

Pidras Pidri hung his head.

"I trust you will no longer deny it," said the Lord Chief Justice sternly.

"No," grunted the young man.

"I shall not make this into a court case," said the Lord Chief Justice. "Although I must say that I highly disapprove of your behaviour! You will, however, have to buy the fake ring from Fernando Dia Porta for three hundred ducats.

And here, Fernando, is your ring. Take better care of it in future. You may both leave."

When the two young men had left, the Lord Chief Justice said to Jiacomo: "I have heard that you, unlike your brother, do not have a trade. Why did you not study law? You would make an excellent lawyer!"

"Really?" said Jiacomo. "Hmm, maybe that's not such a bad idea! I should have thought of it before. Not that I like the prospect of learning all our laws by heart, but you have to be prepared to make an effort if you want to master a profession." And he looked at Mariana.

Laurenzo smiled and said: "So, Jiacomo, have you finally found a job you're suited for?"

The Lord Chief Justice looked from Jiacomo to Mariana, and then from Mariana to Jiacomo, and stroked his chin. "There's just one more thing that I'd like to know, Jiacomo," he said then. "Do you believe in the power of Dia Porta's ring?"

"Why do you ask?" asked Jiacomo, trying to look surprised.

"I was wondering what made you choose to give it to my daughter, Mariana, to keep."

Jiacomo and Mariana both blushed.

"But, Father," said Mariana, "I'm not going to fall in love with someone just because they gave me a ring, no matter how beautiful, old and magical it might be. I wouldn't even accept it... unless I was already in love with the man who gave it to me!"

The Lord Chief Justice smiled. "Aha," he said. "I thought as much!"

Not long after that, Jiacomo married Mariana of Arca. Then each of the twin brothers had a lovely wife, and they continued to live in Bainu, doing the work they enjoyed. Laurenzo made many beautiful pieces of jewellery and Jiacomo became a renowned and respected lawyer, something that many people who had known him previously would have found hard to imagine. And, of course, they and their families and their pets all lived happily ever after.

THE SECRETS OF THE WILD WOOD

TONKE DRAGT

International bestselling
author

PUSHKIN CHILDREN'S

THE
SONG
OF
SEVEN

TONKE DRAGT

PUSHKIN CHILDREN'S

**AVAILABLE AND COMING SOON
FROM PUSHKIN CHILDREN'S BOOKS**

We created Pushkin Children's Books to share tales from different languages and cultures with younger readers, and to open the door to the wide, colourful worlds these stories offer.

From picture books and adventure stories to fairy tales and classics, and from fifty-year-old bestsellers to current huge successes abroad, the books on the Pushkin Children's list reflect the very best stories from around the world, for our most discerning readers of all: children.

**THE MURDERER'S APE
THE LEGEND OF SALLY JONES**
Jakob Wegelius

LAMPIE
Annet Schaap

**BOY 87
LOST**
Ele Fountain